Unsafe Haven

Roxanna Drew, widowed too young, had imagined that the deserted house on the estate of an absentee owner would provide her with a place where her bothersome brother-in-law could not touch her.

When the owner pounded on her door in the middle of a snowstorm, demanding a bed for the night, she was in no position to refuse him. After all, how could she deny him a shelter that was most certainly his?

But was it fair that dour Lord Winn was actually charming, sympathetic, and utterly in need of someone like her, even if he didn't know it yet? It wasn't his fault that his overpowering masculinity reminded her that she had been too long without a husband.

What would people say? She was still in mourning, and there was her lecherous brother-in-law to worry about. Roxanna feared that if Lord Winn spent the night, he would be hard to release in the morning. . . .

Mrs. Drew
Plays Her Hand

by

Carla Kelly

Ⓢ
A SIGNET BOOK

SIGNET
Published by the Penguin Group
Penguin Books USA Inc., 375 Hudson Street,
New York, New York 10014, U.S.A.
Penguin Books Ltd, 27 Wrights Lane,
London W8 5TZ, England
Penguin Books Australia Ltd, Ringwood,
Victoria, Australia
Penguin Books Canada Ltd, 10 Alcorn Avenue,
Toronto, Ontario, Canada M4V 3B2
Penguin Books (N.Z.) Ltd, 182–190 Wairau Road,
Auckland 10, New Zealand

Penguin Books Ltd, Registered Offices:
Harmondsworth, Middlesex, England

First published by Signet,
an imprint of Dutton Signet,
a division of Penguin Books USA Inc.

First Printing, December, 1994
10 9 8 7 6 5 4 3 2 1

 REGISTERED TRADEMARK—MARCA REGISTRADA

Printed in the United States of America

With love to Mary Ruth,
Sarah, Liz, Sandhya, and Jyoti,
daughters and nieces

Who does not tremble when he considers
how to deal with a wife?

—*Henry VIII*

Chapter 1

Roxanna Drew was not a lady to trespass on anyone's property, even if the landlord was out of the country, but she had a blister on her foot, and the grass in Moreland Park looked so inviting. If she took off her shoes and stockings, she could cross that field barefooted and cut three miles off her return route.

"This is the folly of wearing new shoes," she said out loud as she sat on a log at the edge of the woods. She rubbed her heel and contemplated the gentle river of grass that flowed around well-spaced boulders and emptied into a larger meadow. She snapped open the watch that was pinned to the front of her dress. Seven o'clock in the morning. Helen and Felicity would still be asleep, curled up next to each other, and Meggie Watson would be lying awake and thinking about putting on water for tea.

She sniffed the breeze, enjoying the scent of wild roses still blooming into September. Somewhere behind the fragrance was the sharp odor of the sea. She closed her eyes, thinking of the sand dunes, and how wonderful it would be to walk barefoot there. Through the dismal spring and uncertain summer, Helen had wanted to visit the ocean at Scarborough. Perhaps next summer would be soon enough. Winter was coming, and with it, decisions enough to push a seaside visit into the background again.

She took off her shoes and stockings and stretched her toes in the dewy grass. I am not the prodigious walker I once was, she thought as she made no move to rise from her comfortable perch. She smiled to herself—grateful she had reached the point where she could smile about it—and thought of her husband, the dedicated walker. When she was expecting their first baby, he had gently bullied her into walking with him as he made the rounds of his parish. Even when she was awkward with child, he continued to insist on her company. He only smiled when she grumbled about delivering the baby under a hedgerow on one of the miles of country lanes, and was there at her side when Helen made her ladylike appearance in their own bed.

Roxanna leaned forward and rested her chin in her hands. "You were right as always, dear Anthony," she said. Her eyes misted over, but the moment passed quicker than it would have in April or May, when the ground was still raw over his grave.

They had continued to walk together through her next pregnancy, and on until the morning when he sat her down under a distant tree and told her the doctor's suspicions. She knew she would never forget the calm way he looked at her and said, "And if he is right, my dear, he doubts I will see another summer."

He lived another summer, and then another one, but it was from his sickbed that he watched their second daughter, Felicity, take her first steps. He was much thinner by the time Felicity called him Papa and crawled up on the bed to sit beside him. He died as quietly as he had lived, when Felicity was almost four and Helen six, an astonishment to his doctor, who had given him less than a year.

Through a mist of pain that was only beginning to recede now, Roxanna thought of the doctor's surprise at the vicar's ability to hold off death so long. None of you suspected what a tenacious man he was, she thought as she looked at the meadow stretching before her. You saw only a quiet, self-effacing man, never strong, but lit from within by a flame so difficult to extinguish. We Drew ladies took such good care of him. And there is that matter of constant prayer, which most of you regard as sheer foolishness in this age of reason.

Throughout that long, dismal winter as she watched Anthony fade before her eyes and gradually melt away, she promised herself that she would take long walks again, and breathe other air than sickroom air. When he finally breathed his last in her arms, her relief equally balanced her grief. It was time for Anthony Drew, vicar of Whitcomb parish, to quit this life and let his beloved wife see if she cared to go on living without him.

She had taken short walks at first, a mile or two here or there, not far from the village of Whitcomb. Invariably some parishioner in gig or cart would stop and insist that she ride to her destination. Roxanna had not the heart to tell them she had no destination, not really, so she invented enough little errands that filled her drawers with unnecessary notions from the cloth merchants, and more bread than they could eat from Whitcomb's bakeries.

A glance at her dwindling resources convinced her that she had better begin walking across fields, where the danger was reduced of encountering well-wishers and more sympathy than she needed. In rain or shine, she would look in on her sleeping daughters and then walk until she was pleasantly tired. She wore out one pair of walking shoes and started on another, which brought her back to her current difficulty. There was a definite blister on her heel. "New shoes are such a trial," she murmured, and stood up.

She had walked farther than usual, but she knew whose land she trespassed on. It was one of the numerous estates of Colonel Fletcher Rand, Lord Winn, currently on occupation duty in Belgium. Anthony had always made it a point to know something of his parishioners, even those far distant, or those who never attended services, even when they were in the vicinity.

Lord Winn fit both categories. She remembered mailing a Christmas note to Lord Winn in Brussels, begun in Anthony's spidery handwriting and finished in her own firm script. She knew Lord Winn was a colonel of one of the more distinguished Yorkshire regiments. There was more, of course, but she never repeated scandal, and did not think of it, either, beyond a sad shake of her head. "For who of us has not fallen short of the mark?" Anthony would say, and she could only agree.

She started across the field, her eyes on the larger, more distant meadow, ringed about with trees and noisy with birds throwing back their challenge to autumn and shortening days. During the long months of Anthony's illness and death, she sometimes wondered if the Lord was scourging her for thoughtless years of overmuch laughter and quick temper. All emotion had been drained from her now. She lived life on one plane only, and sometimes wondered what it would be like to laugh until her sides ached, or even get really angry. It seemed impossible.

But I know what it is to worry, she thought as she strolled along, breathing in the fragrance of fields ready for harvest. Where are my girls and I to go? And how soon can we get there?

She knew from the day she buried Anthony in the parish cemetery that his older brother Marshall, Lord Whitcomb, would be wanting to give the parish living to another vicar. Until yesterday, Lord Whitcomb had not even spoken to her about the matter, and she was grateful for his unexpected forbearance. He had given her almost six months to collect her shattered thoughts and ruined dreams, and put them away for safekeeping.

His visit yesterday had not been a surprise. He sent a note that he was coming to discuss personal matters. Meggie Watson, Marshall, and Anthony's old nursemaid reminded her little charges that she had promised them a visit to the creek behind the vicarage, where Helen could bait a hook in imitation of her father, and Felicity could churn up the water farther downstream as she searched for pebbles.

Roxanna frowned and sat down on one of the boulders. All things considered, perhaps it would have been better for the girls to have run in and out of the parlor during Lord Whitcomb's visit. "Roxanna Drew, you have earned your suspicions," she told herself out loud, then looked around, afraid the wind would carry her words too far. No one was in sight, not even a cow or horse, so she relaxed again, going so far as to hitch herself up on the boulder and sit cross-legged. She knew it was undignified, especially for a woman dressed in black, but she had more on her mind than decorum.

"I have decided to give this living to Thomas Winegar," her brother-in-law told her over tea and biscuits of her own making.

She nodded, pleased. Mr. Winegar, newly released from Cambridge and ordained, had been filling in during the last year of Anthony's life, even though he had duties of his own of a subordinate nature at nearby St. Catherine's. And hadn't he said something about a new wife soon? Roxanna knew that the future Mrs. Winegar would be as satisfied with her surroundings as the Drews had always been.

"This brings us to you, Roxanna," Lord Whitcomb had said next, as he set down his cup and brushed the crumbs from his impeccable waistcoat.

"I had thought to find a small place in the village," she replied.

Roxanna shivered and then looked around her in surprise. The sun was shining down on her particular boulder, warming her shoulders. Perhaps the chill came from within. Perhaps she did not want to think about Lord Whitcomb.

He had seemed shocked, angry almost, that she would consider such an independent step, reminding her that he had promised Anthony on his deathbed that he would take care of her and the little ones. "I will not hear of such a thing, Roxanna," he said, looking into her eyes and moving closer on the sofa. "You will come to us at Whitcomb."

"I think not, Marshall," she had replied gently. "I do not believe Lady Whitcomb would enjoy my little Indians running about the place, not with her nervous temperament."

There wasn't any need to add that Agnes Drew, Lady Whitcomb, had never reconciled herself to her brother-in-law's some-

what eccentric choice of a wife. On more than one occasion, Roxanna had overheard her to say that "Pretty is as pretty does, but
why in a vicarage?" And there was no distinguished family pedi-
gree to render even a pretty face acceptable. "Better a stout dowry
in a vicarage than a trim ankle," had been Lady Whitcomb's remarks upon that subject, spoken, as were all her jibes, just loud
enough to be overheard. But this was nothing that Lord Whitcomb
had probably not already heard late at night in his own bedroom,
when husbands and wives discuss their relatives and laughed over
them.

Her unexpected resistance, after years of gentle obedience to
his brother, seemed to set off Lord Whitcomb. He got to his feet
and paced back and forth in front of the window as she stared at
him and wondered at his agitation.

"Roxanna, my wife's nerves are her best friends," he had admitted finally, stopping in front of her. He sat beside her again,
closer this time, his knee nearly touching hers. "They are her excuse for neglect of all marital duty." Shocked, she moved away
slightly, hoping he would not follow, and wishing suddenly that
Meggie would return from the creek.

To his credit, Lord Whitcomb picked his words with great care,
even as he inched closer on the sofa. "I was thinking that we
might consider a special arrangement, Roxanna," he said, his
voice quite soft.

It was not in her nature to be suspicious, she thought as she slid
down from the slowly warming boulder and continued at a more
rapid stride across the field, unable to sit still at her memory of
yesterday's searing interview.

"Marshall?" she had asked. "Whatever do you mean?"

He only moved closer until their knees were touching again,
and she could not slide any farther away on the sofa. "I know you
have been missing the comfort of a husband for several years at
least," he had told her, his voice conversational, as though they
chatted about the price of silk or the prospect of a good harvest. "I
can provide that special comfort, and a good roof over your head,
Roxanna." His hand was on her knee then. "And if there was a
son, why, that would be more than Agnes has ever grudged me.
No one would ever need to know that it was not hers."

Roxanna stopped in the middle of the field. She could not remember what had happened next, beyond the fact that in only a
matter of seconds, Lord Whitcomb was standing in the doorway,
his palm against his reddened cheek, his hat in his hand. "I do not

think you fully appreciate your situation," was his only comment as he mounted his horse and galloped away.

Later in her room, as she retched into the washbasin and then tried unsuccessfully to pour herself a glass of water with shaking hands, she reflected on his words. She knew with painful clarity that he controlled whatever stipend she would receive as Anthony's relict. She also knew that her parents were dead and her brothers both in Bombay with the East India Tea Company. She could also assure herself that these circumstances suddenly rendered her even more vulnerable than Anthony's most bereft parishioner.

She hurried faster, grateful at least that they were newly into the quarter, and she still retained a substantial amount of her stipend. If she could find a place to live, and live cheaply, they could probably stretch it to December. Out of wounded vanity, Lord Whitcomb would probably reduce her stipend; surely he dared not eliminate it entirely.

She sighed. So many worries, and now this one, an anxiety so dreadful that she could only question if she had heard Lord Whitcomb right yesterday. Roxanna paused in the field, wondering if at any time in the last three years of Anthony's illness she had ever indicated her longings for marital comfort to Lord Whitcomb. Surely not. No matter how much she yearned for Anthony's love, she had never done anything to make her brother-in-law suppose she was that desperate.

Even if I am, she thought, and then tried to push away that imp from her mind. She forced herself to face the reality that more than once at night she had awakened beside her slowly dying husband and wished he was still capable of making love to her. But I never gave any hint to Lord Whitcomb, she thought. I would never.

Her uneasy reflections took her into the larger meadow, where she could see a dairy herd grazing. As she passed, the Ayrshires looked up at her with that curiosity typical of the breed. Some started toward her. She smiled to herself and hurried across the field, looking back to laugh out loud. Helen would be amused to see a string of spotted cows all following single file in her wake, intent upon knowing her mother's business.

Everyone wants to know my business it would seem, she thought as she came to the fence and climbed over it as gracefully as she could with her shoes still in her hand. She sat on the fence a moment until she had her directions again, and started through the larger meadow.

A short walk showed her that she had reached the lawns of Moreland Park. Sheep grazed around her as she admired the order she saw everywhere. If Lord Winn was still out of the country, he certainly had put his faith in the hands of a loyal bailiff, she thought. She skirted around the manor, observing that no smoke came from the chimneys, Nowhere was there any sign of habitation, and she thought it a pity. The honey-colored stone glowed in the morning sun, and if some paint was needed here and there, it only added to the air of shabby country charm that seemed to reflect from the walls of Moreland. She could imagine the interior, all ghostly with Holland covers on the furniture, and cobwebs and mouse nests. The building cried out for someone to throw open the draperies, raise the window sashes, and get on with the business of turning it into a home again.

She admired Moreland for another moment, smiling to herself at the thought of approaching the bailiff with fifty pounds and asking for a year's lease on the place. He would think me demented, she observed with a chuckle. Still, it was a shame for such a building to remain idle when her need was growing greater by the minute.

She looked at her watch again. Eight o'clock. The girls would be up now, and pestering Meggie for breakfast. And so I should be home, she thought. Oh, I hope Lord Whitcomb does not call again today.

She was crossing the park behind the estate, her eyes on the road that would lead back to Whitcomb, when she noticed the dower house tucked in the shade of Moreland's large trees. She started toward the house as if drawn there by magnets, then stopped and looked toward the road again. I must hurry, she thought, even as she continued until she stood on the front steps of the two-story house.

It was of honey-colored stone, too, and more shabby than the manor, with crumbling mortar, and rain gutters stuffed with debris. She noticed several broken windows as she walked around the house, wishing for a box to stand on so she could peer into the rooms. She found a wooden bucket with the handle missing, and turned it over to balance on it and peer into the front room. She rubbed at the glass with her sleeve until she cleared a small spot and then raised herself up on tiptoe.

"Mrs. Drew, if ye overbalance yourself, I'll be blaming myself."

Roxanna gasped and dumped herself off the bucket and into the

arms of an old man scarcely taller than she. With a chuckle, he se
her on her feet again.

"And barefoot, too? Beware of broken glass."

She did not know him, even as she held out her hand and al
lowed him to shake it. "You seem to know me, sir."

He released her hand and after sweeping off a winter's accu
mulation of rotting leaves, motioned for her to sit on the edge o
the porch. "I'd feel better if you put on your shoes, ma'am," he
said. "My name is Tibbie Winslow, Lord Winn's bailiff. And I've
seen you walking about the place before, Mrs. Drew."

"I hope you do not mind," she said as she pulled on her stockings as discreetly as she could and pushed her feet back into her
shoes. "I am not really one to cause alarm."

He chuckled again and looked carefully as she tugged her
stockings to her knees. "I belong to St. Catherine's parish,
ma'am, and let me tell you we were as sorry to hear about your
husband's death as the folks in Whitcomb parish."

"Thank you, Mr. Winslow," she said quietly, touched by his
matter-of-fact words.

When her shoes were tied, he stood up and patted his pocket.
"Now then, Mrs. Drew, would you like to look inside?"

It was ridiculous, she told herself as she smiled into his face
and nodded, her eyes bright. "If you please, sir," she said. "I like
old houses." And I am desperate to find a place, she did not say.

He opened the door, leaning his shoulder into it when the key
was not enough to allow entrance. "Warped," he grumbled, and
then stepped aside to let her in.

There was a parlor, dining room, kitchen, and library on the
main level, with floors buckled by rain from broken windows.
She skirted carefully around a gaping hole of burned timbers in
the parlor floor.

"Gypsies," Winslow muttered, and motioned toward the second
level, where she found three bedrooms and a modest dressing
room. The roof leaked in all these rooms and the wallpaper hung
in sorrowful tatters, dismal evidence of neglect. As she gazed
about her with growing interest, Roxanna could see what twenty-
five years of off and on war with France and absentee landlords
had done.

Then she did what she never should have done, but what all
women did in a deserted house. As she walked from empty room
to empty room, she began to put her furniture in each place, imagining the girls' bed next to that window, and Helen sitting on that
floor with her dolls and a cozy fire in the rusty grate. She would

take the front bedroom, with its view of the park behind Moreland. She could pull up her chair to the window on cold days and
watch winter birds at the feeder she would hang right under the
eaves.

"I wonder how many fine old homes have been ruined because
too many men have been too busy fighting Napoleon?" she
mused out loud as she mentally rearranged her furniture and put
curtains at each bare window. Broken glass crunched underfoot as
she folded clothes into imaginary bureaus and placed flowers in
phantom vases.

"More than I care to mention," Winslow stated and closed the
bedroom door behind them. "Mind yourself on them stairs, now
then, Mrs. Drew." He laughed. "In fairness to Old Boney, I think
Moreland was deserted long before Lord Winn left Yorkshire. He
got this property by default through a cousin. He has never lived
here. Ain't it a sight how the rich get richer?"

"Oh," she said, stepping carefully around a tread rotting away
from the leaking roof.

She stood on the porch again in a moment, and the bailiff pocketed the key. "Pretty sorry, eh, Mrs. Drew?"

If she had been in a calm mood, she would have nodded, made
some throwaway comment about the sad state of ruined things,
said good-bye, and hurried toward the road that led to Whitcomb.
Instead, she took a deep breath.

"It can be repaired, Mr. Winslow. Oh, sir, how much would
you charge me for a year's rent?"

Chapter 2

Thank God Napoleon is banished to St. Helena, brother. You
have no more excuses now to avoid your family duty."

Fletcher Rand, Lord Winn, colonel late of His Majesty's 20th
Yorkshire Foot, looked up from his newspaper. He settled his
spectacles slightly lower on his long nose and peered over them at
the woman who had administered this opening shot across the
bows.

"Amabel, I wish you would drop yourself down a deep hole,"

he replied, and returned his attention to corn prices in Yorkshire. He cared not a flip for corn prices, but there was no need for his sister to think she had his attention. Corn it would be, until Amabel wearied of the hunt.

"Look at it this way, Winn," said his other sister. "Your eyes are going. Who knows what will go next? I wish you would marry and provide this family with an heir before it is too late."

"Lettice, there is nothing wrong with my virility," he commented, turning the page and directing his attention to pork and cattle futures. "I can refer you to a whole platoon of high flyers in London who were almost moaning to see me return from Brussels."

It wasn't true at all, but that should do it, he thought, in the shocked silence that followed. He returned to pork and waited for the reaction.

It was not long in coming, taking the form of several gasps from Lettice. He waited behind the paper, unable to resist a slight smile. *Now she will fan herself, even though the room is cool. Ah, yes. I can feel the little breeze. Now Amabel will approach her with a vinaigrette.* He took a deep breath. *Yes, there it is. I wonder if Clarice will intervene now. She will clear her throat first. There we are.*

"Winn, you are vulgar. I wish you would not tease your sisters like this. You know we are concerned about you."

He put down the paper to regard his older sister, who sat with her mending at the opposite end of the sofa. She returned his stare, unruffled, unblinking.

"Perhaps you are, Clarice," he said. "But that is because you are married to the juicy Lord Manwaring, and you do not need my money." He glanced at Amabel, who was chafing Lettice's wrists and making little cooing noises. "Amabel, on the other hand, hopes that I will burden some female with a son, and cut out Lettice's oldest, who is my current heir."

"I never considered it!" Amabel declared, dropping her sister's hand. "I only want what is best for you."

The fiction of that statement was not lost on any of the sisters. Clarice turned her eyes to her mending again, while Amabel and Lettice glared daggers at each other. Lord Winn waited for the next statement. It was so predictable that he had to resist the urge to take out his watch and time its arrival.

"It is merely that I do not think it fair that Winn has all the family money," Amabel exclaimed to her sister.

Lord Winn put down the paper, removed his spectacles, and

glared at his youngest sister, who pouted back. Hot words boiled to the surface, but as he stared at her, he was struck by the fact that although almost ten years had passed since he went to war for the first time, the arguments had not changed. Amabel was still feeling bruised because more of the estate was not settled on her; Lettice was smug because her son, a worthy if prosy young fellow, was heir; and Clarice did not care one way or the other.

Nothing has changed, he thought. Nations rise and fall, and the Rands remain as predictable as ever. We continue as we did before, getting each others' backs up, thinking ill thoughts, nursing private wounds that we will throw at each other every time we are together. Next Lettice will give me an arch look and ask if I have heard the latest scandal about my former wife. We dig and hurt and pry and wounds never heal.

Lettice looked at him and motioned to her sister to help her up again from her semi-recumbent position. "Poor man," she began, "you have only just returned, and there is more scandal. Did you know—"

"Stop, Lettice," he commanded. "I do not want to hear any sordid anecdotes about Cynthia. She is no longer my concern."

"I think she is your concern!" Lettice burst out. "She goes about the fringes of our circle, telling whoever will listen that you beat her regularly and"—she gulped and blushed—"and forced her into unnatural acts."

Even Clarice's eyes widened at this news. Amabel sniffed at her own vinaigrette and looked everywhere but at her brother.

Lord Winn rose and went to the window, wishing with all his heart to exchange rainy English skies for the heat and dust of Spain, just one more time. "Sisters, let us not split hairs. I should have beaten Cynthia regularly, but I never laid a hand on her in anger. Never. I do not prey upon women, no matter how they deserve it."

"I didn't really think so, Winn," Amabel assured him.

"And as for unnatural acts—"

"Really, brother," Clarice protested quietly.

"The only unnatural act I ever required Cynthia to perform was to keep within her quarterly allowance," he said, and then grinned into the window, in spite of himself. "I suppose that *was* an obscenity to her." He turned around to face his sisters, struck again, as he looked at them, how lovely they were, and how discontent. "And so, my dears, I trust I am exonerated?"

Lettice nodded. "It is more than that."

"It always is," he murmured.

"My dear brother," she began, in a tone almost loving, "Cynthia does you such disservice. There is not a mother in London who would allow you to come within a furlong of her daughter. I do not see how you can possibly find another wife."

He went to the door then and rattled the knob, giving any servants listening time to scatter from the hall. "As I have no urge to ever marry again, this concerns me not at all. Good day, ladies."

The hall was a welcome relief, but it was only a brief sanctuary. The door opened and Clarice stood beside him. "Fletcher, surely you wish to leave all this to a child of your own someday," she said, gesturing grandly to the ceiling, the floors, and the wider world beyond.

No matter his own disgruntlement, he could not overlook her obvious concern. Lord Winn touched her cheek with the back of his hand. "Why would I want to leave a child quarrels, pouts, and wounded feelings? No, Clarice, that argument does not move me. I shall remain childless."

Clarice was not a Rand for nothing. She followed him to the front door. "Fletcher, you can surely find a woman to love you."

He opened the door. "Ah, but can I find one I can trust? That, it appears, is the difficulty. Excuse me now. I think I will hide in the shrubbery until your sisters find some other target."

Lord Winn strolled down the front steps, his hands deep in his pockets. He frowned up at the gray skies and let the misty rain fall on his face, then turned around and walked backward across the lawn, staring at his home and remembering his arrival, only weeks ago. He had taken up a traveling companion in London, a fellow officer heading home to Nottingham. It was an easy matter to travel that way; although he was not much of a conversationalist himself, Lord Winn did not relish long silences. Major Peck was pleased to chatter on about this and that as the miles rolled by. By mutual if unvoiced consent, both avoided the war.

As they neared Peck's home, the major fell silent, watching for familiar scenes. Before they turned onto the family property, Major Peck looked at him. "Do you know, Colonel, I always wonder if she will want me again as much as I want her."

Winn had chuckled then, a dry sound evidencing no humor. "Well, sir?"

"She always does," Peck replied. "But still I wonder. Is any man ever sure?"

And then they were at Peck's home, a comfortable manor by

the river Dwyer. Before the carriage rolled to a stop, the major's wife threw open the door and hurled herself down the steps and into her husband's arms. Feeling himself a voyeur, Winn looked away from the Pecks as they kissed and clung to one another. He waited a moment, then spoke to the coachman, who unloaded Peck's kit, mounted to the box again, and drove away, while the Pecks still devoured each other in the front yard.

Winn leaned back in the carriage and remembered his last homecoming four years ago after the triumphant march across the Pyrenees. There had been no greeting from Cynthia. He was there for the trial of divorce and his best friend was one of the correspondents.

"Damn," he said softly as he looked up at his home, a pile of gray stone that meant almost nothing to him. His welcome three weeks ago from Brussels had been so different from Major Peck's, with servants lined up in front to drop curtsies, and tug forelocks. His sisters and their husbands had all been there, too, plus their children he could not remember, and who only knew him as the man with the money. Chaste kisses from his sisters, handshakes from his brothers-in-law. There was no one who cared to throw herself into his arms and eat him alive. But he had only a moment ago declared to Clarice that he did not need anything like that ever again, and it must be so.

He found a bench in the shrubbery and sat awhile, wondering what to do with himself. His first inclination on returning to England had been to sleep for a week and eat all his favorite foods, in the hopes of putting on some lost weight. But his good old English cook had retired and been replaced with a French chef, who only rolled his eyes and fanned himself when Lord Winn ventured to suggest that he would like a good roast of beef and Yorkshire pudding.

He had forgotten that Cynthia had replaced the old comfortable furniture with a style he could only call Demented Egyptian. His bed was the same, however. Cynthia never slept in it anyway, and even Amabel, who lived the closest, lacked the courage to replace it. Other than his bed, with the homely sag in the middle, the only thing that was the same was the view from his window. Cynthia had begun one of those ridiculous fake ruins, but his bailiff, in his infinite wisdom, had seen to its removal when the divorce was final.

"And so it goes," he said as he sat in the rain in the shrubbery, waiting for his sisters to occupy themselves with matters other than his own welfare. All he wanted to do now was leave again. His brothers-in-law had made their excuses two weeks ago, mumbling something about duty calling, when he knew it did not. They were men of leisure, even as himself. Lord Manwaring at least had the grace to wink at him as Winn walked him to his carriage. "Don't let'um get on your nerves, laddie," Manwaring had said. "Put Clarice in a post chaise when you can't stand her another minute."

I think I will take myself off, he thought, and started a slow walk to the manor. Unlike that of my wife, I have never doubted the loyalty of my bailiffs, but it is time to see if there is any heart left in my land. He strolled along, his own heart lifting at the idea. He would travel to Northumberland, and make his way back to Winnfield, stopping at his estates along the way. He knew there were some he could let go. Others were willed upon him, and according to law he must keep them, but he would look them over and decide what use to put them. The war was over at last. Napoleon would not be returning this time.

He knew there were homes in Yorkshire where he needed to visit. He would condescend to sit in smoky kitchens and speak to work-worn mothers and fathers of valiant sons, buried now under Spanish and Belgian earth. The good people of Yorkshire would never understand that the condescension was theirs, and not his. He owed his own life to their sons, and not the other way around. All he had done was direct their dying. But they would never understand that, so he would let them make much of him, even as he thanked them for their sacrifice at Quatre Bras and Mont St. Jean and Bussaco and Ciudad Rodrigo, and a hundred other unglamorous forgotten places that took lives as readily as the horrific battles schoolchildren would still be studying, when he was clay in hard ground.

And then he was hurrying faster, this time to the stables. The horse he had just bought at Tattersall's wickered at him as he entered the low-ceilinged stable, but he went first to the chestnut eyeing him from the best loose box. "Now then, Lord Henry," he murmured to his horse in his best Yorkshire accent, " 'av ye summat to tell me, awd lad?"

"Only that ye 'av put t'lad on a brawny pasture, my lord," said his groom from his perch on the railing in the box.

"Mind that Lord Henry's comfortable, Rowley," Lord Winn admonished. "He took me from Lisbon to Brussels, and I won't forget."

The groom only nodded and grinned at his master. "Carrots anytime he says, and sugar tits at Christmas?"

"I'll be back by then, Rowley, but yes, of course." He ran his hand down the old horse's long nose. "And if you should ever see the knackerman eyeing ta' Lord prematurely, you have my permission to shoot the man."

The groom cackled in appreciation and rubbed his hands together. "I'd love to shoot a knackerman!"

Lord Winn laughed for the first time since his return. "I'd like to see that, too. You know what I mean."

"Indeed, I do, my lord. Carrots and sugar tits for the old warrior."

He looked at the groom, struck by the fact that he was an old warrior, too. "Aye, Rowley. And have my new bay saddled and ready to go tomorrow morning early."

The groom nodded. "Have ye named him yet, my lord?"

"Not yet. I'm sure I'll think of something."

He chuckled to himself as he left the stables, remembering last month's final gathering of the regiment in London, when his staff and line officers presented him with a plaque that read, "Colonel Fletcher Rand, Lord Winn—From 1808 to 1816, we trusted him to think of something."

The phrase had become legendary among the regiments. In battle after battle, with the 20th up against many a tight spot, he had ridden Lord Henry up and down the ranks, assuring his men that he would "think of something" to get them out alive. It had worked, too, until Waterloo, when the 20th was almost blasted into a distant memory. Somehow they had survived. When they took him off the field on a stretcher after that endless day, he was still muttering, " . . . think of something."

He shook his head as he went into the house again. It's time to put those memories to pasture, he thought. Now I am a full-time landowner again. I wonder if I will remember how?

His sisters were kind enough to leave him alone for the rest of the day. Over dinner, he told them of his plans.

"I will start in God-help-us Northumberland before it gets too much colder, and see how things are."

"I do not know why you have to leave so soon," Amabel protested. "Your bailiffs have managed well for all these years. Surely after Christmas is soon enough, or even Easter."

"No, Amabel, it is not," he replied quietly. "I want to start now. I will look in on my tenants, too, and be back here before Christmas, I am sure." He looked at Lettice and Clarice. "I am certain you want to return to your own homes, too."

Clarice twinkled her eyes at him. "Tired of our company, Fletcher?"

He winked at her. "Does anything I do ever escape your sharp eyes, madam?"

She made no comment beyond a sharp laugh and a toss of her head.

"When will you leave?" Amabel asked.

"Tomorrow morning."

Amabel's eyes widened. "I am sure that is not time enough to make preparations, Fletcher!"

"Madam, I am ready right now. Pass the bread, please."

"It is not bread, Fletcher, but croissants," Lettice corrected.

"My God, Letty, give it up!"

He left before anyone was up except his groom, pleased with himself to have escaped even Clarice's notice. Beyond a change or two of clothes and linen, he traveled light, remembering that all his estates had the rudiments of soap, razors, and combs. And if he chose to light anywhere for a while, he could always summon a wardrobe from Winnfield.

He thought about stopping in York to visit friends, but changed his mind, the closer he came to that spired city. The friends he had in mind had two eligible daughters, and he did not wish a repeat of his recent experience in London. "No," he told his horse, "I do not need to be cut direct twice in a month. Once will suffice."

The memory smarted. The London Season had ended months before, but Lord Walmsley, his next-door neighbor on Curzon Street, had invited him to a small dinner and dance after his return from Brussels. The dinner passed off well enough, but when he asked one of the Walmsley chits to stand up with him for a country dance, Lady Walmsley had swept down upon him and declared that her daughters never danced with divorced men. She also added that no one would likely receive him, no matter his war record.

His mind a perfect blank, he had bowed to her, nodded to his host, who watched in horror, turned on his heel, and stalked across the ballroom floor, slamming the door behind him so hard that he had the satisfaction of hearing glass break somewhere inside. The next morning, he put his town home up for sale. He looked down at his horse then, grateful right down to his boots that his sisters had somehow not got wind of that development yet.

"So I shall not attempt York, my nameless horse," he said.

But the pull of the place was irresistible. He rode into the cathedral city, remembering happier days when the regiment marched through in full color, blooming with the flower of Yorkshire's finest sons. He had also attended boarding school in York before three years at Oxford, and then the army. He rode slowly past St. Giles, wondering if young boys still scaled the walls late at night. He would not stop to inquire. After his divorce, he was informed in a letter that his name had been removed from the list of trustees for that fine old institution. "Horse, it is a good thing I will never have a son who wants to go to St. Giles. I fear he would not be allowed admittance," he murmured.

He stopped at the cathedral and dismounted, left his horse in the care of a street urchin, and slowly climbed the steps, pausing to admire the facade. The familiar saints gazed down at him with the sorrowing mien of medieval holy men. He shook his head and went inside to the cool gloom, redolent with centuries of incense.

It took a moment for his eyes to adjust to the dimness and then direct their gaze to the loveliness of the rose window over the high altar. He had stood before that altar with the beautiful Cynthia Darnley leaning on his arm as York's archbishop joined them together. Even now his heart turned over at the memory of Cynthia, her hair brighter than guineas, her eyes bluer than cobalt, looking up at him as though her entire future happiness depended on him alone.

What a fool I was, he thought as he sank into a pew and propped his long legs on the prayer bench. Too bad he had to be married before he discovered that she looked at every man that way. Too bad he had the impolite timing to return from Spain unexpectedly and find her in bed with his former roommate from Oxford and best man. Even now his stomach heaved at the memory of her scooting out from under that good friend, opening her eyes wide as she covered herself with a sheet and declared that he should knock first.

And then the bed had turned to blood when he fired at his friend, who sobbed and pleaded for mercy. His hand was shaking; his aim was off. The doctors declared his friend a lucky man. Of course, he would likely never father children now, but that had elicited only a dry chuckle from Colonel Rand as he read the letter from his solicitor over a Spanish campfire six months later. The letter had also included information about the anticipated writ of divorce, which gradually worked its way up to the House of Lords while he fought through Spain and Lady Winn fornicated

through at least a platoon of former friends and relatives, his and
hers. She continued to spend his money at a dizzying speed that
infuriated him almost more than her blatant infidelity. He wasn't
a Yorkshireman for nothing.

The actual trial and divorce decree had ended all that. Somehow Lady Winn had the misguided notion that he would be a
gentleman and let her go after a slap on the wrist. To her furious
dismay, he had paraded that platoon of lovers before the House
of Lords and watched without a muscle twitching in his face as
they described in great detail her peccadilloes. He sat there im-
passively, decorated in his medals, his arm in a sling from Bussaco, a betrayed hero, while the Lords threw her to the dogs.

But now he was a divorced man, and no one would receive
him, either. He stared at the lovely window a moment longer,
watching it change color as the clouds maneuvered around the
noonday sun outside. I suppose I should have kept her, he
thought. At least I would still be received in places where I used
to go with some pleasure. I could have done like so many of my
generation and taken a mistress of my own. So what if our dis-
honor stank to heaven?

He lowered his glance to the altar and knew that he could never
have done that. Lord Winn rose to his feet, yawned and stretched,
overlooking the frowns and stares of the few others at prayer in
the cathedral. The trouble was, I actually listened to the archbishop when he spoke of loving, honoring, and obeying, he reflected to himself. They were more than words or hollow form to
me, thank you, Lady Winn. Damn you, Lady Winn.

He stalked down the center aisle, his hands clasped behind his
back. The glow of candles at the side altar caught his eye and he
went toward it. He tossed a shilling in the poor box and lit a candle from one already burning and replaced it carefully in its slot.

For the life of him, he could not think of anything to propitiate
heaven for. His existence was over at thirty-eight, and it only remained to keep going until death eventually caught up with that
reality and relieved him of his burdens.

But as he stood there, hypnotized a little by the flames, he
knew that it was a sham. He could tell his friends and family that
he never wanted a wife again, but he still could not lie to the
Almighty. "A good woman, Lord," he said out loud. "Someone I
can trust. Is there one anywhere?"

He waited a moment for an answer, got none, turned on his
heel and left the cathedral.

Chapter 3

To his credit, Tibbie Winslow did not stare at her as though she had lost all reason and was frothing about the mouth. He rubbed his chin.

"Come now, little lady?"

The words tumbled out of her. "Oh, Mr. Winslow, please let me rent this place from you!"

He shook his head. "I could'na do such a thing, Mrs. Drew! People would think me a sorry creature to rent you this run-down pile. I am sure if Lord Winn ever visits, he'll just tell me to put a match to it. No, Mrs. Drew." He waved a hand at her and started for the manor house.

She hurried after him, resisting the urge to pluck at his sleeve and skip beside him, as Felicity would have done. "Please, Mr. Winslow. If you can replace the windows that have broken, and just fix the roof, I am sure I can do the rest."

He stopped to stare then. "Mrs. Drew, that's a man's work!"

"Well, sir, I have been doing a man's work for three years and more now," she insisted. "The vicar was too ill for home repair, so I . . . I did it. I can paint and hang wallpaper. I might need some help with the floors, though." She stopped, out of breath, and embarrassed at her own temerity.

She held her peace then, watching Winslow's face as he seriously considered what she was saying for the first time. "You could put it to rights then, Mrs. Drew?"

"If you can fix the roof and the windows, I know I can," she declared, her eyes on the Yorkman as she considered what he would find most appealing about the arrangement. "And all at practically no expense to your landlord. We will save this lovely old house for him, and pay him rent besides."

Winslow looked back at the dower house, which glowed, honey-colored, in the early light of the autumn day. "No doubt Lord Winn would be tickled to find the place cared for," he mused out loud. "And I am thinking there is paint and wallpaper left over from the last renovation at the main house." He took a good look at her and slowly shook his head. "You're such a little bit of a thing. How can you do all that?"

She stood as tall as she could. This is my last chance, she realized, recognizing the look on his face from her own years of living with a man of York. Oh, Anthony, what would you do? She took a deep breath. "My husband always used to say that the dog in a fight was not half so important as the fight in the dog. Mr. Winslow, I can do it, and my girls need a place to live."

"Lord Whitcomb won't take you in?" he asked, his voice quiet, as though someone eavesdropped.

"He will, but I do not wish to live under his roof. I think he would try to make me . . . too dependent." There, she thought as she blushed. Read into that what you will. If you are a man with a conscience, I will not need to say more.

Winslow resumed walking, and her heart fell into her shoes. But he was talking as he walked, and she listened with hope, even as she hurried along and tried not to limp with her blister.

"I've heard rumors about your brother-in-law, Mrs. Drew. Didn't believe them then, but happen I do now," he said carefully, walking casually ahead of her, sparing her the embarrassment of his scrutiny during such a delicate conversation.

Roxanna watched his back as he walked before her, and silently blessed that tenderness of feeling she had noted before in other rough Yorkmen. She waited a moment before she spoke again.

"Well, then, sir, you understand my need," she said at last.

"P'raps I do, miss, p'raps I do," he said, still not looking at her. "Would ten pounds for the year suit you? I would blush to charge any more for a ruin. I can have that roof fixed by this time next week, and the windows sooner."

She was close to tears, but she knew better than to cry. "It will suit me right down to the ground, Mr. Winslow."

He turned around then, his hand stretched out, and shook her hand. "Done, then, Mrs. Drew. And it's just Tibbie to you." He took out the key from his vest pocket and placed it carefully in her palm. "You're not getting a bargain, mind."

"Oh, yes, I am!" she said. "We don't mind roughing it as we fix the place room by room."

He nodded, his eyes bright. "And it might be a project to occupy your mind, if you don't object to my saying that."

She could not speak then, and he looked beyond her shoulder, his own words gently chosen. "Now then, Mrs. Drew, we both have a good bargain. And only think how this will please Lord Winn. I don't remember much about him, except that he loves a good bargain."

Roxanna nodded, clutching the key in her fingers and memorizing its contours. "So do I, Tibbie," she said, smiling at him. "When can we move in?"

Tibbie looked back at the house, his eyes on the roof. "No reason why it won't be ready this time next week, Mrs. Drew. No reason at all."

Her heel scarcely pained her as she walked the remaining three miles to the vicarage. I have a place to live, she wanted to sing out to the farmers she passed, already out in their fields. Instead, she nodded to them soberly, the picture of sorrowing rectitude in her widow's weeds. Inside, her heart danced. She passed the parish church, too late this morning to stop in and see how Anthony did. She blew him a kiss as she passed his gravestone. "Anthony, it won't be as good as it was, but it will be better than it could have been," she whispered as she hurried by.

The girls and Meggie Watson were waiting at the table for her when she hurried to the breakfast room, flinging aside her bonnet and pelisse. Felicity, brown eyes bright, looked up from an earnest contemplation of her cooling porridge.

"Mama, you are toooo slow," she chided. "Didn't you remember that I am hungry in the morning?"

Roxanna laughed and kissed the top of her younger daughter's curly head, still tousled from a night of vigorous sleep. Like herself, Felicity did nothing by half turns.

"Silly mop," she said, her arms around her daughter's shoulders. "You are hungry at every meal. Helen, you seem to have all the family patience."

"Papa and I," Helen corrected gently. She smiled briefly at her mother, a smile that went nowhere, and then directed her gaze out the window again.

Roxanna released Felicity and put her arms about Helen's shoulders. How thin you are, she thought. And how silent. She rested her hands on her daughter for a moment more, thinking of the many whispered conversations that Helen and Anthony had granted each other in those last few months, when he was in continual pain and scarcely anything soothed him except the presence of his older child. Did you absorb all that pain? she thought, not for the first time, as she touched Helen's averted cheek, then sat down at the head of the table.

"We were wondering if a highwayman had abducted you, Mrs. Drew," Meggie Watson said.

"And what would he do with me, Meggie?" Roxanna teased. "I have no money and no prospects."

"Mama, perhaps a highwayman would give *you* something?" Felicity stated as she picked up her spoon.

Roxanna laughed out loud for the first time in months. Tears welled in Meggie Watson's eyes at the refreshing sound, and Helen looked around, startled. Roxanna took her hand and kissed it. "My dear, we do need to laugh. But now, let us pray over this porridge, and then I have such news."

She waited until Felicity was well into her bowl of oats, and Helen had taken a few bites, then put down her spoon. Roxanna picked up Helen's spoon again and put it back in her hand, wishing, as she did at every meal, that she did not have to remind her daughter to eat.

When Helen had taken a few more bites, Roxanna put down her own spoon. "My dears, I have rented the dower house at Moreland Park for us. We will move in a week."

Meggie stared at her in surprise. "Mrs. Drew, didn't that burn down several years ago?"

"It is most emphatically standing, but it does need considerable repair. Tibbie Winslow assures me that the roof will be repaired by this time next week, and the windows replaced."

"Good God," Meggie exclaimed, her voice faint. "Next you will tell us that the floors have rotted away and the walls are scaling."

"I was coming to that," Roxanna said, wondering for the first time at the wisdom of her early-morning rashness. "We'll have to walk carefully until the floors are repaired, but there is nothing wrong with the walls that I cannot fix with paint and paper."

"Mama, I know that Uncle Drew promised us a place at Whitcomb," Helen said. "He told me I could have a pony," she added as she pushed away the rest of her porridge.

He promised me a great deal more, Roxanna thought as she regarded her daughter, but it is nothing I dare tell anyone. "I know he did, my dear, but I want so much for us to have a home of our own."

"We can stay here," Felicity declared as she finished her breakfast and eyed Helen's bowl. "This is where my pillow is," she added, with a four-year-old's unassailable logic.

Roxanna smiled at her younger daughter. "We can move your bed to Moreland, and your pillow. Besides that, my dear, Thomas Winegar is going to be moving in here to become the new vicar."

"Oh," Felicity said, her voice resigned, but only for a moment. She brightened. "He can sleep with you in your bed, Mama."

"Felicity, don't be a dunce," Helen said.

"I think it is a good idea." Felicity pouted as Meggie Watson tugged at her chin, and tried to hide a smile.

Roxanna laughed again. "Daughter, our dear Mr. Winegar is about to marry. He would probably have other ideas. No, we will move to Moreland as soon as we can."

Felicity was never one to release a topic without a good shake. "But will I like it there, Mama?"

Roxanna looked around the table at her daughters, Helen withdrawn again, and Felicity demanding an answer that would create order in her world, topsy-turvy with her father's death. She thought of Anthony, who used to sit in the chair she now occupied. When I leave this lovely home, I will leave part of Anthony behind, too, she reflected. The thought jolted her, and she fought to keep the pain from her face.

"Lissy, you will probably like it as much as you want to," she said finally. "That goes for you, Helen, and ... ." her voice faltered, but she raised her chin higher and waited until the moment passed. "And it goes for me. We will make the best of what we have left."

They were all silent a moment, then Meggie Watson rose. "So we shall! Girls, it is time for lessons."

Roxanna remained where she was as her daughters left the room. Meggie Watson told them to go to the sitting room, but she closed the breakfast room door and sat beside Roxanna. She took her hand.

"Mrs. Drew, did Lord Whitcomb say or do something improper yesterday?"

With a startled expression, Roxanna looked at the older woman and returned the pressure of her fingers. She nodded, unable to speak of something so monstrous. Meggie put her arms around her, something she rarely did. Roxanna allowed herself to be hugged, wondering that the starchy nursemaid would allow such a familiarity, but grateful beyond words for her comfort.

"I feel so helpless, Meggie," she said finally. "There is no one here who can extricate me from this mess, so I must rescue myself." She let go of the other woman. "I wish it were possible for women to make their own way in the world."

Meggie reached out to straighten Roxanna's lace cap, tucking her hair here and there as though she were a child. "There are two of us here, Mrs. Drew."

Roxanna smiled at the dear face before her, grateful again that Meggie Watson had come out of her well-deserved retirement when she learned of Anthony's illness. She felt a twinge of conscience, and took a deep breath. There was no sense in putting off a matter she had been agonizing over for months now.

"As to that, Meggie, I cannot pay you any longer," she said in a
rush of words. "I will certainly understand if you choose to leave
us, for it will not be profitable for you to remain here." She
sighed. "Not that it was before."

Meggie blinked. "Leave you?"

"I can think of no way to pay you now. Lord Whitcomb controls
my stipend, and I fear that after the way he left yesterday, he will
not feel inclined to keep me from the poorhouse." Roxanna felt the
tears prickle behind her eyes. She had spent the last three years
keeping bad news to herself to spare Anthony more pain. To spill
it out now into Meggie Watson's lap seemed like cowardice.

Meggie's eyes narrowed. "He cannot cut you off!"

"No, he cannot do that," Roxanna agreed. "There are laws. But
he can reduce my stipend, and I fear he will." She got up and
went to the window, her hands on each side of the frame, hanging
on as though the room spun about. "I cannot give Helen a pony,
or either child any luxuries. It will be everlasting porridge for
breakfast and twice-turned dresses, and no hope of dowries." She
leaned her forehead against the glass. "I admit I thought about his
offer last night when I should have been asleep, and I was almost
tempted . . . Oh, Meggie!" She burst into tears.

The nursemaid was beside her in a moment, hugging her as she
sobbed. "There now, Mrs. Drew."

"You must think me terrible to even consider such an offer!"
Roxanna gasped and covered her face with her hands.

"No, not at all," said Meggie. "It's easy to think crazy thoughts
when you are desperate." She took Roxanna's hands and gave
them a little shake. "But you're never going to be that desperate,
because I won't leave you."

Roxanna closed her eyes and gathered herself together. "I can
promise you nothing in exchange."

It was Meggie's turn. Her eyes filled with tears. "Tell me, Mrs.
Drew, what do you think is so attractive about a little rented room
in Brighton? I do not think you could get me to leave now, even if
you tried." She hugged Roxanna again, then went to the door.
"And now if I do not hurry, Felicity will think I have declared a
holiday."

As if in response, the doorknob rattled. "Miss Watson, we are
getting ever so weary of waiting," Felicity said on the other side
of the door.

Miss Watson smiled. "She's your daughter, Mrs. Drew!"

Roxanna smiled and nodded. "So Anthony always reminded
me. Thank you, Meggie. Words don't say it."

Meggie put her finger to her lips. "Then don't try. I do think you should get that ten pounds to the bailiff as soon as you can. When Lord Whitcomb gets wind of this, and you know he will, there could be trouble of a legal nature."

"So true," Roxanna agreed. "I suppose we have our morning's work cut out for us."

She gathered up the dishes and left the breakfast room with them when she composed herself. The warm water in the dishpan was soothing to her jangled nerves as she washed dishes and dried them, and thought about the dower house. With the exception of the girls' bed, they would have to leave behind the other furniture. She put away the dishes, mentally sorting out which utensils she had brought to the vicarage as a bride, and which would have to remain. She had her mother's china, of course, but beyond a few pots and pans, the rest belonged to Lord Whitcomb. "And I will not be dependent on you, Marshall Drew," she said out loud, her voice low but fierce.

She separated ten pounds from the pouch hidden behind the row of ledgers in the bookroom, trying not to notice how meager was the amount remaining. She looked out the window at the farmland surrounding the vicarage, ready for harvest now, ripe with the bounty of a Yorkshire summer. It wouldn't be possible to depend upon the farmers bringing her fruits and vegetables now. They would go to the new vicar and his wife. *Somehow we will manage,* she thought again as she retrieved her bonnet and pelisse, found the old pair of shoes and a gum plaster for her heel. In a few minutes, she was hurrying toward Moreland again.

As she almost ran up the long, elm-shaded lane toward the manor house, it occurred to her that she had no idea where Tibbie Winslow would be. Anthony had told her that Lord Winn controlled several estates in the vicinity, and Winslow was responsible for all of them. "Oh, please be there," she said, out of breath, as she resisted the urge to pick up her skirts and race along.

To her immense relief, Winslow stood on the gravel drive that circled in front of the manor, hands on his hips, waiting for the shepherd to herd his flock to the overgrown hay field that was probably the front lawn in better times. She stopped to catch her breath and look around, then sighed with pleasure.

Moreland's yellow stone glowed like rich Jersey butter in the cool autumn noonday. It sat on a small rise, overlooking fields in all directions, fields aching for harvest. An orchard lay to her right, the boughs heavy with fruit. She smiled to herself, thinking of Felicity marching there and climbing up for apples. *Perhaps I will* join you on a branch, my dear, she thought. Moreland was a work-ing farm, burdened with a manor house at once pretentious and ab-surdly dear. The building had obviously grown to meet the needs of an expanding family that had also scaled a few rungs up the so-cial ladder. I wonder they did not tear it down and build something in the grand manner, she thought. I am so glad they did not.

Winslow had seen her by now. He waved to her and motioned her closer. She walked rapidly up the gravel drive, noting the deep pits where rain and winter snows had washed away the peb-bles. As she came closer, she noticed the gray paint peeling from around window frames and under eaves, and windows with no curtains.

"Change your mind, Mrs. Drew?" Winslow asked when she stood beside him.

"Oh, no," she declared, and held out the ten pounds to him. "I wanted you to have this right away so you would not change *your* mind!"

He smiled and took the money, motioning her to follow him. They went into the manor, and she looked around with interest. It was much as she had expected from her first traverse across More-land's lawns only that morning. Everywhere was furniture draped in holland covers. She sneezed from the dust, and sneezed again.

"Needs some work, think on?" was Winslow's only comment as he ushered her into the bookroom and pulled down a ledger. He carefully wrote out a receipt and handed it to her. "I'll write to Lord Winn and let him know what I have done." He looked up at her from his seat at the desk. "He may not care for this arrange-ment," he warned.

"Well, then, it's a good thing I have a receipt," she said as she pocketed the paper. "And I'll hold him to it."

He paused then, and frowned down at the ledger. "There's summat else you should know, Mrs. Drew. Lord Winn has a rather checkered past."

She blew off some dust from the wooden chair facing the desk, sneezed again, and perched on the seat. "I had heard something about a divorce, Tibbie, but cannot see how that concerns me. This is just one of his many estates, isn't it?"

Winslow nodded. "He may come here after Christmas to look over the property. Beyond that, I don't think we'll see him over-much."

"Mr. Drew told me there was a scandal of startling dimensions, but, sir, who of us does not sometimes fall short of the mark?" she said quietly, thinking of her own temptation only the night before.

"If he had the wisdom to hire you as his bailiff, I am sure he shines in certain essential areas."

Tibbie beamed at her. "Mrs. Drew, not everybody can dispense two compliments in one sentence! I've done my best here."

"It shows, Tibbie." Roxanna looked out the back window at the dower house beyond, noting, to her extreme gratification, that the front door was off its hinges and being planed to remove the warp. Another man walked on the roof, testing it carefully.

The bailiff followed her gaze. "I wish I could put more than one man on that roof right now," he apologized. "The harvest is on us, and that's even more than I can spare."

"I am grateful for whatever you can do," she said, and held out her hand as she rose.

He shook it and walked her to the front door. "Would it help if the girls and I came over here and swept out the house?" she asked.

Tibbie shook his head. "No need in the world, Mrs. Drew. We'll have it all right and tight by next Thursday. See you then."

When she arrived at the vicarage, pleasantly tired from her second vigorous walk of the day and thinking along the lines of a brief nap, she was met at the door by Meggie. The set of Meggie's thin lips, and the crease between her eyes were warning enough not to enter. She grasped Meggie by the arm and pulled her out onto the stoop. "Whatever is the matter?" she whispered.

"The very worst thing, Mrs. Drew," Meggie whispered back, barely able to contain her rage. "I sent Helen to Whitcomb for her pianoforte lesson. Lissy tagged along, and told her uncle about the scheme to move. You know how open she is! He's waiting for you in the sitting room. He looks like a leopard ready to pounce."

Roxanna leaned against the door frame, her stomach fluttering as though the breath had been knocked out of her body. "I suppose I was foolish to think that we could keep this a secret until we stole away like gypsies," she murmured, "but I did hope for a few days!"

Meggie shook her head. "We never thought to warn the girls." She sighed. "They wouldn't have understood, anyway."

Roxanna nodded. "Lord Whitcomb is an indulgent uncle to them," she said, her bitterness surprising her. "And he is an upstanding landlord, and an exemplary parishioner, a justice of the peace noted for his fairness! Oh, it galls me, Meggie!"

"Now what, Mrs. Drew?" the nursemaid asked, after the silence had stretched on too long.

Roxanna squared her shoulders and opened the door. "I suppose it cannot be avoided." She stood for a moment outside the closed door to the sitting room, trying to borrow courage from some unknown quarter.

"Should I go in with you?" Meggie asked, her eyes anxious.

Roxanna shook her head, took a deep breath, and opened the door.

Lord Whitcomb was on his feet in an instant, his eyes targeted on her face with a look of such outrage that it took all her willpower not to bolt the room. In her whole life, no one had ever looked at her like that. She forced her feet to move her into the room, advancing even as her brother-in-law strode toward her.

He stopped directly in front of her, so close that she could feel the heat from his body. Roxanna gritted her teeth but refused to step backward. You cannot have that satisfaction, she thought as he stared down at her, his breath coming in short bursts. To her intense satisfaction, he was forced to take a step backward when she refused to move.

"Have you taken complete leave of your senses?" he roared at her.

Roxanna covered her ears with her hands. "We do not shout in this house," she murmured.

Without a word, Lord Whitcomb yanked her hands off her ears and held them pinned to her sides, then grasped her by the shoulders and shook her until the pins fell from her hair. "You idiot! You imbecile!" he shouted as he shook her. "That house is a perfect ruin and I will not allow you to move there! What can you be thinking?"

With a strength she did not know she possessed, she wrenched herself from his grasp. "You have no say in what I do with my family," she said, wishing that her voice did not sound so puny and frightened.

He grabbed her by the neck then, his fingers pulling her unbound hair until she cried out. "Oh, I do not?" he whispered. His face was so close to hers that she could see the pores in his skin. "I am meeting my solicitor at Moreland's dower house within the hour," he hissed at her. "Tibbie Winslow is a reasonable man. I'll send a cart Monday to move you and your goods to Whitcomb. Be packed and ready, you simple woman."

He released her then and threw her back against the sofa, where she doubled her legs under her and put her hands to her face to protect herself. She shuddered as he came closer, then held her breath, praying for Meggie to open the door. But he only stood looking down at her, and when he spoke, his voice was different. It was softer, the malice cloaked in something much worse than rage. It was the voice of a lover, and it filled her with more terror than the fear of a beating. "Oh, Roxanna, you will be such a challenge to me."

And then he was gone.

Chapter 4

Roxanna stayed awake late that night, fearing to sleep because she knew she would dream about the dreadful interview with her brother-in-law. She had sat awake discussing the matter with Meggie until the nursemaid finally looked at her with bleary eyes and said that she had to sleep or she would drop down. Roxanna nodded and took herself off to bed, too, hoping that she was tired enough herself to fall into dreamless sleep.

She could have saved herself the bother of undressing and putting on her nightgown. There was no opportunity to dream, because she did not sleep. She lay in her bed unable to relax, her eyes wide and staring into the dark, listening to the clock downstairs chime its way around the night. Every little murmur and groan of the old house as it settled sent her bolt upright in bed, clutching her blankets to her breast, terrified that it was Marshall Drew, returning to subdue her in a way that made her sob out loud at the mere thought.

Her hands tightly clenched at her sides, she lay still, wondering what she had ever done to encourage her brother-in-law. Had she ever acted in a fashion that would make him think she was interested in him beyond his position as her husband's brother? True, he took occasion to tell her what a pretty ornament she was to the vicarage, but others had told her that, too. She always smiled and blushed, and passed it off. Only when Anthony told her how beautiful she was did it move her. She sighed into the darkness. Of course, when he said that, he was usually in the process of relieving her of her clothes, or kissing her in places that would have amazed his congregation.

She got out of bed and sat at the window, dismayed at the direction of her thoughts. I am so vulnerable right now, she thought. Somehow, Marshall knows this. Do some men possess a shark's instinct for blood in the water? Does he know that I am very ready for a man's body again? This will never do, not if I am to remain an independent woman, with my own say in the future of my body and soul. What he is suggesting is devilish, and I will not yield, no matter how much I want to.

There, Roxanna, you have thought the unthinkable, she told herself, and felt the first stirring of hope. You are a widow of some six months, but your husband has been dead to you for more than two years. You would very much like what no lady talks about, but not from your brother-in-law, and most certainly not as his mistress. You can wait for a better offer. Somehow, you can hold him off, even though you don't really want to. Is that it, Roxanna?

She was still sitting in the window when the sun rose. Her spirits rose too, unaccountably. She had seen herself through another long night in three years of long nights. It was different earlier, she thought as she stared through exhausted eyes at the dew-covered fields and the river shining in the distance as the sun's rays struck it. Before, you mourned your coming loss. Now you mourn your loss and fear for your self-respect. Which is harder?

"Oh, bother it," she said out loud. "Anthony, you were a beast to leave me. How dare you?"

The question took her breath away and left her quivering in the worst pain she had ever known. To think ill of the dead, especially her beloved husband, harrowed her already raw flesh in a torment that was exquisite and brutal by turns. She forced herself to consider her feelings for the first time. Anthony was a beast to leave her with two small children, no home, no money, no prospects, and a lustful brother-in-law. She sat calmly in the window and stared down this living nightmare. The pain settled around her shoulders like an unwelcome shawl, wrapping her tighter and tighter until she could scarcely breathe.

And then when she thought she could not manage another moment, her mind cleared. "But you couldn't help it, could you, Anthony?" she said, remembering his long struggle to remain alive and with her, and the gallantry with which he compelled himself into the pulpit on Sunday mornings when he should have stayed gasping in bed. She remembered the hours he lay listening to her ramble on about this and that, when he was probably screaming with pain inside.

"Oh, Anthony, you did what you could," she said, her words no louder than a whisper. She closed her eyes then, and unaccountably, the pain began to recede, unfolding itself gently, softly, from her shoulders. She leaned against the windowpane, and thought of the everlasting card games she had played with her brothers when they were growing up in Kent. They showed her no mercy, compelling her to play terrible hands to the end, instead of folding the cards and running away to her dolls. At first she cried and complained to Mama, but then she learned to play the hand dealt to her. Sometimes she won, sometimes she lost, but she never threw down a dealt hand again.

"Do your worst, Marshall," she said to the window. "I will beat you at this hand." She smiled then, and resolved to finally write that long letter to her brothers in Bombay that she had been putting off. She owed them something.

But first I must face the lions, she thought as she got up and went to the washstand. The water was cold, but she did not care as she stripped off her nightgown and washed until she was a pincushion of goose bumps. Ruthlessly she looked at herself in the mirror, raising her arm over her head and noting how her ribs stuck out. You have taken perfectly dreadful care of yourself, Roxanna Drew, she thought. You are a skeleton with breasts. This will never do. She dressed quickly, and then looked into the mirror again at her face. It was still pretty, an older Felicity with flashing brown eyes and curly hair, and that relieved her. I would like to hear compliments again, she thought as she pulled her hair back and tied it with a white ribbon. I am sick of black. Surely a ribbon will not matter?

Dressed in black again, she looked out the window and saw a man hurrying across the field from the direction of Moreland. Well, Marshall, did you and the solicitor get to Tibbie as you promised? she asked herself. If the dower house is not to be mine, I will throw myself and the girls on the dubious mercies of the parish poorhouse before I will end up laid in your bed.

Blunt words, she thought as she went calmly down the stairs and opened the front door, smiling her welcome as coolly as though she greeted the ladies of the parish sewing circle.

It was a man she did not recognize from the parish. He tipped his hat to her and thrust a note into her hands, then blinked in surprise when she invited him in.

"My boots is summat muddy," he apologized.

Roxanna smiled wider. "Come in anyway, sir. I do not have any water on for tea, but—"

"We haven't no time for that, ma'am," he interrupted as he stepped inside and she closed the door.

As he waited, cap in hand, Roxanna opened the note from Tibbie and read it quickly. "He has something to tell me?"

"Yes, ma'am," said the worker. "Told me to walk you back. Says there's some ugly John in the neighborhood he doesn't trust."

"Well, I have not had an escort in some time, sir," she said. She wrote a quick note to Meggie, warning her not to let the girls out of her sight, and then wrapped a shawl around her shoulders. "Let us not waste a moment of Mr. Winslow's time, shall we?"

He may have been an escort, but the worker was not a conversationalist as they hurried across the fields. The farm laborers were at work everywhere, scythes flashing rhythmically in the dawn's light, as landowners stole every bit of light for a Yorkshire harvest. She breathed in the wonderful smell of the harvest, and pushed the poorhouse into the back of her mind. Time enough and then some, to think of that.

At least Tibbie is man enough to tell me bad news face to face, she thought as she hurried to keep up with her protector. He could have written it, and sent back the ten pounds with the letter. I hope I do not beg and plead and look foolish.

They hurried up the lane, and she was grateful to be spared the sight of the dower house in the rear of the estate. Tibbie sat on the front steps, waiting for them. "Now then, Mrs. Drew," he said as he stood up and held out his hand.

She shook it. "Well, sir, I thank you for what you tried to do," she said, determined to blunt the knife before he had time to plunge it into her chest. "I am sorry you had to face Lord Whitcomb yesterday. I don't suppose your interview was any more pleasant than mine."

He nodded and smiled at her. "Ooh, he was in a pelter, wasn't he? That's why I have asked you here, Mrs. Drew."

Roxanna squared her shoulders and imagined herself six feet tall at least. "Lay it on, sir," she said calmly. "I can take it."

He blinked at her. "Take what, Mrs. Drew?" He touched her arm briefly, his eyes boring into hers. "You don't think I have cried off?"

"I understand perfectly," she said, and then stopped, her eyes wide. "Tibbie?"

"I should give you a shake for your thoughts, Mrs. Drew!" He sighed. "Although I doubt me that you have a kindly regard for men right now. Come here."

He led her into the house and directly to the bookroom, where he took her arm again and walked her to the back window. She looked out, and felt the tears well in her eyes, just when she was so sure she was too tough to cry ever again.

Four men worked on the roof, with another two at the windows, removing broken shards of glass. Inside the front room, she could just make out other carpenters tearing up the floor. She could not look at the bailiff.

"He came here yesterday with his solicitor, breathing fire," Tibbie said, his voice quiet, but with an edge to it. "Told me I was to return your money and stop work on the dower house immediately. Told me if I did not, he would personally contact Lord Winn and demand it. Said I would lose my job and never find work evermore as a bailiff in Yorkshire."

"Sir, those are hard words and these are hard times. I think he can do what he says."

Tibbie touched her shoulder and she looked at him. "I told him I would die before I would stop work. Told him I had taken your money and signed a paper. Told him to go to hell, ma'am, if you'll excuse me. I also told him to do something else, but I don't think he can."

Roxanna let out a breath she felt she had been holding since she first spotted the man coming across the field to the vicarage. "I would like to have done that, Tibbie. I can say thank you, but the words seem a bit flimsy after what you have done."

The bailiff stuck his hands in his pockets and rocked back and forth on his heels, immensely pleased with himself. "You'll be a good tenant, I am thinking. Maybe there'll be zinnias in the spring in front of t'awd house?"

"Oh, at least," she agreed, determined not to embarrass this man with tears. "I would like to start some ivy on that west wall. It will take a while for ivy, of course, but I intend to stay in this game, sir."

"Ten pounds a year, and you're in, Mrs. Drew," he said and laughed. "And now, I have some harvesting to oversee. True, it may go a bit slower because of the urgencies on the house, but I don't care."

They shook hands again, and he walked her to the front door. "During his volcanic eruption, Lord Whitcomb lathered about having a cart at your door on Monday morning to remove your things to his manor."

"That he did, sir," she agreed.

"Well, how about if I just happen to send a cart Sunday afternoon?"

Roxanna grinned at the bailiff. "I think we could fill it and be off Lord Whitcomb's property before he has time to blink. I really should pay you for that service."

He shook his head. "You've paid your ten pounds, Mrs. Drew. That got you in the game, think on."

The leaves had been stripped from Northumberland trees by arctic winds when Fletcher Rand received the packet of letters. Amabel had forwarded them to the estate he left a week ago, and it had taken another week for them to catch up to him here at High Point.

He wrapped his many-caped driving coat tighter around him and wished he had resisted his sisters' endeavors to see him into a more modish wardrobe before he left Winnfield. He longed for his army overcoat, warm and totally without style. A fire burned in the grate of High Point's master bedroom, but it was a forlorn hope, competing with the wind that insinuated itself through every crack in the window frames. Lord, how do people live here? he thought as he shivered and opened the packet. Especially in October.

He set aside the letter from Amabel, not feeling sufficiently strong to read it until the chill at least was off his feet. The letters from his solicitor could wait, and there were no invitations to anything. He propped his boots on the grating and considered the remaining letter.

It was from Marshall Drew, Lord Whitcomb of Whitcomb Manor. He slit the envelope and spread the closely written pages on his lap, keeping his fingers pulled up into his overcoat as much as he could. He vaguely remembered Lord Whitcomb from his first and only visit to Moreland after the death of a distant cousin twelve years ago, but could form no opinion as he sat and shivered in a drafty manor in Northumberland. He recalled that their North Riding lands marched together across the eastern property line, and that was all.

Fletcher Rand sighed and leaned back in his chair, thinking dully of property lines, entailments, mortgages, summary leases, and quitclaims. His brain was crammed to overflowing with *de donis conditionalibus*, and today's unbarrable entailment—or was that a *quia emptoris*?—on High Point. He longed to leap on his horse, still nameless, gallop to the nearest port, and take a ship to Spain. He seemed to recollect a seaside town on the Mediterranean side of Gibraltar where the food was good and the women more than willing. He could leave all his dratted property in the hands of capable bailiffs and never look a remainder and fee tail in the face again.

But the letter in his lap wouldn't blow away, despite the steady breeze from the closed and bolted windows, so he picked it up and read it. When he finished, he looked into the flames. "My dear Lord Whitcomb," he murmured, "what the hell do I care if a widow is living in my dower house, as long as she pays rent?" He glanced at the letter again, wondering at Whitcomb's obvious bitterness, directed so acutely at Tibbie Winslow and this poor widow and her two daughters. Probably old maid daughters, without a groat between them for a dowry. Too bad.

Winslow had sent him a short note a month ago, describing the results of September's harvest on the North Riding estates, and mentioning at the end that he had leased Moreland's dower house to a vicar's widow, after making a few necessary repairs. And did Lord Winn mind if he took some furniture from the estate to put in the dower house? The widow was bereft of almost any benefit from her former vicarage. Lord Winn did not mind. Lord Winn could not even recall what furniture reposed in Moreland in the first place, so how could he possibly mind?

He sighed, crumbled the letter into a ball, and pitched it into the flames. He would go see Lord Whitcomb in two weeks, drink tea in his sitting room, and maybe offer Moreland for sale to him. He held that property fee simple, thank the Lord, and could dispose of it as he wished. *Then he can do what he wants with that wretched widow,* Rand thought. *Lord knows I do not give a rat's ass for Moreland, or any of these northern estates. I wonder if I give a rat's ass about anything?*

He picked up Amabel's letter when he could no longer avoid it. "And what scheme have you hatched for me, dear sister?" he said, addressing the envelope.

The first page contained a breathless description of the activities of her children, none of whom he could remember. The next page made him frown and mouth obscenities even before he reached her "ever yours in sisterly affection," at the bottom. "Damn you, Amabel," was the most polite thing he muttered as he sent the letter into the flames after Lord Whitcomb's tirade. At least she had not asked for money this time, he had to admit. She had informed him that Louisa Duggett and her parents, Lord and Lady Etheringham, would be spending the Christmas holidays at Winnfield. "I will be pleased to act as your hostess and present you to this diamond of the first water," she wrote.

Lord deliver me from the Etheringhams, he thought. *Their son* had bought a colonelcy and managed to kill himself and most of his regiment at Waterloo, and the only daughter he remembered was rising thirty by now, and gap-toothed. He smiled unpleasantly into the flames, thinking of the Etheringhams, who were without question the most impecunious family in the peerage. *Lord E. must think he can get enough money out of me to stay afloat, and offer his daughter as a sacrifice to a divorced man, in exchange for my respectability again.*

Thank you, no, Amabel, he thought, and then began to wonder where he could spend Christmas this year. His best friends were dead on Spanish and Belgian battlefields. *Perhaps Clarice could tolerate him, and resist the urge to dangle a woman his way. Clarice could probably be depended on to keep his whereabouts a secret from Amabel. He would write her in the morning.*

Lord Winn reconsidered. *The ink was probably frozen in the bottle in this cursed estate. He would finished up his business as fast as possible, direct his horse to Moreland, and write his letter there. It would be a simple matter to clear up this mess with Lord Whitcomb, assure Winslow of his undying affection, visit a few more estates, then beat an incognito retreat to Clarice's manor for the holidays.*

Good plan, he thought, rubbing his hands together and blowing on his fingers for warmth. He cursed Northumberland roundly and stalked to the window. There was snow flying in the air, and despite his ill humor, the sight made him smile. *And so another season turns,* he thought, *and I am older. Still alone, too,* he considered, and leaned against the cold window frame.

But I was alone when I was married, he told himself. In all fairness to Cynthia, he could not blame her for that quirk in his character that isolated him from others. He had always enjoyed solitude. The war only made it worse, he knew. There was something about watching friends blow up on battlefields that led to a certain melancholy, he told himself wryly as he stared out at the snow, which was beginning to stick to the ground now. Others drank their way through the war, or wenched, or took fearful chances. He had withdrawn inside himself until he was quiet to the point that Amabel called him a hermit.

"And so I would be," he said out loud as he went to the bed. He thought about taking off his clothes, but it was too cold. He removed his boots and crawled under the covers, overcoat and all. He shivered until he fell asleep, thinking about Spain, and heat and oranges, and getting the hell out of Northumberland.

He left early in the morning, after scrawling out a note for his bailiff, vowing that he would return in the spring and try to figure out the legal tangle over High Point that had been festering since the days of the first Bishop of Durham, at least. "If it has waited five centuries, it can wait until spring," he wrote in big letters, and signed his name with a flourish. "After all, I am the marquess," he said out loud to the letter as he propped it against an ugly vase on the sitting room mantelpiece. "I can do what I want." He was still chuckling over that piece of folly as he mounted on Young Nameless and pointed him toward Yorkshire.

Lord Winn rode through snow all day until his head ached from the glare of white against the bluest blue of any sky he had seen. And there in the distance, and coming closer, were the Pennines, the spine of England, tall and brooding, and then a delicious pink against the setting sun. There wasn't an inn to be found on the lonely road, but he was welcomed into a crofter's cottage for the night, where the ale made his eyes roll back in his head, and the bread and cheese was far finer than the haute cuisine of his French cook. He slept three in a bed with two of the crofter's children, and was warm for the first time in a week.

The snow began again in the morning, but he rode steadily through the day and into the evening hours, telling himself that Moreland was only over the next rise. He wondered if Tibbie Winslow would have a welcome for him, considering that he was two weeks ahead of schedule, but shrugged it off. He rode doggedly on, thinking of Napoleon's retreat from Moscow.

It was nearly midnight when he rode wearily up the lane to Moreland, lighted by a full moon that came out from behind a bank of clouds like a benediction. The house was dark, which was not surprising, considering the lateness of the hour. To his dismay, he discovered that it was also empty, and he did not have a key.

"Blast and damn," he said out loud into the still night, irritated at himself for crowding on all sail to get to a deserted house in the middle of the night. He cleared off the snow and still holding the reins, sat down on the broad front steps of his property. Despite his disgruntlement, he had to admit that it was beautiful in the moonlight, the snow shimmering here and there like diamonds, the air so still that the trees were diamond-encrusted, too. The orchard to his left was dark and brooding, giving no hint of the promise of apple blossoms in the spring.

"Well, you brilliant man, now what?" he asked himself. The cold was seeping through his coat and his leather breeches, and his toes were beginning to tingle.

He thought of the dower house then, and got to his feet, wiping the snow off his cold rump, then swinging into the saddle again. Perhaps if the old widow wasn't too hard of hearing, or too much of a high stickler, she might let him in to sleep on her sofa. He rode around to the back of the estate, vaguely remembering the direction of the smaller house.

There it was, under the bare trees, smaller than he remembered, but a welcome sight. There was no smoke in the chimney there, either, but a lamp's light glimmered in an upstairs bedroom. That is at least hopeful, he thought as he encouraged his horse with a little dig in the ribs.

He knocked on the door and waited. After a long moment, he heard light footsteps on the stairs.

"Who is it, please?" came a small voice behind the door. She sounded apprehensive, and he couldn't marvel at that, considering the lateness of the hour. The old widow probably didn't have much male company, especially with two spinster daughters.

"I am Lord Winn, and I own this property," he said a little louder, in case she should be hard of hearing. "Could I come in? I think Tibbie Winslow was not expecting me so soon."

The key turned in the lock then, and the door opened upon the prettiest woman he had seen in years, perhaps ever. Her eyes were brown and round like a child's, with high-arched eyebrows that gave her flawless face a surprised expression. *My God, I have never seen skin like that,* he thought as he stared at her loveliness. She was all pink and cream, with dark brown hair tumbling out from under her nightcap. She was dressed in nightgown and a robe too large for her. It looked like a man's robe.

"You may come in, my lord," she was saying as he stood there gaping at her like a mooncalf. "It's too cold to stand overmuch on ceremony, if that's what you are expecting."

He laughed and came into the house after dropping Nameless's reins. "Oh, no, no ceremony. Now tell me, is your mother still up? I must ask a favor for the night."

She tilted her head in a way that he found perfectly adorable. "I am the mother here," she said. "What were you expecting?"

He stared at her in surprise, and she gazed back with that natural inquisitive look that was growing on him by the minute.

"Well, I mean, Tibbie mentioned a widow, and I thought, of course . . . well, you know . . ." he stopped, tongue-tied and feeling like a bumpkin.

"Oh." She looked down at the floor a moment, then back at his face. "My lord, young men die, too. As a former soldier, I am sure you are much acquainted with this phenomenon."

"I am sorry, Mrs.— Mrs.—" he stammered.

"Drew," she said, and held out her hand. "My husband was vicar of Whitcomb parish. Let me help you off with your coat, my lord."

They shook hands. Before he could protest, she grasped his coat from the back, and he had no choice but to pull his arms from the sleeves. For a little woman, she was a managing female, he thought as he obliged her. "I was wondering, Mrs. Drew, if I could sleep on your sofa for the rest of this night?"

She hung his coat on the coatrack by the door. "That will be difficult, my lord, as I do not have a sofa." She picked up the lamp she had carried downstairs with her and held it high so he could look into the sitting room, with the floorboards new and raw, but unpainted, and the wallpaper in tatters. "We're redoing it room by room, and the girls' bedroom was more important."

He looked around the bare room, cold and cheerless in the moonlight that streamed through the uncurtained window. "I certainly hope Tibbie is not charging you too much rent."

She laughed. "Oh, no. I am sure I am cheating you, my lord." She paused, as if trying to gauge his mood. "In the morning, I can show you what we have done with some of the other rooms. They should meet with your approval." He noted the touch of anxiety in her voice, but made no comment upon it.

He took his coat from the rack and carried it into the sitting room. "I can manage all right here on the floor," he said, spreading out the coat.

Her delightful eyes opened wider at that and she shook her head vehemently. "I won't hear of it, Lord Winn," she said, her voice a bit breathless. "I have a much better idea. You may take my bed."

It was his turn to open his eyes wide and stare at her. "I wouldn't dream of that, madam!" he insisted, and felt his cheeks grow warm.

"It's the only solution I will consider," she said firmly, and again he felt himself yielding without complaint to her competent management. "I can sleep with my daughters. There is even a hot water bottle for you." She peered at his face, her eyes filled with concern. "You look as though you have a headache."

"I do," he replied simply, charmed that she would notice, and quite forgetting his headache. "It's hard to ride in snow."

"I have headache powders in my room on the bedside table.

You will feel much better in the morning if you take some. Come, my lord. My feet are bare and the floor is cold."

He shook his head at her forthrightness, then remembered his horse. "Is it too much to expect a stable behind your house?"

"I am sorry, my lord. There is a little shed. You could stable him there until Tibbie arrives in the morning."

She sat herself on the bottom step while he went back outside, hurried his horse around to the shed, and tethered him there. "It'll do, 'awd lad," he said in his broadest Yorkshire as he removed the saddle and covered his back with several pieces of sacking. "We'll find better accommodations for you in the morning."

Mrs. Drew was still seated on the stairs and leaning against the banister, her eyes closed, when he came back in. He stood there a moment, taking in her loveliness, admiring her full lips and the absurd length of her eyelashes. This was a vicar's wife? My God, he thought, in reverent impiety.

"Mrs. Drew?" he said softly.

She opened her eyes, and he almost chuckled at that natural look of surprise on her face. I wonder, can you ever frown? he thought in delight.

"Well, now, perhaps you will come upstairs?" she said. "Duck your head halfway up. The ceiling gets a little low there where the stairs turn."

He followed her up obediently, ducking where he was bid, and breathing in the pleasant odor of lavender that trailed behind her. She hurried up the stairs, her bare feet quiet on the treads. At the top, she held up the lamp for the rest of his ascent.

"This way, my lord," she said, and motioned him into the first room.

There was only the paltriest fire in the grating, but it glowed a welcome at him as he went straight to it to strip off his gloves and warm his hands. While he stood there, she gathered together some clothing from the tiny dressing room off the bedroom, then joined him at the fireplace.

"Good night, my lord," she said softly. "You should sleep very well here. Tibbie arrives around nine at the manor house, so you will have time to breakfast with us before you go, providing you like porridge."

"I love it," he lied, perjuring his soul without a whimper. "Thank you for your kindness, Mrs. Drew. This is such a shocking intrusion."

She gave him that wide-eyed look. "Not in a vicar's household," she said. "We've sheltered many orphans of the storm who looked more weary than you. Good night then, my lord. If you need anything, why, you'll probably find it about where you would find it in your own house."

She closed the door behind her, and he smiled at her ingenuous reply. Still smiling, he looked under the bed, and laughed out loud. Sure enough, there was the chamber pot. You are a diplomat, madam, he decided as he shed his clothes and crawled gratefully between Mrs. Drew's warm sheets. They smelled wonderfully of lavender, too, and he relaxed and felt the tension leave his shoulders. You cannot imagine how weary this orphan is, he thought as he closed his eyes in sleep.

Chapter 5

He slept soundly and well, stirring only once when he dreamed that someone was pounding on his back. "Stop it, Threlkeld," he muttered, dreaming of his aide-de-camp, dead now this year and more at Waterloo, who used to wake him up for urgent messages with a thump to the kidneys. "Stop it," he murmured again, and dropped back into dreamless sleep. The bed was firm in all the right places, and he was warm for the first time since he had laid eyes on Northumberland in October.

When he woke finally, the sun was streaming in the window as though yesterday's snowstorm had been a bad dream. He lay comfortably on his side, drowsily gazing at the bare branches that tapped on the window glass, and imagining them full-leafed and green in summer. His back was deliciously warm and he started to close his eyes again.

They snapped open and he sucked in his breath. Who *was* that cuddled so close to him? He pulled the sheet up higher across his bare chest, looked over his shoulder, and found himself staring into a second pair of lovely brown eyes, round and wide open.

"Where did you put my mother?" she asked, sitting up and tucking her flannel nightgown down over her feet like a proper little lady.

She couldn't have been much over four, but as he smiled into her charming face, Lord Winn was delighted with her calm air of competency, so like her mother. You were certainly fashioned from the same mold, he thought as he tucked the blankets about his bare body and sat up in bed, propping the pillow behind him. I wouldn't have thought it possible.

But she was obviously waiting for an answer. In fact, she was getting a little impatient. She pursed her lips in wondrous imitation of her mother, then to his delight, sighed and laid her head on his blanketed thigh. "I wish you would tell me," she muttered, then closed her eyes again.

She was irresistible. I must remind myself that I do not care for children, he thought as he touched her curly hair tentatively, then rested his hand on her small shoulder. She sighed again and snuggled closer.

"No wonder I was so warm last night," he said softly. "My dear, I did not put your mother anywhere. In fact, do you wager?"

She looked at him with those big eyes and frowned. "I don't know what that is," she asked, her voice full of suspicion.

He grinned. "Of course you do not. You are a clergyman's daughter," he said quite matter-of-fact. "Well, I would be willing to lay down good money that your mother is going to come running in here any minute, looking for you. Can you reach my watch there on the night table?"

She sat up again and found his watch next to his reading spectacles, which she put on. He laughed out loud at the sight, and she peered at him over the top of the glasses. She held out the watch to him, but he shook his head.

"You open it, my dear. Can you tell the time?"

After a moment of concentration, with his glasses dangling on the end of her short nose, and her tongue between her teeth, she snapped open the watch, and held it up in triumph.

"Excellent! Now, do you know your numbers?"

She nodded. "The little hand is by the seven, and the big hand is on the six."

He winced. "Seven-thirty! You certainly keep army hours here."

She put the watch to her ear and kept time with the ticking. He took his spectacles from her. "I will give your mother another five minutes to come bursting in here. What do you think?"

She grimaced and snapped the watch shut, dangling it in front of her face by the long gold chain. "She will be here sooner."

"Well, I say five minutes. This is a wager, my dear, a bet. If she comes in after five minutes, I win. If she comes in before, you win."

"What do I win?" the little one asked, flopping onto her back and resting her head on his thigh again.

"What do you want?"

She thought a moment, still dangling the watch from its chain. "I would like a pony for Helen."

Her answer moved him beyond words. He thought suddenly of Amabel and Lettice, and their constant bickering. He touched her hair again, winding a curl around his finger.

"It's too much, isn't it?" she said, more to herself than to him. "Then I would like a skein of yarn, instead."

"For what?" he asked, marveling at the size of the lump in his throat.

"So Mama can make me some mittens. It snowed last night." She handed back the watch, and then her eyes opened wide. "But suppose you win?"

He couldn't think of anything he wanted more than just to stay where he was, but was spared the necessity of an answer. He heard a door open, and someone calling, "Felicity? Felicity?" in a low voice.

"I lost," he said. "Here she comes. You are Felicity?"

She nodded. "I could hide under the covers."

He clutched his blankets. "Not a good idea, Felicity! It's too late to duck from the wrath. By the way, my name is Fletcher Rand. Perhaps we should shake hands."

"That is a strange name," she said as she solemnly shook his hand and Mrs. Drew knocked softly on the door.

"So I have always thought," he agreed. "Call me Winn. Come in, madam. I think I have what you are looking for."

The original pair of round, brown eyes peeked into the room. Mrs. Drew, still in robe and nightgown, opened the door, her marvelous complexion a deeper pink at the sight of his bare chest.

"I am so sorry, Lord Winn . . ." she began, then let her gaze go to the window. "I never thought . . . Felicity does that . . . Oh, I hope she didn't push on your back with her feet! She nearly tumbled me out of bed once."

He laughed out loud and slid down under the covers again to spare the widow his hairy chest. "So that's what it was! I had an aide-de-camp who used to wake me up with a chop to the kidneys. I'm a heavy sleeper, ma'am, or so he used to tell me. Felicity and I have already introduced ourselves, and I have taught her to wager."

"Such dissipation!" Mrs. Drew exclaimed. "I suppose you were wagering how soon I would miss her?"

He nodded. Felicity, still resting against his thigh, nodded too. "I won, Mama."

"Of course you did, you scamp! You know me a little better than our sorely tried guest." She held out her hand to her daughter. "Come, my dear. Let us leave this gentleman in peace."

Felicity sat up and looked back at him, her eyes merry. "Yarn and a pony, or just yarn?"

To his intense amusement, Mrs. Drew put her hands on her hips and pursed her lips. "Felicity! Next you will tell me you wagered for a castle in Spain!"

"Mama, I would never. What good is that?"

Mrs. Drew turned away for a moment to hide her smile. "Spoken like a true Yorkwoman!" she murmured, then shook her finger at him. "Lord Winn, if you have set Felicity on a life of dissipation and crime, I will lay the blame entirely at your door."

"I think it will not come to that," he protested. "And truly, I have been marvelously entertained. "Don't be too hard on her."

"She is a scamp!"

Felicity stood up on the bed and opened her arms wide for her mother, who came into the room, picked her up, and whirled around with her, nuzzling her neck until she shrieked. She carried her to the door, set her down, swatted her lightly on the bottom, and pointed her in the direction of her own room.

"Lord Winn, really, forgive us."

"Nothing to forgive, Mrs. Drew," he assured her. "She's better than a hot-water bottle."

Mrs. Drew smiled then, and went to the door. "Lord Winn, in a few minutes I will have a can of hot water for you. I'll knock on the door when it is ready. There will be some coal, too. Not much, I fear, because it is so dear this season." She turned to leave, then looked back, hesitating. "If you wish, you can find Anthony's shaving gear in the dressing room. I . . . I left it there."

"Thank you, Mrs. Drew," he replied, rubbing his chin. "I must have left my saddlebags in the shed last night."

"Well then, please use what you can find here. We'll eat when you are ready."

She closed the door, and in another moment, Lord Winn heard her admonishing Felicity in firm but quiet tones. He lay still another moment, considering his early-morning bed partner. *I wonder if Felicity would like red mittens or green ones? Red, I think. And where can I find a pony?* He got up and pulled on his small-clothes and breeches. Soon there was a knock at the door. After waiting a modest moment for her to retreat, he opened the door and brought in the hot water and a very little coal.

"So coal is dear," he said as he dumped the hot water in the washbasin. "I think I shall save this, then."

He washed his face, but couldn't bring himself to use the razor belonging to the late vicar. He stood a moment in the dressing room, breathing in the lavender fragrance from Mrs. Drew's clothing, then pulled on his shirt.

Still tying his neckcloth, Lord Winn came downstairs and followed his nose to the kitchen, where Mrs. Drew, dressed in black with her hair pulled back tidily under a lace cap, was stirring the porridge. Felicity counted spoons, while a tall, thin woman brewed the tea and eyed him with vast suspicion.

"Lord Winn, this is Meggie Watson. She was Anthony's nurse-maid, and came to help us out when . . . things were difficult. Now I do not know what I would do without her. Meggie, Lord Winn."

He nodded to her, then ruffled Felicity's hair. "And you are in charge of spoons? Did you count out an extra one for me?"

She nodded, intent upon her work as she gathered up spoons and napkins. "I am to behave myself, Lord Winn, if you do not make it difficult."

Mrs. Drew laughed out loud, then covered her mouth with her hand. "Felicity! Be a little kinder to our landlord!" she insisted, and gave her daughter another gentle swat. She looked at him then. "Couldn't you find Anthony's razor? I was sure it was in the dressing room."

"As to that, Mrs. Drew, a man would always rather use his own blade," he said as he finished tucking in his shirt and pulled on his riding coat, which someone had thoughtfully draped in front of the fireplace. "I'll retrieve my gear from the shed and shave after breakfast, if the sight of a day's growth doesn't upset anyone's appetite."

"I think we can manage," Mrs. Drew allowed as she removed the pot from the stove.

"My lord, perhaps you could hurry along Helen," Miss Watson suggested. "I sent her outside with a bucket of water for your horse."

"She still isn't back?" Mrs. Drew said. "I don't wonder. She gets dreamy-eyed around horses."

"So do I, madam," he said as he opened the back door.

The back steps were deep in snow, except where Helen had walked, so his first task of the morning was to clear them off.

When he finished, the air was moving briskly through his lungs and he looked about in appreciation. There was no wind, and not a branch or bush rustled. The diamonds of snow and ice still jeweled the trees and the ground, and the silence was almost as intense as the blue sky. I wonder why people live in cities? he asked himself as he followed much smaller tracks to the shed.

There he found Helen, nose to nose with his horse, saying something to the big gelding that was generating a wicker of appreciation. He paused in the doorway, unwilling to intrude on the formation of a friendship, and content to admire this other daughter of the lovely Widow Drew.

You must be the image of your father, he thought as he leaned against the door frame and regarded the young girl before him. Her hair was blond and free around her shoulders. She had pulled up a box to sit upon and her posture was impeccable. He could almost imagine her in a riding habit and seated sidesaddle upon a fine horse of her own. She was slim and elegant, with a profile almost regal.

She turned then, and her blue eyes were nearly the color of the sky outside. "I like your horse," she said, then got down off the box, suddenly shy. She remained beside his horse, but Lord Winn had the feeling that had he not been standing in the door, she would have bolted.

He stayed where he was, unwilling to see her disappear. "I like him, too. Are you Helen?"

She nodded, her eyes on his face. He regarded her calm beauty, and found himself irrationally jealous of her dead father. Mr. Drew, you must have been a handsome man, he thought as he smiled at the vicar's elder daughter.

"Thank you for watering my horse," he said, moving closer slowly, as he would approach a skittish colt. "I hope Tibbie has some corn in the stables behind the estate."

"He does, because he puts his own horse there when he comes," she offered. "There are no horses now, my lord." Her voice was wistful, but he did not remark on it.

She couldn't have been more than six or seven, but there was a maturity in her voice that saddened him, somehow. Perhaps I have seen too many children in Spain growing up faster than their years, he thought. I recognize that voice, no matter what the language. Helen, you hide your loss with dignity.

He joined her beside his horse, rubbing the animal's nose as Helen stroked his shoulder with a sure hand, standing on tiptoe to reach him. He slowly moved the box closer to the horse, and to his delight, she allowed him to give her a hand up onto it.

"What do you call him?" she asked as she ran her fingers through the horse's mane, straightening the tangles.

"I haven't named him yet."

Her blue eyes widened at such neglect, and for a moment, he saw her mother's expression in them, too.

"Perhaps you can think of something," he offered hastily, unwilling to suffer her measuring regard. I am short of the mark, he thought with amusement. "I will entertain any and all suggestions."

She nodded, her face serious. "I will ask Mama. She names everything." The briefest smile lit her face, then was gone. "She even named our pigs, which Papa said always made it rather hard to eat them."

He smiled at her. "Did she name them Ham and Bacon?"

Again, that brief smile. "No, my lord! One was Columbine and the other Cynthia."

Lord Winn burst into laughter, transfixed by the idea of his former wife as a sow rooting in a vicar's barnyard. "Magnificent, my dear!" he said, when he could speak. "That is more amusing than you know. We shall apply to your mother for a name. And now—"

"Lord Winn! Helen!"

Helen sighed. "We are both late to breakfast, my lord."

He nudged her shoulder gently. "Does this mean we are in the basket?"

She regarded him candidly. "I think I would be, if you were not here, too, my lord."

He helped her down from the box. "Strength in numbers, Helen, is an element in military strategy. Shall we?"

Mrs. Drew waited for them at the back door, with Felicity beside her, looking impatient.

"Lissy does not like to wait for her meals," Helen confided in a whisper that he had to bend down to hear. "She even likes oats."

Lord Winn smiled, pleased to be taken into this quiet child's trust. He wondered what Tibbie Winslow would say if the first thing he inquired about at Moreland was where he could buy a pony. And some coal. And red yarn for Felicity.

Helen skipped ahead, walking in the wider tracks he had made, her blond hair rippling and shining in the cold, clear air. "Mama, you must think of a name for Lord Winn's horse!"

Mrs. Drew twinkled her eyes at him, and his heart nearly stopped dead in his chest. "I'm sure I'll think of something," she said, and she touched Helen's face briefly and helped her unbutton her coat.

He nodded, remembering his plaque at Winnfield from the 20th Foot with those very words inscribed upon it. *And how is your generalship, madam?* he wondered as he followed Helen into the kitchen.

Felicity tugged Helen toward the breakfast room, and he stood with Mrs. Drew a moment as he removed his coat and she regarded her daughters.

"You have met my family now, sir," she said.

He looked down into her laughing brown eyes, and his heart started to beat again, but a little faster. "Charming, Mrs. Drew, simply charming. And I don't even like children very much."

She stared back at him. "My lord! Everyone likes children!"

"I do not," he said firmly. "My sisters' children fight with each other and only greet me to ask for things. Dreadful brats."

Mrs. Drew lowered her gaze from his face. "Oh, dear, and didn't I hear Felicity petitioning you for yarn?"

He took her by the elbow and guided her toward the breakfast room, where Felicity was standing at the door, her head tilted and her hands on her hips. "My dear Mrs. Drew, that was a wager and she won it fair. I am always scrupulous in gambling debts." He stopped her and leaned closer to her, breathing in her lavender fragrance. "Tell me, how much yarn does it take to make a little pair of mittens?"

He could almost feel her reluctance. "Oh, I wish you would not."

"Mrs. Drew, you would have me avoid a gambling debt? You wound my honor. How much yarn? I insist."

"Oh! One skein, my lord."

He bowed in her direction. "Done, then, madam. Of course, the labor will be yours. I wish all debts were so easily discharged."

She only smiled and shook her head, then helped Felicity into her seat with the books on it. "Sit over there, my lord. If we wait much longer, Felicity will rise in open rebellion, and it is not a pretty sight."

He did as he was told and was startled when Mrs. Drew took his hand on one side, and Helen on the other. He looked at the widow, his eyes questioning her.

"My lord, we always pray this way. Will you say grace?"

"It's been years, Mrs. Drew," he protested, even as he clung to her fingers.

"I can help you, Lord Winn," Helen offered.

His eyes were still on Mrs. Drew. To his amazement, they filled suddenly with tears. She swallowed several times, and bowed her head. Moved beyond words, and not understanding, he bowed his head, too.

"Yes, if you please, Helen," he said. "I'm a bit rusty. No one prayed much in Spain."

"Please bless us, Oh Lord, and these thy gifts," she said softly.

"Amen," he finished. When he opened his eyes, Mrs. Drew was in control again. She filled their bowls and Felicity tackled hers at once.

He had never eaten better porridge.

While Helen was clearing off the table, Mrs. Drew looked out the window. "Ah! Tibbie is at the estate now, Lord Winn," she said.

The news did not please him particularly. He rubbed his chin. "I really need to shave first," he temporized.

"Certainly, my lord. Meggie, will you pour another can of hot water for Lord Winn? Helen, when he finishes, perhaps you will show him to the right entrance?"

Helen smiled shyly and nodded. Felicity regarded her mother. "I am to come, too."

Mrs. Drew knelt beside her younger daughter, and put her forehead against Felicity's. "My dearest, you would disappear in a snowdrift. This is Helen's duty."

They looked at each other eye to eye until Lord Winn wanted to laugh. He touched Felicity's head. "Felicity, perhaps you could get that leather pouch with my razor and shaving bowl from my coat pocket and carry it upstairs?"

She nodded, mutiny forgotten, and skipped into the kitchen. Helen grinned and followed her. He gave Mrs. Drew a hand up.

"Masterfully done, my lord," she said. "One would think you had practice."

He winced. "I have already told you my feelings regarding the infantry, madam! It is but a fluke."

She only smiled, then touched his arm as he started from the room. "I must apologize for my weakness a moment ago."

He started to protest, but she shook her head. "My lord, Helen has said more this morning than she has since . . . well, in months. I do not know what magic you are working, but it makes me happy."

"It is horse magic, madam, that is all," he said, keeping his voice light, even though he felt another lump rising in his throat. "And you have promised us a name."

He could see tears threatening again, and he felt an absurd desire to pull her close and let her weep, but he did not. "And now I must shave. Excuse me, Mrs. Drew, or Felicity will become impatient."

So that is it, Mrs. Drew, he thought as he mounted the stairs, untying his neckcloth. I wish I had time to be drawn into your little circle here in the North Riding. Too bad I do not.

Felicity perched herself on the bed and watched as he pulled down his shirt and draped a towel around his shoulders. Her face was serious, her lovely eyes wide as he lathered up and began to shave himself. He propped his shaving mirror on the bureau, and watched her through it.

When he was halfway done, another pair of brown eyes regarded him from the open doorway. "Felicity! Leave Lord Winn in peace!"

"I do not mind, madam," he said as he tilted his face up to shave under his nose.

"Mama! He is shaving himself! And he is standing up!" Felicity whispered, her voice filled with wonder. "Can you imagine?"

He laughed and flicked some soap at her. "Of course I am, you absurd child! How else would I shave?" he said, and glanced at her mother. To his consternation, her eyes were filling with tears again. This time, she turned away and her shoulders began to shake. Quickly, he wiped the soap from his face, and picked up Felicity, depositing her outside the door and closing it behind him. Without another word, he took Mrs. Drew in his arms. She buried her face in the towel around his neck and sobbed.

My God, what a strange family this is, he thought as she cried. He wasn't sure what to do, except put his arms around her and let her weep. Her tears seemed to come all the way up from her toes.

In another moment, she pulled herself away from him and wiped her eyes on his towel. Her face was fiery red. "I am so ashamed of myself," she said at last.

"Mrs. Drew, what happened? I don't understand," he asked, lathering up again to finish his face. "I wish you would tell me."

"I used to shave my husband and Felicity always watched," she said, her words coming out in a rush. "In her young life, she has never seen a man shave himself while on his feet."

"I had no idea," he murmured.

"I know you did not, my lord. She never knew her father as a well man. Excuse my tears, please. I don't know what's the matter with me," she said as she opened the door. "I should be beyond this by now."

Felicity came back in, her face cloudy with hurt feelings. Lord Winn set her back on the bed, took some lather off his face, and liberally deckled her cheek. To her delight, he laid the blunt side of his straight razor against her cheek and scraped it off. She shrieked with laughter and then ran from the room to show her sister. He looked around. Mrs. Drew was gone.

To his disappointment, she did not reappear after he came downstairs again, dressed and ready. Helen held his riding coat by the front door.

"I hope you are not upset, Lord Winn, but I led your horse to the front door."

He grinned at her and opened the door, then picked her up and set her on his horse. "We'll come back for the saddle later," he said as he took the reins and walked alongside as his horse broke a trail from the dower house to the estate.

"That's the door to the back entrance by the bookroom," Helen said.

"Well and good, my dear, but let us go to the stables first," he said. "I feel certain you can show me where they are."

The stables were substantial, but only one horse resided within. "That is Mr. Winslow's horse," Helen offered, then leaned down confidentially. "He's not really much of a horse." She touched his shoulder, her eyes lively. "But Mr. Winslow is not much of a rider."

They chuckled in conspiratorial fashion and then he lifted her off his horse. Helen skipped ahead to a loose box and opened the gate. "You could put him in here, my lord," she said.

He led his horse into the box and Helen closed the gate. He leaned on the gate, regarding his horse. "My dear, surely this box already belongs to another horse. It is all set up with hay, corn, and water. I thought you said there were no horses here usually?"

Helen blushed and looked at her feet. "I fixed it that way. I like to pretend I have a horse." She looked up at him then. "Mama thinks I am helping the housekeeper over here, but sometimes I come to the stables instead."

"I'll never tell," he promised, and crossed his heart. In another moment, she was gone.

"Helen, you are a fairy sprite," he murmured, and turned back to his horse again.

"Lord Winn! I thought I saw you from the bookroom window!"

He turned around to see his bailiff, Tibbie Winslow, standing in the door of the shed. Winslow came toward him with that dignity that he recognized as pure Yorkshire, and held out his hand. "It's been a few years, hasn't it, my lord?"

Winn nodded. "A few, Tibbie." He looked around him. "You seem to be well in control here."

"I can show you better in the bookroom, my lord. Ledgers are all right and tight, and we had a good harvest, we did. Will you join me inside? I know you're a busy man, going from estate to estate. I'll not hold you up here at Moreland."

"Certainly, Tibbie. I will only be here a few days, and I do need a prompt inventory." Lord Winn followed his bailiff to the stable door, then stopped. "Tell me, where can I find a pony?"

Chapter 6

From an upstairs window, Roxanna watched Lord Winn and Helen leave the dower house, her heart lifting to see her daughter lean down from atop his horse to speak to him. She hugged herself and shivered, even as she smiled. Oh, Helen, how good to see you in conversation with someone again, Roxanna thought.

She made Helen's bed quickly, fluffing the pillows, then went to her own room. Lord Winn was obviously not there, but she felt a moment's reticence in opening the door. In a way she could not understand, it seemed to be his room, too, and not hers alone.

"Of course, Roxanna, this is his house," she reminded herself as she opened the door and closed it behind her. She bit her lip in dismay. The coal she had rationed out for him was still sitting in the scuttle. "Lord Winn, you will think I am such a nip-farthing."

Well, you are, Roxie, she thought as she went to the bureau. You have another month to go in this quarter, and then you can face the reality of what damage your brother-in-law will have done to your next quarter's stipend. It was a discouraging thought, so she forced her mind into other channels. Bad news could always keep.

Lord Winn had left his shaving mirror on the bureau, and there were his soap and brush. She swished the brush around in the washbasin, breathing deep of its fragrance, trying to remember when she had last smelled shaving soap. Toward the end, it had been too painful to shave Anthony, so she had stopped. She

picked up the soap container. " 'Limón de España,' " she read,
" 'un jabon de hidalgos.' The soap of gentlemen." She sniffed
again, enjoying the lemon fragrance, more than slightly tart, and
as subtle as a bolt of lightning. "Nice," she decided as she
screwed on the lid, dried the brush, and replaced his shaving gear
in its leather pouch with the razor. Helen would probably enjoy
another trip to the estate to return it to him.

She looked around to make sure he had not left anything else,
and discovered his spectacles on her night table. There was no
case for them, so she wrapped them in a handkerchief of hers and
placed them on the bureau, where Felicity could not reach them.
He had left his shirt in the dressing room. She fingered the material. "Fine linen, my lord," she commented. "Nicely made, too."
She rubbed the material against her cheek, breathing in the slight
lemon fragrance and a pleasant combination of sweat and
woodsmoke. The fabric was soft from many washings, and as she
held it out, she noticed a European cut to the design. "How long
have you been away?" she asked as she folded it carefully and
added it to the pile on the bureau.

She made her bed, noting the indentation of Lord Winn's head
on the empty pillow next to hers. *I wonder if men have an instinct
about these things?* she thought as she fluffed her pillow and
straightened the blankets. After Helen was born, she had claimed
the side of the bed closest to the door, so she could be up quickly
in the night. She started to fluff his pillow, but changed her mind.
She traced her finger over the indentation, then pulled the bed-
spread over both pillows. *I really should change the sheets,* she
thought, but knew she would not.

Roxanna went to the window again, looking for Helen, and
wishing she had not made such a fool of herself in front of Lord
Winn. *He must think me a certified ninnyhammer,* she thought, *to
cry over a man with shaving soap on his face. I must learn not to
let little things set me off, or else life will be a misery. I must
learn to go to bed at a decent hour, and not read myself into a stu-
por until I am too tired to do anything but sleep without dreaming.
And I really must go through Anthony's things and see what I can
give away to those in need. When Helen asks for spice cake, I
must not keep making silly excuses, just because it was Anthony's favorite dessert. I have to move on.*

She gazed out the window with dull eyes, seeing not the
sparkling winter landscape, but the years yawning before her like
an endless cavity with nothing to break her fall. She stood another
minute at the window, then hurried from her room. Today she had

promised Meggie they would strip the remaining wallpaper from that last wall in Meggie's bedroom. Soon the upstairs would be done, and she could tackle the sitting room at last. By spring, the dower house would be finished. And then what will occupy my mind? she wondered.

Glowing with the cold, Helen returned from the estate, and skipped back just as happily with Lord Winn's property, while Felicity glowered from the breakfast room window. "It's not fair," she declared to her mother, who only smiled and kissed her cheek.

"Of course it is, my dear," she told her daughter, taking her on her lap, and hugging the warmth of her. "Didn't you get to spend the night with him? Lissy, you are such an imp! When will you learn to stay in your own bed? I cannot imagine what he thinks of us."

"Well, he has promised me red yarn," Felicity allowed at last. She leaned back against her mother, pacified. "And do you know, I first asked for a pony for Helen?"

Roxanna rolled her eyes and held her daughter closer. "No more wagers with Lord Winn," she said firmly. "I doubt he will be here much longer than a day or two, but I will not have you making any more wagers!"

The yarn arrived in early afternoon with Mrs. Howell, the housekeeper who came occasionally to Moreland for basic maintenance. Roxanna welcomed her in, shook the snow off her cape, and sat her down to tea in the breakfast room.

"Mrs. Drew, this is for you, with Lord Winn's compliments," she said, pulling out a red skein from her bag. "And this blue skein is for Helen. He told me to match her eyes."

Roxanna blushed and took the skeins on her lap, looking up into Mrs. Howell's inquiring face. "Oh, it was a foolish wager he lost with Lissy. This is his payment, and I am to make mittens."

Mrs. Howell laughed. "He seems a most pleasant man, for all the stories I have heard about him." She paused, and took another sip of her tea, regarding Roxanna over the rim of the cup.

"There was some scandal, wasn't there?" Roxanna said carefully, looking around to make sure that Felicity was still napping upstairs, and Helen engaged in lessons with Meggie. This is none of my business, she thought. Why do I care?

Mrs. Howell pulled her chair closer, eager to continue. "Aye, indeed, Mrs. Drew! A mighty scandal. Worthy of them Romans, think on. 'Twas five or six years gone now, I recall. Something about Lady Winn servicing half the bucks in London whilst he, poor man, fought Ney and Soult in Spain!"

"Mrs. Howell!" Roxanna said, her cheeks on fire. "Dear me! Was it that bad?"

"That and more, lassie," she stated, pouring another cup as calmly as though scandal was mother's milk. "If that wasn't embarrassing enough, instead of just hushing it up and demanding crim. con. money from the more flagrant offenders, what did Lord Winn do but parade them all through the House of Lords for a regular trial. Complete with juicy details."

"No!" Roxanna gasped. "How dreadful for him!"

"Him? Him?" Mrs. Howell demanded. "I hear the entire Winn family was mortified nearly to death. It put old Lord Winn over the edge and into his coffin, it did!" She looked about her. "I hear that no one in London receives him for showing such bad manners. It could have been a quiet divorce. I guess them earls and lords and what-alls do it all the time."

"He must have been grossly offended by his wife," Roxanna said quietly. She thought absurdly of the lemon shaving soap. "Some people are not subtle, Mrs. Howell. Perhaps he really loved her."

"Oh, aye, lassie, happen he did," Mrs. Howell agreed. "I am sure it tickled his male pride, at the very least and all. But to do such a thing to your family?" She was silent, finishing her tea.

"No one receives him?" Roxanna asked. "That seems wrong. What of the former Lady Winn?"

Mrs. Howell snorted, and pushed back the teacup. "The ways of the aristocracy is beyond the ken of you and me, missie, I don't mind saying. What does the former Lady Winn do but marry one of her lays? She's Lady Masterson now, and isn't she seen everywhere?"

"Sounds as though she was before," Roxanna murmured, then blushed again. "Oh, excuse me, but that was a rude comment. But it isn't our business, is it?"

"Well, it might be a little, Mrs. Drew," said the housekeeper. "I've promised myself to Moreland for these next few days for an inventory of the estate's contents."

"Yes, I hear he has been looking over his estates," Roxanna agreed, relieved to change the subject. "Does he own much land around here?"

Mrs. Howell stared at her with wide eyes. "Mrs. Drew, where have you been? He owns half of the North Riding, I am thinking, plus land in Northumbria and Durham, not to mention his own seat somewhere to the south of York."

"Goodness, no wonder he wants to get out from under some of that," she said. "Imagine the responsibility. Well, I only hope he does not decide to sell Moreland."

Mrs. Howell stood up and held out her hand. "As to that, I do not know." She looked around her at the pleasant breakfast room. "It would be a shame, with all the work you have done."

Roxanna thought of her brother-in-law. "You don't know what a shame it would be." She shook herself mentally. "Well, let us hope Lord Winn leaves Moreland alone. Thank you for the yarn, Mrs. Howell."

The housekeeper put on her cloak again and opened the front door. She breathed deep of the cold. "The snow's melting. It'll likely be gone before too much longer."

"Until it settles in again and winter begins in earnest," Roxanna reminded her. "Mrs. Howell, if you need any help with that inventory, I will gladly offer my services."

The housekeeper put her hand to her mouth and laughed. "And wasn't that the other reason I came over here? I must be in my dotage, my dear. Yes, would you help? Tibbie and Lord Winn are riding to Retling Beck tomorrow to check the books there, and I am beginning then. Eight o'clock? And wear an old dress."

Roxanna smiled. "That's all I have!" she teased, then her face fell. "But it isn't black."

Mrs. Howell patted her arm. "Don't worry, dearie. I'll never tell. Tomorrow then?"

"Yes. Eight o'clock."

She was there before eight, wearing a dark green wool dress and accompanied by Felicity and Helen, each with new mittens. Mrs. Howell received them in the warm house, and Roxanna could not overlook Helen's smile of pleasure.

"It's so warm here, Mama," she said.

Roxanna ignored Mrs. Howell's inquiring gaze and held her chin up higher. "Yes, my dear. We do keep our home rather cool, don't we? Perhaps Lord Winn is used to Spain."

Felicity twirled herself around. "I think I would like Spain then, Mama."

Roxanna laughed. "I think you would like any place with hot sun and opportunity for mischief! Now then, Mrs. Howell, tell us what to do."

Mrs. Howell gathered the girls to her. "First, there are cinnamon buns in the breakfast room. Lord Winn said to leave them there for you two. When you finish, stack the dishes, and then find us. I think you can start dusting. The scullery maid will show you where the rags are."

Roxanna followed the housekeeper into the main hall. Mrs. Howell had removed the holland covers from the furniture and she looked about her in delight. "What a fine old piece," she commented, admiring the pianoforte in the sitting room. She played a chord, wincing at the sound. "A bit out of tune."

"I wouldn't know, Mrs. Drew," the housekeeper said. "It all sounds the same to me." She ran her hand over the newly polished wood. "Lord Winn was in here last night. He played something, and told me to have it tuned before it gave him a headache."

"He plays? How delightful," Roxanna said. "See there, Mrs. Howell, he can't be all bad!"

"Well, I wouldn't care to get on his dark side," Mrs. Howell said. "Come, my dear. You can tackle the linen room. I'll inventory the silver. Tibbie says there's enough of that to pay even the Prince Regent's debts."

She spent all morning in the linen room, writing down in her careful hand the sheets, pillow slips, bedspreads, towels, and handcloths, and culling out those obviously lost to mice. She admired the ornate embroidery on some of the sheets, wondering if they dated back to the days of Queen Anne, herself. When she couldn't stand to look at another sheet, she walked through some of the upstairs bedrooms, her eyes wide with wonder at the stately beds, most of which would be too tall for her to crawl into without a stepladder. Felicity and Helen tagged along with her.

"Helen, think how high we could jump on these beds!" Felicity said to her sister.

"Mama would not approve," Helen admonished, even as she grinned at Roxanna.

"Lord Winn wouldn't mind. I am sure of it," Felicity declared.

Roxanna took a firmer grip on her younger daughter's hand. "And you, you ragamuffin, are destined to never know!"

They returned to the dower house when the shadows were lengthening across the back lawn, pleasantly tired and eager for the dinner Meggie had promised them. Roxanna looked at Felicity. "I insist that you take off your mittens for dinner," she said firmly.

Felicity looked mutinous until Meggie brought in the covered roasting pan. She sniffed the fragrance and looked at her mother.

"No food until your mittens are off, Lissy," Roxanna said, trying to subdue the laughter that welled inside her. Oh, Lord, was I this difficult as a child? she thought. Probably.

Felicity did as she was told. The nursemaid, her eyes lively, made them close their eyes. Roxanna opened them to see a roasted leg of mutton before her, the meat moist and ready to be carved. She gasped in surprise.

"Meggie, where did this come from?"

"Mrs. Howell said she bought too much and Lord Winn told her to see that we got some for our dinner."

Roxanna frowned. "We can't make such generosity a habit," she said, hesitating even as she held the knife in her hand. "What will people think?"

"Roxanna, he's only going to be here a couple of days!" said Miss Watson.

"Mama, it's been a long time," Helen added.

She sighed and looked at Felicity, who already had a finger in the gravy that pooled in the bottom of the platter. "Very well," she grumbled. "I may have to take Lord Winn to task, but we will eat to bursting tonight. Pass your plate, Helen. Lissy! Wait your turn. Oh, we are forgetting grace!"

It was a good dinner, complete with Yorkshire pudding covered in gravy so creamy that Helen sighed. "Mama, you know what Papa would say," she commented as she leaned back finally and pushed away her empty plate.

Roxanna looked at her daughter. You have never spoken of him, she thought as she set down her own fork, fearful that her hand would tremble. "You tell me, dear," she said, her voice low with emotion.

Helen sat up straight, and put both elbows on the table in an imitation of her father that made Roxanna close her eyes for a moment. " 'Well done, Mrs. Drew. It couldn't possibly be any better, not even if the Lord Almighty himself sat for dinner,' " Helen said, pitching her voice lower.

Felicity laughed and clapped her hands. Helen burst into tears, and then they were all crying, and laughing, and hugging each other, until Meggie hurried in from the kitchen where she was removing the plates, and joined them. Roxanna pulled both girls onto her lap and held them close to her, feeling better than she had in a long time.

Helen blew her nose vigorously on a table napkin. "Mama, do you mind?"

Roxanna shook her head, her lips on her daughter's hair.

"Somehow, it makes me feel better to talk about Papa."

"Me, too, dear," Roxanna said. "Let's do it whenever we feel like it."

After the girls were in bed, she went onto the front porch, breathing deep of the cold air, more content than she had felt in months. She drew her shawl closer, surprised at her own peace of mind. For someone with such an uncertain future, Roxanna Drew, you certainly are as merry as a grig. She smiled to herself, then found herself listening, her head tilted to one side.

She could hear the faintest sound of a piano coming from the estate. She listened harder, and her grin widened. The piano tuner must have found his way through the melting drifts, after all, she decided, as she strained her ears and concentrated until she identified a Beethoven sonata. It ended with a flourish and a crash of chords, just before her toes started to tingle from the cold. She clapped her hands softly, and went inside, closing the door behind her.

Her teeth chattered as she undressed and crawled into bed, wishing almost that Felicity would climb in with her for warmth. But I must not encourage that, she thought. Gradually, the heavy blankets warmed her and her eyes closed. Before she drifted to sleep, she ran her hand over the indentation in the other pillow. The scent of lemon shaving soap was long gone from the room, but she imagined it anyway, and places like Spain where it was warm.

Lord Winn and Tibbie returned from Retling in the afternoon, when she was trying to count the sheets and stack them back on the shelves. At the sound of horses' hooves on the gravel drive outside, Helen set aside the towels she was folding and looked out the window.

"Mama, can I go to the stables? Maybe Lord Winn will let me curry his horse!" she asked, her eyes lively.

" 'May I,' not 'Can I,' " Roxanna corrected absently as she began her count again. She looked up as Helen tugged on her arm. "Of course, my dear. Only do not make a nuisance of yourself."

"Mama, I would never!" Helen declared. She looked at Felicity, who slumbered on a pile of rejected linen, still wearing her red mittens. "Now, Lissy might."

Roxanna put her finger to her lips. "Then don't wake her, silly!" She returned to her count, stacked the sheets, and opened

yet another carved chest. At least it is the last one, she thought. I
wonder if the inmates of Moreland ever threw out anything? She
opened the chest and gasped out loud, then looked around to
make sure she had not wakened Felicity.

The chest was full of lace, beautiful lace, old and yellow now,
but still possessing the power to amaze. She carefully lifted out a
tablecloth and napkins, tracing over the delicate design with one
finger, almost afraid to touch it. I wonder if any of this is salvage-
able? she thought as she set it aside and turned her attention back
to the chest.

There was a smaller tablecloth, and then a christening dress.
She sighed with pleasure and held it up, admiring the tiny
stitches in the wool and the lace edging around the tiny cuffs
and hem. How many generations of babies have worn this? she
wondered. And what a pity it is to stick it unused in a chest.
She looked about her at the shelves and chests, full to bursting
with so much to offer. Such bounty for an empty house, she
thought.

She heard firm footsteps in the hall outside, and looked up
from her contemplation of the christening gown in her lap. She
smiled. It was Lord Winn.

"Good afternoon, my lord," she said, and put her finger to her
lips, indicating Felicity with a nod of her head.

He was dressed in riding clothes, the top boots and leather
breeches of the country gentleman he was, his coat open and
his neckcloth comfortably loose. You don't stand much on ceremony, do you? she thought as her glance took in his graying
brown hair, with the indent where his hat had rested, and his
handsome green eyes. I did not notice before how green they
were, she thought as she returned his smile with one of her
own. He was just tall enough, and just broad enough to look
substantial, without any suggestion of overweight. You look
healthy, she thought, and then blushed at such a foolish observation.

"Now what did I do to make you blush?" he whispered, coming
closer.

She shook her head in confusion, not about to admit to her
thoughts. "I am still embarrassed over my piece of foolishness
yesterday," she murmured. There. He didn't need to know that
she was measuring him, and not finding him wanting in any way.

"Already forgotten, Mrs. Drew," he said cheerfully, then
peered at Felicity. "Nice mittens."

"She refuses to take them off, except for meals," Roxanna said, happy to change the subject.

He shook his head and grinned at her. "What's that?" he asked, pointing to the bit of lace in her lap.

She held it up for him to admire. "It is a christening gown, my lord. Imagine all those little stitches for one wearing."

"Beyond me," he said. "Most children should be drowned at birth, anyway."

"Lord Winn!" she exclaimed, then pursed her lips when he told her to shush and looked at Felicity.

"I have already told you my opinion of children," he whispered. "I intend never to have any." He watched Lissy. "She won't take them off, eh? Did you make them too tight?"

She put her hand to her mouth to keep from laughing out loud. "No! Lissy finds you 'top 'o the trees,' my lord. If she were a puppy, she would follow you from room to room, I am sure! It's a good thing for you that your stay here is not long."

He nodded. "I suppose," he said, without any particular enthusiasm.

The silence made her uncomfortable, but he did not seem to notice as he walked around the little room, his hands behind his back. "Damned lot of sheets," he commented finally, when he finished his circuit. "Take anything you want, Mrs. Drew."

"I could not—" she began.

"Of course you can," he insisted. "Take that christening gown, too. You'll likely marry again won't you, Mrs. Drew? You'll find a use for it, unless I am grossly overestimating the abilities of most Yorkmen."

"I—I hadn't really thought of it," she stammered in confusion.

"I'm sure that once you are out of black, the men of the North Riding won't waste any time," he said, and strolled back into the hall, leaving her to stew in her muddled thoughts.

Roxanna blinked and stared after him. You have such a nice walk, Lord Winn, she considered as she watched him. It's somewhere between a saunter and a . . . Oh, Lord, Roxie, mind your thoughts.

She pulled out the rest of the chest's contents, suddenly eager to be done with the inventory and back in the dower house. She applied herself to her task, finished the list, and was about to wake Felicity when she heard more steps in the hall, light steps, Helen's steps, and she was running. She tiptoed into the hall in time to catch Helen in her arms.

Her daughter's breath came in rapid puffs as Helen grasped her about the waist. "Is something wrong?" she asked anxiously, kneeling beside her daughter.

"Oh, Mama! You cannot imagine! Mama!" Helen said, her eyes shining.

"What, my dear?"

"It's a pony! Lord Winn says it's part of Felicity's wager. Oh, Mama, come look!"

Chapter 7

Oh no!" she exclaimed. "My dear, we can't possibly . . ."

But Helen was tugging her down the hall. She took a last look in the linen room to make sure that Felicity still slumbered, then hurried down the stairs and out to the stable with her daughter.

She paused in the stable's entrance. Lord Winn was leaning comfortably on the gate of a loose box, resting his arms on the top rail. He looked at her and winked at Helen. Roxanna sighed and came closer, her lips set in what she hoped was a displeased expression. Lord Winn moved over obligingly and she stood next to him, too angry to look in his direction. Helen clambered between the rails and put her arms around the little animal's neck.

"Oh, Mama, he's the most beautiful horse I have ever seen!"

Roxanna stared straight ahead at the pony. "Lord Winn, I ought to call you out for this!"

"You and who else, madam!" he said, his voice full of amusement. "I told you I always pay my gambling debts."

"My lord!"

"Are you swearing or addressing me?" he asked, and then laughed, turned around when she gasped, and leaned against the railing with his hands in his pockets. "Name your second, Mrs. Drew. I would recommend Felicity. Is it swords or pistols at twenty paces?" He peered at her face. "You know, the way your face is so nicely arranged, it's hard to tell if you're truly angry at me."

"I am angry, my lord," she assured him.

He leaned closer and nudged her shoulder. "What could I do? There was this little pony at Retling Beck, and the stable keep there is half blind and past ready to retire from my services. I couldn't leave him there. And what better hands could he be in than your daughter's?"

"You know this won't do!"

He took her by both shoulders, his touch gentle but firm. "Why not? I have an empty stable here, and someone who will take excellent care of my property." He peered closely at her. "What is it, Mrs. Drew? Do you not relish being under obligation to a man who is not a relative?"

"It is rather improper, my lord," she said. "Surely you must see that?"

He released her, and resumed his casual position against the gate again. "Perhaps you would like it better if I gave the pony to your brother-in-law Lord Whitcomb, then he could bring it over here, or you could keep it in his stables. Would that be better?"

He spoke casually enough, and she knew that he was sincere, with no idea what his words meant to her. Still, she could not repress a shudder. She felt nauseated then, and desperate to leave the stable before she disgraced herself yet again before this well-intentioned man.

"No, that would be much worse," she managed. "I would far rather be under obligation to you. Excuse me, my lord."

Her anguish must have showed in her voice, because as she started from the stable, he turned quickly to look at her, and grabbed for her arm.

"Hold on, Mrs. Drew!" he called after her, but she ignored him and walked faster, her hand to her mouth, her whole aim in life at that moment centered on getting out of the stable before she threw up.

She made it, but barely, hanging her head over some bushes around the corner of the building. Luckily, her stomach was nearly empty, so she was wiping her mouth with the edge of her apron when Lord Winn caught up with her. He stood there in open-mouthed surprise as she calmly patted the sweat from her forehead and turned to face him.

"My lord, I do not wish to discuss my brother-in-law with you or anyone else. And yes, Helen may keep the pony on your property. Excuse me." *Please don't stop me,* she thought as she looked at him.

To her chagrin, he took her by the arm and gazed into her eyes. "Mrs. Drew, what is the matter?" he asked, his voice firm.

She glanced away, wishing that her voice did not sound so puny. "It is not something I am prepared to discuss with you, my lord." She tried to pull away, but he tightened his grip. She looked into her eyes again, remembering her dreadful interview with Lord Whitcomb, and his hand on her arm. "Oh, stop!" she pleaded.

He released her arm immediately, his face flushed. "Mrs. Drew, if I am not mistaken, there is something quite wrong here. I wish I knew what it was."

She shook her head. "Lord Winn, this is a matter between me and Lord Whitcomb. I cannot see how it can possibly concern you, especially since you will be leaving any day now. Please let it go at that."

He wanted to say more, she knew he did, but Helen came out of the stable then, and he stepped back.

"Mama, you must name the pony," Helen insisted, tugging her toward the stable.

Roxanna glanced around at Lord Winn, who stood regarding her, a frown on his face and his hands thrust in his pockets again. "It seems I am needed elsewhere, sir," she said, her voice calm again.

"What do you think, Mama?" Helen asked as they stood in front of the loose box again.

Roxanna gathered up her skirts and climbed up a rail for a better look. To her surprise, Lord Winn picked her up and set her on the top railing. She rested her hand on his shoulder to steady herself, and tried to look stern. He gazed back at her, his eyes innocent.

"You are a difficult person to remain angry with, my lord," she murmured.

"Oh, well, you need only ask my former wife about that," he said mildly.

She blushed. "And you are exasperating." She looked down at the pony. "A name, Helen? Let me think."

Lord Winn moved slightly, and rested his arms on the railing again as she took her hand from his shoulder. "I am sorry, Helen, but you will have to wait in line. I believe your mother had promised to name my poor nameless beast," he explained. "I have a prior claim. Isn't that right, Mrs. Drew?"

He smiled up at her, and she nodded. "Yes, I did," she agreed, and shifted herself to regard the big hunter in the other loose box. She started to smile. "Of course! Why didn't I think of it sooner?" She looked down at Lord Winn, "You should call him Ney, my lord."

Helen frowned and shook her head in disappointment. "Oh, Mama! That will never do. You cannot name a horse Neigh."

But Lord Winn was chuckling to himself. "N-E-Y, madam?"

"Exactly. I assume you have a working knowledge of that foxy Frenchman, and after all, this is a hunter."

"Happen I did know Ney reet well," he said, looking at her then but not seeing her. "He was a worthy opponent the length and breadth of Spain, and I must admit to a mild regret when Louis had him executed. Well, only a mild regret. Ney, it is, Mrs. Drew. It is an excellent name for an old Peninsula man's horse." He reached out and touched Helen's head. "You're right, my dear. Your mama has a facility for this."

Roxanna held out her arms to Lord Winn. "And now, please help me down, my lord. If Felicity wakes up and finds me gone, I know she will rush upstairs to try to bounce on one of your beds. It is a temptation no four-year-old can resist."

He helped her down. "Or forty-year-olds, madam. That almost sounds fun."

"You are hopeless, my lord," she murmured as she straightened her dress, then laughed in embarrassment. "That was rude of me. Excuse it, please."

Why do I seem to say and do the most stupid things around Lord Winn? she asked herself as she hurried into the manor again. Thank goodness he is not staying here beyond a few more days, or I would make a complete cake of myself. As it is, I have cried all over his bare chest, and thrown up in his bushes, and now I call him names. Oh, dear. She stopped outside the linen room door and leaned her forehead against the cool wood for a moment. I could almost tell him about Lord Whitcomb.

Felicity still slumbered on the pile of rejected sheets, her red mittens a splash of color against the yellowing fabric. Roxanna sat down, her eyes soft as she regarded her younger daughter. There had been enough yarn left to make a little cap. Another evening would see it finished, and then Lissy would have something else she could not bear to take off. She thought about Lord Winn, wondering how it was that someone so adamantly opposed to children could be so good with them at the same time. Drown them at birth, indeed, she thought. You could no more do that than fly to Madagascar, my lord. Or could you?

She gave herself a little shake. Roxanna Drew, you know next to nothing about Lord Winn, beyond the fact that he is your landlord, and kind to your daughters. And he was the center of a huge divorce scandal. He is not received in his former social circle, or so Mrs. Howell says. She thought about her husband, wondering how he would treat someone with Lord Winn's reputation. Anthony was kind to everyone, but even he had his limits. "And so should I," she said as she kissed Felicity and woke her up.

The snow was gone by morning, but a bone-chilling cold settled in. It was almost a relief to hurry to the much warmer manor house to complete the inventory with Mrs. Howell. Even Meggie Watson came along this time. Lord Winn and Tibbie were already out riding, and Helen quickly disappeared into the stable, after assuring her mother that she would keep her coat well-buttoned, and her mittens and cap on. With a determined expression, Meggie headed for the library to begin her inventory. Lissy followed Mrs. Howell into the breakfast room to see what Lord Winn had left behind, and Roxanna continued her inventory with the second-story bedrooms, writing down the contents of each room.

There were six bedrooms, so she went quickly to work. She would have worked faster, but each room presented the temptation to stand gazing out the south-facing windows, looking down from their situation on Sutton Bank to the Great Plain of York. It stretched away, resting now in winter's early grasp, but fertile and only waiting for spring and the bite of the plow in the soil. There would be lambs dotting the landscape, too, and calves, and long-legged colts that Helen would exclaim over, and follow with her eyes as they trotted, stiff and clumsy, along the fences. Both of her babies had been born in the spring. I must be quite in tune with the land, she thought as she sat in the window seat, put aside her paper and pencil, and rested her chin on her gathered-up knees.

"I do that, too, Mrs. Drew. Lovely view, isn't it? Moreland is more charming than I remembered."

Startled, she looked around in surprise and reached for the inventory pad again.

"No, no. Don't let me disturb you," Lord Winn said as he sat on the edge of the bed. He still wore his riding coat, but he held his muddy boots in his hand.

"Well, I am hardly discharging the duty Mrs. Howell requested today," she said, even as she turned her gaze outside the window again. "Do you know, sir, this view reminds me that there is not a season in Yorkshire that is not beautiful."

"Even winter?"

She nodded, and looked at him, still resting her cheek on her knees. "I like the holly on the snow, and the sky so blue it looks as though it will crack with the cold. Stars seem larger in the winter, or have you noticed, my lord?"

"You're talking to someone who campaigned outdoors through too many winters," he said. "Now I prefer a fire, and a good book, and a comfortable chair a bit sprung in the seat, like me. Ah, yes, Mrs. Drew, I was waiting for that smile! You would have to show me what was so enchanting about a tromp through the snowy woods."

She stood up and reclaimed the pad and pencil again. "All you require for that are two little girls who need to wear off endless energy before they can sleep."

"Or you, madam?" he asked. "I seem to notice a lamp in your window rather late at night."

"Perhaps," she replied, suddenly shy. "Excuse me, my lord."

"Don't bother with the next room, Mrs. Drew. It's mine, and I am not particularly tidy."

"Very well, my lord."

He stood up, still tall in his stockinged feet. "Would you call me Winn?"

"That's rather too familiar, my lord,"she murmured, and left the room.

He followed her into the hall. "What's your first name, or may I be so bold?" he asked.

"It is Roxanna, and no, you may not be so bold," she replied, trying to suppress a smile. *Here I am in my oldest dress, with an apron wrapped practically around me twice, my hair probably dusty, and you are trying to flirt. How absurd.*

"Anyone ever call you Roxie?"

She shuddered. "Only my brothers! Don't remind me."

He laughed."Very well, Mrs. Drew." He opened the door to his room and tossed in his muddy boots. "If I dare not call you Roxie—"

"You dare not," she interrupted.

" . . . and you intend to 'my lord' me to death—"

"I do," she interrupted again. "My lord."

"You are a bit of a trial, Mrs. Drew," he said. "Look now, I have completely lost my train of thought."

"I have not lost mine, sir," she said as she opened the door to a bedroom across the hall.

He followed her into the bedroom, and she laughed out loud. "Sir, leave me to my duties! You are so persistent!"

"Yes, rather like Felicity," he said. "I remember what it is, Mrs. Drew. Could I ask Helen to ride with me this afternoon? I am going into the village to see my solicitor, and it would be a good distance for her pony."

"Your pony," she reminded him.

He rolled his eyes at her. "You know, your perpetually pleasant expression is exasperating! Just when I think you will return an unexceptionable comment, you surprise me. Let us call it a loan, madam!"

She smiled again and looked around the room. "Let me see, a bed, a bureau, a clothes press." She wrote them down. "Yes, my lord, Helen may accompany you. A wing-back armchair, a footstool . . . Very well, sir, a loan."

He was gone then, whistling down the hall. What an odd man, she thought as she continued the inventory. After a quick lunch in the kitchen, Meggie took Felicity home for a nap, and Helen left for the village, riding alongside Lord Winn's tall hunter. Roxanna watched them, proud of the way her daughter sat so erect in the saddle. Lord Winn had found a sidesaddle somewhere in the stable loft, Tibbie had polished it, and Helen sat it like the lady she was. "I wish you could see her, Anthony," she said as she watched from an upstairs window.

In the final bedroom, she made the mistake of sitting down on the bed to rest a moment. Before she knew it, she was lying down. Lord Winn is right, she thought as she closed her eyes. I do stay up too late each night. I wonder if it will ever be easy to sleep without Anthony there?

When she woke, the room was in shadow. She got up quickly, finished her inventory, and hurried down the stairs. Mrs. Howell waited for her at the bottom, her hands on Helen's shoulders.

"We were about to send out a search party for you," the housekeeper said. "Helen's been eating macaroons this past hour with Lord Winn." She tittered behind her hand. "Lord Winn was of the opinion that you were asleep on one of the beds. I told him that was ridiculous."

"Oh! Yes, ridiculous," she agreed, holding out her hand to her daughter. "Come, my dear. If we delay much longer, Felicity will be tapping her foot by the front door and reminding us that she is starved."

They hurried along, almost gasping with the cold. "How was your ride, Helen?" Roxanna asked.

"Oh, Mama! It was such fun!" Helen exclaimed, and Roxanna blessed Lord Winn for the enthusiasm in her voice. "Because I was so good in the solicitor's office, Lord Winn took me to the Hare and Hound for trifle and ladyfingers."

"And now macaroons here?" Roxanna teased. "We'll have to roll you into the house, if you keep up such dissipation!"

"Lord Winn ate more than I did, especially the trifle," Helen confided. "He says his French chef at Winnfield hasn't a clue about 'reet good Yorkshire food with bark on it.' "

Roxanna widened her eyes. "A French chef? Oh, my! Somehow, I don't think that was his idea."

Helen nodded, her eyes merry, then she stopped. "Oh, but, Mama, he said he is leaving tomorrow."

Roxanna digested that news as they walked along in silence. "I will miss him," she said finally. Yes, I will, she thought. It had been a pleasant diversion to have someone as interesting as Lord Winn tumble into their limited society.

"Mama, do you think I could write him?" Helen asked as they scraped the mud off their shoes on the edge of the back porch.

Roxanna considered the question. "If you were older, I would say it was too forward. Since you are six, perhaps it will be unexceptionable, my dear."

"Mama, you could write him, too, and I could add a letter to yours."

Roxanna shook her head, amused at her daughter's enthusiasm. "Now that would *not* be proper! Besides, my dear, what could I ever have to say that would interest a marquess?"

She opened the door, then stepped back outside in surprise, wondering for the briefest moment if she had stumbled onto the wrong property. The dower house was warm. She and Helen stared at each other, and she opened the door cautiously this time.

It was still warm, deliciously so. They hurried inside to keep the cold out, and Felicity looked up from her contemplation of the silverware destined for the dinner table. Meggie Watson smiled at her from the fireplace, where she was lifting off the kettle of mutton stew.

"Meggie, what is this?" she asked as she removed her cloak and bonnet.

Meggie ladled the soup into bowls and managed a rare joke. "I believe it is called heat, miss! I was just sitting here this afternoon, when a coal wagon drove up. The man dumped a load of coal in the shed without so much as a by-your-leave."

"It must be a mistake," Roxanna said, even as she stood before the massive fireplace that covered one end of the kitchen and turned around, reveling in the warmth. "I have no hope of paying for this. Do you think he meant to deliver it to Moreland?"

"I asked him, Mrs. Drew," Meggie said. "He wouldn't say. You'd have thought he was deaf. Or addled."

"It cannot be correct," Roxanna insisted.

"I am sure you are right." Meggie looked her mistress in the eye and set her lips in a firm line for a brief moment. "But all the same, I brought in enough to warm this house tonight. You can take it up with Lord Winn in the morning."

"I will take it up with him tonight!" Roxanna said, already dreading the interview. "He is leaving tomorrow morning."

I wish I were not one to put things off, Roxanna Drew told herself two hours later after she tucked her daughters in their warm bedroom, told them a story about a prince rescuing two little girls in distress, and then knelt on the floor for their prayers without freezing her knees. She knew she should have gone over much sooner, but she couldn't bring herself to leave the warmth of the dower house. I could even do my mending tonight, she marveled. My fingers are still nimble.

Instead, she pulled on her cloak again and girded her loins to face a rather different lion. He will probably tell me some cock-and-bull story and insist that I keep all that lovely coal, she thought as she hurried along, her head down against the wind that grabbed her about the neck and shook her. This much solicitude borders on impertinence, and so I will tell him.

Mrs. Howell answered her timid knock. "Mrs. Drew, nothing is wrong is it?" she asked, holding the door open wide.

Roxanna came inside gratefully and laid her cloak on the hall table. "No, not really. Well, yes, actually. I need to speak to Lord Winn. He hasn't gone to bed yet, has he?"

Mrs. Howell chuckled. "Oh, my, no! He stays awake till all hours, prowling about the house, standing by the window, or just looking into the flames." She tilted her head toward the sitting room. "And now since that pianoforte is tuned, he has a new toy."

Roxanna smiled in spite of herself and listened to the sound of Mozart rippling through the closed door. "He's rather good, isn't he?" she asked.

Mrs. Howell walked with her down the hall. "As to that, I wouldn't know." She took Roxanna's arm and leaned closer. "Sometimes he even sings." The two of them chuckled together.

Mrs. Howell knocked on the door.

"Come in, please," Lord Winn said.

Roxanna took a deep breath and raised her chin higher. Onward, Roxie, she told herself.

He was standing by the piano, his pocket watch out, when she came through the door and Mrs. Howell closed it behind her. He regarded it a moment, then snapped it shut.

"Felicity should be here, my dear Mrs. Drew. I think I would have lost another wager."

"Oh, now, see here, sir . . ." she began, coming toward him, fire in her eyes.

He sat down at the piano again, straddling the piano bench this time. "You see, I thought you would come right away to scold me. But look, you have waited least three hours." He put on his spectacles. "Pull up that stool, Mrs. Drew. You can turn the pages while I play. My Mozart is rusty and I need the music."

She sighed in exasperation, and he looked at her over the top of his reading glasses. "You don't read music?"

"Of course I do!" she said. "My lord—"

"There you go again, swearing. I am distressed at such laxity in a vicar's widow," he said smoothly as he turned toward the piano.

"I would like to thump you! No wonder you can't stay married!" she burst out, then gasped at her impudence.

Lord Winn leaned forward and rested his forehead on the piano, laughing. He laughed until he had to clutch his side. "Oh, Mrs. Drew, that hurts my Waterloo souvenir!" he managed finally. "And don't frown at me like that, or blush. Your face just won't let you look serious."

"Oh, you! What I said was dreadful," she admitted, sitting on the stool beside the piano. "I don't know why that came out."

"You were upset with me for dumping coal all over the yard and warming up that glacier," he said calmly. "And I *am* exasperating." He began to play an allegro, and her eyes went automatically to the music as he played. "Watch closely now. You need to turn . . . ah, very good. You'll do, Mrs. Drew."

She stared at the notes before her, wondering what to say. This will never work, she thought as she turned another page. "I cannot accept that coal, my lord."

"Hush, Mrs. Drew. I have to concentrate on the allegro passage. You can scold me during the andante. Heap coals on my head during the largo, eh?"

She couldn't help herself. She snatched up the pages he was playing, rolled them into a tube, and struck him over the head with them. He laughed as he played doggedly on from memory, and she hit him again, then collapsed with the giggles on the stool. "You would try a saint!" she protested as she laughed and hit him one more time for good measure.

He rescued the music while she laughed, and continued playing, a grin on his face and his eyes on the music. "I do like a hearty laugh, Mrs. Drew. When you are through, we can get down to the business at hand."

She wiped her eyes on her sleeve finally. "Oh, forgive me! I haven't laughed like that since . . . Well, it's been a long time. And I still can't take that coal. Will you pay attention to me, my lord?"

He stopped playing, and straddled the bench again, looking into her eyes until she wanted him to start playing instead. "Mrs. Drew, there is a clause in your contract. As your landlord, I am required to provide coal."

"That is a hum, and you know it, my lord," she said quietly.

He took her hand. "Dear lady, I have spent the last two miserable months—or is it three now?—traveling from estate to estate, staring at deeds and titles and clauses until I am practically blind with it, and if I tell you that the Moreland holding has a clause about coal, you can bank on it that I am right. Cross my heart and hope to die."

"You had better show me the deed," she said, pulling her hand away.

He put his face close to hers. "It is in Latin, you exasperating female!"

She did not back away. "Next you will tell me you found it in your personal copy of William the Conqueror's Domesday Book!"

His eyes brightened and he took off his spectacles. "How did you know? Have you been in my library?"

She leaped to her feet, resisted the urge to thump him again, and took a turn about the room. "Very well, sir, we will accept your coal. Arguing with you is like trying to stop water flowing."

He turned back to the piano and played a wonderful minor chord. "Now you understand! Excellent, Mrs. Drew. There is hope for you yet. Pull up that stool. Do you know Mozart's Piano Duet in C sharp minor?"

She stood looking down at him. I could go home right now, she thought. I probably should. But I am tired of worrying and contriving. Very well, sir, let us play a duet. She sat down and pulled the stool closer while he spread out the parts.

"Just the andante, please, my lord," she said, her back straight, her hands poised over the keys. "I need to get home to my girls."

"Very well, madam," he agreed, his voice gentle. "I know you do. Are you ready?"

"Not too fast," she cautioned. "I have not done this in a while."

"I will take my time," he said, and smiled at the music. "And then when we are done, we will discuss your brother-in-law, who paid me a visit tonight. He wants to buy this place from me."

Chapter 8

Her hands faltered on the keys. He reached over and touched her wrist lightly, then continued the melody.

"Keep playing, madam," he said, his eyes on the music. "The first rule of dealing with such men is not to show any fear."

"But I am afraid," she said. "I am terrified."

"You must not show it. I suspect a deep game here, but we're going to finish this andante first. Excellent, Mrs. Drew. You're a steady one."

The andante concluded. She put her hands in her lap, and continued to stare at the music. Lord Winn closed the piano and put away the music in silence. He shifted to face her, but she could not bring herself to look at him.

"Do I go first, or you?" he asked quietly.

"I wish you would, my lord," she replied. "I want to know what happened tonight before I say anything." You are sitting too close to me, she thought, and felt that same panic that had nearly overwhelmed her during that quelling interview with her brother-in-law.

To her relief, he got up and stood before the fireplace. "I ran into Lord Whitcomb in the village this afternoon. He was surprised to see Helen with me. By the way, Helen was delighted to see him."

Roxanna looked up for the first time. "I am sure she was. He has always been kind to her, and to Felicity."

"And to you, Mrs. Drew?"

She nodded, unable to speak.

"He asked if he could visit tonight on a matter of business." Lord Winn poured himself a glass of port from the table by the

fireplace and offered her one. She shook her head. "He wasted no
a minute in telling me that he wanted to buy Moreland. Said he
would pay any price."

Roxanna shivered, and met Lord Winn's eyes. "Come closer to
the fire, my dear," he urged. "Or is it cold that you are feeling?"

She shook her head and remained where she was.

"I asked him why he was so eager to have Moreland. Told him
I would gladly sell him Retling Beck, but he wasn't interested in
that property."

He came closer and leaned against the piano. "Mrs. Drew, he
said he wanted Moreland so he could keep a better eye on you. It
seems he made a perfectly kind offer to move you into Whitcomb
Park, but you would have none of it." He sat down again by her
on the piano bench. "He wonders if you possess all your facul-
ties."

She sat absolutely still as her insides churned. She could feel
the color draining from her face. The room seemed too hot and
too cold by turns and she closed her eyes. In another moment,
Lord Winn had raised his glass of port to her lips. She drank, and
felt her color return. He set it beside her on the piano.

"You need this more than I do, Mrs. Drew," he said. He
touched her cheek, and withdrew his hand quickly when she
flinched and pulled back from him.

"I think I am beginning to understand what is going on," he
commented. "But you need to talk about it, my dear."

Roxanna looked into his eyes again. Can I trust this man, she
asked herself, or is he just another Lord Whitcomb? God knows
his reputation is much worse than my brother-in-law's. To everyone in the North Riding, Marshall Drew is an excellent landlord,
husband, parishioner, and friend. On the other hand, Lord Winn is
a wild card, a man steeped in scandal, someone mysterious from
farther south. What do I really know of him?

He returned her stare without wavering. "Mrs. Drew, you already trusted me enough this afternoon to take your daughter riding," he said. "I strongly suspect that your daughters mean more
to you than your life."

She nodded. "They *are* my life now. Very well, sir, I have to
trust you, don't I?"

"I believe you do."

She took a deep breath and let it out slowly. "Lord Whitcomb
wants to get me into his bed." She shivered again. "That's bald,
isn't it?"

He nodded. "Bald, but it covers the subject," he said as he got up and took a light blanket off the sofa, which he wrapped around her shoulders. She clutched at the fabric until her knuckles were white, but he made no comment.

"His own wife is a disappointment to him, or so he told me. He thinks I should . . . accommodate him, in exchange for a pleasant life at Whitcomb Park. My daughters would have every advantage." She turned away because she could not bear to look at him. "And if . . . if I had a child, we could pretend it was his wife's. It seems she cannot have children, and I am obviously capable of this."

She jumped up then and stalked to the fireplace to grab hold of the mantelpiece and stare into the flames. " 'We will keep you in the family,' he told me, as though I were a plaything, a man's bauble! Oh, God, what could I do but leave?" The words were torn from her and she shivered again. "He controls my parish stipend as Anthony's relict. He cannot eliminate it, but he can reduce it, and probably will, out of spite. I thought if I could rent the dower house, I might be able to make ends meet, no matter how much he shaved from my allowance."

"Have you no male relatives to apply to for protection?"

She shook her head. "My parents are dead these five years, and my brothers are both officers in the East India Company, situated in Bombay. I have no one in England to turn to, Lord Winn, and no one would believe me if I told them what Marshall was planning."

"Probably not. On the face of it, he seems as upstanding as your late husband must truly have been."

She walked to the piano to stand in front of him. "Do you believe me?" she asked, her voice barely audible to her own ears.

"I do, most emphatically," he replied, his voice as quiet as hers, but filled with a conviction that made her sigh with relief.

"I'm so cold," she said suddenly. "I cannot seem to stop shivering." She tried to smile. "Since you have arrived, I have done nothing but make a cake of myself. What you must think!"

"I think you are quite a valiant lady, but far out of your depth, Mrs. D.," he said as he tugged the blanket tighter around her shoulders.

She questioned him with her eyes. "What do you mean? What can he do beyond what he has already done, if you will not sell him Moreland?"

"Rest on that, at least, Mrs. Drew. I will not sell him Moreland. And so I told him."

"Was he angry?"

Lord Winn smiled. "Oh, a little. Less than you would suspect. I think he must have another plan, but I do not know what it is. I cannot think he has power to harm you here, and I've never been one to borrow trouble from tomorrow."

Roxanna nodded. "I remember a sermon once along the lines of 'sufficient unto the day is the evil thereof.' "

"Matthew 6:34," he said absently, then noticed her wide-eyed gaze. "Yes, I read the Bible, Mrs. Drew! I've even been known to go to church! Not recently, however," he added. "I don't think the Lord is too pleased with me lately."

She sipped the port, then handed it back to him. "Perhaps you are too hard on yourself, Lord Winn."

"Perhaps," he agreed. "At any rate, you needn't worry about your situation here."

"I feel safe enough, as long as you do not sell Moreland." She frowned. "But . . . but I cannot dictate the terms, my lord. This is your property, and if you choose to sell it, then we will leave. It's as simple as that."

"My dear, seldom is anything simple."

She did not know what he meant. He wasn't looking at her, but beyond her and out the window. Somewhere a clock chimed. She counted the chimes in the quiet room, and got to her feet.

"Oh, it is so late! I am sorry to have burdened you with my problems, Lord Winn, but then, you did ask," she said as she held out her hand to him. "I certainly wish you a happy journey tomorrow. Are you returning to your principal seat?"

He nodded, and shook her hand. "I think so. I have to strategize where to spend Christmas this year. It must be a place where I will not get into any trouble, and my sisters will not try to manage me."

"Good luck! My girls will miss you."

He nodded. "Tell Felicity I said to take off those mittens occasionally, and assure Helen that I will answer any and all letters."

"I hope she will not plague you," Roxanna said.

"I don't she how she could," he said, then looked into her laughing eyes. "And you, Mrs. Drew, will you miss me?"

She considered his question, and chose to answer in the spirit of its asking. "Why yes, I will," she replied promptly. "I've laughed with you, cried on you, thrown up in your bushes, and thrashed you with your own music score." He started to laugh, and she held up her hand. "It is nice to know that I can feel something again, my lord, even if it is merely rage and nausea!"

He was still laughing when she hurried down the hall, pulled on her cloak, and opened the back door. She waved her hand at him. "I enjoyed the duet, my lord," she called. He bowed to her and she thought him charming.

It was even colder than when she left the dower house, but Roxanna walked slowly home. Poor Lord Winn. You will wish you had never set eyes on Moreland, she thought as she picked her way carefully through the hardening ground. Widow Drew and her daughters are rather a lot of trouble for ten pounds a year.

She let herself in the front door, and stood for a moment in the empty sitting room. I will tackle this room right away, she thought. I can have it done and furnished with a sofa and chairs from Moreland by Christmas, if I can beg those items from Tibbie. Oh, dear, Christmas. I fear it will be sparse this year.

It was easier than usual to sleep, she discovered. Meggie had thoughtfully provided a warming pan between the sheets, and the grate was furnished with enough coal to keep the chill away. She snuggled into the blankets, thankful to be warm for a change. As sleep came closer, she stretched out from habit to put her feet on Anthony's legs, and drew back when no one was there. "Oh, drat!" she said out loud. "When will I stop doing that?"

Lord Winn stood by the bookroom window and watched until Mrs. Drew was safely inside the dower house. He locked the door and sauntered back to the sitting room, where he poured another glass of port and sat down at the piano again. He held the wine up to the light.

"Here's to you, Lord Whitcomb," he said. "I can empathize completely with your desire to slide Mrs. Drew between your sheets." He drank it down, and poured another drink. "And here's to you, Mrs. Drew. Truth to tell, Roxie dear, I'd like to see you between mine."

He drank the second toast more slowly, playing one-handed through the andante of the duet, wondering why he had been chosen, out of all the people on earth, to be such a fool. "I am an ass, Roxie Drew," he said softly as he concluded the andante, then went back and played her part. "You would no more consider this divorced man as prospective husband material than walk naked through York."

Restless, he went to the fireplace and stared into the mirror over the mantelpiece. Discounting all that, Winn, if she possibly could, you are nearly forty, with graying hair, catty green eyes, and a sharp tongue. A bit of a misanthrope. Mrs. Drew would want children, and you cannot abide the idea of ushering little ones into a miserable world of greed and squabbling relatives. It's a good thing you told yourself that you don't wish to marry ever again, because it's not going to happen with Mrs. Drew, be you ever so in love.

He winced and looked away from the mirror as he remembered the times he had told Cynthia he loved her. Well, you did love her, Winn, he reminded himself. He poured another drink, sloshed the wine onto the carpet, and wondered why the decanter looked farther away from his arm than before. "And here's to you, Cynthia," he said, and drank steadily. The thought of you kept me alive through many a battle, when I wanted to run screaming from the field, he considered. I owe you that.

He picked up the decanter and drank from it. Damn good thing I didn't know what you were doing in our bed while I was thinking noble thoughts in Spain, though, he told himself. Damn good thing. He sat down on the floor by the fireplace. "You are drunk, Lord Winn," he observed, and reached for another bottle on the table. It was too far away, so he abandoned the idea, contenting himself with the last drops from the decanter.

His mind was clear enough. He lay down on the carpet in front of the fireplace, enjoying the warmth on his back, and stared up at the crumbling plaster swirls in the ceiling overhead. Roxie Drew, I was a dead man from the moment you opened your door to me at midnight. I should have just put a gun to my head and blown out my brains on your doorstep. I could look at you, listen to you, watch you for the rest of my life and never get bored. I wonder what you look like when you sleep. When you're angry. When you make love. I would like to know.

Lord Winn put his hands behind his head. This will never do, he thought. A man can go crazy thinking things like that. I can understand Lord Whitcomb's predicament. "Poor sod," he murmured. "You've had to admire her for years and not touch. Did you hold her in your arms to comfort her when Anthony died? How did you manage that, Lord Whitcomb?"

His eyes started to close. Well, at least you are safe from that pile of dirty laundry, Mrs. Drew. I'll never sell Moreland. And since I'm leaving tomorrow, you're safe from another ugly customer.

When he woke, the coals glowed dull red in the grate and the candles had burned down beyond the wicks into waxy puddles. He sat up and rubbed his head, wondering what campfire he had nodded off beside, what battlefield he rested on. In another moment, he recognized his surroundings. He stood up, stretched, and found an unlit candle, which he lighted from the coals.

The hall was dark. Mrs. Howell had long ago gone to bed below stairs. He raised the candle to look around the hall. "A bit shabby, my lord," he told himself. "Could use some refurbishing, rather like you."

He mounted the stairs slowly and walked down the upper hall to his room. "Good night all," he called to the empty rooms. "Sleep well, everyone."

Mrs. Howell woke him in the morning with a can of hot water, coal for the grate, and a reminder that breakfast was ready, and wasn't he leaving? He dragged himself onto his elbow, uncomfortable in his clothes, and wishing he had possessed enough dexterity last night to have at least unbuttoned his pants. Mrs. Howell folded her arms and regarded him with the proprietary disfavor that was the particular gift of female servants old enough to be his mother.

"I know. I know. I am disgusting," he growled. "I'll be down in a minute, Mrs. Howell."

"Take your time, my lord," she muttered as she left the room. "You can only get better."

He took his time, shaving carefully, dressing with more care than usual, and wishing he had time for a haircut. That could wait for Winnfield, he thought, where his valet languished. He combed his hair, glad at least that while it was graying, it was not thinning. Chickering could scold him for being such a shaggy beast, and probably would. Then Amabel would descend again, full of plans for Christmas and her palm up for money. He winced at the thought and put his hands to his head, pressing hard against his temples.

He pulled on his boots, packed his saddlebags, and took a last look around the room. Mrs. Howell could put the books back in the library, he thought, then he looked at the one on top. He pulled out the handkerchief he had been using for a bookmark and sniffed it. Mrs. Drew had wrapped his spectacles in the handkerchief, and he had been meaning to return it. The lavender was gone now, but he tucked the dainty square out of sight in his pocket.

Mrs. Howell waited for him outside the breakfast room. "You have a visitor, my lord," she whispered.

He hauled out his watch. "At seven o'clock in the morning

someone has come calling?" He groaned, pocketed his watch, and went into the room after squaring his shoulders.

He looked around and could not see anyone. "Hello?" he called. "Anyone here?"

Felicity peered out from one of the wing chairs. She grinned at him, and he smiled back, unable to resist her any more than he could resist her mother.

"I thought you would never come down," she scolded, and took a napkin from the table. "I am starving."

He laughed out loud and looked down on her over the back of the chair. She tipped her head up to return his stare. He rested his arms along the back of the chair and admired her red cap, noting that she had removed her mittens at least. Red was definitely Felicity's color. Probably her mother's color, too. He took her plate.

"What will you have, my dear?" he asked, peering at the sideboard. "I don't see any porridge."

"That's all right," she said generously. "I can have that at home. I would like some bacon and a cinnamon bun most especially."

"Very well," he said as he grinned and selected her choices, adding a baked egg. "You'll eat an egg, too."

He set the plate before her and filled his own, marveling how rapidly his headache had disappeared. When he sat down, she took his hand for the blessing, and his cup nearly ran over.

They ate in silence. When Felicity finished her bacon and bun, she wiped her hands carefully on her napkin and looked at him with those eyes that made his heart crack a little. "Aren't you going to wager?" she asked.

He let out another shout of laughter and she grinned at him. "Do you know that you are a certified rascal?" he asked.

"Mama says I am a scamp."

"She's right," he agreed. "No, I am not going to wager. If I do, and lose, your mama will ring such a peal over my head."

"She would never!" Felicity said, shocked, her eyes wide.

"Trust me on this one, Lissy," he said. "She would." He leaned back in his chair and looked at his breakfast guest, who tackled the egg last. "You know, if you had eaten the egg first, then it would be out of the way, and you could have saved the best for last."

She nodded. "Mama puts things off, too."

"Oh?" he asked, hoping for more information about Roxie Drew from such an unimpeachable source.

"She says bad news always waits. So do eggs." She finished the egg and looked at him expectantly. "And I am depending on you to give me another cinnamon bun!"

He laughed again, then heard rapid footsteps coming down the hall. "Lissy, I think your tenure in my breakfast room is about to end."

"I had hoped she would wait until I had another cinnamon bun," Felicity commented, her disappointment evident.

He leaped up and put another one on her plate and then opened the door as Mrs. Drew had raised her hand to knock on it. "Mrs. Drew, what a delightful surprise, and so early!" he commented as she just stood there, looking at her daughter.

She was dressed, but her hair was still down around her shoulders, wavy and brown. Although his brush with marriage had been brief, he knew better than to make any remarks upon her appearance. *She would smite me if I told her how beautiful she looked with her hair that way,* he thought, as he ushered her in and pulled back a chair for her to sit in. *Or at least, Cynthia would have. Of course, Cynthia never got up before eleven o'clock, so what do I know?*

"Lord Winn, I hope you have not been making any bets," she said as she glared at her daughter. "Felicity, you are enough to try a saint!"

"Have a cinnamon bun, Mrs. Drew," he said, and brought the whole dish over to the table. "I told Lissy that her credit wasn't that good at present, so we had better not wager on your approximate arrival."

"Thank heavens for that!" she declared, and to his delight, sat down in the chair he pulled out. "I would love a cinnamon bun. Lissy tells me they are wonderful." She took a bite and rolled her eyes, to his infinite enjoyment. When she finished it, she turned to regard her daughter. "I thought I sent you upstairs to get Helen out of bed, and what do I find but that you have escaped!"

"I wanted to say good-bye to Lord Winn," Felicity said, then grinned. "And eat his cinnamon buns."

Mrs. Drew laughed. She ruffled her daughter's curly hair, then looked sideways at him. "Only think how much more peaceful your life will be soon with no little scamp to plague you!"

Dead dull is more like it, he thought, but returned her smile. "The funny thing is, I haven't minded it," he said, then put his napkin on the table and pushed back his chair. "But I do have to leave."

Mrs. Drew rose, too, and held out her hand for Felicity. "Then we will see you off from the front steps, sir. By all means, my dear, put on your mittens!"

"Then to earn your breakfast, you can carry my saddlebags out to the front," he told Felicity and pointed to them by the door.

He chuckled as she tugged the saddlebags down the hall, intent on her duty, then strolled along more slowly with Mrs. Drew, savoring every moment of her presence. "Mrs. Drew, I have instructed Tibbie to spend more of each day here at Moreland. I think Retling Beck will be sold within the month, and I prefer that he spend more time here."

"Why, sir?" she asked. "Are you worried about my brother-in-law?"

He took her by the arm, holding his breath that she would not bolt from such familiarity. To his relief, she did not. "Let us say, I am cautious, Mrs. Drew. If he tries anything, Tibbie can get me word."

She nodded and moved along slowly at his side. "Very well, my lord. I will be finishing the sitting room at the dower house now, and if there is anything you wish done here, I am at your disposal."

How I wish you were, he thought. I would take you upstairs and we wouldn't come down until spring. "Do remind Tibbie when the coal gets low," he said instead. "That clause in Latin covers coal until the warm weather returns."

She stopped and looked up at him. "Don't try me, Lord Winn!" she began. "Yes, I will let him know. And thank you."

Felicity had tugged the saddlebags out the front door, where his horse waited, saddled and bridled. He took them from her and fastened them onto Ney, who whinnied and stepped about at the prospect of removal from Moreland. "Slow down, lad," he cautioned. "We haven't left yet."

There was nothing to remain for. He had finished his business at Moreland. He could return to Winnfield and suffer any variety of plaguey attention from his relatives, now that he had visited this estate. Mrs. Drew stepped back inside and came out with his riding coat and hat. He shrugged into the coat and rescued his hat from Felicity, who was trying to put it on. "Fits me better than you, Lissy," he said as he clapped the low-crowned beaver hat on his head and moved toward his horse again.

"Wait one minute, Lord Winn!"

He turned around, his heart pounding, as Mrs. Drew came toward him.

"You can't leave here without buttoning your coat!" she scolded as she stood on tiptoe and started at the top. "Don't you have a muffler? Suppose you get a cold?"

Felicity looked up at him. "She does that to me, too," she commiserated.

His eyes lively, he allowed Mrs. Drew to button him into his coat. "There!" she said and stepped back. "Now you can leave." She held out her hand. "Thank you again for all you have done."

He took her hand, wanting to sweep her into his arms and kiss her until she begged for breath. "It's been a pleasure, Mrs. Drew."

Felicity leaned against his leg, so he knelt down and kissed her cheek. "Take care of your mother," he said. "And don't make any bets with strangers. Give Helen a kiss for me." And your mama, he told himself, as he swung into the saddle. I feel as though I am leaving my wife and child, he realized with surprise. We have discussed mundane affairs, she has made her last adjustments to my person. We will say good-bye, except that I am not a husband or a father, and there will be no return anytime soon. I am imagining what isn't there.

"Can I finish the cinnamon buns?" Felicity called to him.

He laughed and waved his hand, then put spurs into Ney's ribs.

Don't look back, you idiot, he told himself as he set his face south down the lane of bare-boned elm trees, ragged now with descending winter. He would write Clarice and tell her he was coming for Christmas, the Etheringhams be damned. He could stop back here in the spring on his way to Northumberland to straighten out that pernicious deed on High Point. By then, Mrs. Drew should be out of mourning, and probably the center of attention of several of the North Riding's gentlemen. If not, at least he should be sufficiently recovered from his brush with love to risk a brief stop here on his journey to nowhere.

He reached the end of the lane and stopped. It was safe to turn around, he thought. They would be inside by now, and he could savor one last look at an estate that was infinitely more dear to him than any other he owned. He turned around for a last look, and they stood there yet, mother and daughter, far away now, but watching him still. He could make out the red dashes that were Felicity's mittens.

As he looked, Mrs. Drew raised her hand again.

"That does it," he said. "Ney, I hate to disappoint you, but we're not going anywhere today."

He wheeled his horse about and started back up the lane. He wanted to gallop, but he forced Ney into a sedate walk, trying to give himself more time to think of a plausible reason that he would be returning. Mercifully it came to him as he traveled the lane again. He reined in his horse in front of Mrs. Drew and Felicity, who could hardly contain her excitement.

"Mrs. Drew, I am the veriest coward," he said as he dismounted. "I find that I cannot face my relatives for Christmas. I have a proposition for you. And don't look wary! How would you like to direct the refurbishing of Moreland? It's a lovely old home with much promise." Like me, he thought. Please, Mrs. Drew.

Chapter 9

"Mama, I think Lord Winn is not easy to argue with."

Roxanna looked up from the baseboard where she was peeling away the last of the sitting room wallpaper, tattered from years of neglect. She laughed in Helen's dirty face and touched another smudge from the end of her finger to her daughter's nose. "My dear, he is impossible!" She leaned closer, her eyes twinkling. "Perhaps he is deranged. Let us do what he says before someone hauls him away to an asylum and we do not have a sitting room."

"Who is deranged, madam?" asked Lord Winn from the entrance, where he was scraping his muddy boots. He draped his coat over the newel post and came into the room dressed in a faded shirt and patched breeches.

"You are, my lord," she replied as the wallpaper came away with an enormous rip and a showering of plaster that left Helen gasping. "Oh, dear, Helen, come out of there! Lord Winn, you do not need to do this before we start on Moreland. And surely you don't have to help with this work."

"Of course I do," he replied as he dusted the plaster off Helen's head and pointed her in the direction of the kitchen and Meggie's attention. "I think it's in that old Latin contract," he said and grinned at her.

"You will remind me," she murmured.

"Of course! Besides all that, Mrs. Drew, I hate to leave things unfinished, and I enjoy this kind of work. We'll have this room plastered and repapered by the end of the week, and then you can

turn your attention to Moreland, where I will use you unmerci-
fully until that grand old place is up to snuff." He grinned and
ripped off the piece above her head that she could not reach. "At
least now you'll have a sitting room to collapse in every night
after I've wrung you out!"

"I suppose that is fair warning," she said, ducking from under
his arm and turning her attention to another section of the wall. "I
recommend that we tackle the sitting room and library at Moreland first. That way, should you choose to entertain during the
holidays, at least they will be done."

"Oh, I won't be entertaining, Mrs. Drew," he said as he pried
off the rest of the baseboard under the window and the glass shivered. "Don't you know I am not received anymore?"

"I had heard," she replied cautiously.

"Hasn't everyone?" he replied, his voice affable. "I am a beast
and an ogre for creating a scandal where there did not need to be
one." He stood the baseboard in the corner. "I should have been a
gentleman about my former wife's numerous indiscretions, and I
was not."

This is not a conversation for my ears, Roxanna thought as she
pulled off the layers of wallpaper. Why is he telling me this? she
thought, knowing that her face was rosy with embarrassment.

"And now I have embarrassed you," he said quietly, looking at
her. "Perhaps I am still not a gentleman." He turned back to the
wall to pry up another section of baseboard.

She watched him in silence for a moment, admiring how easy
the work was for him, and remembering how hard it was for Anthony to even hold a spoon in his hand toward the end. I wonder,
Lord Winn, do you work hard all day so you can fall asleep without dreaming at night? I know I do. But he was speaking to her,
and she forced her mind back to the present.

"Your silence tells me that you agree," he said, putting his back
into the pry bar.

"Oh, no! I wasn't thinking of that," she apologized, speaking
louder to be heard over the creak of the wood.

He stopped and leaned against the wall, shaking his head at her.
"Mrs. Drew, here I give you the perfect opportunity to learn all
the unsavory details, and you are not interested! You are a disappointment to your sex!"

"Really, Lord Winn!" she protested.

"Yes, really! Or is it that you have already formed your opinion
of my character?" he asked, his voice subdued now.

She looked at him then, considering his question seriously.

"Why, yes, I suppose I have." She paused, watching him, and the way his eyes never seemed to leave her face. "I think you are very kind, sir," she concluded, wondering what it was about her that always seemed to take his whole attention. I must have plaster in my hair, she thought. Is my bodice too low? Surely not.

"You should have seen me in the House of Lords, passing that legion of lovers in review by some very startled peers," he said. "No one thought me kind then."

"You were hurt, weren't you?" she asked. She looked into his green eyes, calmly observed the pain there, and plunged ahead. "I personally think infidelity is a dreadful circumstance. Perhaps that makes me old-fashioned, but—"

"That's two of us then, Mrs. Drew," he interrupted. "I took my marriage vows seriously. Too bad Lady Winn did not."

"You must be a rare member of the peerage, indeed," she said before she thought.

He laughed. "You have definitely formed an opinion of my class! And you would be right, in the main, Mrs. Drew." He ripped up the rest of the baseboard, then sat back on his heels. "But, no, I am not kind."

She smiled then, thinking of red and blue mittens, and a pony, and coal, and a leg of mutton. "Well, as to that, I suppose you are entitled to your opinion and I to mine."

They worked in silence then. In a few moments, Lord Winn was whistling under his breath, absorbed in his efforts. When she finished stripping the wallpaper, she paused to watch him a moment, admiring the play of muscles under his shirt as he strained at the baseboards, and remembering when Anthony would have thought nothing of such a task. She remembered their first year in the vicarage, and the times he carried her upstairs for an afternoon romp in their bedroom that would have scandalized his parishioners. She sighed, and then looked guiltily at the marquess, hoping he had not heard.

To her chagrin, he turned around with that searching regard that further discomfited her. "Mrs. Drew, if you have time to sigh like a schoolgirl and be so idle, give me a hand here."

She hurried forward and grasped the board he indicated. "You pull while I pry, and if the whole wall doesn't come down, I'll be through with this."

Roxanna did as she was told, gritting her teeth against the shriek of the wood. One more deft nudge of the pry bar and the whole baseboard came off in her hands. She sat down with a thump as the dust and plaster swirled around them.

"Are you all right?" he asked, kneeling beside her. "Nothing injured?"

"Just my dignity," she said and remained where she was on the floor. She gazed around the room in dismay. "Oh, my. You really think it will be done by Friday?"

He wiped his hands on his breeches. "I am certain of it. Which reminds me"—he looked toward the entrance to the front door—"do my eyes deceive me, or is that a clean child in the doorway?"

Felicity giggled. "Meggie says I am not to enter this room," she reported to her mother.

"Sound advice," Roxanna said.

"Lissy, let me engage your services," Lord Winn said as he settled on the floor, his long legs crossed. "Hand me that scroll of wallpaper by my coat."

"Just toss it in, love," Roxanna said.

He caught the roll of paper and spread it out between them. "What do you think?"

Roxanna leaned forward, careful not to touch the paper. It was a floral pattern, delicate and springlike, the lightest shade of blue, and obviously expensive. "It's beautiful, my lord," she breathed.

"Good! I thought so, too."

"Is it for your sitting room?" she asked. "What an excellent choice."

"It is for yours, madam," he said. "I was in Darlington earlier this morning, and this caught my eye in the warehouse."

"Oh, dear, Tibbie didn't tell you?" she asked, dismay and regret mingled with equal parts in her voice.

"Tell me what?"

"We've been doing the rooms here with leftover paper from earlier renovations at Moreland. This is much too expensive, my lord."

"But I like it," he said. "I bought it for this room because it reminded me of you and your girls. And I don't like to be argued with."

"He doesn't, Mama," Helen agreed from the other doorway into the dining room and kitchen.

"My lord!"

"There you go again," he said as he rolled up the paper and tossed it back to Felicity. "You really have to let me use it on the walls here, because it matches the carpet I purchased at the same time."

Impulsively she touched his sleeve. "And yet you will tell me that you are not kind?" she asked, her voice low.

He got to his feet and held out his hand for her. "Kindness has nothing to do with it, Mrs. Drew," he assured her as he lifted her up. "It is mere expediency. How would it appear if the carpet did not quite fit with the sofa and chairs I ordered?"

Roxanna glanced at Felicity. "Lissy, hand me back that roll of paper. I intend to beat Lord Winn over the head with it!"

Felicity laughed and clapped her hands. "Can we watch, Mama?" she asked, while Helen opened her eyes wider. "Mama, he is a marquess!" she reminded her mother.

"He is a scoundrel," Roxanna said. "And now you will say it is in the Latin charter."

To her further embarrassment, Lord Winn ruffled her hair. As she coughed from the plaster dust, he went to the entrance and pulled on his coat. "I wouldn't dare, Mrs. Roxie Drew," he declared. "If you and the girls will wipe down those walls, I'll send the plasterer over here this afternoon. Good day, Mrs. Drew. Don't get in a snit over small things."

And he was gone, shouldering his roll of wallpaper like a musket, and leaping lightly over the muddy spots in the front yard. Helen watched him go, then closed the front door. "He likes you, Mama," she said quietly. "Do you like him?"

Roxanna sat down on the stairs and held out her arms for her daughters. "Of course I like him," she said, hugging her girls, even as they sneezed from the plaster on her dress. "You'd have to be made of stone not to like Lord Winn."

Felicity nodded, and rested her head on Roxanna's lap. "Mama, do you think Papa would have liked him?"

Why that should bring tears to her eyes, she did not understand. "I am sure he would have, my dear," she said, and kissed Felicity, and then Helen. She hugged her girls close, comparing and contrasting. Physically, they were two completely different men, she thought, Anthony tall and slender, Lord Winn shorter by a little, and built sturdy like a Yorkshire barn. She rested her cheek against Helen's hair, reminded of Anthony's blondness and his graceful ways as she looked at her elder daughter. He had been everything she wanted in a husband. Too bad he was gone before they had time to do more living together.

But both men were kind. She considered her dead husband a moment, aware for the first time that his kindness everyone took for granted, because he was a vicar. With Lord Winn, such kindness was unexpected. Roxanna ran her hand through Helen's silky hair. Why is it that I suspect he is selective in his kindness? she thought. And why on earth has he singled us out?

She closed her eyes a moment. When she opened them, Felicity was watching her. "Mama, are you sad?" she asked, her voice anxious.

Roxanna hugged Felicity. "I don't know what I am, Lissy, but I don't think I am sad."

The plasterers descended on the dower house after a hasty rub-down of the walls that left Meggie retreating upstairs to nod over a book, and Roxanna and the girls sneezing even as they with-drew to the kitchen. "Why does every home improvement seem to fill a whole house?" she asked Tibbie as he got the workers started.

"That's what my wife always wonders." He pulled a folded note from his pocket. "It's from Lord Winn. He said he won't take no for an answer."

Roxanna glanced at Helen's expectant face as she opened the note. "My dears, it seems we are to dine at Moreland tonight." She sighed and looked at Tibbie as her daughters clapped their hands. "We are such an imposition on that man!" She pointed to the note and read out loud. " 'I do not think you would care for stewed plaster, or fricasseed plaster, or plaster hollandaise, which, I believe, is on the menu in the dower house tonight. I will request cinnamon buns for Lissy.' "

"Mama, he will spoil us," Helen declared solemnly as she read the note in her mother's hand, then ruined the effect by grinning at her sister. "I like it!"

Roxanna shook her head at Tibbie, who shrugged his shoulders. "Think of it as getting a wonderful return on your ten pounds, Mrs. Drew!"

Lord Winn dressed more carefully for dinner than usual, changing waistcoats several times, thinking that he ought to write to Chickering for more clothes. He combed his hair and wondered if the village had a barber. Not that it would help much. Cynthia used to complain that no matter how elegantly he dressed, he al-ways looked as though he belonged on a farm. "Happen I do," he murmured to the mirror. There was no question that he was seri-ously wanting in high looks. "But I am rich," he told himself. "I can have anything in the world I want—except Mrs. Drew." He raised his chin and tied his neckcloth. "And that, Fletcher, is the cruelest kind of poverty."

He considered Mrs. Drew as dispassionately as he could, com-paring her to Cynthia, who was without question the most beauti-ful woman he had ever seen. He was only one of many suitors that season who'd dangled after Cynthia Darnley, second daughter of Sir Edwin Darnley, enraptured by her ash-blond beauty and eyes the color of cornflowers. She was tall and elegant of form, with an aristocratic curl to her lips that he'd thought enchanting at first. Her nose was chiseled from the palest marble, and Brummel himself had rhapsodized over Cynthia's profile until little portraits of her appeared, white against a blue background, all over London. "Chiseled" was certainly the operative word, he thought. Cynthia, you were chiseled from an entire block of marble. Lucky me. Thank God there was a war on and I had to leave you. I can only wish Lord Masterson good luck.

He sat on his bed, wondering for the thousandth time if things would have been different if he had been able to devote all his time to her. He concluded, as always, that it would have made no difference. "Cynthia, you were just bound to be too much trouble," he said, and got up to change waistcoats again.

Mrs. Drew, on the other hand, has more than beauty going for her, he considered as he looked in the mirror, tugged on the waistcoat, then reached for his coat. If anything, she was thinner than Cynthia, as though she didn't take any thought to her own health. While Cynthia's fashionable slimness was due to a daunting regimen of vinegar and boiled potatoes that used to take away his own appetite, Roxie Drew was thin because she worked too hard, slept too little, worried too much, and wasn't loved sufficiently.

But, oh, those eyes. He knew, as sure as he stood there in his stockinged feet, that he could look at her all day and never grow weary of the view. In fact, when they were working in the sitting room, he'd caught her questioning gaze when he stared too long. It would never occur to Roxie Drew that she was worth a second and third glance, he decided. Her marvelous skin was not a city pallor, but a rosy country hue, and her wonderful high-arched brows and brown eyes, round as a child's, made him want to take her in his arms and just hold her until moss grew over them both and they blended into the landscape.

"Rave on, Lord Winn," he said as he looked at himself one more time. He was reminded then of Cynthia's favorite pose in front of the mirror, and was immediately disgusted with himself. "At least she thinks I am kind," he said as he closed the door behind him and went downstairs. But I would rather be a dashing lover, he thought as he shot out his cuffs and hoped Mrs. Howell had remembered cinnamon buns for Felicity.

After a few minutes of standing in the hall, he opened the back door at a tentative knock coming from rather low on the door panel.

"It's me, Felicity," he heard on the other side of the door, "and we are cold!"

Helen and Mrs. Drew were laughing at Felicity when he opened the door. It was easy to bow and usher them in, mouthing something about "three of the prettiest women in England on my doorstep," and meaning each word utterly. He looked into Mrs. Drew's enchanting eyes. Cynthia would have simpered at such a compliment, but Roxie just grinned at him and said "Thank you," quite prettily.

Dinner was a remarkable success, and it gave him the greatest pleasure to lean back in his chair, admire the diners around him, and pretend they were all his own. Mrs. Drew ate a healthy serving of everything, and he felt himself relaxing as she leaned back, too, her hand on her stomach.

"Mrs. Howell is a wonder," she said finally as she wiped cinnamon glaze off Felicity's cheek and nodded to Helen.

With another glance at her mother, Helen got to her feet and stood beside his chair. "Mama says I should play a song for you on the piano, Lord Winn," she said.

He pushed his chair back. "Aha, you are to be the evening's entertainment, my dear?" he asked.

"Not precisely," Helen replied. "You are, sir. Mama is going to cut your hair while I play for you."

He laughed and looked at Mrs. Drew, who was taking a pair of scissors and a comb out of her reticule. "You're serious," he said.

Mrs. Drew stood up and took Felicity by the hand. "Of course I am, my lord," she replied. "I never say anything I do not mean. Tomorrow I will be struggling with wallpaper again and you do need a haircut. It will have to be tonight, if you are to pass yourself off with any credit in this neighborhood."

He allowed himself to be led along the hall by Felicity, with Helen beside him, her back straight, her lips firm, as though she contemplated an execution rather than a recital. After soliciting a dish towel from Mrs. Howell, Roxie Drew joined them.

Helen stood by at the piano bench while he adjusted the height. She played a tentative chord and smiled at her mother. "Mama, only think how fine it will sound when I can reach the pedals!"

"Oh, most emphatically yes, Helen. Take off your coat, now then, Lord Winn," Mrs. Drew commanded.

Anything, he thought. She pulled out a straight chair and made him sit in it while Helen began "Für Elise" and Felicity settled herself on the sofa, her ankles crossed and her hands folded in her lap. He watched her, then glanced up at Mrs. Drew, who stood behind him. "Do you wager?" he asked, his voice low.

She chuckled. "I would not give her beyond thirty seconds of such gentility." He watched in amusement as Felicity sighed and flopped back on the couch to stare up at the plaster swirls in the ceiling.

"The civilizing process is a long one, Lord Winn," Mrs. Drew commented as she removed his neckcloth with a practiced hand and unbuttoned his top button. "I don't see Lissy rushing it, either, do you?"

My God, he thought as her warm fingers tucked the dish towel around his neck. I could die right now and be in paradise, breathing lavender and listening to "Für Elise." To his continued delight, Mrs. Drew stood in front of him, pursed her lips with that expression that made him want to shout "Yes!," and stared at his hair. She combed his hair carefully, smoothing it with her hands, then stepped behind him and began to snip. "This is certainly the least I can do, after all your many kindnesses," she said, and he felt her breath on his neck as she clipped away. He closed his eyes with the bliss of it all as Helen launched into something that sounded like Vivaldi and Lissy watched him, her eyes slowly closing.

"We have a casualty from all those cinnamon buns," he whispered.

"I am sure I will be the second one," she said. "I ate too much, but then, Meggie Watson insists that I need to put on some weight."

As a former husband, he knew that any addendum to that statement would have got him into trouble. He remained silent, relishing Mrs. Drew's proximity, and the heavenly way her bosom brushed his head once or twice as she cut his hair and hummed along with Helen's performance. She was soft beyond belief, and he closed his eyes in gratitude to a merciful God who was sometimes surprisingly kind to miserable sinners.

When she finished, she rested her hands on his shoulders for a brief moment. He could have cried when she removed them and walked to the mirror over the fireplace. "Come here, my lord, and tell me what you think," she said.

He followed and gazed into the mirror at the two of them standing together. I think I would like to kiss you, he told himself. "It's fine," he said, running his hand along the back of his neck. "In fact, much better than my valet usually does."

She grinned into the mirror at him. "I am happy to have the chance to do something nice for you."

I have so many other suggestions then, he thought, each of which would earn me a slap in the chops. Instead, he returned some comment, and to take his mind off Roxie, glanced at Felicity, who was sleeping soundly on the sofa. Helen played the last chord of the Vivaldi.

"Shall I play some Bach now?" she asked.

Mrs. Drew shook her head, and he wanted to cry out in disappointment. "No, my dear. I think it is time we were leaving."

"It's a lovely piano," Helen said, her voice wistful.

"Then I think you should practice on it as much as you like," he said, extending his arm to Roxanna. "And do play the Bach, Helen. Mrs. Drew, may I just take you upstairs to show you what I have in mind for the second floor?"

He didn't have the slightest idea what he wanted for the second floor. Perhaps if they strolled through the rooms, her lavender scent would linger after she was gone. He looked up at the crumbling plaster scrollwork in the ceiling. "I think you can see what needs to be done down here."

"Oh, yes," she said, and after a slight hesitation, took his arm. "I would like to use that same wallpaper in here that we are putting into my sitting room. It's just the right touch. We'll be only a moment, Helen."

Upstairs, he took her through the room and babbled something about colors and heavy furniture that must have sounded more intelligent than he thought, because she nodded and seemed to regard his comments seriously.

"Exactly so, my lord," she said, standing at the window in the last bedroom. "Moreland is a wonderful old farmhouse that woke up pretentious one morning. I would like to strike a happy medium and return some of that innocent quality to it."

Anything, anything at all, Mrs. Drew, as long as it takes you months and months. Her next words were a cold water bath.

"This won't take any time at all, sir," she said, fingering the ornate damask draperies. "I will lighten the walls with more modern paper and paint, and replace these drapes with lace, or even muslin." She sat on one of the unyielding beds. "You might want to reconsider these mattresses, my lord. And I know of a warehouse in Darlington with lovely bedspreads, too."

He watched her as she perched on the bed and felt the sweat start down his back, even though the room was cool. "I bow to your judgment," he said, his voice calm, his mind in outrageous turmoil. "Just make it look like a home."

She laughed and got off the bed, to his relief. "That's easy, my lord! I'll loan you jackstraws and blocks to trip over in the middle of the night, enough clutter to drive you distracted, and suspicious marks and rings on things that no one admits to."

He tucked her arm in his again and picked up the lamp from the bureau. "Well, new bedspreads and curtains will do, I suspect, and more modern furniture."

"Oh, that's right," she returned, closing the door behind them. "Didn't you say something once about children being the curse of the earth?" She looked about the hall, doubt in her eyes. "I do not know that a house without children is really a home, but I'll do my best to make it so here at Moreland. And now I really must be going, my lord."

Felicity was still asleep on the sofa when they returned, and Helen was gathering up her music. "Just leave it there, my dear," he said as he helped her into her coat. "If we can convince your mother that Ney and your pony need some exercise, we can ride tomorrow, and then you can come back here to practice."

Helen, her eyes dancing, looked at her mother. "Oh, please!"

"I am sure that will be fine," Mrs. Drew said. "You can work on that Mozart piece you were practicing"—she paused, then continued smoothly enough—"at your Uncle Drew's house."

"I can help her if she needs it," he offered.

Mrs. Drew widened her eyes in mock surprise. "Why, Lord Winn, how *kind* of you!"

He smiled at her little joke, and picked up Felicity. "I am kindness itself," he said, grateful that at no point in the evening could she read his thoughts. *Actually, I am wondering how on earth I can convince you to marry me, and coming up absolutely dry.* The reflection pained him.

Some of this agitation must have crossed his face then, because Mrs. Drew touched his arm. "Lord Winn, are you all right?" she asked. "Is it a war injury? I can wake up Felicity. You needn't carry her."

"Oh, no!" he assured her. "It's nothing. Perhaps I shouldn't have pried so energetically on those baseboards. Lead on, Helen."

Snow was in the air again. Mrs. Drew turned her face up to the heavy clouds in the night sky. "I think there will be snow by morning," she said softly. "And I do not think it will leave much before spring now, my lord."

"Winter comes early to the North Riding," he said, loathing

himself because his conversation could go no deeper than the weather, or the price of bedspreads.

"It's November," she said. "Not so early."

He carried Felicity upstairs to the bedroom that she shared with Helen, and stood watching as Mrs. Drew deftly removed her shoes and stockings, slid her out of her dress, and tucked the blankets around her. She kissed Helen good night and then joined him in the doorway.

"I sometimes stand here and wonder how I got so lucky," she whispered to him.

"Lucky, madam?" he said. "Some would say you were not so lucky." It sounded bald to his ears, but it was honest. He wanted so much to touch her, but he could only make bracing statements.

"Lucky," she said again, her voice firm. "I have my girls."

Her quiet words humbled him as nothing else could. I have more estates than ought to be legal, and more money than some countries, he thought. Mrs. Drew isn't even sure if she will have a quarterly allowance after December, but she is lucky and I am not.

Her head came just past his shoulder. How easy it would have been to kiss her, but he knew he did not dare. A few more perfunctory words, a nod or two, and he was outside again, looking up at the dower house. He walked back quickly as the snow began to fall, resolving to write Amabel in the morning and tell her that he had no intention of spending Christmas at Winnfield this year. The Etheringhams could go to hell, for all he cared. Perhaps he could spare a day or two with Clarice and Frederick, but that was open to debate.

To his gratification, the upstairs hall did smell faintly of lavender yet. He was a long time getting to sleep.

Chapter 10

The sitting room was done by Friday afternoon, true to Lord Winn's prediction. Roxanna sighed with pleasure and wiggled her stockinged feet in the carpet, then leaned back on the sofa. The only bad moment had come during the unloading of the furniture. She knew enough about quality workmanship to know that Lord Winn had squandered what Meggie called a king's ransom on the sofa, chairs, and end tables now placed so companionably in the compact room. It was the kind of furniture that she and Anthony would have admired in a warehouse, but never selected, no matter how much they wanted to.

"I think he's up to something," Meggie said from her perch on one of the wing chairs before the fireplace.

"Lord Winn?" Roxanna asked. "Oh, Meggie, that's preposterous!" She patted the cushions into place. "I do own to some guilt that he spent so much, but, Meggie, he has the money. If he chooses to do this, I wouldn't argue." She smiled. "Even Helen will tell you what a waste of time it is to argue with him. And truth to tell, it *is* his house."

"All the same, Roxanna, be a little wary," Meggie warned. She settled herself in the chair, and in a moment was snoring.

Roxanna tucked her legs under her and gazed out the window, curtained now with lacy strips the same pale blue as the wallpaper. If I want to worry about something, Meggie, let me worry about my brother-in-law, she thought. She had not seen Marshall Drew since her removal to the dower house, but he was on her mind more than she cared to admit.

She had known him for eight years, since her marriage at age nineteen to his younger brother, and while she did not study his career about the North Riding, she knew that Lord Whitcomb never failed to get what he wanted, whether it was a parcel of land, or a colt to train for the Scarborough races. It was a quality that Anthony shook his head over more than once, then confessed to her that he did not know if what he felt was envy or approbation at this doggedness in his brother.

We are safe here at Moreland, she reminded herself, then stood to put more coal in the grating because she felt a chill. She remained at the window, hugging herself, and admiring the shocking blue and white landscape of a Yorkshire winter that never failed to move her. A child of Kent, she had been raised in a milder climate. The bite of December in the North Riding, with trees iced and streams silenced, and hills almost grotesque with drifted snow, awed her. Everything seemed to hibernate, in the hopes that deep sleeps would produce spring sooner. Even Felicity slowed down, and offered less objection to an afternoon nap.

She was discovering that she thought of Anthony more in the winter, waking up at night to wonder how cold the graveyard was, and how deep the snow there. He seemed farther away under that additional burden of snow, as though the distance now was more than miles. She had cried yesterday when she couldn't remember whether his birthday was January 16 or February 16. What else will I forget? she wondered as she stood before the window.

I wish I were not so restless, she thought. I wish I could relax like Meggie, and sit in one spot without leaping up to pace about a room, or search for more to do, when I have already done everything around here that needs to be done.

She knew what she missed, what drove her to ceaseless activity, but there wasn't anyone to discuss the matter with. Meggie had never married, and Mrs. Howell, well, Mrs. Howell would only stare at her. Proper ladies didn't talk about what she needed. For the first time also, she found herself wishing she had been less interested in Anthony's body when he was alive, and able to gratify her love. Roxie, if you had been a bit less eager then, perhaps you wouldn't feel such a sharp edge now, she scolded herself.

"Oh, bother it!" she said, then put her hand over her mouth when Meggie woke up and looked around. "I am sorry, my dear," she exclaimed, contrite.

Meggie watched her, but she could not help herself as she paced in front of the window, feeling like a pet mouse on a wheel. She stopped finally and lifted her cloak from the peg by the front door. "Meggie, I am going for a walk. Lissy is napping on my bed, and Helen is reading in her room." She was out the door before Meggie could ask any questions.

She swung the cloak around her shoulders and took a deep breath of the bracing air. All was silent now, the stream by the house quieted by ice, the birds far south. The only sound she heard was the impatient crunch of her shoes on the crusty snow.

The lane that led from the main road to the manor house was

free of snow, something Lord Winn insisted upon. She started down the road, feeling better already as the cold circulated through her lungs and her cheeks began to tingle. I shall become a champion walker, she thought, and giggled at the notion. Anthony, the lack of your husband's comfort will turn me into the healthiest woman who ever strode the hills of the North Riding. The doctors will have to take my heart out and beat it to death so I can die at a decent old age.

She was still smiling when she reached the end of the lane and started back. As her mind cleared, she considered Christmas, which would be sparse, but not impossible. Someone, probably one of her husband's former parishioners, had sent her an anonymous five pounds, so there would be a goose and other good things, and perhaps enough for a small gift for each girl. She would like to have afforded something for Mrs. Howell, Tibbie, and even Lord Winn, but that was out of the question, particularly for Lord Winn. What could she possibly give to a man who had everything?

"Mrs. Drew, are you practicing for a footrace?"

Startled, she looked over her shoulder and up into Lord Winn's eyes, as he sat on Ney.

"You should not sneak up on a person like that," she scolded.

He reined in his horse and she stopped, too, as he hitched his leg over the saddle. "My dear Mrs. Drew, I was whistling something rather loud from *The Magic Flute!* This was not a sneak approach. What is occupying *your* mind?"

"None of your business!" she said crisply, then repented. "Well, actually, I was wondering what I could give you for Christmas since you already have everything."

To her amazement, Lord Winn began to blush. She laughed out loud. "Well, whatever it is, I am sure it must be illegal or immoral! Surely nothing a vicar's widow could possibly satisfy."

He had to laugh at that, but it sounded rueful to her. He peered down at her as he swung his leg back in the stirrup. "Mrs. Drew, you are a rascal. I think I understand Felicity better now."

"I am no such thing, sir!" she protested, and walked alongside his horse. "You are the rascal."

He was silent for most of the lane, then he reached inside his coat pocket. "Mrs. Drew, you'll appreciate this," he said as he pulled out a sheet of paper and handed it down to her.

She looked at it with interest. "Very good, my lord. You've ordered enough wallpaper and paint to get the whole job done. Tibbie told me this morning that he has arranged for the plasterers to return. They promise to tackle the ceiling in your sitting room the first thing on Monday morning."

"Well, then you'll have to suffer my presence in your sitting room occasionally until it is restored," he replied and pocketed the paper again.

"You may drink tea with us this afternoon, my lord," she offered. "Everything is finished, just as you promised, and Helen and I made gingersnaps this morning."

"Tea *and* gingersnaps?" he quizzed. "Strange isn't it, Mrs. Drew? Two years ago, I was dining on puppies—don't tell Lissy—and strained pond water somewhere in the Pyrenees."

She made no comment as they continued slowly up the lane. What a different life you have lived, she thought. "I should think that after all those years of deprivation, you would seek out the company of your friends, or at least your relatives, at this time of year," she said finally as they approached the curving drive before the manor.

He dismounted and handed the reins to his groom, who must have been watching for him. "My dearest friends lie dead on battlefields all over Europe, and I only quarrel with my sisters. Oh, now, Mrs. Drew, don't take it so to heart!"

"I'm not!" she declared, even as her eyes filled with tears.

She held her breath as he took off his glove and touched her cheek, then leaned close to whisper in her ear. "Don't ever cry over me, my dear. I'm not worth that. I have everything, remember? You said so yourself."

She dabbed at her eyes, embarrassed. "I say stupid things, don't I?"

"No more than I," he replied, his voice suddenly hard. "I have the advantage over you, my dear. I *do* stupid things." He took off his hat and bowed to her. "I think I will skip tea this afternoon, Mrs. Drew. Some other time."

And then he was gone, hurrying inside the manor without a backward glance. She stood a moment longer in the driveway, her heart even heavier than before, then turned and walked back to the dower house.

I must have said the wrong thing, Roxanna Drew told herself many times in the coming weeks before Christmas. I wonder what it was? she asked herself as she threw herself into the renovations at Moreland. She removed paintings, shifted furniture, stripped wallpaper, and learned to patch with plaster as the work proceeded in the manor. At the end of each day, she was deliciously tired and no good for anything except a quiet dinner, and then blissful sleep.

Lord Winn did visit in her parlor on several occasions while his own sitting room was a tattered ruin. He drank tea, played cards with Helen, read to Felicity, and even listened to Meggie Watson's animadversions on the current government. He spoke but little, and too many times, Roxanna could almost feel the sadness in him. No one else seemed to notice, and she wondered if she was just imagining his low state, because he said and did all that was proper.

Or perhaps because I feel low, I have imagined others are so afflicted, she considered one afternoon as she straightened up from scraping paint from a window frame. She backed up against the wall to straighten her spine, wondering why the closer Christmas came, the worse she felt. As she stood there, she remembered something Marshall had said to her just after Anthony's funeral. "My dear, the holidays and birthdays will be the worst," he had told her. As much as she disliked thinking about Marshall, she had to agree with him.

Christmas without Anthony would not be Christmas, not really, she reasoned as she tackled the frame again. They always decorated the sitting room with greens, and hung a wreath, but she had not bothered yet. Meggie had reminded her only last night that it was time to start on the Christmas cooking, but the conversation had drifted off to nothing.

I simply must exert myself for the girls' sake, she thought as she left Moreland that evening. She thought of her brothers, glad that she did not have to report to them how badly she was playing her hand right now. "We will make gingerbread cookies tomorrow," she said out loud. *But no mistletoe this year,* she added to herself, remembering the sprig that dangled last year over Anthony's bed. The stockings would have to go up. *Maybe if she spaced them wider apart on the mantelpiece, Anthony's wouldn't be missed.* "Oh, God," she cried out loud, and stopped in the snow. "I can't face it."

She stood there in the snow until her feet started to grow numb, then continued into the house, ashamed at her own whining. *I still have so much,* she thought. *Why must I dwell on what I do not have?*

Helen met her at the door with the news that Lord Winn was in the parlor and would stay to dinner. Roxanna sighed. *Why tonight, when all she wanted to do was go to bed and curl up in a little ball?*

"I gather from that sigh that you wish I would take my mutton at Moreland, Mrs. Drew," Lord Winn said from the doorway into the sitting room.

He was still dressed in his riding clothes, and leaning comfortably against the door. She did not want to look at him because she knew her face was bleak, but courtesy demanded some response. She glanced in his direction and mumbled some pleasantry, and then he promptly straightened up and spoke over his shoulder to Helen, who had been out riding with him.

"Helen, I think you and Lissy should see what Meggie needs in the kitchen. Come, come, march like soldiers."

When they were gone, he came closer and took her arm. To her vast relief, he didn't say anything, only gave her a little shake. It was enough. She squared her shoulders and came into the parlor, grateful to sit down before the fireplace.

"If Moreland is too much, I can get some more help," he said as he sat in the other wing chair.

She shook her head, not looking at him. "It's not Moreland, my lord, and you know it. I will be glad when it is January and this holiday is behind us."

"There will always be something else, my dear Mrs. Drew," he commented, pushing the footstool her way. She propped her feet on it, sharing it with him.

"I know," she agreed. "And I will take each event as it comes and not think too far ahead." She smiled into the flames. "I refuse to be defeated by death."

"Bravo, Roxie Drew," he said softly. "I get through days like that, too."

She looked at him in surprise. "Somehow I never thought . . ." she began, then stopped.

"That I loved her?" he finished. "Oh, I did, Mrs. Drew. I suppose I mourn a little too, wondering if Cynthia and I were casualties of the war, or if all this dirty business would have happened, anyway. I conclude it would have, then I kick myself for loving her."

Impulsively she touched his sleeve, then drew her hand away, embarrassed at her forwardness. "I'm sorry," she said simply. "It's hard to let go, isn't it?"

She cried then, leaning back in the chair and letting the tears slide down her cheeks. To her relief, Lord Winn said nothing, but let her cry in peace. He left the parlor in a moment, and she heard him supervising her daughters in the breakfast room. She dried her eyes, blew her nose, and settled more comfortably in the chair. Her eyes closed and she slept.

When she woke, the house was quiet, and the fire much lower in the grate. She looked around in surprise, and saw Lord Winn in the other chair again. "Goodness, what time is it?" she asked, sitting up in alarm.

"Nearly midnight, Mrs. Drew," he said. "Meggie and I put the girls to bed. Lissy cut up a bit stiff because I did not carry you up to bed and tuck you in, too, but I assured her you would rather not wake up that way."

Roxie chuckled. "Trust Lissy to worry. You could have at least wakened me for dinner."

He shrugged. "Why? You needed a nap."

"Why, indeed?" she agreed. "Do you think there is any food left?"

"Mrs. Drew, I made you a sandwich, and found a bottle of ale from somewhere, if that won't disturb your gentility."

She laughed as he went to the kitchen and returned with the sandwich and a dark brown bottle.

"Do you require a glass?"

"Of course, my lord! I am not dead to propriety,"she teased, and accepted the glass that he pulled out from behind his back.

The sandwich was delicious. "I am always amazed that sandwiches taste better when someone else fixes them," she said between bites.

"You should try my horse meat on a stick over a cow dung fire," he said. "You don't even need seasoning."

She laughed again and he joined her, after taking a swig from her bottle of ale. "You are a man of many talents, Lord Winn!" she exclaimed.

"Oh, I am," he agreed affably, putting his booted feet on the footstool again. "I've decided to go to Clarice's for Christmas," he said, changing the subject. "She's not too far from here, but far enough from Amabel, who, by the way, wished me to Hades in her last letter."

"Your sisters!" she said. "Of course, I am certain you wrote Amabel a perfectly gentlemanly letter explaining why you did not choose to entertain the Etheringhams and their daughter," she continued, trying to keep the amusement from her voice.

"Of course!" he stated in mock seriousness. "How could you doubt it? I only mentioned casually that I would not stud for the Etheringhams to cut Lettice's son out of my succession. I do not understand why she took offense at that."

Roxanna rolled her eyes, grateful that the gloom in the sitting room hid the color that she felt rush to her cheeks. "Lord Winn! You are a trial to your sisters!"

"Yes, ain't I?" he agreed cheerfully.

"You know, you could always fall in love again and marry," she commented as she finished her sandwich and set the plate on the floor. "What then?"

He was a long time in replying. "I doubt marriage is possible," he said finally as he stood up to leave. He bowed over her hand. "Mrs. Drew, go to bed. Tell Helen we will go riding in two days. I'll leave Christmas Eve morning for Clarice's place."

She walked him to the door. "Very well, sir! We will take good care of Moreland while you are gone."

He paused in the doorway, his overcoat half on. "By the way, I have taken the liberty of purchasing presents for your daughters."

She started to protest, and he put his finger to her lips.

"A riding crop for Helen and some rather pretty barrettes for Lissy. That is completely unexceptional, Mrs. Drew."

"Well . . ." she stalled.

"All you need to do is say 'Thank you, Lord Winn, you shouldn't have,' and leave it at that." He shrugged into his coat.

"Thank you, Lord Winn, you shouldn't have," she repeated.

He winked at her and closed the door.

She shook her head and climbed the stairs. "Telling his sister he wouldn't be a stud . . . ," she muttered as she opened her bedroom door. "Brothers are a dreadful trial."

Roxanna saw Lord Winn only briefly in the next two days, and then from the window as he rode out to Retling Beck with Tibbie and his solicitor. They must have returned long after she finished chipping paint for the day, and by then she was involved in the Christmas baking she had been putting off and did not think about him much.

At any rate, she tried not to, but this was rendered difficult by the discovery of a large goose on her doorstep the following morning. Lissy stared at the plucked and bound bird and looked up at the sky, her eyes big. Roxanna turned away to avoid laughing at her daughter. "My dear, I think it may be a gift from Lord Winn," she said, when she could speak.

Lissy nodded. "Not from heaven?" she asked.

"Well, not precisely, my dear! Here, help me carry it in."

Lissy's "goose from heaven" found its way to Meggie in the kitchen, and then onto the cold side porch with the other perishables she had baked earlier.

"It will be cookies today, girls," Roxanna announced to her daughters over porridge. "Your favorite kind."

Helen looked up from her bowl, her eyes troubled. "Papa's,

too?" she asked. "Please, Mama, I don't want to forget him," she burst out when Roxanna hesitated.

Helen pushed back her chair and ran from the room. Roxanna bit her lip, poured the rest of her oats into Lissy's bowl, and followed Helen upstairs. The door was closed, so she knocked on it quietly, and then entered.

Helen lay on her side, facing the window, staring out at the bleak landscape. Roxanna sat beside her, rubbing her back as Helen cried. "I thought I would like Christmas," she said at last after she blew her nose on the handkerchief Roxanna held out to her. "Why is it so hard this year?"

Roxanna leaned against the headboard. "Helen, I think it is hard because we want to remember Papa, and we want to go on, at the same time."

Helen looked at her through red, swollen eyes. "Will it be any easier next year?" she asked as she rested her head in her mother's lap.

"I suppose we won't know until next year, my dear," Roxanna said honestly. "We won't ever forget Papa, but I suspect our feelings will change and mellow."

Helen was silent. Roxanna hugged her close, looking forward to the dark and cold of January as never before. "My dear, we will make those cookies with almond paste that Papa liked so well. I wish we could gather holly and greens like we used to, but we don't have a gig."

Helen blew her nose again and managed a watery smile. "Oh, it will be all right if we just have the cookies. And will we read from the Bible on Christmas Eve?"

Roxanna smiled at her daughter, because she knew it was expected of her. "I don't see how we can possibly avoid it!" she teased, keeping her voice light. "Now you wash your face, and we'll go downstairs and start on the cookies." She gave Helen a little pat. "Didn't you promise to go riding with Lord Winn this afternoon?"

Helen nodded. "Five Pence needs the exercise."

"Five Pence?" Roxanna asked. "You finally named your pony?"

"Lord Winn did, Mama," Helen said from the depths of a washcloth. "He said my pony was as fine as five pence. He's almost as good at naming as you, Mama."

The morning was devoted to cookies, and the whole dower house smelled divinely when Lord Winn rapped on the door that afternoon for Helen. He stepped inside the house when Roxanna

opened the door, took a deep breath, and staggered back against
the doorsill while Felicity laughed and clapped her hands. Even
Helen grinned, to Roxanna's relief.

He took Helen by the shoulder. "My dear, you cannot possibly
expect me to take you riding without a little restorative. I'd like at
least one of each of those smells, please."

She and Felicity hurried off to the kitchen for some cookies as
Lord Winn watched them go, an appreciative smile on his face.
"Charming," he murmured. "Mrs. Drew, you and the late vicar
are to be congratulated on your offspring."

"Why, thank you!" she exclaimed. "Now, you will eat with us
tonight? I know Mrs. Howell has left for Darlington already."

He bowed and accepted promptly as the girls returned. He
scooped up a handful of the cookies Helen held out to him.
"Come, my dear. Our horses are turning into hay burners. Race
you?"

They returned just as dinner was ready. Roxanna spooned up
bowls of potato soup, Lord Winn said grace this time, and they
began dinner. Lord Winn ate in silence, then held out his bowl for
more.

"Mrs. Drew, Helen has informed me that the sitting room is
quite bare without greenery," he said as he lifted his spoon again.
"I have advised her that we will take the gig on that road toward
Whitcomb tomorrow morning for holly and whatever else appeals
to us."

Roxanna looked at him in surprise. "But you're leaving for
your sister's tomorrow, aren't you?"

"Well, I was," he temporized, dipping a chunk of bread in the
soup. "I rather think the greenery is more important than an early
start. Clarice can wait a few hours for my scintillating appearance."

"Very well," Roxanna said dubiously. "I wish we were not
such a chore to you." He opened his mouth to speak and she interrupted. "And this is *not* in the Latin charter!"

"My dear, I didn't know you had read it," he said smoothly,
then returned to the soup.

"It really is a trouble to you," she said later as he came downstairs from telling the girls good night.

"Not at all, Mrs. Drew," he insisted, and gently took her by the
elbow to steer her into the parlor. "Helen needs to have some con-
tinuity right now."

Roxanna went to the window and stared out at the darkness.

"She was feeling in the dumps this morning about forgetting her papa."

"So she told me."

She turned around to face the marquess. "I seem to get deeper into your debt each day. But we do need to gather greens tomorrow." She hesitated. "I feel it, too."

He nodded and picked up his overcoat. "Excellent, Mrs. Drew! How pleasant you look when you do not argue with me!" He was gone with another wink, and she had no time to feel sorry for herself.

They didn't leave before afternoon, because Lord Winn discovered another paper he had to sign at Retling Beck to secure the sale of that manor. When he returned with a gig, they piled in and left Meggie waving at the front door and giving all manner of cold-weather advice that no one remembered.

It was almost too cold to talk. "We'll keep this short," he assured her as he reined in on the Whitcomb road. "Mrs. Drew, if you would oblige me by driving this horse up the lane and then back, the girls and I will hunt the wild holly. Come, Felicity."

He tucked Felicity, shrieking, under one arm, and broke a trail through the snow for Helen, as Roxanna sat in the gig, blessed him, and wiggled her toes to keep them warm. *I wish you would not leave,* she thought. *It's too cold and I will worry.* Then she scolded herself for being a ninny. *Roxie, he crossed the Pyrenees on foot once with a starving army,* she told herself. *Surely he is beforehand enough to negotiate the distance to his sister's estate without coming up against disaster.*

She took the horse and gig up and down the lane twice before they returned with a burlap sack bulging with greenery. It was a tight fit in the back now for Helen, so Felicity sat on her lap for the return journey. In a moment Lissy was asleep, her face turned into Roxanna's warmth. The marquess glanced at her. Roxanna flashed him her most appreciative smile.

"I'll leave right away and spend the night in Wisner. I'll be at Clarice's by the middle of tomorrow afternoon," he said, still looking at her.

I wonder why he does that? she thought, then took his arm to point out the fact that the gig was wandering from the road. *I know I am not a beauty. He must be lonelier than he lets on.* She stared ahead, hoping that Clarice would find one or two interesting women to drop in on Boxing Day, for her brother's benefit.

"Well, are you expecting company?" Lord Winn asked as they approached the dower house.

She looked at the horse, blanketed and miserable, tied to a tree in the dower house yard, and shook her head. "I can't imagine anyone who would visit on Christmas Eve. Come, girls, let's see who our company is."

"The horse looks familiar," Lord Winn said. He stopped the gig and jumped down to help Roxanna with Felicity. Helen pulled the burlap bag from the back and accepted a hand down. "I think I will help Helen with the bag, if you don't mind."

"You're just nosy, my lord," Roxanna teased, "wanting to know who visits a widow on Christmas Eve!"

"Guilty as charged," he said cheerfully.

Helen and Felicity ran ahead, calling to Meggie to hurry with the string and shears to create a wreath, and Roxanna came more slowly. The marquess closed the door behind them. She came into the parlor, shaking the snow off her cloak.

She did not recognize the man who sat on her sofa, but he leaped up the moment she entered the room, and then looked in surprise at Lord Winn, who followed her in.

"Lord Winn! I was told . . . I thought you were gone for the holiday," he said as he tugged a wax-stamped document from his overcoat pocket.

Roxanna looked from the man to Lord Winn, curious about the frown that appeared on the marquess's face. "No," he began, and she wondered at the wary tone. "Should I have been?" Lord Winn turned to her. "Mrs. Drew, since he has no manners, let me introduce the sheriff of this district, Reggie Cowans. Mr. Cowans, is your business with me or with Mrs. Drew?"

She frowned at the marquess. *I wish you would be a little more friendly,* she thought as she reached out to shake hands with the sheriff. *And here he is, impatient with waiting. I wonder if he would like tea?*

She gasped as Cowans slapped the document into her outstretched hand and bolted for the door. "It wasn't my idea!" he shouted over his shoulder as he ran from the house.

"Good God!" the marquess exclaimed. He took her by the shoulder as he stared down at the papers in her hand. "I don't know what this could possibly be, Mrs. Drew, but I think you ought to sit down before you open it."

"Nonsense!" she exclaimed as she broke the seal and spread out the pages. She read a few words, then sank to her knees before Lord Winn could grab her. She dropped the document as thought it burned her fingers, and covered her face with her hands.

Lord Winn snatched it up, his face white. "My God," he said softly as his eye scanned the first page. "Mrs. Drew, this is a writ of removal." He sat down hard on the sofa, running his finger down the document. He sucked in his breath and stared at her, dumbfounded. "Lord Whitcomb means to take your children in three days!"

Chapter 11

There was a great roaring in her ears, blocking out what Lord Winn was saying to her, even when he grasped her by the shoulders and spoke right into her face. She noticed finally that she was sitting on the sofa, and that someone—it must have been Lord Winn—had placed her hands in her lap.

She sat there, and finally heard someone, his voice urgent, saying, "For God's sake, make a wreath in the kitchen and keep the girls out of here! Meggie, do you have any brandy?"

As her vision cleared, she saw Lord Winn holding out a glass to her. She tried to reach for it, but it seemed miles away and her hand was shaking too badly. In another moment, Lord Winn gripped her shoulder, put the cup to her lips, and made her drink.

"You were saying something," she managed to gasp, after the brandy began its work.

He sat beside her, his arm tight around her shoulders, as though to stop her trembling. "You simply must get hold of yourself, Roxie," he ordered softly. "The girls cannot know what is going on. It would destroy them."

She nodded, clenching her jaw closed to keep her teeth from chattering. She knew she should remonstrate with him for calling her Roxie, but it suddenly seemed so unimportant. He could call her anything, and it would not matter. Marshall Drew was coming for her children. She closed her eyes and leaned against the marquess.

Her senses on edge, she jumped and opened her eyes at the rustling of paper. Lord Winn had spread out the pages on his lap, reading them quickly, turning the pages. "Damn," he said several times softly, but with great venom.

"Tell me," she said, wishing that he would put more coal on the fire. She was numb with cold. But how could that be? A fire roared in the grate.

He shook his head. "No time now." He looked at his watch. "Roxie, we have to decorate this room with greenery and help hang a wreath. Then we'll eat dinner. What do you do then on Christmas Eve? Roxie? Come on, my dear. Speak to me."

"We read something," she said, her voice dull to her ears. "I wish I could remember what. Something."

"The Bible?" he suggested gently.

"Bible?" she repeated. "Oh, yes, the Bible. Something in St. Luke. I can't remember what. Why would we read Luke? I wish I knew."

She stared at the marquess. He put his hands gently on her neck and gave her a little shake and then spoke distinctly, as though to someone deaf.

"Roxie, you've been dealt a dreadful hand by your brother-in-law," he said. "Are you going to play it?"

Am I going to play it? she asked herself and thought of her brothers, teasing her when she threw down a bad hand and ran from the room. "Of course I am going to play it," she replied automatically, and took his hands from her neck. "Of course I am."

She sat still a moment, and gradually began to feel warm. She sighed and burrowed closer to Lord Winn, grateful for his warmth. She could hear the clock ticking over the mantelpiece now, and the girls laughing with Meggie in the kitchen. I cannot lose them, she thought. I must be in control. She sat up straight then, and the marquess relaxed his grip.

"We read the story of the First Christmas from Luke, my lord," she said calmly, even as her stomach churned and roiled. "We hang our stockings, and the girls go to bed."

"Good girl," he said. "When they're in bed, we're going over to Moreland to take a real look at this and figure out what we're going to do."

To her indescribable relief, he said, "what we're going to do," and not, "what you're going to do." She turned to look him in the eyes. "Thank you for not leaving me in this alone."

"I wouldn't dream of it," he replied, standing up, and pulling her to her feet. Her legs buckled under her, but he held her up until she could stand on her own.

"Mama?"

It was Helen, and she was holding out a red ribbon. "Mama, are you all right?" she asked anxiously.

I am dying, she thought as she squared her shoulders and smiled at her daughter. "Of course I am," she lied smoothly. "I think I was just a little too cold out there. Do you need me to make a bow?"

Helen nodded. Lissy came into the room, struggling with a wreath as tall as she was. Roxanna sat on the edge of the sofa as Meggie hurried to Lord Winn, a question in her eyes. There were whispered words between them, then Meggie gasped and turned away to face the window.

"Now, my dears, let us go in the kitchen, so I can lay out this ribbon on the table," Roxanna said as Meggie began to cry softly.

Startled, the girls looked at Meggie, then followed their mother into the kitchen. As they watched, she willed her hands to stop shaking, and made a bow for the wreath. It took three tries, but received Helen's approval finally. Under her direction, Helen threaded a needle and bound the bow to the wreath with a few careful stitches.

"Excellent!" Roxanna declared and took a step back for the full effect. "I am certain we can get Lord Winn to hang it over the mantelpiece. Is there enough holly left for a small wreath at the door? Hand it to me carefully, Helen. I can do that."

She fashioned a holly wreath, surprised that she could not feel the sharp pricks of the leaves. It is as though I am watching someone else do this, she decided. Nothing hurts, because it is not happening to me.

"Mama, it's beautiful," Lissy cried, her arm resting on Roxanna's leg as she worked at the kitchen table.

Roxanna bent down and kissed the top of Felicity's head, breathing deep of her child's fragrance. She rested her head against her daughter's curly hair for a moment and closed her eyes, trying to imagine life without her.

"No," she said firmly. "It is not possible."

Lissy looked at her with those brown eyes so like her own. "Mama, *I* think it is beautiful!" she argued.

"Oh!" Roxanna said. "Of course it is. I was thinking of . . . something else. Let's put it on the front door."

By the time she returned to the sitting room, Meggie was fully in possession of herself and helping Lord Winn arrange the large wreath over the fireplace. Roxanna hung the holly wreath over the knocker. It was beautiful, she thought, the shiny green and red contrasting so elegantly with the white door. I will not think about the end of the week, when my brother-in-law will knock on this door to take my daughters from me.

She and Meggie prepared dinner in tight-lipped silence while Lord Winn and the girls sang carols and draped the holly and greens about the sitting room. Meggie looked up once from the onion she kept mincing over and over. "He's a cool one, Mrs. Drew," was all she said. Roxanna could only nod her head in agreement.

She did not attempt dinner, knowing that if she raised her fork to her lips, she would throw up. By pushing the food around on her plate, she managed to look busy enough to fool Lissy, who was always involved in her own meals anyway. Helen regarded her with a frown.

"Mama, you should eat," she scolded. "Don't you like fricassee?"

Roxanna patted her stomach. "What I really need is a glass of soda and water. I think I ate too many cookies this morning."

Helen nodded, accepting this reasoning, and finished her food. Lord Winn even asked for seconds. "You're a good cook, Mrs. Drew," he said. "I could grow stout with my legs under your table."

She smiled at him. "Don't blame me! It's all those cinnamon buns that Lissy insists on at your house."

There, she thought, that was a reasonable volley of conversation. We almost sound normal. She glanced at the clock. Another two hours of this charade and I can put the girls to bed and fall apart.

After dinner, while Meggie cleaned up in the kitchen, Lord Winn settled himself on the sofa, took Felicity on his lap, and accepted the family Bible. "Luke 2, my lord," Roxanna reminded.

He looked up at her in genuine amusement. "I know where it is, Mrs. Drew!" he declared. "You must not persist in thinking that I am a heathen." He turned the pages. "Ah. Here we are. 'And it came to pass in those days that there went out a decree from Caesar Augustus that all the world should be taxed . . . ' "

Her arms around Helen, Roxanna leaned back against the sofa and closed her eyes, the majestic words like a balm flowing over her whole body. As Lord Winn read, his voice that interesting combination of Yorkshire brogue and cultured diction so familiar to her ears now, she forced herself to think about that first Christmas. She thought next of her eight Christmases with Anthony, then folded them in her memory and tucked them away in her heart. Next year will be better, she thought. It has to be.

Helen was disappointed that there was no stocking for Lord Winn to tack onto the mantelpiece. "You could take off your boot and let me have that one," she reasoned as Roxanna hung the Christmas stockings.

"Oh, you wouldn't want either one," he assured her. "I believe there is even a hole in the toe of one and in the heel of the other."

Helen's eyes opened wide. "But you are a marquess!" she exclaimed.

Lord Winn laughed. "A title has nothing to do with it! You should have seen me in Spain. Even my breeches had holes in them there. Let me bring over a clean sock in the morning." He looked down at Felicity, who slumbered in his lap. "Here, Mrs. Drew. Take the Bible and let me get Lissy upstairs."

She and Helen followed him up the stairs. The floor was cold, so Helen's prayers were short. Felicity didn't even wake up as Roxanna dressed her in her nightgown and tied on her sleeping cap. Lord Winn stood looking down on her. "If that were anyone but Felicity, we could call it the sleep of the innocent," he whispered. Helen giggled, and crawled into bed beside her sister. She held out her hand.

"Good night, Lord Winn. I hope you have a happy Christmas."

As Roxanna watched, he turned away, the muscles in his face working. Tears started down his cheeks. She touched his shoulder and sat on the edge of Helen's bed as she left the room. "I am sure he will," she managed to say. "Perhaps the holidays are hard for him."

"But he has us," Helen asserted, keeping her voice low to avoid disturbing Lissy.

And such a lot of trouble we are for ten pounds, Roxanna thought. She kissed her daughter good night. "When you wake up in the morning, you will smell Lissy's heavenly goose cooking."

And my goose is already cooked, she thought as she hugged Helen, then closed the door behind her. Lord Winn was already down the stairs and into his overcoat, the writ in his hand, his eyes red.

"Get on your cloak, Roxie," he ordered. "We're going to Moreland. You can cry in peace over there and I can throw things."

She nodded and let him help her with her cloak. "I'll be back in a while, Meggie," she said. "Please try to sleep."

"I couldn't possibly, Mrs. Drew," Meggie said.

Lord Winn took her hand and hurried her through the snow to Moreland, his face grim. She half-ran to keep up with him, and then he shortened his stride. "Sorry," was all he said as they traversed the distance.

The estate was dark and cold. He let her into the bookroom and lit a lantern, then dumped coal in the grate and started a fire. "I'm going to the stable to wake up my groom," he said as he looked at the little flame. "I'm sending him for Tibbie."

"Tibbie?" she asked.

He nodded. "He may be the only cool head in the bunch, Mrs. Drew. I'll be back."

She pulled up a chair close to the fire and reached for the document that Lord Winn had thrown down on the desk. The Latin phrases mingled with the English words and leaped out at her like little imps to torment her. She shuddered and pushed it away.

By the time Lord Winn returned, the fire glowed in the grate, and her hands were warm for the first time all day. He sat down heavily in the chair and swiveled it around to face her. "Did you read it?" he asked.

She shook her head. "I can't bring myself to touch it."

"I understand that, Roxie," he said simply. "He has been granted a writ of removal by the lord magistrate in York."

"York?" she questioned. "Why there? It's so far away!"

"Exactly," he said, scooting his chair closer until they were knee to knee. "The writ can only be answered in York, my dear."

"Then we will start out tomorrow," she said, her eyes on his face.

He shook his head. "To enter a pleading you have to have a court hear you. There's nothing in session right now." He leaped to his feet and slammed his hand on the desk. "Damn that man! There are no Common Pleas, or Assizes, or even Chancery Court open between now and at least January 6," he shouted. "Quarter sessions doesn't start for another three weeks! Mrs. Drew, he has humbugged you!"

She sagged back in the chair, her mouth open. "My God," she said softly. "Can I not at least bring a plea before a justice of the peace?" she asked.

He grasped her by the shoulders. "And who is this district's JP?" he demanded, his eyes fierce.

She began to cry. "It is Lord Whitcomb!" she sobbed. "But . . . how can he do this? Why can he take my children?" She cried as he took her in his arms and held her close.

"It's in the document, my dear," he said, holding her off a little to look at her face. "He claims you are an unfit mother because you moved your daughters into a dilapidated house with floors and roof missing. As the only living relative in England, he is empowered to take your daughters from your influence."

Roxanna stared at him, her tears forgotten. "But the house is beautiful now! How can he say that?"

Lord Winn was thumbing through the document. "Look you here. 'The house is in execrable condition, with peeling wallpaper, parts of the roof missing, and the floor entirely gone in the sitting room. The structure is unsound and dangerous for children. By reason of the fact that Mrs. Anthony Drew, relict of Anthony Drew, is obviously of unsound mind, I claim her children as my own to raise.' "

"How can he do this?" she murmured, looking over his arm at the words. "It is not true now about the house."

He sank down in his chair again. "And how is a magistrate in York to know that?" he asked quietly. "And why would a magistrate in York have cause to doubt Lord Whitcomb's testimony to the state of your house? He is a district justice of the peace, and by everyone's acknowledgment, a gentleman." He spit out the word like venom.

She let the words sink in as she read where he pointed, looking up finally. "I have no legal recourse, have I?" she asked.

"None whatsoever, Roxie," he agreed. "None that I can see, at least."

"I have to turn my daughters over to him on Friday," she said, her voice calm. "And myself, too, I suppose. He will have me after all, because he knows I would never let them go without me. And I cannot do a thing about my upcoming ruin."

They were both silent, staring into the fireplace. In a few minutes, Lord Winn put more coal on the grate, then rested his boots against the fender. He reached for her hand. "We can enter a pleading in the middle of January when quarter sessions convenes."

"That will be too late," she said. "He's a strong man, Lord Winn. I do not think I will have much of a chance to resist him." She shuddered. "I am already afraid of him. Excuse my blunt words, but I know he will hurt me," she said frankly. Her voice broke then. "We can't do anything? Oh, God, tell me there is something we can do!" She sobbed into her hands.

"You could grab them and run, but why do I think he will be watching the roads?" he said, handing her his handkerchief.

"Of course he will," she said, her voice muffled in the handkerchief as she blew her nose angrily. "And when I am apprehended, it is only one more indication that I am of unsound mind. Even a January pleading in quarter sessions would not convince a judge that I was a fit mother. I cannot run."

"No," he agreed, "you cannot. And I doubt anyone would take the word of a woman suffering from derangement of grief against Lord Whitcomb's calm testimony. As far as the world knows, all he wants to do is offer you and your daughters a good home with him and his lady, and you have irrationally resisted his good offices by moving into a ruin." He sighed. "I might add, the house is on the estate owned by a notorious divorcé of dubious character. Humbugged," he repeated. "Trussed up better than a Christmas goose."

"Oh, don't say that!" she pleaded.

"If I weren't so angry, I could almost admire his cleverness," he said, then sat up, listening. "I believe Tibbie is here. Roxie, light another lamp and go to the kitchen. I think there is a bottle of rum on the table. Bring it back here with some cups."

When she returned, the marquess was sitting on the edge of the desk, telling Tibbie the story. She calmly poured rum for the three of them. Tibbie accepted his absentmindedly, his eyes on the document before him. He looked up finally.

"I think I understand how he could give such a description," he said, and held out his cup for more.

"Say on, sir," Lord Winn declared.

The bailiff looked at Roxanna. "Remember when he and his solicitor came here to talk me out of renting you the house?"

She nodded. "Yes. And I was so afraid you would yield."

"Well, after they left in such a fit, one of the workers came to tell me that they were going through the dower house, room by room. He said the solicitor was taking notes!"

"That explains how he knew so much," Lord Winn said. "Well, Tibbie, any suggestions? We're fresh out of ideas."

The bailiff shook his head. "You need to see a solicitor, my lord."

Lord Winn managed a laugh with no humor in it. "He left yesterday for Edinburgh for the holidays. The only other solicitor in the village is retained by Lord Whitcomb." He rose heavily to his feet and paced in front of the window, his hands behind his back. "I cannot believe how cleverly we have been diddled!"

"Yes, and the sheriff even thought you would be gone today," Roxanna said, joining him at the window. She leaned her forehead against his arm for a brief moment. "I am so grateful Helen had to have her greenery. I could not face this alone."

He put his arm around her. "I can't see that my presence here is making one scintilla of difference, Roxie dear," he admitted frankly.

As they stood at the window, staring out into the snow, Tibbie Winslow began to chuckle. It started as a low rumble in his throat, then welled into such a hearty laugh that they turned around to gape at him. As they watched, he reached for the handkerchief Roxanna had abandoned and dabbed at his eyes.

"Have you lost your mind?" the marquess snapped.

Tibbie looked at Roxanna and then at Lord Winn. He nodded. "It'll do in a pinch," he said to himself. "It'll do."

"What will do?" she demanded. "Oh, Tibbie, you are driving me distracted!"

He spread his hands out on the table and looked up at them with glittering eyes. "It's simple. Lord Winn, all you have to do is marry Mrs. Drew! Then Lord Whitcomb can't touch her or the girls. It's so simple."

She gasped and released her hold on Lord Winn. "Tibbie, that is out of the question!"

"Why?" he asked simply.

"Well, because it just is," she said, looking at the marquess for confirmation. "Surely Lord Winn will agree. Tibbie, I believe you owe him an apology for such an absurdity."

To her bewilderment, the marquess was looking back and nodding, his expression completely unreadable.

She stared at him. "You can't be considering this seriously!"

"And why not, Mrs. Drew?" he said at last. "Tibbie, you may have hit upon the only thing that will humbug Whitcomb."

Tibbie agreed, his eyes bright. "Just the way you two were standing there, you know, like she fits under your arm, made me think of it." He looked at Roxanna. "He's a good man, Mrs. Drew."

"A bit shopworn," Winn said, his eyes light now with something besides despair. "But I could be the answer to your current dilemma."

Roxanna sank down into the chair. "Surely you don't want to do something that drastic, my lord. I mean, what a crazy notion this is!"

"It's not so crazy," the marquess argued, sitting on the edge of the desk. "If you and your daughters are my chattel, according to law, Whitcomb can't do a thing. That would solve your problem."

"Yes, but—" she began helplessly.

"And if you marry me, then Lettice, Amabel, and even Clarice will be off my back forever," he continued with relish, unable to disguise his growing enthusiasm. "I would count that a blessing!"

He reached out to shake Tibbie's hand. "Sir, you are a genius! I am sure I do not pay you enough!"

Tibbie glanced at Roxanna and allowed himself a little smile. "My lord, I think this will require some convincing on your part." He grinned at Roxanna. "I think something in the stables is needing my attention."

"What?" Roxanna snapped. Everything was happening too fast. She wanted to curl up somewhere and think about matters, even as they were racing toward a conclusion she had no control over.

"Happen I'll find out when I get there," he said quickly as he nodded to Lord Winn and backed out of the room with the speed of someone half his age.

Lord Winn closed the door behind his bailiff and strolled to the window again, his hands clasped behind his back, not looking at her. He waited a long moment to speak, as though choosing his words with impeccable care. "Mrs. Drew, I need hardly remind you that you are at *point non plus*, if ever anyone was."

"I suppose I am," she agreed, her eyes lowered, the words dragged out of her.

There was another long silence. He finally turned around and looked at her. She couldn't bring herself to meet his glance, so he knelt by her chair and raised up her chin with his fingers until she had no choice.

"Marry me, Mrs. Drew," he said softly. "And let me assure you from the outset that this will be a marriage of convenience."

"That is hardly fair to you, sir," she protested, when she could speak.

He continued to look into her eyes. "Oh, Mrs. Drew, it is entirely fair. I really have no desire to commit any more matrimonial folly. You already know my ideas on children of my own. I will deed Moreland to you upon my death and provide you with an income now. Beyond a few visits a year to make sure that all is well, I'll not trouble you with my presence. It will drive my sisters crazy, but what can they say, really?"

She was still silent, staring at her hands now.

"And Mrs. Drew, should you form a more agreeable attachment in a year or so, I am sure we can arrange a very quiet annulment."

"But this is all so cold-blooded!" she burst out, unable to contain herself. "Fletcher, I cannot do this to you."

He smiled. "Well, at least you acknowledge that I have a first name. That is a step in the right direction. And yes, you are right.

It *is* cold-blooded. We are trying to save your daughters and your virtue," he reminded her.

She nodded, unable to dispute his line of reasoning. "But—"

"Do you like me even a little bit, Roxie Drew?" he asked suddenly.

"Oh, of course!" she said. "How could I not like you?"

"Well, you need only ask Cynthia for a whole list of reasons why not," he replied, a twinkle in his eyes. "My dear, this will solve your problem and mine, too. Marry me."

She looked him in the eyes. I am not even a year through my mourning, she thought. My God, I am still in black! The village will be scandalized. His relatives will be aghast. A sudden smile played around her lips. The girls will be delighted, and we will be safe. The smile left her face. And I have no choice, none at all, but by God's blood, I will play this hand.

"I will marry you, sir," she said.

Such a light came into his eyes that she gazed at him in surprise. When he saw her expression, his own became more sober again. He held out his hand and they shook on it. He sat at the desk again, and leaned back in his chair. "Very well, Mrs. Drew. We certainly haven't three weeks to cry the banns. It will have to be by special license."

His chair came down with a bang and he slammed his fist on the table. "Damn!" he shouted, and she jumped. He touched her arm, his eyes filled with distress. "I'm sorry, my dear. I just remembered. I cannot get a special license. The only way I can remarry is with a writ from Chancery Court and with the approval of the Archbishop of Canterbury himself."

He went to the window to stare out at the snow as her heart sank again. She was beyond tears. And so even this wretched plan will not work, she thought. I am doomed to be Lord Whitcomb's mistress. God help me.

She watched with dull eyes as Lord Winn paced the little room, pausing at last in front of a map of England and Scotland. He stared at it, and as she watched, his shoulders relaxed and his hands came out of his pockets. He picked up the lamp and moved closer to the map.

"Oh, Mrs. Drew, we'll get that bastard another way," he said, the note of triumph undisguised in his voice.

"How?" she said at last, afraid to hope.

"We're about seventy miles from the Scottish border," he informed her, his voice filled with enthusiasm again.

"I know that! I do not think I need a geography lesson right now, my lord," she said. "How will this solve our—"

She stopped, leaped to her feet, and hurried to join him in front of the map. "You are not thinking for one minute . . ." she began.

He was nodding as his finger traced the route. "Oh, yes I am, Mrs. Drew, think on. If we can catch the mail coach, we can be in Gretna Green on Boxing Day. My dear, we will have to marry over the anvil."

She blinked her eyes and leaned against the wall, the breath knocked out of her. "Sir, is that legal?" she asked.

"Most assuredly. It's just a bit . . . well, the word *ill-bred* does come to mind."

She was silent, contemplating the enormity of such a step. What will people think? she asked herself, then shook her head. What did it matter? Her girls would be safe, no matter how scandalous the wedding.

"I will do it, my lord," she said slowly. "I have no choice."

"No, you do not, my dear," he sympathized. He held out his hand again and she extended hers slowly until they were clasping hands. He gave her hand a shake, but did not release it.

"Well, Mrs. Drew. In for a penny, in for ten pounds, in your case. Let's go find Tibbie."

Chapter 12

Sleep was out of the question that night. After a lengthy conversation with Meggie, in which they both cried and clung to one another, she filled the girls' stockings and sat in the parlor until even the coals grew dull in the grate. What have I done? she asked herself over and over. Did I have any choice? The answer was always the same. She was as much at the mercy of Lord Winn as Lord Whitcomb.

It distressed her that she knew even less about Fletcher Rand than she did about her brother-in-law, and yet she was ready to join her life to his in the most intimate bond. I could say I was taking him on faith, she thought, but that almost seems like blasphemy. I am doing this because it is the only way I can save my daughters. I must trust my future and my daughters' futures to someone I scarcely know.

She went upstairs to bed finally, knowing that she needed at least part of a night's sleep before the trip tomorrow. The marquess had warned her that it would be a difficult journey. She undressed and brushed her hair, then crawled into bed.

She was still awake when the room began to grow light again, lying there thinking about the night before her wedding to Anthony. She had stayed awake all night then, too, but with a difference—excruciatingly in love with the vicar and wanting him so much that she did not know how she could contain herself until the wedding.

This time was different. Her friends and Anthony's former parishioners would be scandalized at her hurried marriage over the anvil to a divorced peer. Sweet Roxanna Drew, who never spoke a word out of turn or did an improper thing in her life, was eloping to Scotland when their beloved vicar was hardly settled in his grave. Will they think I married Lord Winn for his wealth? she asked the ceiling. Will they conclude that I had to get married to beat the stork? Will they call me deranged? An opportunist?

She knew she could always start a story circulating about Marshall Drew and his infamous offer, but that was even more repugnant to her than what the villagers would be thinking of her marriage to Lord Winn. Suppose Lissy and Helen heard the rumors about their uncle? She sat up in bed and pulled the covers around her. They must never know what an odious man Lord Whitcomb was. She refused to betray Anthony's memory and the Drew name that way. Better that people should wonder about her, and not lose faith in the Drews, and what they meant to the North Riding.

Roxie, you are not being fair to yourself, she thought. You are getting security, but at the price of a warm man in a warm bed. Lord Winn has made it perfectly clear that he does not covet your body. You are going to be taking a lot of long walks for the rest of your life. She knew that once she said her vows over the anvil, there would never be anyone else. She could no more look around for another husband and seek an annulment from Lord Winn than fly. Her word, once given, was given.

I have made an empty bed, and now I must lie in it, she told herself as the sun came up. But did I ever have a choice? Lord, you have dealt me another wretched hand. Is that any way to treat someone?

The room grew lighter. There was no wind outside, and she

could not see any snow falling, which was a relief. At least we will not be frozen in a blizzard in the Pennines, she thought as she lay back and listened for the girls. I am making such a sacrifice for them, and they must never know. Anthony, I trust this is what you would have me do. I can think of nothing else, and as God can witness, I have thought all night.

Her eyes closed then in weariness. She slept for a few minutes before she heard the door open, and Helen and Lissy threw themselves on her.

"Happy Christmas, Mama!" Lissy shouted as she pried open Roxie's eye to make sure she was in there.

"Felicity, have a few manners," Helen scolded, and then crawled into bed with her mother.

Roxanna held her close, and pulled Lissy up beside her. "Happy Christmas to you, too, my darlings."

"Can we go downstairs now, Mama?" Lissy begged.

Roxanna took a deep breath and cuddled her daughters on either side of her. "First I must tell you something. I do not know if you will understand, but you must know." She paused, then plunged ahead. "Lord Winn and I are going to Scotland this afternoon to be married."

"Oh, Mama, how famous!" Lissy exclaimed as she clapped her hands. "Can we come, too?"

Roxanna shook her head. "I am sorry, my dear, but it's too cold, and we have to hurry." She looked at Helen, who lay still, staring at the ceiling, even as she had earlier. "My dear?" she asked.

Helen was silent a long moment before she spoke. "Mama, why do you want to forget Papa so soon?"

Roxie felt her heart break as she gathered Helen closer. "Oh, never even think that, my dear! I could never forget Papa."

"Then why are you doing this so soon?"

Why indeed? she thought. It is for your protection, Helen, but I cannot tell you that. "Let us say, it is for our benefit."

Lissy sat up and looked across Roxie to her sister. "Helen, you know you like Lord Winn!"

"Yes, of course," she agreed. "But I do not understand."

Roxie could only kiss the top of her head, hold her close, and say, "You'll have to trust me, Helen, that I am doing what is best for all of us. Please believe me."

Helen nodded finally. "I trust you, Mama," she said at last, but her voice was wistful. "But, Mama, do you ever wish things were different? Why is life so strange?"

Roxie could not speak as she held her daughter. Is this what we do now? Do we take life an hour at a time? Do we wish for what once was, or do we move ahead on this new path? She held her daughter off from her so she could look into her eyes. "My dearest child, we move forward," she said firmly. "The less we look back, the better."

It felt like betrayal, like a corkscrew spiraling into her heart, each turn more painful than the one before. She calmly stared down the hurt in Helen's eyes, even as she wanted to run around the room screaming and pulling at her hair.

"Forget Papa?" Helen whispered, and Roxie felt another turn of the corkscrew.

She shook her daughter gently. "Never! But, my dears, we must put him in a special place now and turn a page in our book."

Helen sighed and leaned against her mother again. "I wish could understand," she sighed.

So do I, Roxie thought as she forced a smile in Felicity's direction. I am glad you are too young for this, Lissy.

"I do not have to call him Papa, do I?" Helen asked.

"No, my dear. I expect he will want you to call him Winn, though."

Felicity tugged at her mother's nightgown, then rested her head in Roxie's lap. "What will you call him?"

Roxie fingered Lissy's dark hair. "I really don't know. He has always been 'my lord,' or Lord Winn."

"His name is Fletcher," Lissy offered.

"It seems a little strange."

Lissy brightened and sat up. "Mama, you can name him like you did Ney!"

Roxie laughed. "I do not think he would take kindly to that!" She kissed her daughters. "Come, my dears. Let's go see if Father Christmas found us here in the dower house."

The house was smelling wonderfully of cooking goose when Lord Winn knocked on the door. Felicity let him in, wearing all four of the barrettes he had left in her stocking. She twirled around so he could admire the dress Roxanna had made. He smiled and covered his eyes. "Such beauty if positively blinding, Felicity." He handed her another package. "Open this now, and remember, you have to share."

Roxanna knew she should have come forward when she heard his knock on the door, but she felt suddenly shy. You are a goose, Roxanna, she thought as she stayed in the sitting room and watched Lissy and the marquess. He was dressed more elegantly than usual, his boots polished and his neckcloth arranged with more thought than was typical. She watched as he knelt beside her daughter to talk. Lord Winn, for all the things you say about children, you have the good instinct to speak on their level.

Lissy ran into the room, holding out the box she had opened. "Mama, it is chocolate! Oh, please, may I have one?"

"Of course you may. Did you tell Lord Winn thank you?"

Lissy put her hand to her mouth in dismay, turned, and curtsied. "Thank you, Lord Winn," she said breathlessly as she popped a chocolate in her mouth, then dashed into the kitchen calling for Helen.

"I had no idea the effect of chocolate on that one," Lord Winn mused as he watched her go and rose gracefully to his feet. "Is there anything she doesn't like?"

His tone was light, and she knew it was her duty to match it. "She is not overly fond of aubergine in any form. I cannot disguise it enough."

"Then she and I are at one on that issue," Lord Winn agreed as he sat beside her on the sofa. "You don't ever need to serve it, except in times of famine." He reached in his pocket and pulled out a narrow package. "Happy Christmas, Roxanna," he said.

She took the package after a moment's hesitation. "I do not have anything for you, my lord," she said.

"Next Christmas will be soon enough," he replied somewhat enigmatically. "I would be happy enough now if you would call me Winn."

"Very well, Winn," she replied as she opened the package. She held her breath as she opened the box, dreading something expensive. She stared, then took out a tin-stamped medal on the end of a leather string. "What is it, my l—Winn?"

He grinned and took it from her. "It's a good luck charm I got from a Portuguese fisherman when he fished me from the water three parts drowned after our ship sank off Cabo San Vicente. You've earned it."

Her eyes lively, she held still as he draped it around her neck. He kissed her on the forehead with a loud smack that made her giggle, despite her discomfort at his nearness.

"I didn't think you'd accept anything else, and by God, it got me through eight dreary years without a fatal injury."

She fingered the medal then looked at him. "Thank you," she said simply as she tucked it inside her dress. "I don't know that there's anything I need more right now than a little good luck."

"That's what I thought. You're welcome," he replied, then stood up and held out his hand for her. "Let's hurry up that goose in the kitchen. We want to catch the mail coach."

Tibbie and Emma Winslow arrived just as Lord Winn began to carve the goose. Roxanna showed them to their seats, apologizing for this shocking intrusion on their holiday.

"Think nothing of it, Mrs. Drew," Tibbie said as he tucked a napkin under his chin. "Emma and I will be delighted to keep an eye on things while you're gone." He tilted his head toward Meggie Watson. "I think between the three of us that you can count on it."

Roxanna nodded, her eyes serious, then looked down at her plate. This is all a dream, she thought. In a moment I will wake up, and Anthony will be carving the turkey. Then she touched the leather thong around her neck and sighed.

"White meat or dark, Roxanna?" Lord Winn was asking. He swallowed as he watched her, and she realized he was keeping a check rein on his emotions, even as she was. The thought comforted her as nothing else could. In for a penny, in for a pound, indeed, she thought as she held up her plate and asked for white meat, please.

Tibbie turned to Helen and Lissy. "My dears, go into the kitchen a moment. You'll find a pudding that Mrs. Winslow brought along. Can the two of you bring it in here?"

Helen and Lissy both jumped up from the table. "Mind you take it out of the bowl and find a plate," Tibbie called, then turned back to Lord Winn when they left the room, his eyes serious. "Lord Whitcomb has his people watching the inn where the mail coach stops, my lord. He doesn't mean for Mrs. Drew to even try to get through to York."

"Damn!" Lord Winn exclaimed. "That means we have to catch the coach in Richmond."

"I'm not even so sure the road north is open," Tibbie continued. "I heard something about a road crew at work."

"We'll manage either way," Winn said, his expression grim. "Damn that man. With someone watching, we can't go south or north on the highway, at least until Penrith, on the other side of the Pennines."

The girls returned with the pudding and he smiled at them, joking with Lissy that the pudding was bigger than she was. You're a cool one, Lord Winn, Roxanna thought as she forced herself to smile, too. No wonder Soult and Ney lost Spain for Napoleon, if the other soldiers they fought against were anything like you.

After the dinner, Lord Winn and Tibbie returned to Moreland, their heads together, engaged in earnest conversation. Her heart pounding, her thoughts on the journey ahead, Roxanna read to Felicity and tucked her in bed for a nap. Helen and Mrs. Winslow were busy in the kitchen with dishes. She listened to the comforting domestic sounds as the clock struck one.

She pulled on her warmest dress, a woolen petticoat, several pairs of stockings, and her riding boots that she had not worn since well before Helen's birth. Something old, she thought, looking down at her boots, and something new to me, as she fingered her necklace. She went into the dressing room and found Anthony's woolen muffler, wrapping it around her neck. "Borrowed and blue," she whispered as she leaned against the wall until she had the strength to stand upright.

She looked in at Felicity one more time. The barrettes caught the fire's glow and twinkled back at her. I would die for you, she thought. Is that what I am doing? She closed the door quietly.

Lord Winn returned on horseback, bundled in his military greatcoat and wearing boots with no polish and deep scratches in the leather. He dismounted as she opened the door.

"I thought we'd both ride Ney," he explained. "Helen tells me you're not much of an equestrienne."

"She's right," Roxanna agreed as she pulled on her mittens. "Is Ney up to this?"

"Roxie, you don't weigh much," he said. "And he has a grand, brawny heart. Besides all that, we'll keep each other warm. Are you ready?"

No, she thought, I am not. She hesitated at the door, and knew that he could tell exactly how she felt.

"Ready or not, madam, you haven't a choice," he reminded her, his voice firm, even a little hard.

She took a deep breath and closed the door behind her. "Then I am certainly ready."

He mounted again, then held out his hand to her, pulling her up in front of him in the saddle. "It's a tight fit," he said in her ear as his arms went around her and he grasped the reins tighter. "Too many cinnamon buns, Roxie."

She chuckled because he expected it, then stared in surprise as Tibbie came toward them in the gig, dressed in Lord Winn's greatcoat and low-crowned beaver hat. He waved a gloved hand at them, and turned the gig toward the lane overlooking the Plain of York.

"He says he and his missis were followed to Moreland," Lord

Winn said as they watched the bailiff drive slowly south. "Let's watch from here a moment."

He backed Ney off the lane and into the orchard, with its concealing hedgerow. "Happen he was right," he whispered in her ear. "Your brother-in-law is not taking any chances," he observed as two horsemen followed the gig at a distance. "He still thinks either you or I will be making a break to the magistrate in York, and he means to stop you even before you reach the mail coach."

"But why is Tibbie doing this?" she asked.

"Diversionary tactic, my dear. He'll give the men someone to follow while we try another road." He wheeled Ney around toward the hills nearby. "We will ride east for a few miles then turn west and north, in case anyone else is curious." His cheek was next to hers. "I trust you know some back trails, Roxie."

She nodded. "I can guide us through to Richmond without getting on the main road."

"Good girl! You'd have been an asset in Spain."

They entered Richmond as the clock in the church there chimed two. The road was closed, true to Tibbie's prediction. Without even pausing, Lord Winn ignored the warning of the road crew and continued steadily toward the great bulk of the Pennines, that spine of England so green and inviting in the summer, but white now, and stark with winter. The road was a narrow lane between shoulder-high drifts, a mire of freezing mud that Ney picked his way through carefully, slipping occasionally, but guided by Lord Winn's firm hand on the reins. He steered mainly with his knees, digging in sometimes with his spurs when Ney hesitated. Roxie admired his horsemanship, even as she blinked at the glare of the snow and kept her chin down in Anthony's muffler.

She had never been so cold before, even crammed up against Lord Winn in the saddle they shared. The inside of her nose prickled; she tried to breathe through her mouth, but that pained her lungs. She gasped for breath several times, and then Lord Winn pulled her muffler up over her nose.

"Breathe through your nose," he ordered, his own voice muffled. "Keep your head down. And let me know if you can't feel your fingers or toes."

They continued steadily upward, never looking back, but concentrating on the road before them that wound past villages sleeping in the grip of winter. As they plodded toward Scotland, Roxanna imagined people in their houses decorated for the holiday, toasting the season with loved ones, warming themselves with a Yule log. In the distance, through fields bare now of roads, and with stone fences scarcely showing above the snow, she saw lonely crofters' cottages, the smoke brave against the sky.

The sun was low and still they had not reached the summit. She protested when the marquess handed her down and made her walk. He joined her as he led Ney along, his arm tight around her shoulders. "My feet were getting numb," he said. "Keep your head down, Roxie." She nodded, too cold to speak, until he prodded her. "Yes," she replied distinctly, knowing that he wanted to hear her voice.

It was dark when they reached the summit. The wind picked up then as the sun fled from the freezing Yorkshire sky, and whipped around them until her head began to ache. Can we see to go on? she wondered, and then noticed the full moon rising.

"Think of it as the retreat from Moscow," Lord Winn said as they struggled on in the early dusk. "Speak to me, Roxanna."

"You weren't there, were you?"

"Lord, no, my dear. That was Napoleon's little blunder. It was cold enough over the Pyrenees." He managed a dry chuckle. "And here I thought my campaigning days were behind me." He put his cheek next to hers for a moment. "At least you smell better than my lieutenants."

They rode slowly into the night then, the air so cold that it almost hummed around them. Lord Winn pummeled her once to point out the northern lights. She gazed at their green splendor, her mind too dull to appreciate the beauty before her. She thought of Helen and Felicity asleep in their bed, and closed her eyes.

He wouldn't let her sleep, but prodded her awake again and again. "Keep your eyes open, Roxie, or I'll make you walk," he insisted, his own voice slurred with exhaustion.

The moon was beginning its descent when she finally noticed that they, too, were traveling down hill. The thought gave her heart and she sat up straighter in the saddle, grateful for what little warmth Lord Winn gave off. Minutes or hours later—she could not tell—he pointed with his riding crop.

"Penrith," he said, a note of triumph in his voice. "By God, Roxie, we've done it."

Penrith before dawn was as still as the crofters' cottages on the high passes. They traveled the quiet street and Lord Winn dismounted before an inn proclaiming itself The King and Prince. He pounded on the door a long time before the keep stuck his head out of an upstairs window.

"Come back when it's morning," the man protested. "I've got no room."

"Typical for Christmas, wouldn't you agree?" Lord Winn murmured as he stepped back in the street. "Let us in, anyway," he ordered. "We've come from Richmond tonight."

The window slammed shut, and Roxanna's heart sank. To her vast relief, the door opened in a few minutes.

"Richmond?" the keep asked as he tucked his nightshirt into his breeches. "You must be daft. The road is closed."

"It certainly is," Lord Winn murmured. "For God's sake, build us a fire."

In a few more moments, they stood before a roaring fire, ale in hand. The landlord pointed to the settle against the wall. "No room, but you can rest there. I'll take your horse around back."

"Stable him there for a day," the marquess said as he reached slowly into his coat. "Lord, but my fingers hardly work," he grumbled as he took out a handful of coins with stiff hands. "When does the mail coach from the west road come through to Scotland?"

"Two hours. You can rest here."

Lord Winn made her drink the ale, then led her to the settle. He sat down and pulled her head into his lap. She protested, even as her eyes closed. "Shut up, Roxie," was the last thing she remembered hearing.

The mail coach was late, and she hardly recalled climbing onto it. They slept, leaning against each other, until they crossed the Scottish border. When she finally opened her eyes, the sun was blinding on the snow, and they were in Gretna Green. She looked over at Lord Winn, who still slumbered. Here we are, she thought. I will hold hands with this strange man and be married by a blacksmith. She pulled out the charm he had given her and held it up to the light, hoping the luck had not disappeared with the end of the war.

"Well, so far our good fortune is holding," Lord Winn commented as he watched her.

"I thought you were asleep," she said, shy again. She tucked the necklace back into her dress, where it rested against her skin.

"No, no, madam," he said lightly. "I've got wedding jitters." He smiled at her and gave her shoulder a squeeze. "Well, let's get off and find the blacksmith."

The village blacksmith was dawdling over a late breakfast when they interrupted him. He came to his door with his napkin still tucked into his shirt and a thick slice of ham in his fist. Roxanna stared at the meat as her mouth watered. She remembered goose, but it seemed years ago.

"Come back tomorrow," he growled and started to close the door.

Lord Winn stuck his foot in the door and shouldered his way in. He strode to the table and slapped down a handful of guineas. "Now!" he demanded, his voice full of command. He leveled a stare at the blacksmith that probably had struck terror into many a soldier from Spain to Belgium. Roxanna felt herself standing up straighter.

The blacksmith stuffed the ham in his mouth and strolled to his table. He fingered the coins, letting them drop through his hand. "Maude," he bawled over his shoulder finally. "We've got some customers. Look lively." He glanced from Lord Winn to Roxanna. "You must really want to get married today," he commented. He winked at Roxanna as he still chewed the ham. "I like winter weddings, myself, dearie. Good cuddling afterward."

Roxanna blushed and he laughed, his mouth still full. "Oh, Maude, you've got to see this one! When did we last have a blushing bride?"

"That's quite enough," Lord Winn snapped.

The blacksmith almost came to attention. He swallowed the great lump of ham. "Hurry up, Maudie!" he called, when he could speak.

The blacksmith's wife joined them from the kitchen, wiping her flour-covered hands onto her apron. She nodded to Roxanna and then riveted her eyes to the pile of gold coins on the table. She nudged the marquess. "Pound for pound, couldn't ye have snabbled a bigger one for all that money?"

His jaw working, the marquess stared at her until she retreated to stand beside the blacksmith, muttering, "I didn't mean nothing by it."

Her nose in the air, she pulled out a piece of paper and plumped herself down at a writing desk by the fireplace. She dipped the quill in the ink and looked at Roxanna. "Name and age?" she demanded.

"Roxanna Maria Estes Drew, twenty-seven," Roxie said, her voice a whisper. She reached for Lord Winn's hand and clutched it in her fear. The pen scratched on the paper.

"You, laddie?"

The marquess's hand tightened around hers. She looked at him in surprise. *You are as frightened as I am*, she marveled.

"Fletcher William George Winfrey Rand, Marquess of Winn,

thirty-eight," he said, and repeated it when the blacksmith's wife looked up in surprise.

"We don't get too many lords up here," the blacksmith commented, rubbing his hands together. "Spinster or widow?" he asked Roxanna.

"Widow," she said.

"You, sir? Bachelor or widower?"

"Does it matter?" Lord Winn asked, his voice grating like sandpaper.

"For the book, my lord."

"I am divorced." He reached in his pocket and slapped down an official-looking document.

The blacksmith read it through carefully as the marquess's grip tightened around her fingers. He looked down at her hand and loosened his hold when he noticed her pained expression. "Sorry," was all he said.

"So this is why you came to Scotland?" the blacksmith asked as he gestured to the document.

"Why else, sir?" Lord Winn answered, trying to keep a lid on his irritation.

"It appears in order," the man said at last. He looked toward the door. "It's too cold for the anvil, my lord. Do you mind?"

"Of course not," he replied. "Just marry us."

The blacksmith motioned to his wife to hand him his jacket. He pulled it on, trying to brush off the more obvious stains, and picked up a well-thumbed book from the table. He looked at his wife in irritation. "For God's sake, Maudie, take off your apron! This is a marquess!"

Lord Winn turned his head slightly, and Roxanna felt his shoulders shake.

"I could sing a wee hymn," Maudie offered.

Lord Winn couldn't help himself. He started to laugh, then looked down at her. "Oh, my," he said. "Roxie, were you ever in a stranger situation?"

She shook her head and took a firm grip on his hand. "Marry us, sir," she told the blacksmith. "We'll manage without the wee hymn."

It was the service of the Church of England, read with the glottal stops of a lowland Scot, standing before a peat fire. The stately words rolled off her like rain and she admired them all over again, despite the bone weariness that was even now making her eyelids droop. She only had the courage to glance at Lord Winn once and discovered, to her embarrassment, that he was looking at her with an expression that, if it was not tenderness, was a close relative.

We are safe, she thought as she murmured yes, and the marquess answered in the affirmative, too, his response more confident. The blacksmith assured them that they were man and wife now, and was there a ring?

The marquess reached into his waistcoat. He held the ring out to her. "Will this do?" he asked.

It was a plain gold band, wide and softly glowing in the light of the fire.

"I am sure it is too large," he apologized. "We can have it cut down later." The marquess slid the ring onto her finger, where it dangled. He took it off and placed it on her thumb instead. "For now," he assured her.

The blacksmith nodded in approval. He clapped the marquess on the arm. "She's all yours, laddie, my lord. Take good care of her."

"I intend to," Winn replied, a slight smile on his face.

"You can kiss her, my lord," Maude suggested as she put on her apron again.

Roxanna stood still as Lord Winn grasped her by the shoulders. She closed her eyes and raised her face to his as he kissed her. It was such a brief kiss that she felt a slight disappointment.

"Well, laddie, you've done it now," the blacksmith said as he removed his coat and looked at his breakfast table with some longing. "I always offer a little advice." He paused. "That is, if you don't mind, my lord."

"Say on, sir," Lord Winn stated in amusement, his arm tight around Roxanna's waist.

The blacksmith cleared his throat. "It's good advice, my lord, especially since you've ridden this hobby horse before."

"Don't remind me," Winn murmured.

"It's this, laddie," he said, leaning closer and winking at Roxanna. "Always do what they want."

The marquess grinned. "Very good, sir," he said. "And now if you can direct us to an inn, we are falling down with exhaustion."

The blacksmith winked at Roxanna and grinned as she blushed. He handed the marriage lines to her. "Try the Bonnie Charlie," he suggested. "Down two blocks. You'll see it. I hear the sheets are usually clean."

He was sitting down to his meal before they even closed the door. Roxanna handed the marriage lines to the marquess. "Here you are, Lord Winn."

"Nope. Try again, Roxie," he said as he tucked the paper in his coat.

"Oh, very well, then! Fletch," she replied, her eyes straight ahead, her lips firm. "That's what I'll call you."

The keep at the Bonnie Charlie found them a room near the eaves, apologizing because his wife's relatives were visiting for the holidays from Fort William. "It's a good room," he assured them as they climbed the narrow stairs. "Not much view, but then, not many of my patrons waste time on that!"

Roxanna turned away in embarrassment and the marquess handed another coin to the landlord.

"When does the next mail coach to Carlisle come through?" he asked.

"Three hours."

"Knock on this door in two and a half hours then, and have some food ready."

When the door closed, Winn turned around. "Well, my dear, if I do not lie down I'm going to fall down." He took off his coat and waistcoat and loosened his neckcloth. "Could you help me with my boots?"

She did, tugging them off, then sitting down so he could help with hers. He pulled back the covers, unbuttoned his breeches, and lay down with a sigh. His eyes closed and he was asleep in minutes.

Roxanna arranged his clothes over the back of a chair and unbuttoned her dress. She lay down next to the marquess, gradually relaxing as his warmth spread to her. She touched the ring on her thumb and closed her eyes.

Chapter 13

She woke to loud knocking on the door. Go away, was her first thought, then she raised her head slightly. "Yes, thank you," she said, and the knocking stopped. She lay back down again, held firmly in Lord Winn's grasp. He had pulled her up close against his chest while they slept, his arm draped over her.

She lay still and looked at his hand, admiring the handsome

signet ring he wore. He was warm, so warm, and she was more comfortable than she had been in ages. The pillow was soft, and she felt her eyes closing again. No, she told herself, just before she drifted off to sleep again. We have to catch that mail coach.

Roxanna eased out of the marquess's grasp and tried to tug down her dress. In another moment, Lord Winn rolled onto his back and continued to sleep. She looked down at him. Why is it that men look like little boys when they sleep? she wondered.

His eyes opened and he smiled at her. "It's time to get up," she said.

"Damn." He sighed, and closed his eyes. "I'm finally warm for the first time in at least a day. Thank you for not digging me in the back like Lissy."

"I would never—" she began, then laughed. "You're quizzing me."

"Ah, yes. How astute you are, Mrs. Rand."

Mrs. Rand. She got out of bed quickly, pulling down her dress and looking for her boots. Get used to it, Roxie, she told herself. At least it sounds less formidable than Lady Winn. "My goodness," she said out loud.

"That's pretty strong language, Roxie," Lord Winn said mildly as he ran his hand over the stubble on his chin. "Did you just have a vision I should know about?"

She blushed as she pulled on her boots. "It just occurred to me that I am a marchioness, my lo—Fletch." She stood up and looked out the window. "I don't feel like one."

Lord Winn laughed. "That is funny. Cynthia always felt like one. Damned near ruined me, too. I'll call you Mrs. Rand, when you get tired of hearing 'Roxie.'"

She turned to regard him. "Well, it is not as though it will be much of an issue."

"No," he agreed. "I'm heading for Winnfield as soon as this matter with your wretched brother-in-law is taken care of. Despite her serious irritation with me, Amabel did inform me that I have piles of correspondence on my desk at home and daily notices from my solicitors." He winked at her. "But if you do get any mail at Moreland addressed to Lady Winn, don't send it back, hear ye? I do intend to write you."

They ate quickly in the tavern, bolting down their coffee when the coach announced its arrival from Dumfrees with a blast on the tin horn. The coach was crowded. By putting his arm around her and crowding in close, they managed to stay together. I wish I could talk to you, Roxanna thought as they bowled along. She glowered at the other occupants of the coach and wished them elsewhere, but no one disappeared.

As they traveled steadily south, the sunny morning gave way to clouds that drooped lower and lower. Lord Winn's attention was taken up with the weather, but she snuggled in closer to his chest, preferring to ignore it. *And what if it is snowing?* she thought, then shut the idea from her mind. *Time enough to worry about that later.* She chuckled.

The marquess leaned toward her. "What?"

"I was just thinking that if I don't look out the window I won't be frightened. Helen accuses me of putting off bad news."

"Do you?"

"I suppose I do, Fletch," she replied. "I've noticed in the last few years that you can put off anything, because bad news is always still there when you have the strength to face it."

"I have a better idea, Roxie," he said. "Let me worry about it for you."

His face was close to hers. Impulsively, she kissed his cheek. "Thank you, Lord Winn," she replied. "That's quite the nicest thing anyone has said to me in a long while."

It was his turn to blush this time. He squeezed her shoulder and looked out the window again. "Roxie, you're a funny thing."

Snow was falling by the time they reached Penrith. As the marquess handed her down from the coach, Roxie looked up at the sky in dismay. Winn touched her cheek. "I told you to let me worry, my dear," he murmured.

"This could be tricky," she said, unable to help herself.

"I have faced worse things, and so have you, Mrs. Rand," he told her. "What's a little snow?"

Little snow, indeed, she thought four hours later as they dismounted yet again to flounder through drifts too deep for Ney to carry them. They toiled toward a summit that seemed to move farther and farther away the more they struggled. Only through strenuous effort could she keep herself from looking back to see if Penrith was still visible. *That would be discouraging in the extreme,* she decided, *so I will not do it.*

Lord Winn walked Ney ahead of them to break a trail. "You know something, my dear?" he asked as they labored along, out of breath.

"What?"

He reached behind for her hand and she took hold of him. "In addition to being rather nice to look at for extended periods of time, you don't complain."

"Your compliments are so charming," she replied, amused, as she slipped on the snow and he stopped to steady her.

"Well, I don't tell just anyone these things. Ah, Roxie! The summit. Let's rest a moment and consider this situation."

There was nothing visible for miles around except snow. The sky was blue again, and the wind only idle puffs. Roxie put her hand up to shade her eyes from the glare. "It's beautiful," she said. "Do you feel like we're the only two people on earth?"

He draped his arm on her shoulder and leaned on her a little. "Yes, nice isn't it? Except that I am cold and my feet hurt, and my stomach is growling, and my eyes are starting to burn from the glare. Unlike you, wife, I do complain."

She leaned against his arm. "For a marriage of convenience, this one is certainly taking on adventurous overtones, my lord."

She felt rather than heard his chuckle. "Things can only get better, Roxie," he said as he straightened up and whistled to Ney. "Let's see if this noble beast will carry us for a while."

They continued into the afternoon, traveling a little faster when they reached the area cleaned by the road crew, then slowing down when snowdrifts claimed even that narrow passage. She felt stupid with sleep as she lay back in Lord Winn's arms. He rested his chin on the top of her head as they inched along.

"I should tell you," he said as the sun set, "I wrote to Clarice before we left, advising her of my marriage. If I know Clarrie, she will pass the word to my other sisters." He tightened his grip on the reins and dug in with his knees as Ney slipped onto his haunches. "I expect that will solve my problem. Since I am no longer matrimonial fodder, that will keep shabby genteels like the Etheringhams off my back."

She sat up a little, until he pushed her back gently with his hand against her chest. She relaxed again. "Did you tell them . . ." She paused, not knowing how to phrase her question.

"That it is a marriage of convenience?" he finished. "No. That's none of their business, is it? What we have done is between us, Roxie. You need suffer no embarrassment over this from my family."

"I owe you such a debt," she said softly. "If ever I can repay you, only tell me how."

He was silent, and she wondered if he heard her. "Oh, Roxie," he said finally, and nothing more.

There was no question of stopping for the night, even though they passed crofters' cottages with lights in the windows, and saw, in the distance, the comfort of two farmers herding in their cows from some desolate pasture.

"My God, my hands are cold," the marquess said finally, after an hour of silence. "Roxie, can you take the reins for a while?"

"Of course," she said as he handed them to her. "Maybe I should make you some mittens like Lissy's, instead of those leather gloves."

"I recommend it. Mind you make them brown, though, and not Jezebel red. Now if you don't object, I'll get really forward, Mrs. Rand," he continued, stripping off his gloves with his teeth.

When she said nothing, he reached inside her cloak and under her sweater. He wrapped his arms around her breasts, tucking his hands up under her armpits. "That helps," he said after a few minutes, the relief evident in his voice.

"I can hold the reins as long as you need," she said, enjoying the warmth of his fingers, too, as they gradually thawed.

"I remember killing a horse once in a blizzard and opening him up to tuck my hands in his entrails," he said, his tone conversational. "I won't do that to you, however."

"Thank you, Fletch," she responded.

As his hands grew warmer against her body, he became more conversational again. "Roxie, we used to dig up French graves, dump out the corpses, and burn the coffins to keep warm."

Roxanna shuddered, more wide awake than she had been for miles. "Those days are over," she reminded him.

"I hope so. If you keep prodding Ney, he might not have to give up his guts."

"You wouldn't . . ."

"Of course I would, Roxie. We have some business this morning with your brother-in-law. Do you think I would let my affection for a horse stop me?"

No, I do not, she thought. You are a hard man, Lord Winn. How grateful I am that you are on my side.

They walked past Richmond just as the sun was coming up. She staggered through the snow as Lord Winn kept a firm grasp on the back of her cloak. Once he slung her over his shoulder and kept walking doggedly along, until she cried, pounded on his back, and made him set her down.

Past Richmond the road was clear and they mounted Ney again. There were even farmers on the road now bringing goods to market, who stared at them as they rode slowly by. Lord Winn rubbed his chin.

"We must look like desperate characters," he told her.

"Speak for yourself," she said, wondering why it was so difficult to even move her mouth. She felt frozen solid, Lot's wife in wintertime, turned to a pillar of ice.

The sun was up, illuminating the Great Plain of York as they reached the end of Moreland's tree-lined avenue. Lord Winn reined in his horse. "I have never been so grateful to see anything as these elms," he told her as he sat there a moment, then gathered up the energy to dig his heels into Ney again. "Come on, old champion. Let's get Roxie Rand home before we have to chip her out of my saddle."

The dower house looked unbelievably welcome as Lord Winn twitched on the reins and Ney stopped, his head down, the journey over. Winn let the reins drop, but made no effort to dismount. "I can't move, Roxie," he said finally. "Can you throw your leg over the saddle and get down?"

She shook her head, too tired to speak, too exhausted to cry. As she sat there in misery, wondering if they would die from the cold just outside her door, she saw Helen's face in the window, and then jumping up and down, Lissy, too. "Oh, thank God for early risers," she murmured as the door opened and Helen ran out in her nightgown and bare feet, calling for Tibbie.

In another moment Tibbie followed. He stared at them in open-mouthed amazement. "We heard the roads were all closed from Scotland to Carlisle. Did you manage?"

In answer, Lord Winn tugged Roxie's mitten off her left hand and held it up in triumph so the bailiff could see the ring stuck firmly on her thumb. "It was a grand wedding, Tibbie," he said. "Only don't ask!"

Tibbie chuckled as he reached up for Roxanna. "And I suppose you can't move, Mrs. Drew . . ." He paused. "No, it's Lady Winn, now, isn't it?"

"It is, indeed," Lord Winn said. "Any sign of Lord Whitcomb yet?"

"Not yet. We'll give him another hour to drink his tea and put a silly smirk on his face, damn his hide."

"Tibbie, no!" Roxanna murmured, and looked meaningfully at her daughters. Tibbie pulled her from the saddle and she gasped at the pain. She sank into the snow and just lay there as Helen hugged her and Lissy knelt beside her, touching her face.

"Oh, Mama! Couldn't you have waited until it was warmer?" Helen asked, her eyes filled with concern. "Lissy, feel how cold she is."

Roxie shook her head and managed to reach her hand up to

touch Helen's face. "I've never been better, my dearest," she whispered, meaning every word.

With a groan that seemed to well up from the soles of his boots, Lord Winn dismounted and leaned against Ney. He regarded Roxie as she lay in the snow at his feet. "Mrs. Rand, you truly have been more trouble than any tenant I ever encountered." His eyes smiled into hers. "And I would do it over in a minute." He groaned again and leaned away from his horse, reaching down for her hand. "But not in the next one hundred or two hundred minutes, let us say."

His arm around her waist, Helen and Lissy right beside him, they tottered into the house, collapsing onto the sofa. Roxanna stared at the wreath over the fireplace. Was it only three days ago that they had decorated the sitting room? It seemed like years. She uttered no protest as Meggie pulled off her boots, then stood shaking her head at the sight of her feet.

Lord Winn leaned forward and pulled up her skirt to her knees, even as she protested feebly. "Don't worry, Meggie," he said. "No white patches. I recommend that you set up the tub in front of the kitchen fireplace and start warming some water. That should thaw out Mrs. Rand." He shivered involuntarily. "And I'll see what I can find at Moreland."

"It'll have to wait."

They looked at Tibbie, who stood at the window. Summoning strength from somewhere, Lord Winn got to his feet and joined him.

"He's not wasting a moment," Winn said as he removed his overcoat, wincing at the exertion. He reached into the pocket for the marriage lines, and held out his hand for Roxanna. "On your feet, my dear. Let's not forget our manners. Helen, I want you and Lissy to go upstairs and stay there with Meggie and Mrs. Winslow until your uncle leaves. Give me no grief, please."

There was something of firm command in his tired voice that stopped any argument the girls might have offered. He helped Roxanna out of her cloak and sweater, slowly unwinding the muffler from her face, and then leaned against her, forehead to forehead, as Lord Whitcomb's carriage drew to a stop in front of the dower house. He straightened up as Lord Whitcomb rapped sharply on the knocker.

"Open it, Tibbie," he said, very much the colonel commanding.

Lord Whitcomb came in, followed by the sheriff. He stopped in the open door, staring from Lord Winn to Roxanna.

"I told you he was still here," the sheriff murmured to Lord Whitcomb.

Marshall Drew came forward. He removed his coat, looked around for someone to take it, then shrugged and draped it over a chair. He walked farther into the room, past Lord Winn, until he stood before Roxanna, who dug her toes into the carpet and refused to step back.

"Where are they? I have come to claim your daughters, Roxanna." He paused and then coughed delicately into the back of his hand. "Of course, you may accompany them, if you choose, but they are mine now by consent of law."

"No, they're not," Lord Winn said. "And I'd like you to leave."

With a nod, Lord Whitcomb indicated the sheriff to come closer. "This may be your property, Lord Winn, but you can have nothing to say about this matter. It is between Mrs. Drew and me."

Lord Winn limped from the window to stand beside Roxanna. His arm went around her waist. "I have every right to speak, sir." He smiled at her and handed her the marriage lines. "Perhaps you'd like to have the honor, my dear."

"With pleasure," she said, her voice low but carrying an intensity that filled her whole body, driving out the exhaustion and the pain and the worry of the last few days. She slapped the document into her brother-in-law's outstretched hand. "I have a writ of my own, Marshall."

His eyes widened as he read once through the brief paper, then again. "This is not possible," he said, throwing it down.

"Pick it up before I break your neck," Lord Winn ordered.

Whitcomb pushed it aside with his foot. "It can't be official," he protested, his voice rising even as his face turned red.

"Ask any magistrate. Take it to the House of Lords, if you choose," Winn replied, biting off each word. "At least we will not fool you and diddle you and frighten you with an unanswerable writ delivered the day before Christmas! Lord Whitcomb, how dare you terrorize this woman like that?"

His words hung in the air between them, the loathing unmistakable. Roxanna trembled at the fervor of the exhausted man who stood beside her. I do not know why you are fighting my battle, she thought as she looked from him to Lord Whitcomb, but thank you. I can never repay you, Lord Winn, not if I live a thousand years.

"You're really married?" Whitcomb asked, as though he could not believe the paper still at his feet.

"It was the only road you left open to your sister-in-law!" Winn shouted. "She and her daughters are my chattel now and if you do not leave this house at once, I will ask this sheriff to arrest you!" He came forward and took Lord Whitcomb by the neckcloth, jerking him off his feet. "They are my property now!" he snapped, each word distinct.

With a gesture of revulsion, he released Lord Whitcomb. "You offend me, sir," he said finally. "I don't ever want to see you again."

Whitcomb made no reply. He picked up the marriage license and read it again, shaking his head. He handed it to Roxanna. "I hope you have no cause to regret this piece of folly, Roxanna," he said at last, his voice heavy with disdain.

"I regret not one thing, Marshall," she said, hoping she sounded as determined as Lord Winn. "Please leave."

He stared at her another long moment and she gazed back, her spine straight, her shoulders squared. You will have to blink first, for I will never do it, she thought. Never.

He looked away finally, and groped for his overcoat, as though he could not see it. She let her breath out slowly as he pulled on the coat and walked to the door. He turned back suddenly and she held her breath again.

"What do you know of this man?" he asked. "I could tell you things."

Roxanna reached for Lord Winn's hand, grasping it to her stomach. "I know he will never let me down, or scare me, or threaten me, or take what is mine, or violate my mind, as you have tried to do." Her voice trembled with emotion. "Go, Marshall. We can have nothing more to say."

Without a word he turned on his heel and stalked from the room, leaving the door wide open. In another moment, the carriage was retreating down the lane. Tibbie closed the front door. "Some people have no manners," he murmured.

Lord Winn raised Roxanna's hand to his lips, kissed it, then rubbed her fingers against his two-day-old beard as she laughed and tried to pull away. "Now who is humbugged?" he said as he released her.

Roxanna sat down in relief, holding the marriage lines tight in her hand. She wanted to say something else to Lord Winn, but her eyes insisted on closing. In just a moment I will open them, she thought as she fell asleep sitting on the sofa.

She vaguely remembered a warm bath in front of the kitchen fireplace, with Meggie scrubbing her back and scolding her for taking such chances, even as the old nursemaid cried with relief that "her girls" were safe. She dimly recalled the smell of lavender shampoo, and then the delicious feel of a rough towel on her skin, and the pleasure of sliding between flannel sheets with a footwarmer at the bottom of the bed.

She slept solidly for the rest of the day and then all night, waking in the morning only with the arrival of Dr. Clyde, who had come at Lord Winn's insistence. He thumped her soundly, listened to her breathe in and out, and scrutinized her fingers and toes.

"You'll do, Mrs. Drew—no, no, Lady Winn," he corrected himself. "Nothing wrong with you that a good rest won't cure, and some of Mrs. Howell's cooking. She's back, by the way, with her sister to help cook." He tucked the blankets up to her chin again. "Of course, I assured Lord Winn that you were stronger than a French pony and more fit than most crofters, but he insisted I put you through your paces."

She rose up on her elbow. "Is Lord Winn all right?" she asked.

"Well, he lost a toe, madam. Told me not to tell you."

"No!" she exclaimed, feeling a wave of extraordinary guilt. "Nothing else?"

"No. You were both lucky, in my estimation." He replaced his listening tube and closed his black satchel. "I can't see why the hurry, but then, I never argue with the aristocracy."

And I'll never tell you, she thought. Lord Whitcomb may be a scoundrel of the first water, but that Drew name still means something to me. "You are sure he is all right?" she asked.

"He's already up and using a cane. Says he's leaving in a day or two for Winnfield." He shook his head, as if questioning the wisdom of the entire peerage. "I almost don't doubt him. Good day, my dear. Stay out of snowdrifts, mind."

She lay back as Meggie fluffed the pillows behind her. "Where are the girls?" she asked, when the house seemed too quiet.

"Helen is riding with Tibbie, and Lissy is jumping from one foot to the other outside the door, waiting for me to let her in."

Roxanna held out her arms. "Lissy! Come here at once, my love. I need a hug!"

As she hugged Lissy, she noticed that her wedding ring was gone. "Meggie, did I lose my ring?" she asked in sudden alarm. "I thought it was on my thumb when we arrived here."

"It was," Meggie assured her. "Lord Winn removed it before Tibbie took him back to the manor. He said he would have it sized."

Lissy napped with her that afternoon until Meggie carried the sleeping child to her own bed with the whispered announcement that Lord Winn was coming up the stairs.

Oh, dear, she thought as she reached for a brush, wondering what her hair looked like. He should not be climbing stairs, with his foot so uncomfortable. She brushed the tangles from her hair and listened to his slow tread on the stairs. In another moment, he rapped on the door with a cane.

"Come in, please," she said, setting down the brush and wishing she had on something more attractive than faded flannel. Don't be a goose, Roxie, she scolded herself. He couldn't possibly care.

He opened the door and leaned on his cane, wincing as he crossed the threshold. He stopped to admire her. "Mrs. Rand, you look as fine as five pence," he said. "How do you do it?"

"At least I have all my parts," she replied. "Do sit down, Fletch."

He ignored the chair she indicated and sat heavily on her bed. "I suppose the doctor told you," he grumbled.

"Did you really think he would not?" she questioned. "Will you be all right?"

"Certainly! It was only a toe," he assured her. "And don't look so wide-eyed! Well, do, actually. I like your expression. Seriously, Roxie, at Waterloo I spent the better part of a long afternoon in the middle of a square, holding my insides in. I think I can suffer the loss of my little toe without getting too worked up." He leaned closer. "Anyway, I should know better than to wear socks with holes in them."

She touched his arm. "You're pretty tough, Lord Winn," she said.

"So are you, Roxie. I can't fathom any other woman going through all that and then sitting here looking so pleasant." He chuckled. "And the doctor assured me downstairs that you are right as a trivet." He considered a moment, then plunged on. "He also assured me that no one has babies as nicely as you do, and he wished me happy."

Roxanna grasped the blankets and slid down in the bed until her face was covered. She started to laugh then, despite her embarrassment. In another minute she sat up again. "You'll have to forgive Dr. Clyde," she said, apologizing for the doctor, and unable to look him in the eye. "Only think how glad you will be to leave in a few days. This neighborhood could become unbearable."

"Yes, only think," he agreed, sounding anything but cheerful.

She watched his expression. "Does your foot pain you?" she asked, forgetting her own discomfort.

"I suppose," he agreed, his thoughts obviously concentrated somewhere besides his little toe. After a moment he reached into his pocket and took out her ring. "Hold out your hand, my dear."

She did as he said, and he slid her wedding ring on her finger, where it belonged.

"Perfect," she said, holding her hand up to the light. She clasped her hands in her lap. "I truly do wish I knew how to thank you for all you have done." She shook her finger at him. "And even you are not so brazen as to tell me it's part of the rental agreement!"

He twinkled his eyes at her then, his momentary melancholy forgotten. "Happen there is something you can do, Lady Winn," he said as he reached into his pocket again and pulled out a letter. "Read that."

She eyed the letter while he rested on the bedcovers. "It's not from Lord Whitcomb, is it?" she asked with suspicion.

"Oh, no! Nothing like that. Apparently since we suffered your relative yesterday, it's my turn tomorrow. Read it, Roxie."

She picked up the letter and read it through once and then again, her eyes wide. "Does this mean . . ."

He nodded and laughed at the look on her face. "Most assuredly, my dear wife. My sisters, husbands, and children are descending on us here tomorrow."

"Oh, no," she said in dismay.

"Oh, yes! And you thought a trip over the Pennines was bad!"

She gulped and twisted the ring on her finger.

"Happy New Year, wife," he said as he winked and kissed her fingers. "You are in for a real scrutiny."

Chapter 14

Lord Winn propped his aching foot on the chair next to Roxie's bed. What he really wanted to do was lie down beside her, breathe deep of her lavender fragrance, work up his nerve to kiss her, and see where it led. She looked so adorable sitting there, staring at the letter, her mind already going a thousand miles an hour.

"You could have warned me this might happen," she accused.

He wanted to laugh. Have you any idea how very married you sound right now? he asked himself as he shook his head and looked serious. "I really had no clue they would do this, my dear," he replied, remembering contrition as a useful tool from his first marriage. Not that it ever worked for long with Cynthia, he thought as soon as the words were out of his mouth.

"I am sure you did not," she replied, to his intense gratification. "Please do not think that I am blaming you. These things happen, don't they?"

Oh, excellent. No blame, and does she appear concerned at *my* discomfort? As he tried to look casual and admire her at the same time, Lord Winn was struck all over again that Roxanna Rand was a distinct cut above any woman he had ever known before. He wondered if he dared rest his hand upon her leg, which had produced such a shapely outline under the blanket. After a moment's reflection, he concluded that his credit was not that high yet, despite this promising beginning. He would attempt something else.

"Roxie, you'll have to excuse me if I lean back," he said. The wince was genuine, he was sure of it.

His cup nearly ran over when she helped him lie back at the foot of the bed, and tucked one of her heavenly lavender-scented pillows under his head. Surely it wasn't his imagination that her hands lingered a moment longer than necessary on his neck as she positioned the pillow. Since his long legs dangled off the bed, she leaped up and pulled the chair closer, resting his wounded foot in the seat again. He had never seen such an attractive flannel nightgown. It was worn from many washings, and the fabric was thin enough now to exhibit the outline of her hips to great advantage.

"Much better," he managed.

"I should scold you, of course," she said, trying to look stern, and failing utterly because her face was not constructed upon stern lines. She went to the bureau and rummaged around until she found a pencil and paper. She plumped herself back in bed while he watched appreciatively, then crossed her legs Indian-fashion. She poised the pencil over the paper.

"All right now," she said. "What do you want me to do to get ready for this onslaught?"

Roxie, you are amazing, he thought as he put his hands behind his head. He took a deep breath, wondering how far he would get.

"Roxie, they think we are happily married newlyweds, and not, you know, pursuing this as an arrangement of convenience."

She pursed her lips and regarded him, and he fought the urge to take her in his arms and damn the pain in his former toe. "The girls and I will move to Moreland at once to perpetuate this notion," she said, and wrote on the page. "There are six bedrooms there, one of which is in the depths of renovation and not suitable for anything." She looked up and blushed. "The girls will take one room." She hesitated. "And I suppose I will have to share your chamber to accomplish this subterfuge."

Better and better. Roxie, you are a sensible woman. "I suppose," he replied, keeping his voice offhand. "There is a cot in the dressing room which I can use for the duration of the vis—"

"I won't consider that!" she interrupted, indignant. "I will take the cot and you can have the bed!"

"Wrong, Roxie. I'll take the cot," he said, grateful right down to his bandage that she was still consenting to sharing the bedroom.

"I insist," she said. "After all, I have all my parts."

He laughed. "Roxie, it's only a toe! I still have nine others, plus all my fingers."

She looked at the paper. "Well, I suppose we can fight this out tomorrow night."

Oh, God, Roxie. "I am sure we can."

She wrote on the paper. "That will free up the dower house. Who do you want the farthest away?" She grinned at him over the paper and his heart seemed to change rhythm.

"Amabel, without question," he said with no hesitation as she wrote. "Clarice and Frederick and their children will occupy two more bedrooms at the manor, and that will leave—"

"One bedroom for Lettice," she said. "Did you not say she was a widow?"

"Yes. Edwin, her only child, is my heir. I do not believe he will be coming."

"Well, it's a good thing," Roxie said. She unlimbered herself from the covers and flopped down next to him on her stomach, pointing to the paper. "See here? That fills the bedrooms. Their servants can go below stairs. Amabel and hers will be in the dower house and I'll sleep in your dressing room!"

"Roxie!" he declared as he turned sideways to face her. He surrendered to her good-natured expression. "Oh, very well. Have it your way."

To his delight, she leaned her head on his arm for a moment.

"Good for you, Fletch. Didn't that blacksmith advise you to always do what I want?"

He groaned and ruffled her hair before she could move away. "I suppose you will remind me of that now and then!"

To his dismay, she grew quiet. She left his side and returned to her own pillow. "There won't be much opportunity for that. Didn't the doctor tell me you were leaving in a couple of days?"

"Yes, I am," he said, forced to agree. "I have a mound of correspondence at Winnfield, and most of it concerning these pesky deeds of title to all my land. Was ever a man so cursed with wealth?" He chuckled and put his hand over his heart. "So if you want to get anything out of me in the next few days, that will be your golden opportunity."

She regarded him with an expression he was unfamiliar with. "You know, I will miss you," she said frankly.

He raised up on his elbow, unable to allow that to pass unanswered. A thousand witty things came to mind, but none of them were fine enough to say to this woman he loved. "Thank you," he said simply, cursing himself for the lameness of his delivery. "I don't know when anyone has ever missed me before."

To his further amazement, tears came to her eyes. She reached out and touched his arm, then sat back. "Now you'll have to leave," she said firmly as his heart sank. "I have a lot to do before your sisters get here, and I need to get dressed."

"Oh, very well," he replied, relieved that she was not ejecting him forever. "You'll have to help me up."

He didn't need any help. He remembered a time after the battle of Bussaco when he had sewn up his own arm because the surgeons were too busy. But, Roxie, you don't know that, he thought as he allowed her to help him to his feet. He leaned on her, breaking into a sweat as his fingers just brushed her breast. It was almost more than he could bear when she came closer and dabbed at the perspiration on his forehead.

"Oh, you are in pain!" she said, her voice filled with remorse. "I wish you had not climbed the stairs!"

He should have been ashamed of himself, but he was having too much fun to feel any remorse of his own. "I'll be all right," he managed, trying to sound gallant, and grateful that none of his former comrades in arms were around to hoot at him and make rude noises.

"I'll be fine," he assured her, feeling just a twinge of guilt at his performance. "If you can arrange affairs here, I can have Tibbie marshal his forces to move your things next door anytime you say."

"Very well," she agreed. "I can put Meggie on it right now, and I'll be at your house in a moment." She turned him around and gave him a push toward the door. "Is Mrs. Howell about? She and I will need to discuss menus and make beds. Go along, now, Fletch. I'll see you soon enough."

He descended the stairs carefully, a smile on his face. He stopped halfway down and looked back at the closed door. I am married to that magnificent creature, he marveled. The impossible has happened, and I really can't thank Lord Whitcomb enough for his perfidy. My stars, life is strange.

True to her word, he soon found Roxie at Moreland, deep in consultation with Mrs. Howell and her sister, Mrs. Hamilton. He peeked in on them in the kitchen and was shooed away by all three ladies. It may have been wishful thinking, but he thought Roxie winked at him. He was content to limp to the sitting room and play through Haydn's Second Piano Sonata, the perfect antidote for a disordered mind. Cadence and calm, Fletcher, he told himself as he followed the score. Spain wasn't won in a day; neither will Roxie be.

"Take your time, Fletch," he heard from the doorway and stopped, startled, wondering if she could read his mind. Please no, he thought. In another moment Roxie stood beside him, her hand resting lightly on his shoulder, her other arm full of sheets.

He continued, almost overwhelmed by her lovely presence as she looked at the music then sat down beside him on the piano bench, the sheets clutched in front of her now. "You need a metronome," she said, then glanced at him, her brown eyes merry. "What's the hurry?"

I am thirty-eight and deep in love, he thought. That's the hurry, my dear. "I always seem to rush Haydn," he temporized, racing one-handed through the rest of the page as she laughed. "There! Can I help you now?"

They made beds until Meggie and Tibbie brought over the clothes from the dower house, Lissy and Helen trailing behind, their arms full of possessions.

"You will be in here," he said to Roxie's daughters as he opened the door to the room next to his. "Will this do?"

Helen gazed around the room, open-mouthed. "It is so large!" she declared. "Oh, Mama, I do like this wallpaper you chose."

Roxie was already putting clothes away in the bureau. "Actually, I think Winn picked that out in Darlington. Oh, and the bed is so soft, Lissy. You'll find that most agreeable."

But Lissy was already sitting in the window seat, looking out as dusk tinged the Plain of York far below. "Is this the whole world?" she asked in awe of the view.

He limped over to sit beside her. She patted his arm, looking up at him for an answer. "I think it must be," he replied as he looked into her brown eyes and fought an absurd urge to cry.

"Then I am glad we are all here," she said, leaping up to jump on the bed before he disgraced himself with tears. He sat there a moment longer, trying to regain some measure of control.

But Roxie was watching him, a frown on her face. She told the girls to carry their boxes into the dressing room, then joined him at the window. "That look on your face tells me that we are already too much trouble," she said, the anxiety evident in her voice. "I am sorry. Sometimes Lissy is rambunctious. I'll remind them to be a little calmer while you are still here."

"It's not that," he said, wanting to spill out his heart to her.

She touched his forehead. "Oh, it's your foot, isn't it? I think you should lie down until dinner."

He nodded. "Yes, I am sure that is it." He rose and she took him around the waist, as though she had done this a hundred times before. "Lean on me and I'll get you to your room."

He did as she said, marveling at her resilience. *I suppose you have done this often with Anthony,* he thought as she helped him into his room and off with his shoes. *Mrs. Rand, I am no invalid, except that my heart has been pierced through and through as never before.*

He did sleep, which surprised him, and gave him some slight justification in his own eyes that perhaps his foot was partly the culprit. To his delight, Roxie and the girls brought their dinner upstairs and ate with him in his room. When they finished, Lissy tucked herself under his arm and insisted that he tell them all about his nieces and nephews who were coming to visit. He remembered as many names as he could, wishing that he had paid closer attention to his sisters' various birthings. Roxie rescued him finally.

"Have a heart, Lissy!" she scolded and sat down beside him, gathering her daughter in her arms. "He was away in Spain for eight years fighting Napoleon. Perhaps Lord Winn needs to become reacquainted with his own relatives!"

Lissy considered that and nodded. "Do you think they will like us?" she asked.

"I like you," he replied. "Who cares what they think?"

"We do, Fletch," Roxie said, her voice firm. "And I think you should, too. Come along, girls, let's go home for our last night in the dower house."

Lissy blew him a kiss as Roxie led her out of the room. Helen remained behind, sitting quietly in the chair beside the bed. She began to gather up the dishes, then set them down and came closer. He watched her, again struck by her quiet dignity, and afraid to break into her silence. He took his chances and held out his hand to her.

He smiled when she took his hand. Still she was silent.

"It's difficult, isn't it, Helen?" he asked at last. "Please don't think that I will ever try to take your father's place. That will never be my intention."

She was still silent, but as he held his breath, she sat on the edge of the bed, and for the briefest moment, touched her cheek to his hand. It might never have happened; he could have dreamed it, except that her eyelashes brushed the back of his hand and he knew he would never forget the feeling. In another second she was darting to the door. But she paused and raised her hand to him in a gesture of friendship.

"Good night, Winn," she whispered. "I hope you feel better tomorrow."

He never slept more soundly in his life.

The Rand sisters came in one steady invasion the next afternoon. Lissy had bounced in with the news that a whole train of carriages was trundling down the lane. "Mama, there are so many of them!" she said, then hurried to the window.

Lord Winn peered over his spectacles at Roxie, who sat beside him on the sofa, darning his socks. "I can't face it," he moaned as he put down his book.

Roxie only laughed and threw a sock at him. "We are supposed to love our relatives," she said, then amended under her breath, "except for Lord Whitcomb."

"Well, he loves you, Roxie," he joked, and ducked as she dumped the basket of socks on him.

Helen stared at her mother in amazement. "Mama!" she gasped. "You've never done anything like that."

Roxie paused, surprised. "No, I suppose I have not," she agreed. "But I enjoyed it, Helen." She threw a last sock at him. "And he deserved that. Oh, foul!" she exclaimed as he threw the socks back.

They were still gathering up socks, sitting on the floor and laughing when Mrs. Howell opened the door to announce Amabel, Clarice, and Lettice, with husbands and children in tow.

"Oh, dear," Roxie said under her breath when Lettice raised a lorgnette to her rather prominent eyes.

Winn grinned at his sisters, and threw a sock at Amabel. "Happy Christmas!" he announced, flopping back on the carpet to toss another sock over his head at Roxie.

Clarice stared at him, then began to chuckle. "Winn, you're certifiable," she declared as she came forward and stepped over him, her hand outstretched. "You have to be Roxanna, my dear. No one else but a wife would stay in the same room with this lunatic. I am Clarice and this is my husband Frederick. Fred, help up your brother-in-law. He seems to have done injury to his foot."

Roxie raised up on her knees and shook hands as though she did this every day. "Welcome to Moreland," she said, tucking her hair under her lace cap. "I was darning socks and your brother was being outrageous."

"I'd like to know who began this attack," Winn said as he held out his hand to his brother-in-law.

"You deserved it," Roxanna replied.

Lord Winn allowed his brother-in-law, Lord Manwaring, to help him back to the sofa. "My God, Winn, where did you find one that juicy on such short notice?" Fred whispered.

"It was just the most bare-faced piece of luck, which I will never explain to you," the marquess whispered back. "Good to see you, Fred," he said out loud, then turned to Roxie. "Fred, meet my wife, Roxanna. And these are her daughters Felicity and Helen."

Lord Manwaring bowed, then kissed Roxie's cheek. "Welcome to the family, m'dear. You're a brave one."

Amabel still stood in the doorway, transfixed. Lord Winn grinned at his youngest sister. Never saw me have any fun before, did you, Amabel? he thought. He waved her in. "Cat got your tongue, Amabel?" he asked. "This is a rare occasion, indeed. Let me make you known to my far-better half. Roxie, this is Amabel. And Lettice. Sisters, such a pleasure to undergo your scrutiny! I hope we measure up."

"I cannot imagine what they must think of us," Roxie told Lord Winn that night as she sat at the dressing table in his chambers and brushed her hair.

"Let me answer for Fred," he spoke up from the bed, where she had fluffed his pillows behind his head and given him his book and spectacles. "He wonders where I found such a beautiful wife."

She clapped her hands in genuine delight. "Really? He thinks me beautiful? How diverting."

"Roxie, sometimes I think you have cotton wadding where your brains should be," he remarked, putting down his book. "Don't you ever stand still long enough to look in a mirror? I wish I had a sock to throw at you."

She rolled her eyes and looked at him through the mirror. "Don't remind me! I do not think Amabel was impressed."

"Amabel has had a poker up her bum as long as I have known her," he responded, sinking lower and returning his attention to the book.

He sighed with pleasure as she sat in the chair by his bed. "And you would say all those outrageous things at dinner!" she scolded. "You needn't look so pleased about it, either."

Lord Winn took a last look at the page and closed the book. *I do not know what I have been reading anyway,* he thought as he watched his wife's lively face. *It might be the records from last year's Corn Exchange or merchant marine lading bills. Roxie, I see only you. I'm the one with cotton wadding for brains.*

"Well?" she was prompting.

He drew his legs up, wincing a bit. "I don't think our reproductive proclivities are any of her business, do you? Lettice's son is my heir, and I intend to leave it that way. You know my views on the subject."

He knew she would blush, and she did, the rose coming into her cheeks as he watched. "But did you really need to make those remarks about stud fees among the peerage?" she persisted. "And now Helen is asking me questions. Dear me, Fletch. She's only six."

He took her hand, running his fingers over her wedding ring. "I am sorry, my dear. It was rude of me." He sat up straight again, wishing he had the nerve too pull Roxie onto his lap. "But Amabel is such fair game!"

Roxie sighed and rose to her feet. "My brothers were just the same!" She shook her head at him. "Fletch, they will be here one more day and so will you. Do try to be pleasant."

She went back to the dressing table and tied on her sleeping cap. His heart sank. *And now you will leave me for the other room,* he thought. "What will you do for me if I am a model of rectitude tomorrow?" he asked, stalling her.

"I will probably sink into a coma at your feet," she responded promptly and kissed her hand to him. "Good night, Fletch. I hope you sleep well."

I would sleep better if you were in my bed, he told himself as he nodded to her and smiled. She went into the dressing room and closed the door behind her. He listened, but she did not turn the key in the lock. At least you trust me. Damn, what a burden.

He took off his glasses and turned down the lamp. If I must leave the day after tomorrow, how soon do I dare return? At what point will she look at me and see a husband, and not a convenience? Anthony, you must have been quite a fellow.

He tried to make himself comfortable, but all he could think of was Roxanna Rand in the next room. And Clarice and Fred in the room beyond, and Lettice, and Amabel in the dower house probably complaining to her mouse of a husband about the accommodations. He wished he could evict them all and woo his wife in the day remaining. I know so little of the sensual arts, he thought as he stared at the ceiling. There was only argument as I grew up, and then war, and bitterness and divorce. He remembered a Spanish proverb then, and smiled into the gloom—"Patience and shuffle the cards." But I am not a patient man.

The next day began in a more promising fashion, with the company lured to the breakfast table by Mrs. Howell's cinnamon buns and a ham that suited even the critical Amabel. While he sat at the table after breakfast chatting with Fred, Roxie organized a snowball fight on the front lawn. He went to the window to watch, finally opening the window quietly to scoop snow from the ledge and plaster his wife when she wasn't looking. He barely closed it in time, laughing as a snowball splattered onto the glass by his head.

Lord Manwaring watched him from the breakfast table. "She's a ripe one, Winn," he said, and nudged his wife. "Don't you think so?"

Clarice only smiled and finished her tea before speaking. "She's a delight, Winn. But why do I think there is much more here than meets the eye?"

I cannot fool you, he thought as he regarded his older sister. He sat down beside her. "Because there is."

"Tell me, brother," she asked quietly. "I won't say anything to my sisters."

He looked from his sister to her husband, leaned back, and told them the whole story, leaving nothing out. He was relieved that Clarice had the good sense not to make any comment as he spoke quickly, hurrying to finish before the snowballers trooped indoors for a continuation of breakfast. "And that's it," he concluded. "She's sleeping on a cot in my dressing room, and we are trying to present a good face to all of you. I wish you had not come, actually."

Fred chuckled. Clarice touched Lord Winn's hand. "You love her, don't you?" she asked, her voice soft for a sister of his.

"Clarrie, I can't begin to tell you how much I love her," he replied. "That's the damnable part. If she were merely agreeable, this would be an easy arrangement. But she is a darling and I want her so much." He shook his head. "But I have to be patient now, and return to Winnfield, and leave her here. It chafes me."

He heard the front door slam, and excited voices in the hall. "Well, now you know. Wish me success, Clarice. Maybe I can return here in the spring . . ." His voice trailed off.

To his surprise, she came up behind his chair and hugged him. "We do wish you well, my dear." The door opened and his nieces and nephews tumbled into the room, snowballs in hand, to continue the fight indoors. "But now I would duck, if I were you, Winn!"

As the day wore on, the thought of leaving sank him lower. His mood was not improved when yet another post chaise rolled to the front driveway at Moreland and released from its confines Lettice's son and his heir, Edwin Chandler. If that was not enough to throw him into despair, the carriage also disgorged two of Edwin's Cambridge friends, all watch fobs and seals and too-tight pantaloons.

"Uncle! What a pleasure!"

Why must he be so cheerful? Lord Winn thought as Edwin shook his hand vigorously, introduced his friends whose names he promptly forgot, then toddled off to find refreshment, looking about with interest as though he already owned the place. *I wonder he does not follow me from estate to estate, counting the silver,* Winn thought sourly. *Why did I never notice that about him before?*

Roxie was the perfect hostess, smiling at the new arrivals, and even listening with what appeared to be interest at yet another of Edwin's prosings about life at university, the price of things, and other bits of noninformation that made Lord Winn's head and toe throb simultaneously.

The only crisis passed quickly enough. Roxie whispered to Mrs. Howell to clear up that yet-unfinished chamber, and try to locate a third bed from somewhere. Mrs. Howell thought a moment, assured her that she could find something, and hurried off to do her duty.

He managed to capture Roxie for a private word before dinner as she was hurrying to make a tisane for Amabel's headache, brought on, Amabel was sure, by "all these children shouting."

"This is not what I had in mind for a peaceful holiday," he said, draping his arm over her shoulder as she headed for the kitchen. "Hold still a minute, Roxie," he ordered, when she remained in motion.

She slowed down to oblige him, and looked up into his face, a question in her eyes.

"Why isn't this driving you crazy?" he asked, out of sorts with her that she could be so cheerful in the face of relentless relatives.

"It's simple, Fletch," she replied, offering no objection when he put his hands on her waist to stop her. "I like Clarice quite a bit, and Fred, too. Lettice is a prosy windbag but she means well, and Amabel was put here on earth to test mortals."

He let out a shout of laughter and smacked a kiss on her forehead. "You're a wonder!"

"No, I am not," she argued and gently moved out of his grasp. "I would trade you one Lord Whitcomb for at least ten of these people. Twenty. Thirty."

He could not disagree. "Never thought of it like that." He resisted the urge to pat her on the fanny as she hurried off to the kitchen.

He suffered Edwin's after-dinner chatter, and couldn't hurry through the brandy and cigars fast enough. He was starved for a glimpse of Roxie. Somehow, when she was close by, he felt less inclined to speak his mind to his relatives. *Do I just feel* safe *around that little lady, I who have fought Napoleon's legions across half of Europe? I wonder how soon I can tear a page from Amabel's book and plead a headache?* he thought as Edwin blew another puff of smoke in his direction.

But when they rejoined the ladies in the sitting room, Amabel was on one of her rampages. She lay on the sofa, wincing as Helen softly played a rather fine Scarlatti he had been teaching her. Roxie turned the pages and Lissy leaned against her. Roxie patted the chair beside her, but Amabel was too quick.

She dragged herself upright. "Brother, I have something to say to you about the sale of your London house," she began.

"Don't start on that, Amabel," he warned. "There is nothing for me in London anymore."

"You might have considered the rest of us," she burst out, holding her head and ignoring the twitterings of her colorless husband seated beside her. "It is just another example of your selfishness!

If society sees fit to cut you direct, I don't know why you need to take it out on us! Wasn't it enough for you to tumble Papa into an early grave? Perhaps Cynthia was justified."

"Damn you, Amabel."

"No, Winn! You are the villain here," Amabel shouted.

Lettice gasped and dug for her smelling salts. The air was thick with tension as he felt his own anger rising. Out of the corner of his eye, he could see Clarice starting toward her sister, but a calm voice interrupted them all.

"No, Amabel, not here," Roxanna said. She rose from her seat at the piano and stood in front of him, leaning back against him as if daring him to move. "I cannot permit you to rip at my husband that way. You may return to the dower house now, or silence your tongue. This is our home, not yours, and we do not speak that way."

Her words were quietly spoken but they carried to the far corners of the room. My God, Roxie, he thought as he gently rested his hands on her shoulders. She was trembling, but she did not take her eyes from Amabel. Helen continued with the Scarlatti invention, and soon his relatives were conversing with each other again. Amabel said nothing more.

Roxie returned to the piano bench and soon Edwin reclaimed his attention, demanding to know what it was really like at Waterloo. When he looked around finally, she was gone, and so were her daughters. Clarice was regarding him with something close to fondness.

"I think we can see ourselves to bed, Winn," she said. "Good night."

Chapter 15

Roxie wasn't in their bedroom so he knocked quietly on the next door, and opened it when Lissy called out. She lay in the girls' bed, a daughter on each side of her. Lissy sat up and motioned to him. "Mama tells the most wonderful stories," she said. "You can lie down, too."

He did as she said, finding himself a spot at the foot of the bed where he could grab Lissy's toes and make her shriek. Soon even Helen was laughing. When Roxanna finished her story, she kissed her daughters and sat on the edge of their bed as they said their prayers.

"Good night, my dears," she said as she snuffed the candles and then closed the door behind her.

He followed her to their room, chagrined that she had not once looked him in the eye. You must be so disgusted with my relatives, he thought as he closed the door behind them. I am so ashamed of them. And myself.

"Roxie, I . . ."

She turned around then, her eyes bright with tears. "You have every right to be upset with me," she began, raising her glance to meet his. "I just couldn't bear to hear Amabel go on that way, digging at you like a harpie. I know I have no right."

He pulled her close to him. "You were wonderful, my dear. Thank you."

She stepped back to look at him, astonished. "You're not angry?"

"Heavens, no," he said and released her. "I don't know when any husband has ever been so adroitly defended. Anything you want from me? Just name it, up to one half my kingdom."

She laughed then, relieved laughter. "I have my limits, sir," she said. "I do not think Amabel and I will be on speaking terms, but perhaps she will not harrow you up again in my presence. Here, let me help you off with your shoes. I noticed you've been gritting your teeth since dinner."

"It was the company, not the toe," he assured her, but allowed her to assist him. She took off his sock, and stared in dismay at the blood on the bandage.

"Sit right there," she ordered, and went to the washbasin.

"Roxie, I can take care of it," he insisted.

"I am sure you can," she agreed, returning with a tin of water and a cloth. "You've been taking care of yourself for far too long. Do allow me my penance for getting stern with your relatives."

"Really, Roxie," he protested as she knelt by the bed and carefully lifted off the bandage.

It looked disgusting, but she did not even flinch as she dabbed at the crusted blood around the sutures. "I suppose you will now bluster and protest and tell me that you rode your horse all across Europe with your bowels hanging out, and your nose on by a flap of skin only, and your backbone open to the spine," she murmured as she worked, her hands expert.

He laughed. "Yes, I do go on like that, don't I?" he agreed. "How insufferable for you."

She stopped and sat back to look up at him. "There's no shame in letting someone do for you, Lord Winn. Hold still."

He looked down at her in self-conscious amusement. "It doesn't look too appealing."

"It is nothing, really. You should have seen Anthony's bed-sores before he died," she murmured as she dried off the wound. "His skin was breaking down and we couldn't do a thing about it," she said, her voice matter-of-fact. "I cried a lot, but not when he was conscious."

There wasn't anything he could add to her artless statement, but admire her sensible courage in silence. He pointed out the fresh dressings on his bureau and let her re-bandage his foot. "That should keep you until morning," she said as she stood and gathered up the old bandage. "Let me look at it again before you leave."

"Yes, doctor," he replied.

She grinned then. "I do become somewhat managing, don't I?" she said.

"Yes, you do," he agreed as he untied his neckcloth. "But I am tired, and don't intend to worry about it tonight." *I feel old, too,* he thought as she helped him from his coat and arranged it over the back of a chair. *And bitter, and disgusted with myself, and missing you already.*

"Well, good night, Fletch," she said and went into the dressing room with her lamp.

She was out in a moment, her eyes wide. "Do you know where Mrs. Howell found that extra cot for Edwin's friend?" she asked, her face red.

There is a God, he rejoiced. *Play this carefully, Fletcher,* he told himself, as he continued unbuttoning his shirt. "Your bed?"

She nodded. "I suppose I can find enough blankets in the linen room to make a pallet on the floor."

He shook his head, trying to appear casual. "I'm afraid you're out there. I'm sure Mrs. Howell gathered up the last of the blankets to make up those beds for Edwin and his friends." He pulled out his shirttails. *Do this right, Winn,* he thought. "Do you trust me, Roxie?"

"Yes," she said. "But . . ."

"Well, then, I will share my bed, as long as you promise not to touch my foot. I'd probably shriek and then my sisters would come running." He shuddered elaborately.

She stood there at the door of the dressing room for a long moment as he regarded her.

"In for a penny . . ."

" . . . in for ten pounds," she finished. "Oh, very well! It seems I do not have a choice. Why has this become my Christmas refrain?"

She returned to the dressing room and he hurried into his nightshirt, wishing that his hands would stop trembling. Winn, you are too old to be coy, he thought as he put on his dressing gown, took out his book, and lay down on the bed.

Roxie came out in a moment, wearing Anthony's dressing gown with the sleeves rolled up that he remembered from his first sight of her two months ago. She went to the dressing table and took the pins from her hair, shaking it out with a sigh. She started to brush her hair, and the crackle was pleasant to his ears. He put down the book and watched Roxie over the top of his spectacles as she brushed out her long hair and hummed to herself.

He screwed up his courage and closed the book, going to stand behind her at the dressing table. "Hand me your brush," he said as she watched him in the mirror, her eyes wary. She did and he brushed her hair, pulling the brush vigorously through the length of her hair from root to stem. It fell nearly to her waist in a glorious wave of dark brown, lively with electricity.

"Oh, much better," she sighed. "Helen tries, but she doesn't have the force to make that feel so good." She closed her eyes in pleasure. "I've thought about cutting it."

"Don't you dare," he said, his whole body on fire, hoping that he did not sound like he was panting. "There now."

She pulled the mass of hair over her shoulder. "Wonderful. This excuses all your social blunders of this evening, Fletch."

He laughed and sat down beside her on the bench. "Roxie, you're too easy to please."

She tied on her sleeping cap and went to the bed, standing there a moment in reflective indecision. "This really isn't a very good idea," she said dubiously.

He took a deep breath and removed his dressing gown and got into bed. "Well, the floor's too cold to stand there ruminating too long, Roxie," he said, and blew out the lamp. "Maybe you'll lose a toe tonight."

He held his breath as she still stood there. "Oh, bother it," she said at last and took off Anthony's robe. She crawled into her side of the bed and punched down the pillow, wrapping her arm around it and looking remarkably like Lissy.

He turned to face her. The moonlight came in through the draperies he had forgotten to close, and her skin was lit by the soft glow from the window. She chuckled. "Do you know, I almost laughed out loud this morning when Lissy threw a snowball at Lettice!"

"She has a good throwing arm," he agreed, relaxing and letting the mattress claim him. The fragrance of lavender surrounded him and he felt more peace than at any time he could remember. "But I don't think she expected Lettice to throw one right back!"

They laughed together. He took her hand. "Good night, Roxie," he said softly. "Thanks for coming to my rescue."

She gently eased her hand from his loose grasp. "Someone has to save you from yourself," she replied, her voice sleepy.

He lay there a moment, contemplating all manner of mischief, and rejecting it. Ah, well. "Good night, Roxie," he said again. He raised up on one elbow to kiss her chastely on the cheek. She had started to turn away from him as he leaned over, and they cracked heads.

He thought about it later, recognizing the event as a pivotal moment similar, somehow, to Wellington's decision to attack Quatre Bras and bring on Waterloo. Once begun, inescapably engaged. They could have laughed, said good night, and turned over again, but they didn't, and the chance turned into something wished for but not expected.

Even moments later, he couldn't be sure who began it. Did she grasp him around the neck and pull him closer? Did he kiss her on the lips, and then do it again when her arms went around him? Her lips were as soft as he imagined, gentle and demanding at the same time. She sighed and moved closer, her hands in his hair now, her body sliding under his as though she belonged there.

He hesitated a moment, his thoughts wild. I will not regret this, he considered as he tugged up his nightshirt, but, Roxie, will you? He rested lightly on her then, his mind screaming one thing, his body another. And then she said, "Please," her voice filled with as much desire as he felt himself, and he understood perfectly.

He gave her time to divest herself of her nightgown, helping with the buttons, and then he was captured in love, devoured by it, overwhelmed as never before—and his memory was excellent. She was a woman starving, and it gave him the most exquisite joy to pleasure her over and over again until they were both boggled with exhaustion. Even then, she allowed him to leave her only with the greatest reluctance.

"Roxie, I weigh too much," he said finally.

She relaxed her grip then even as she protested. He lay beside her, his mind completely blank. Then the cool night air reminded him that the blankets were somewhere and he searched for them. She lay watching him as he covered her. He smiled and picked up her hand, letting it drop to the mattress again, limp as a rag doll.

I shall not say anything, he thought as he lay back next to her. I shall lie here and breathe lavender and Roxanna, and it will be enough. Everything I ever did in life before this moment is of no consequence. I have been baptized with love and I am clean as never before.

Roxie sighed, and he turned his head to look at her, raising up on one elbow.

"I should be ashamed of myself," she murmured. "I can't imagine what you must think." As he watched her lovely face, tears slid onto the pillow.

Careful, Fletcher, he thought. Say the right thing for once. Don't laugh off her genuine remorse at breaking so thoroughly your idiotic marriage of convenience, or at giving me a glimpse of the intensity of female love I wasn't sure existed. There's more here than even she understands.

He touched her face. Please God, the right thing. "Tell me, Roxie, and tell me frankly: when was your husband last able to pleasure you?"

She closed her eyes. "He's been dead nine months now, and before then . . ." She sighed again. "It was two years before then that he had the strength. I suppose nearly three years."

"That's a long time for a healthy young woman, Roxie," he said.

She hesitated, then thought better of speaking.

"Tell me, my dear," he urged. "Please don't be shy."

"I enjoy making love so much," she whispered, and then covered her face with her hands. "Oh, God, so many nights I wanted to touch Anthony and turn him into someone healthy, anyone. I cannot tell you how many miles I have walked over these hills, trying to wear myself out!"

He did chuckle then. "I seem to remember surprising you once on one of your forced marches."

To his relief, she laughed softly. "Yes." Her voice turned serious again. "But this is not something good women talk about, I suppose."

"You can talk to me," he replied. "Let me say that I feel . . . oh, I don't know . . . honored almost, to have given you something you needed. And Roxie, there's no shame in wanting what I gave you."

She shivered, and sat up to find her nightgown, buttoning it slowly as she looked at him in the moonlight. "Then I thank you, sir," she said, quite serious. "I do regret that I trampled on our convenient agreement."

"No regrets, Roxie," he commanded. "I don't think either of us had much control over this circumstance. We can overlook it."

"I know, but . . ."

She lay down again. He put his arm out, inviting her into his embrace, but she shook her head, clutching her pillow again, but still looking at him. "I feel such relief," she said finally and then closed her eyes.

He watched her, loving her with all his heart. At some point, Roxie, he vowed silently, you'll consider me and see a real husband. I can wait until that happens. He touched her hair and she moved a little closer, more into his warmth.

"Roxie, are you still awake?" he whispered.

"H'mmm."

"If you wish more refreshment again before morning, I'm a light sleeper."

Her voice was drowsy. "But you said once that your aide-de-camp had to punch you awake," she murmured, her face in the pillow.

"He wasn't Roxie Rand. Good night, dear."

She woke him before morning, rubbing his back, and her love was even more thorough. At first, he hoped everyone at Moreland was a sound sleeper, and then he didn't care.

When he got up and dressed in the morning, Roxie was still sleeping, her arms thrown out like a child, her hair fanned around her face. He built a fire for her, wincing at the noise the coals made, but chuckling to himself at the soundness of her slumber. Roxie, not only are you rendered boneless by intercourse, but deaf also, he thought, a smile on his face. And I feel like I will live a thousand years now. Such immortality you bestow, my love.

They were all assembled and deep into breakfast before she came down. Winn patted the chair beside him. "My dear, I was afraid you would sleep through our departure."

"Oh, no," she replied, not looking at him as he poured her coffee, just a hint of unruly color in her cheeks. "You're all leaving at once?" she asked.

"Winn is ever so far behind on *our* family affairs at Winnfield," Amabel said, effectively snubbing Roxie from the family circle.

"I am sure he is," Roxie replied smoothly, smiling at him as he handed her a cinnamon bun.

"I think you should join him there, my dear," Clarice said.

Don't meddle, he thought. Let her take her time, Clarice. "Oh, sister, this is a delicate matter," he said out loud. "Helen and Lissy need some time to work around to this change in their lives. We'll take things as they come."

"I suppose it was rather a rush," Amabel said, her eyes on Roxie. "Are you even out of mourning yet?"

Winn could hear everyone take in a breath and hold it. He looked at his wife, who calmly set down her knife and fork. Go get her, Roxie, he thought.

"Yes, it was a rush, Amabel," she replied. "And no, I am not out of mourning yet. You can think what you choose. I really don't give a hearty damn." She nodded to Clarice to pass the eggs as Amabel choked on her tea and left the room coughing.

Edwin giggled. Fred grinned at the departing Amabel, and Lettice glowered at him. "You're a quick one," Clarice said, smiling at Roxanna. "It's hard to render Amabel speechless."

Roxie blushed. "I don't make a practice of that," she assured her sister-in-law as she touched a napkin to her lips. "Now, can I help anyone pack? Amabel, perhaps?"

I do not know what is coming over me, she thought as she allowed Lord Winn to pull back her chair from the breakfast table. I don't make a career of setdowns. She glanced at her husband. And I don't, as a general rule, leave fingernail tracks all across a man's back. I certainly hope I didn't draw blood. Oh, my. What must he think of me? The sooner they are all gone, the better for my piece of mind. Or what's left of it, at any rate.

"Roxie, come with me to the bookroom a moment," Winn was saying to her. "We need to discuss a little business."

She allowed him to take her arm and stroll with her down the hall. She noticed that he barely limped now.

"Your foot is better this morning?" she asked.

"Yes, and everything else, too," he replied, a slight smile on his face.

Better let that one pass, she thought as she sat next to him at the desk and he indicated the ledgers in the glass-faced cabinet.

"Tibbie handles all the estate matters, planting, lambing, and so forth," he was saying, when she dragged her thoughts back from last night to the present. He held out a smaller book. "I've settled a yearly allowance of five thousand pounds on you, Roxie. You can keep a record here."

She gasped. "Five thousand pounds?" she repeated. "Fletch, I was managing on two hundred pounds!"

"A paltry sum," he declared as he replaced the ledger. "You'll be wanting a new wardrobe when you're out of mourning in a few months."

"Yes," she agreed, "but I was thinking more in terms of muslin, and less of cloth of gold and ermine!"

He laughed and took her hand. "You really are a wife after a Yorkshireman's heart, Roxie dear! I'll bet you even turn up your petticoats, and scrape butter off bread to conserve."

"Doesn't everyone?" she asked blithely, grateful for his light tone, especially after last night's heavy doings. "I am sure that will be more than ample for my needs, and see to the finishing of the renovation here."

"My dear, that comes out of estate funds." To her relief, he looked up from his contemplation of her when Lord Manwaring called to him from the front hall. "Use your allowance on yourself and the girls! No arguments. Fred is anxious to be off. He knows it's best to travel with Amabel on a full stomach."

She allowed him to help her up, but she held him back for a moment. He looked at her and shook his head.

"If you intend to apologize again for what happened last night, I won't listen," he said softly. "I had a delightful time, and so did you, and let's leave it at that for now."

She sighed.

"And don't sigh and flog yourself," he continued. "What I do want you to do is write me occasionally, and let me know how things go on here." He led her into the hall, her arm tucked through his. "See my solicitor in the village for funds, and I think his wife knows a good piano teacher, if you find you haven't time."

"Aye, sir," she said, amused.

"I'm trying to think of everything," he protested and tugged at the loose hair under her cap. "I've left our marriage lines with him, and a fair copy of my divorce papers, and a statement of chattel. I can see no further difficulty from Lord Whitcomb on that head."

"Very well," she said, hurrying to keep up. "Ah, here comes your farewell committee. Good morning, my dears!"

Lord Winn picked up Felicity, who was still rubbing sleep from her eyes, and continued down the hall beside her. He looked across Roxanna to Helen. "Helen, I trust you will continue riding. I have arranged for a rather gentle little mare to be delivered to your mother. With saddle, of course."

"You needn't have—" she began.

"Roxie, it is so hard to do nice things for you!" he protested, amusement evident in his voice. "Well, nearly always," he amended, his eyes roguish. "Helen, teach your mother to ride. She might find it useful."

"Yes, sir," Helen replied, taking her commission quite seriously. "And I will practice my Scarlatti."

"You'll be back in a few days?" Lissy asked, her hands on his face.

He stopped then and gave her his full attention. "No, my dear, I won't," he said at last.

"But when?" she persisted as he set her down and opened the front door.

"I don't know," he said.

Roxanna knelt beside her daughter, hugging her close, and feeling an absurd urge to join in Lissy's sudden tears. "Lord Winn has a lot of business to attend to," she explained. "We were . . . lucky to have him here as long as we did, Felicity."

Lissy sobbed, stopping only when Lord Winn picked her up again and held his handkerchief to her nose. She blew, and then threw her arms around him in another flood of tears.

Roxanna looked away, the pain of departure suddenly real. I owe you so much, Lord Winn, she thought. She gathered together her own disordered thoughts, and tried to smile and nod at Edwin Chandler and his friends, standing there with baggage in hand. You've rescued my daughters for me, and given me enough income to live on for the rest of my life. I have a beautiful home now, and nothing to fear or worry about. Why do I feel so dreadful?

It was an unanswerable question. Lord Winn, his face a study in discomfort, gently pried Lissy's hands off his neck and handed her daughter to her. Lissy watched him. "I want to know when you are coming back," she stated, each word distinct, the model of her mother.

Yes, Roxie thought, tell us when.

"Lissy!" he began, exasperated. He looked at Roxanna. "That depends on a lot of things," he said, "none of which you will understand."

"I want to know," she demanded.

Clarice stepped to her brother's side then and nudged him. "As a parent of some years, I recognize that tone, Winn, even if you are unfamiliar with it. Four-year-olds want answers, brother."

Roxie nodded to Clarice in complete agreement. "Yes! Don't they?" So do I, she thought, and I am much older than four.

Lord Winn thought a moment then cleared his throat. "Very well, Felicity Drew," he said and put his hand on her shoulder. "I will make a flying trip back here in March with my York solicitor. We have to return to Northumberland to settle up a rather pesky deed, and I trust the snow will be gone then." He knelt by her again. "Now. Will that satisfy you?"

Lissy was silent a moment, tears forgotten. She blew her nose again on Winn's handkerchief. "Mama, can we mark a calendar?" she asked.

"I am sure we can, my dear. Now don't plague Lord Winn anymore."

"I am not a plague, Mama," she replied with dignity. "I am merely a trial."

And so the Rands were laughing when they entered the carriages drawn up for them. Lord Winn tied Ney's reins to the back of his brother-in-law's carriage, then came up the front steps again, walking slowly, reluctantly, almost. He took Helen's hand in both of his hands.

"Take good care of your mother," he said, his voice strained.

Oh, dear, she thought. I hope you are not getting a cold, too, from all these comings and goings.

"I will," Helen assured him. "And I will write."

"Excellent!" he kissed the top of her head, then picked up Lissy again. "You are not even a trial, Lissy. Admire that view of the Plain of York for me," he told her. "I live at the other end of it, think on."

She nodded, and touched his face again. "March?"

"Just three months, Lissy."

And then it was her turn. What do I say to you? she thought as he took her by the arm. I like you a lot. God knows I have used you down to a burned wick. It's even quite possible that you know me better than Anthony did. You've seen me through one of my worst experiences.

"I don't know what to say," she admitted, tears in her eyes.

He hugged her close, taking her breath away with the strength of his grip, and then he released her.

"You'll think of something someday, Roxanna," he said.

"You're sure of that?" she murmured.

"No, I am not," he replied, his words honest. "But then, I always was a fool where women are concerned. Take care, Roxie. Think of me occasionally."

He kissed her then, put on his hat, and took another long look at the three of them standing close together on the front steps. He turned his back on them, hurried down the steps and into a carriage. He did not look back, but they stayed on the front steps until the carriages were only a speck on the road.

"Well, my dears," she said at last, when she finally noticed that Lissy was barefoot and Helen shivering. "Let's finish the cinnamon buns and find Meggie. There's much to do."

The hall was so empty, with no quick, firm steps of a military nature. There was no Haydn played too fast in the sitting room. The cinnamon buns didn't taste the same, and even Lissy left the last one unfinished on her plate. When she suggested that Five Pence needed some exercise, Helen shrugged and continued to sit there until Roxie reminded her.

"We are feeling sorry for ourselves," she declared finally. "Come, girls, it's time to get dressed."

She shooed them upstairs to their room and went into the room she shared with Lord Winn. The bed was a mess, she thought, but what fun. She sat on his side a moment, wishing that it was still warm and still smelled of him.

It did not. She peeked in the dressing room, but all his clothes were gone. So was his shaving gear, his book, and his spectacles. She straightened the bedcovers and noticed something white under the bed. She pulled out his nightshirt and laughed softly. So that was where it ended up, she thought as she hung it on a peg in the dressing room.

There was a calendar next to the clothes hamper. She found a pencil stub and drew an X through December 30.

"January, February, March," she said. "And what then, Roxie? What then?"

Chapter 16

If it wasn't the snowiest winter on record in the North Riding, then it was second cousin to the snowiest, Roxanna decided as she marked the last X through January 31 and crumpled the page into the fireplace. She sat on the hearth and poked at the coals. February would be long, she knew, fifty days at least. Then would come March, and Tibbie and the shepherds would be on the alert for ewes snuffling about, looking for a likely spot on the thawing ground to drop their lambs. And the wind would blow, and she and Lissy would continue to spend too much time at dusk looking across the Plain of York.

Helen seemed to adjust quickly to Lord Winn's leaving. She devoted long hours in the stable to Five Pence, and cajoled Roxanna into currying the Empress Josephine, her mother's new mare and parting gift from Lord Winn. Roxanna had to admit that she was looking forward to a break in the weather so she could ride the pretty animal.

"Mama, she likes you," Helen declared.

"Well, I do believe I like her," Roxanna replied, stroking the horse's nose.

"I am going to draw a picture of the Empress to send to Lord Winn," Helen said as she handed Roxanna a bucket of grain. "Do you think he will like that?"

"I am sure he will," Roxanna said.

"You'll mail it?"

"Of course. But don't tell Lissy. It think it almost makes her more sad to send letters because it reminds her that he is not here."

Helen turned back to Five Pence and began to curry the pony. "She'll get over him, Mama," she said, her voice matter-of-fact, a little cold, almost. "I have."

"My dear, you sound a wee bit bloodless," she scolded, startled from her contemplation of the Empress.

Helen leaned against her pony. "Mama, I do not want to like

someone else who will just be leaving, like Papa," she said calmly. "It's too hard to do."

Roxanna sat down on the grain bucket and pulled Helen close to her. "Oh, my dear, I wish you did not sound so adult," she whispered into Helen's ear.

Helen only cuddled in close to her mother, her eyes filled with misery. "Mama, I miss him, too." She sat up. "Why, Mama? He wasn't here that long. Why do I miss him?"

Roxanna cradled her daughter close again. "Well, he had a way of filling up a room, didn't he?"

"He did." She moved off her mother's lap and back to Five Pence again. "I am forgetting things about Papa, too. Will I do that with Lord Winn? Why does that have to happen? I try and try to remember . . ." Her voice trailed away.

I have no answers, my love, she thought that night as she sat in the bookroom, long after the girls were asleep. She picked up the picture of her horse that Helen had drawn, folded and addressed to the marquess. "My husband," she said out loud, wondering why it seemed so distant now. He had been gone a month and more. Even their tumultuous night together was fading around the edges now. She put her head down on the desk. I shall have to start taking long walks again when the snow stops. If it ever stops.

He wrote once a week, in response to their letters. Lissy usually received pictures he had drawn, sketches of Winnfield, mainly. One sketch was of the picture gallery with a series of forbidding, pop-eyed faces glaring down from the cobwebbed walls, and a note, "Wish you were here," scrawled across the top in spooky handwriting that made them all laugh.

To Helen he wrote horse advice, and sent along music, one sheet a Mozart exercise, and another a work of his own creation that Helen played over and over. "So you do not care?" Roxie said to herself as she heard Helen humming the tune and rehearsing it endlessly.

Her own letters from Lord Winn could have been read from the pulpit on Sundays, prosaic bits of news about Parliament's latest blunder, or more often, the business venture he was involved in that took him to London for several weeks. "Mind you," he wrote, "soiling my hands with business makes me smell of the shop to some of the high sticklers I know; but since I seldom have any dealings with the *ton* anymore, it hardly matters. They can be proud; I choose to be richer."

It was an intriguing venture, and so she wrote him, asking for more details about the canal system he was investing in. He responded promptly with maps and schematics of the canals. She pored over them, feeling complimented somehow that Lord Winn would not dress them down or simplify them because she was a woman. He seemed to know that she could follow them, and she did. To Lissy's delight, one of the canal maps had a small boat sketched in, with a pirate on a plank who looked something like Lord Whitcomb.

His letters to her were nothing special, no intimate references to make her tuck them under her pillow to hoard and read over and over again. But she read them over and over anyway, chiding herself as she did so. What are you expecting, Roxie? she asked herself. It impressed her how forcefully his personality came through his words. He could almost be there, except that he was not, and they all felt the poorer for his absence.

"Do you think he misses us as much as we miss him?" Lissy asked her one night after prayers and before she blew out the lamp.

Roxanna sat on the bed, looking into Lissy's eyes, so like her own. "Oh, I am sure he is very busy with his canal venture, my love, and all the activities of his estates."

"Do you think if I told him I missed him, he would come sooner than March?" Lissy persisted, even as her eyes started to close.

"I think you ask too many questions!" she said, avoiding the issue.

Without question, she missed him. Even long before their precipitate marriage, she had enjoyed waking up in the dower house with the thought that perhaps if she worked on the renovation at Moreland, she might run into him during the course of the day. He always had something to say, some observation to make, that cheered her. True, he could be outrageous, but it was worth a blush to really laugh again.

As February began to slide toward March, she thought she understood why his letters were so businesslike: he obviously did not choose to further whatever relationship might have begun between them. The thought pained her a little, even as she scolded herself for thinking there would ever be more. She had made a marriage of convenience and that was all it was, barring one slip. Everyone's human, she thought, and then blushed. Maybe some of us more than others. But it was only a onetime moment, obviously of little importance to Lord Winn.

Or so she reasoned as she and Mrs. Howell busied themselves with some early spring cleaning, in the hopes that would bring an end to the eternal snows of 1817. And then it was March 5, a year since Anthony's death, and Lord Winn sent a note accompanying a bolt of burgundy dimity. "Dear Roxie, how about a walking dress of this? I found it in London and thought it would look especially nice on your back. More to follow. Winn." Two days later, a carter arrived with bolts of material, lavender, soft gray, blue and white, and a note pinned to one bolt of green fabric: "Is there enough for you and the girls? I can send more. I probably will. You know me. Winn."

Meggie laughed over that note. "Enough?" she asked, pointing to the bolts that they stashed in the linen room. "We could outfit an army from this. Someone ought to tell Lord Winn that current fashions don't require whole bolts. Well, Roxanna? You're woolgathering again."

Guilty, Roxanna looked up from the note. "You know me," she read again as she dragged her attention back to Meggie. No, I don't know you, Lord Winn, she thought. And yet I know you awfully well. Lord, what a mull. "Yes, Meggie? I'm sorry. Say again?"

It was springtime material, but spring was still just a dream in the North Riding. Roxanna summoned a modiste anyway, and plotted and planned wardrobes for her and her daughters as the snow fell and the wind whistled around Moreland's well-insulated windows. When the weather broke, she promised herself a whole day in Darlington to look at hats and silk stockings.

When she finally completed the wallpaper and painting in Lord Winn's bedroom, she declared the renovation complete. True, the bedcovers and furniture were still definitely Queen Anne in a house more Regency now, but that could wait for a trip to the warehouses in Richmond. Curtains could wait, too. The matter interested her less and less. What was the point of renovation? She and the girls had their rooms completed, and Lord Winn was not selling Moreland. The other bedrooms would only remain empty.

And then it was March. Lissy triumphantly threw away her February calendar page. "Mama, he said he would come in March, didn't he?" she asked for the umpteenth time. She stood still only long enough for Roxie to button her nightgown and then ran to the window seat. "Do you think I will be able to see him from this window when he comes?"

Helen joined her. "Lissy, he might not come."

Lissy shook her head. "He said he would."

Oh dear, Roxie thought as she watched them both in the window seat. We have got to get over our melancholy. And we cannot spend all our days waiting for something to happen. Please, Lord, a break in the weather, she prayed that night.

She heard the wind howling as she shivered in bed and clutched her pillow close to her. Go to sleep, she told herself, even as she listened and dreaded the snow that would follow soon. But as she listened, she heard a different sound. The wind was coming up from the south, accompanied by the welcome drip of water from the long icicles outside the window. Spring was coming.

For two days, the winds blew warmer and gradually the ground began to emerge from the long sleep of a Yorkshire winter. Snow was everywhere still, but they could walk outside now and see the dark soil again. And here and there crocuses poked up through the snow.

"Come, girls," she said after breakfast. "Put on your oldest shoes. We are going walking."

She thought it would take some urging, but the girls were almost as restless as she was. The wind cut across the dale as they left the house, but it was warmer than the blizzards of January. Lissy tugged on her beloved red mittens and held up her hand.

"Mama, they almost do not fit!"

Roxanna smiled at her daughter, and examined her mitten. "That means a new pair next winter." She looked at Helen. "And for you, too?"

Helen nodded. "But let us not talk about next winter, Mama," she said. "Let us put it off, as you like to put off things."

They laughed together, grateful to be outside.

They passed the dower house, looking almost like a doll's house now, after the spaciousness of Moreland. "Do you know, Helen," she murmured, "I think I will ask Meggie if she would like to move in there."

"Why, Mama?" Helen asked. "She likes it with us."

"Every woman should have a home of her own," Roxanna said decisively. "Before she came here, Meggie only lived in rented rooms." She took her girls' hands and walked more purposefully toward the park beyond the house. "I will ask Lord Winn what he thinks."

It was really too cold to be walking long, but the meadow seemed to open up for them. And there in the distance were sheep. Lissy ran ahead, waving her arms. As Helen and Roxanna watched, she stopped and looked down at one sheep, then hurried back to her mother.

"Mama, it is grunting and grunting," she said, giving a demonstration that would have made Lord Winn laugh, Roxanna decided. "Is it sick?"

Roxanna shrugged. "Let us see." She hurried closer, and discovered the ewe deep in labor. She knelt in the mud beside the sheep and fingered its bedraggled wool, looking about for help. "Helen, see if you can find Tibbie or one of the shepherds," she asked as the ewe grunted, then panted softly, looking vaguely disturbed.

Helen was gone a long time and the wind blew colder. Lissy knelt beside her, grunting along with the ewe. Her nose was red and she shivered in the wind.

"This will never do," Roxanna said at last. "In for a penny . . . ," she muttered as she took off her cloak and rolled up her sleeve.

"Mama, what are you doing?" Lissy asked in astonishment as Roxanna inserted her arm into the ewe.

"Call it a courtesy," she said as she rummaged around and discovered a wonderful tangle of legs inside the ewe. The animal only looked back at her once and continued chewing placidly. "Goodness, Lissy, there are at least two lambs in there!"

Lissy leaned closer. "Mama! Do you know what to do?"

"I think I can figure out this puzzle," she grunted as she pulled on two legs, pushed back two others, then hooked her forefinger into an eye socket as another unborn lamb licked her wrist. "Stand back, Lissy! This may be like a cork in a bottle."

By the time Tibbie arrived, there were two lambs shaking themselves off and contemplating the ewe's udder. "Well, well, Mrs. Rand," he said as he squatted to watch her continued efforts. "No. You keep going. This last one ought to slide right out like an oyster. Grand work, Mrs. Rand! You'll put my shepherds out of business!"

As Roxanna sat back on her heels, her fingers aching, Lissy stared at the three lambs. She listened with satisfaction as the sheep made its odd purring noise and the lambs at the udder settled down to more serious matters.

"Mama, you are wonderful!" Helen declared as she ran up with a shepherd.

Roxanna accepted a piece of toweling from the man. She was bloody and covered with mud, but smiling with satisfaction. Spring had come to this harsh land at last, bringing new lambs. Perhaps it would bring Lord Winn back for a visit.

That evening Helen wrote a narrative to the marquess of her mother's exploits in the meadow, while Lissy drew a picture of the three lambs. Over her daughters' protests, Roxanna vetoed

Lissy's first picture of her arm in the sheep. "I think Lord Winn has sufficient imagination to figure out where lambs come from," she assured her children as she added her note about the dower house and Meggie, and sealed it with the pictures.

The next day was warmer, so while Lissy napped under Meggie's watchful eye, she and Helen rode their horses into the village to post the letter. The Empress Josephine was a well-mannered mare, Roxanna decided as they trotted along amiably. Lord Winn obviously knew his horses.

"Mama, have you ever seen a finer day?" Helen exclaimed, her face turned upward like a sunflower to the sky.

"Never, my dear," she agreed, struck all over again how different this year was from last year, when they were all claustrophobic in black and numb with Anthony's death. As they rode along, glorying in the North Riding spring, last year's tears and agony seemed to fold into the earth. She felt at peace finally, as if the disappearing snow was taking with it the unquiet in her heart. It had been a long year. She was glad it was over.

They returned to Moreland by way of the graveyard in Whitcomb parish. The snow was gone from Anthony's grave, and there were crocuses in bloom. They dismounted and came closer, admiring the beauty of the flowers against the scrollwork of the tombstone. Roxanna took Helen's hand and swallowed an enormous lump in her throat. "Helen, let us return tomorrow and plant daffodils," she said, speaking through her tears.

"Oh, yes, Mama, and then something else for summer." Helen's eyes were bright with tears, too, but she was smiling. "Papa would like that. Columbine, Mama."

Roxanna nodded and took her daughter by the shoulder as they turned away from the graveyard. And maybe woodbine, too, she thought, and holly later. There should be some part of Yorkshire for all of Anthony's seasons here. She looked back one last time at the crocuses, their petals giving way now in the sharp wind. "To everything there is a season," she thought, remembering a sermon given in the strength of his better days. This was yours, my love.

Lissy watched all week for the postman; Lord Winn did not disappoint her. While the others stood by, she opened a letter and pulled out a sketch of Roxanna, her eyes wide with disbelief, sitting up in bed and clutching her blankets as three lambs jumped over the footboard. Roxanna chuckled over the note at the bottom: " 'Little lamb, who untangled thee? Dost though know who untangled thee?' " she read. "Lord Winn, you should be shot for such a mangling of Blake!"

As the girls decided where to pin the picture in their room, Roxanna read the accompanying letter. He had given his whole-hearted approval of Meggie's removal to the solitary splendor of the dower house. "Heaven knows she deserves an occasional break from Lissy's enthusiasms," he wrote in his rapid scrawl. "It was good of you to think of it, Roxie." Her heart warmed as he informed her that he had settled three hundred pounds a year on Meggie Watson with his solicitor. "I'd say her service was above and beyond the call of duty, wouldn't you, wife?" he continued. Wife, she thought. It sounds good.

The rest of the letter brought a frown to her face. Oh, dear, Helen was right, she thought as she continued on the next page. "I fear I cannot return in March as I had promised," he wrote. "I must go to Northumberland by way of Carlisle, as we have another canal backer to cajole there. I wish it were not so. Please tell the girls how sorry I am. Perhaps I can visit later in the summer, when negotiations are settled. Winn."

That is somewhat indefinite, my lord, she thought as she scanned the last page again. What would you rather I read into that? She looked from the letter to the picture, wondering at the contradictions. Are you as confused as I am? Likely, she told herself. But now comes the hard part.

It could have been worse, but I am not sure how, she decided an hour later after she closed the door to the girls' room. Lissy was asleep now, tears drying on her face, crushed by her news of Lord Winn's nonarrival. She had stormed and wailed, then refused to sit in the window seat for her nighttime perusal of the Plain of York. Roxanna went to her own room and lay down on the bed. To her mind, Helen's reaction was worse. She had flinched at the news, then her shoulders drooped as she looked at Roxanna. "Mama, at least with Lord Winn we don't have so much to tuck away in our minds," she said quietly, then turned away to sit in her chair by the fire.

I suppose every family needs a realistic member, she thought as she stared at the ceiling. Lissy and I hope and dream, and Helen keeps us tethered to the ground. I doubt she will ever put off things like I do, but oh, she can break my heart. There was no point in blaming Lord Winn. He was a busy man, and once cut adrift from the loose ties of Moreland, quite in demand in his busy world. It was no wonder he had forgotten them. She would be a fool to think otherwise.

She went to the window for her ritual look across the wide plain. *And he never promised you anything more, Roxanna,* she told herself. *Look what he has done already.* She smiled to herself. It would be sufficient. Lonely, perhaps, but sufficient. "I shall close that book, too," she said and then chuckled. "Not that it was ever open very far, anyway."

In the morning, she wrote a proper letter expressing their regrets, but saying nothing that would cast blame, or express the deep disappointment of her daughters. As she left the bookroom to look for Tibbie, Helen ran up with a letter, too. "For Lord Winn," she said.

Roxanna took it. "I trust you said nothing to cause Lord Winn any discomfort," she said as Tibbie came into the hall, motioning for her to bring the letters.

Helen shook her head. "I don't think so, Mama. Mostly I had a question about Five Pence. Do you think he will have time to answer it?"

Roxanna shrugged, and handed both letters to Tibbie. "He's obviously a busy man, my dear. Thanks, Tibbie."

The last week in March saw the roads freed finally of mud from the thawing snow. It had taken no cajoling on her part to talk the girls into accompanying her to Darlington to select bedcovers and material for curtains in the almost-completed bedrooms. There had been the dresses to pick up from the modiste, too, and a careful look at bonnets, which rendered Lissy bored beyond belief. Only the bribe of luncheon in a real tearoom bought Roxanna enough time to purchase silk stockings and several lengths of ribbon to refurbish old dresses.

It was a good luncheon. Lissy ate everything brought to her, and even Helen finished most of her meal. As they waited for dessert, Roxanna played her final card in cheering up her daughters. "My dears, I was thinking that a month at Scarborough this summer would be something fine. What do you think?"

"Mama, the seashore!" Helen gasped. "Really?"

"I remember making such a promise last year," Roxanna replied. "What about you, Lissy?"

She hesitated. "But what if Lord Winn decides to visit while we are gone?"

Roxanna sighed inwardly. *Oh, Lissy, let it go! I have.* "Well, we can let him know our plans so he will not come then."

"But suppose that is the only time he can visit us?" Lissy argued, with all the maddening persistence of a four-year-old.

"Don't be a nod," Helen said, her voice firm. "Think of sand castles and pony rides along the beach. And raspberry ices, Mama?"

"Of course."

Lissy thought, and then nodded. "I like it."

"Very well," Roxanna said as the dessert arrived. "August, then, in Scarborough."

They rode home singing loud songs, to the amusement of the coachman, and glorying in the unexpected warmth of early spring. Even the news that they must return to the classroom with Meggie tomorrow did nothing to dilute her daughters' noisy triumph over winter. "For we have gotten lax in our studies, now that Meggie has moved to the dower house," she reminded them. "Tomorrow, it is spelling and penmanship again."

And thank goodness for that, Roxanna said in the morning as she waved her daughters off to the classroom Meggie had established in her upstairs bedroom at the dower house. She debated over her new dresses, then hurried instead into a faded muslin which had once been blue. Climbing tall ladders does not require much fashion, she thought as she draped the tape measure around her neck and pulled the ladder closer to the window in one of the empty bedrooms. Now that she had finally chosen the material, she needed to measure windows. I have put this off too long, she thought. Why do I do that?

"I wish you would not dangle yourself atop tall ladders."

She blinked—it couldn't be—then reached out for the top of the window to steady herself. "Lord Winn?" she asked, and then turned around slowly on her perch.

"I thought I was Fletch to you," the marquess said, leaning against the frame of the open doorway, still wearing his many caped riding coat and hat. He tossed his hat onto the bed. "Obviously my credit is a little lower with the females of the Drew/Rand family right now. Do get down, Roxie! You make me nervous."

She hiked up her skirts and climbed down the ladder. She stopped halfway down and smiled at him. "You came after all," she said softly.

She didn't know what it was about her smile that made him stand up straight and stare back at her. I don't know about your expression, she thought as she descended and shook her skirts out. I wonder if I am in trouble?

She decided she wasn't when the marquess shrugged out of his overcoat, tossed it after the hat, and took her in his arms. Well, that's a relief, was her last coherent sentence before he kissed her, held her off for a moment, then kissed her again. In another moment she was flooded with desire, drenched in it, craving his body even as he pulled away and went back to the door.

Drat, she thought, her hands stopped on her buttons. To her relief, he was only closing the door and locking it. She went back to the buttons again, wondering why, out of all her clothes, she had put on the dress with so many. He turned back to help her, but his fingers were shaking, too.

"Roxie, is this dress valuable to you?" he asked finally.

She shook her head. "It's years old."

"Good." He grasped the front of it and ripped it open, sending the buttons clattering to the floor. "Now then, Roxie."

It was an easy matter to wriggle out of her chemise and petticoat as he tugged off his boots. He looked up at her, his eyes admiring what he saw. "You've been eating better, my dear," he managed. "Lord, Roxie, you could almost be an eye-popper!"

She laughed, sat on his lap, and started on his shirt. "You say the most romantic things, Fletch."

After that, words drifted from her brain in odd little bursts. I'm glad that door is locked, she thought as she shoved aside a coat and hat, and rolls of wallpaper, and took the tape measure from her neck. No sheets on this bed, she thought as he laid her down onto it. "Frills," she muttered, then devoted her whole attention to more pressing matters.

"Frills, eh! I am a frill?" he asked later as she rested herself on him. "Don't move. You're fine. But frills?"

She closed her eyes in vast contentment. "I was merely pointing out that there are no sheets on this bed, and your head is resting on a pillow of wallpaper."

"And your bum is covered with goosebumps," he added in most unloverlike fashion, running his hand over her backside. "Can you reach my overcoat without moving?"

She did, and he pulled it over both of them, then dug in one of the pockets, taking out a folded sheet. "I honestly do not have time to be here," he explained.

"I'll move," she offered, remaining where she was.

"Don't you dare! Take a look at this letter."

She spread out the letter on his chest. "It is from Helen," she said, and looked into his eyes.

"Read it. You'll see my primary reason for this visit, all frills aside, Roxie dear."

She did as he said, then rested her head on his chest. "Thank you for coming, my lord," she murmured.

He picked up the letter. "What could I do? That part about 'getting used to disappointment' sliced me to the bone." He put his arms around her again, running his hand over her back. "And the thing is, she was so matter-of-fact. There's not an ounce of pity in that letter. I wish she could still be a child, despite all that's happened to her. That's why I had to come."

"Helen never deals in self-pity." Roxie kissed his chest absent-mindedly. "I wish . . . well, I don't know what I wish. She will be so glad to see you."

He sighed and gently relocated her to the bed, sitting up to rummage for his watch, which he snapped open, shaking his head. "It's nine-thirty in the morning, Roxie," he said, his voice filled with wonder. "I don't recall that I ever did this before so soon after breakfast." He grinned at her. "What about you?"

She grinned back, even as she reached for her chemise. "Well, vicars do not keep regular hours, my lord," she hedged, her face red. She giggled. "Anthony used to swear it helped the digestion."

They dressed quickly. "Drat, there's no mirror." The marquess complained as he held out his neckcloth.

"Let me help," she replied, tying it expertly. She paused halfway through. "How could you manage this?"

"Well, I took off my clothes . . ." he began, his eyes roguish.

"Lord Winn, you're risking your credit! You said you were busy."

"I am," he agreed as he tucked his shirt into his pants and looked for his waistcoat. "After Helen's letter came, I told my solicitor that we were by damn going to go to Carlisle another route, even if we had to ride all night in a post chaise—he hates inconvenience, Roxie."

She put her hand to her mouth, her eyes wide. "And now you will tell me you have left that poor man sitting downstairs in the parlor!"

He nodded. "Well, yes."

She burst out laughing. "You are a rascal!"

He held up his hands in self-defense. "I did not plan this! Really! You are the one who gave me that look from the ladder, Roxie." He let her help him into his coat, and ran his fingers through his hair. "I can just drop in on Helen and Lissy and say hello now."

He took her hand and she felt her heart flop about in her chest. "My dear, we need to consider our arrangement," he said.

She nodded. "It does bear serious thought."

"Write me," he urged as he grabbed up his hat and overcoat.

"I'll be at Carlisle this week, and then High Point in Northumberland. I want to know how you feel."

"I'm not sure I know," she protested.

He grabbed her hand again and kissed it, then pulled her close to him. "Roxie, you need to decide if I am to be an everyday husband or an occasional convenience. Good-bye, my dear." He opened the door, then looked back at her. "If you hurry, you can make it to your room and find another dress before my solicitor sends Mrs. Howell on a hunting expedition."

She dressed quickly in her room and then went to a back bedroom, where she watched the dower house as Lord Winn ran in, and then came out a few minutes later, carrying Lissy, Helen at his side. He kissed them both, waved good-bye, then rejoined the solicitor in the post chaise. In a moment they were gone from view, heading north toward the Pennines.

It was almost hard to conceive that he had even been there at all, so quick was the visit. Except for the fact that she felt hugely content and her buttons were spilled everywhere on the floor, Lord Winn's visit might have been a product of her imagination. She went back to the other bedroom, replacing the rolls of wallpaper and hunting for her tape measure. She found it, but sat on the bed, staring at her hands. It's a good question, Roxie. What do you want?

Chapter 17

It was a good question, and one that she asked herself several times every hour, no matter how involved she was with other matters. *What* do I want? became her refrain as she supervised the hanging of the curtains in that bedroom. What *do* I want? she asked herself, changing the emphasis as she listened to Helen practice her Scarlatti. What do I *want*? was the question that chased around in her head when she should have been paying attention to Lissy's somersaults in the orchard.

Her brain told her that it was much too soon after Anthony's death to have formed a rational opinion about another man. If you truly loved Anthony, her mind scolded, you wouldn't even have thoughts about another yet, even if he is your husband now. "Bother it," she said out loud in church that Sunday during the reading of the Gospel, which caused a few heads to turn in her direction. She retreated behind her prayer book to tell herself that was a rumdudgeon notion. You couldn't put a timetable on love, as if it were a mail coach.

But is this love? was the next logical question. She glared at the vicar, wondering why he was prosing on and on about the atonement and resurrection, when she was wrestling with the more weighty matters of existence. Without question, she enjoyed Lord Winn's body. She slid lower behind her prayer book, hoping the Lord God Almighty wouldn't be troubling Himself at the moment to monitor her unruly thoughts. And the interesting thing is, she considered when she stood to take communion, neither time did I compare Fletch to Anthony. Beyond the basics, their lovemaking was not alike. She glided up the aisle, her eyes on her folded hands. Anthony had been a leisurely man, restful almost in his patterns, while entirely satisfying. Fletch was an adventure, a tumult. Oh Lord, she thought as she opened her mouth for communion. I shall be struck dead here at the altar, and what a pity that will be.

The Lord did not strike her dead, but she knew better than to take any more chances. She forced herself to concentrate on more mundane matters, such as why Lissy was staring cross-eyed at the lady in the next pew, and was it fair that the man over by the window had shoulders as broad as Fletch's? She could almost feel Lord Winn's back under her hands . . .

"Drat," she whispered under her breath, causing Helen to look up at her with a startled expression.

"Mama," she warned in a low voice. "You should behave yourself."

It's too late for that, she thought mournfully. Much too late.

They walked home across the fields to Moreland, Lissy stopping to blow dandelion puffs and dance around in the warm breeze of late March, as unexpected as it was richly deserved by the hardy souls of the North Riding. She walked with her hand in Helen's, miserable because Lord Winn was not there, her mind a tumult because she could not speak to him and hear his lovely Yorkshire brogue, with all its old style words that she, a transplant to this shire, could never master without sounding fake. It pained her that she could not see him lounging about in that casual way of his, or playing the piano with his sleeves rolled up and that look of concentration on his face, his long legs tapping out the rhythm.

She stopped suddenly in the middle of the park. Helen smiled and let go of her mother's hand, flopping down in the new grass, while Lissy danced around them both. I am an idiot, she thought as she dropped down beside Helen. How could I ever have considered Lord Winn just a convenience? Oh, well, he is a magnificent convenience, but that is only part of it, she amended, stretching her arms over her head in the soft grass. He is also someone I like to talk to, to walk with, to tease, to flatter, to laugh with, to admire, to worry about. I am in love again.

I wonder when it happened? she thought as she held up her left hand and regarded her wedding ring. Have I been in love with him since I first saw him looking so dejected on my doorstep? Was it when he let me cry all over him while he was shaving? Or maybe when he got that determined look in his eye and said we were going to Scotland, no matter what.

"Mama, are you listening to me?"

Lissy was sitting on her, staring into her eyes. Roxie grabbed her and rolled over with her in the grass, growling, as Lissy shrieked and tried to leap away. Helen giggled and threw handfuls of grass at them both.

"Come, my dears," Roxie said finally as she stood up and brushed off the grass. "I know you are starving, Lissy, and I have a letter to write."

She wrote to Lord Winn after dinner, debating whether to post her message to Carlisle or Northumberland, and choosing the latter finally. I have already delayed a reply to a pressing question, she reasoned, and he may have left Carlisle for High Point. This way, it will find him, she assured herself as she applied a wafer. She gazed at the letter, a smile on her face. I suppose he will respond promptly with one of those silly sketches of me.

The letter was on its way in the morning, and Roxanna busied herself with more spring cleaning. Two or three days at most, she thought as she finished hemming the last curtain in the last bedroom. Perhaps he will even show up again. That would be the best of all.

When he did not return a reply that week, she put it down to business. By the end of the second week, she was trying not to think about it. By the end of the third week, she had a bigger problem than Lord Winn's apparent lack of interest in her declaration of love through the mail.

She noticed it first one morning when she woke with a

headache and the urge to throw up. "Lord, this is unkind," she moaned as she sat up in bed and eyed the washbasin, wondering if she could get to it in time. She made it only just, retching until she thought her liver and lights would appear in the basin, too. She crawled back into bed and threw the covers over her head.

She was feeling much better until Lissy ran into her room and bounced on the bed. The motion made her gorge rise again, except that there was nothing left to heave. "Oh, Lissy, not now!" she gasped, her hand over her mouth.

Lissy ended her with real surprise, then rested her head against her mother. Roxanna flinched at the pain in her breasts. I must be coming down with something, she thought as she carefully settled her little daughter against her.

"Mama, you promised to take us riding in the gig," Helen reminded her over breakfast. "Remember? Tibbie said there were new calves in the upper pasture."

"Well, then, let us get ready," Roxie declared as she pushed away her uneaten breakfast and forced down the rest of her tea. She stood by the table, nibbling on a piece of dried toast, and wondering what else she could do today to forget that Lord Winn was not interested anymore. She shrugged. Perhaps she would just take a nap that afternoon. She had been so sleepy lately, and it was a convenient way to pass time.

They found the calves in the upper pasture, and Tibbie there, too, admiring the herd. "This is more like, Lady Winn," he said. "It's always a pleasure to communicate good news to Lord Winn."

"Oh? And have you heard from him lately?" she asked, hoping her voice was casual.

"Aye, ma'am, think on," he replied. "Only yesterday I got a letter asking about spring planting."

"Where did he write you from?"

"Why . . . Winnfield, of course, ma'am. He's been back from Carlisle for these two weeks and more."

Tibbie eyed her speculatively, and she managed a smile in his direction. "I suppose we'll hear from him one of these days," she said. "Come, girls. You have lessons."

She was grateful that her daughters wanted to sit in the back of the gig, take off their stockings and shoes, and dangle their bare feet over the edge. That way they wouldn't see her tears and ask questions. She drove slowly, reminding herself that Lord Winn had been jittery about the married state, and adamant so many times about not wanting children. Certainly it followed that he really would not care to assume any other relationship with her except the one that now faced her. Whatever he had said that day in the unfinished bedroom had obviously been because his emotions were carried away temporarily. He had chosen not to respond to her letter, and she would have to live with that. I should have known, she thought. I should have been wiser. She dried her eyes on her sleeve. Perhaps Tibbie will find me some estate business to work on to keep me occupied. Does he need a barn built? a road constructed? I fear it will have to be a major project.

The bailiff was happy enough the next morning to send her to the village with an order for grain and a letter for Lord Winn's solicitor. Emma Winslow had brought them by the house after breakfast with the news that Tibbie was in bed with a cold.

"At least, that's what we think it is," she said as she handed Roxanna the letter. "Mind you, and wasn't my husband shaking with chills and fever when he came home yesterday?"

"I'm sorry," Roxanna said. She touched Emma's arm. "Well, you know, lots of soup with onions in it will mend him."

"Aye, ma'am, and a mustard plaster, think on."

She rode the Empress Josephine into the village and discharged Tibbie's business, riding slowly home, then dismounting and leading the mare because the motion was nauseating her again. Goodness, I hope this is not catching, she considered as she sat under a tree finally and let the reins drop. I wonder if it's what Tibbie has? The Empress cropped grass by the side of the road as Roxanna leaned back to watch.

I haven't felt this bad since I was expecting Felicity, she thought as nausea surged over her. Her eyes closed, and then she sucked in her breath and sat upright again. Surely not. She stared at the Empress, trying to remember when her last monthly had been. The end of February? The first part of March? Not that she had had any reason to keep records for the last few years. No need at all, Roxie, she thought, except that you and Lord Winn sported pretty heavily at the end of March. If you weren't such a nincompoop, you'd remember that so much fun does make babies.

"This is another unkind hand," she declared out loud, and then rested her forehead on her drawn-up knees. Mind you, Lord, I suppose someday I will appreciate the exquisite irony, she told God Almighty with some asperity, but not now. I have written a declaration of love to a man who doesn't want children, and who is content apparently to have a wife in Yorkshire to keep his relatives at bay so he can get on with his own life undisturbed. And now we've fetched a child. Lord, I am not laughing.

Her next thought was to write him immediately. She discarded that idiotic notion as fast as it came to her mind. How would it look, Roxie, to follow your letter of love with the casual announcement that in eight months he would be a father? He would think you had declared your love expeditiously, to blunt his wrath when the glad tidings become inevitable. He would think you dishonest. Better not to say anything.

She looked down at her belly in dismay. You can put this one off for only so long, Roxie. He'll have to know eventually, and then he will be furious. He will not believe that you really do love him to distraction.

I think I shall run away to Canada, she thought as she got up, held onto the tree until it stopped leaping around, then slowly mounted the Empress again. I shall move into the interior and become a shepherdess. We will change our names and join an Indian tribe.

She patted her belly. "Oh, well, little one," she said out loud, smiling briefly when the Empress pricked up her ears. "I am sure your father will be dreadfully upset with me." She rested her hand there. "It's not your fault, however, and I shall never blame you." And I will have something of your dear father forever, even if he did not choose to remain with us himself. It is better than nothing.

She was through crying by the time she returned to Moreland. The girls would have to know eventually, but it could wait several months at least. Thank goodness current fashions are kind to the expectant mother, she thought, and I never have been one to show early. Maybe I'll have thought of something by then, or at least started learning whatever language they speak in Canada. Perhaps Australia would be better.

Her disquieting thoughts kept her awake all night, and she braced herself for another session with the washbasin in the morning. She was still hanging over it, her face white and perspiring, when Mrs. Howell knocked on her door.

"Lady Winn, Emma Winslow is below. It seems that Tibbie is not well at all. Can you come downstairs?"

"Yes," she gasped, wiping the bile from her lips. "Give me a moment."

Give me three months, actually, she thought grimly as she dressed. I'll feel fine then, and ready to tackle dragons—maybe even Lord Winn. But I have ten minutes to look agreeable.

She shoved away her own discomfort when she opened the bookroom door on Emma Winslow, who leaped up from her chair, her eyes red.

"Lady Winn, Tibbie is terribly sick! I have summoned Dr. Clyde, and he tells me that influenza has broken out in Richmond!"

Roxanna took Mrs. Winslow by the hands, sat her down again, and calmly poured her a glass of sherry. "Surely it is too late in the season for influenza," she said, remembering other outbreaks. Anthony even had a funeral sermon just for the flu season, she remembered with a pang.

Mrs. Winslow sipped the sherry, then shook her head. "Those were my very words to Dr. Clyde, but he said it was entirely possible." She looked up at Roxanna. "Tibbie wondered if you could ride out to the west pasture this morning. They're dipping sheep today, and someone needs to supervise."

"Of course," Roxanna said. "Tell him not to worry about anything."

Mrs. Winslow retreated to her handkerchief again. "He's so concerned! It will be such a burden on you."

"I'll be fine, my dear," she replied, drawing strength from some reservoir she must have forgotten about. "I can check Tibbie's farm record from last year and see what needs to be done until he is well again. Tell him not to trouble himself."

Mrs. Winslow nodded, gave her a watery smile, and left. Roxanna sat back down in Lord Winn's swivel chair, holding very still against any sudden motion. She took a deep breath and reached for the farm records.

"Stay at Moreland, Lady Winn, and keep your circle of visitors small," Dr. Clyde told her three weeks later, stopping in on his way back to Richmond. His eyes were red-rimmed from lack of sleep, and he looked as though he slept in his clothes. "I only wanted to stop by here to tell you that. This is a wicked flu. Is everyone still well?"

"Everyone except Tibbie," she replied. He had found her in the stables after a long day in the fields, trying to get the energy to remove the Empress's saddle. "Oh, thank you, sir. I seem to be too tired to lift a saddle these days."

He peered at her closely, and put the back of his hand to her forehead. "You don't feel warm. Can you identify any other symptoms, Lady Winn?"

Oh, can I ever, she thought as she shook her head. "No, Dr.

Clyde. I am just tired." She managed what she thought was a rather fine smile. "Surely it will be better when Tibbie is about on the estate again."

He set down the saddle and removed the Empress's bridle, turning her into the loose box. "That'll be some time yet. You've written Lord Winn, of course," he said. "He needs to get you another bailiff."

"No, actually, I have not written him. He's a busy man, Dr. Clyde. We'll manage."

He walked with her to the back door, but shook his head when she invited him in to dinner. "I'm needed back in Richmond," he explained as he mounted his horse again. "And my wife said something about a bed, and clean clothes in a house I vaguely remember as my own. I think I even have children."

"Oh, dear," she said and held out her hand to him. "Take care, Dr. Clyde. There's nothing wrong with any of us here that won't keep."

She could not keep her eyes open over dinner, even through Lissy's lively chatter about Meggie's drawing lesson that morning, and Helen's description of their afternoon's expedition to the stream to find watercress. Silently she blessed Meggie Watson for her cheerful taking over of the girls so she could spend her days in the saddle seeing Moreland through the busy season of sowing, shearing, and calving.

Mrs. Howell approached her after dinner, when Helen had taken Lissy into the sitting room to practice a duet. "Lady Winn, I know how busy you are." She prefaced her remarks. "It's my sister, Mrs. Hamilton. You remember how she helped out at Christmas?"

Roxanna nodded, knowing what was coming next. "Is she ill?" she asked quietly.

The housekeeper nodded, tears in her eyes.

"Then you must go to her at once," Roxanna murmured, her arm around Mrs. Howell. "We will manage. I know I can ask Meggie to come back over here and help in the kitchen. Isn't there a scullery maid left?"

"Aye, ma'am, Sally," Mrs. Howell replied. "She can cook, too, even though she's young."

"Excellent! And you know, I imagine Helen could help, too," she said as they walked along together. Calm, calm, Roxie, she told herself. We can eat simply, and the dust can wait. "I think you should leave as soon as possible. Can the groom take you in the gig tomorrow morning?"

Mrs. Howell was gone after breakfast, waving her handkerchief from the front drive, and then sobbing into it. Roxie stood there a long while, wishing she had time to admire the handsome, full-leafed lane and the orchard close by, the apples large enough to be visible. She rested her hand lightly on her belly. She could feel the bulge now, as slight as it was. You must be a stubborn little one, she thought as she watched the gig retreat down the lane. Considering your father, why am I surprised at that? Here I have been riding and riding for weeks now, and I even fell off the Empress once. You must be well seated in there. Thank God for that.

She walked slowly to the dower house, wanting a word of comfort from Meggie. I really should tell her about the baby, she thought as she tapped on the door. She's so good with children. And with me. I'd like to put my head in Meggie's lap and make everything go away for a while.

There was no answer. She knocked again, louder this time. She stepped back finally and looked at the open windows in the upstairs bedrooms. "Meggie?" she called, cupping her hands around her mouth. "Meggie?"

In a moment she was wrenching open the front door and running up the stairs, her heart in her throat. She pounded on Meggie's door, then burst into the room, her eyes wide at the sight before her.

Meggie Watson looked up at her from the floor where she had fallen. She was shaking all over, and trying to speak. Roxanna threw herself down beside the nursemaid. She touched her forehead, drawing her hand away quickly, alarmed at the warmth there. Meggie could only shiver, and stare at her.

"Oh, my dear, not you, too?" she said as she helped the woman into her bed. "Don't try to speak. Just rest. I'll—I'll think of something."

Meggie died three days later, attended at the end by Helen because Roxie was supervising the first cutting of hay in the upper meadow. She used to enjoy watching the rhythm of the workers in the hayfield as they cut and stacked the hay. But now, influenza had ripped such a swath through the North Riding that she had to help pitch the hay into wains because there were too few men to work the fields. When she rode back that evening, her arms and back on fire from her exertions, she saw Dr. Clyde leaving the dower house.

"I'm sorry, Lady Winn," he said. "The flu is hardest on the young and the old."

"Oh, no," she whispered, too tired to work up more emotion. "Please tell me Meggie will be better."

"My dear, didn't you hear me? She is dead," he said. "Helen rode to tell me."

Her mind numb, she dragged herself into the dower house, where Helen and Lissy sat on the sofa, their arms around each other, both too stricken for tears. Wordlessly, she sank down at their feet and gathered them in her arms. Lissy said nothing, but burrowed in close to her, holding tight as though afraid she would disappear, too. Roxanna clung to her daughter, then touched Helen. "My dear, I am so sorry I was not here," she murmured.

Helen regarded her with those searching eyes so like Anthony's. "Mama, I think you should write to Lord Winn," she urged. "We need some help."

Roxanna shook her head. "Helen, we have been such a trouble to him for so long."

"Mama, don't you like him anymore?" Helen asked. "We have not sent letters or pictures in such a long time."

Oh, I love him, she thought. Nothing would make me happier at this minute than to crawl into his lap like Lissy here and turn all my miseries over to him. But I dare not. I am too much trouble, and he has already done more than any man could be expected to do, considering the nature of our agreement.

"I just want to carry on without bothering him," she said. It sounded lame, but it was the best she could do without tears.

There was no funeral for Meggie Watson. The epidemic had reached such a stage that the doctors forbade mourners to gather in large groups, for fear of passing on the contagion. It tore out her heart to watch Meggie's simple coffin bundled into a farm wagon and destined for the burying ground without anyone there to lament her passing. She stood with her daughters on the front steps as the wagon rolled away, acutely aware of Meggie's devotion, and wondering what to do now, with Mrs. Howell gone, and Tibbie still too ill to do more than sit up in bed and look distressed when they visited him.

She lay awake a long time that night, too tired to sleep, going over and over in her mind all the activities of the days and weeks that seemed never to end. What if I have left something out? she thought. She hoped it would rain, so she could find an excuse to stay inside, and not risk falling off the Empress again. How nice it would be to sit still, and really, how much safer. She knew she should not be in the saddle.

Thank God you are still so small, she thought as her hands rested on her belly. Perhaps she could write Lord Winn after all, and plead for help. She could assure him that he needn't come himself, but at least loan her a bailiff from another estate untroubled with illness. She reflected a moment and sighed. Since he had not been interested enough to answer that letter she sent to Northumberland, he probably would not come. And even if he did, he would never notice. Men really weren't so observant.

"Roxanna, you are a great looby," she said as she patted down her pillow and tried to find a cool spot. "How long can you keep this baby a secret?" She couldn't bring herself to voice her greatest fear, the one that dogged her all day and left her sleepless at night. When he found out, suppose Lord Winn was so angry that he divorced her? She knew he could do it. And then will I be at the mercy of my brother-in-law again?

The thought so unnerved her that she got out of bed and went to the window. She opened it and breathed deep of the fragrance from the park. Somewhere she could smell orange blossoms, and it calmed her. She stared at the moon, so full and benevolent, wondering how the night could look so serene when people were dying of influenza and her own life was a turmoil. Soon high summer would come. The flu could not hang on forever, and perhaps she would find the courage to tell Lord Winn, before he discovered it himself, or heard from others.

She climbed back in bed, trying to compose her jitters. Her eyes were finally closing when the door opened. Fletch, is that you? she thought, caught halfway between awake and dreaming. I wish I looked better.

Helen ran to the bed, her eyes wide with fear. Roxanna sat up and grabbed her daughter. "My dear, what is it?" she asked, holding her close.

"Mama! Lissy is so hot! And she is coughing like Meggie did." Helen started to cry, a helpless sound that made Roxanna suck in her breath. "Mama, I don't know what to do! Look what happened to Meggie!"

Roxanna closed her eyes in agony, seeing in her mind Helen standing helpless as Meggie died before her. She gathered her child close as she sobbed, even as she got out of bed, her heart and mind on Lissy. "Helen, you did everything you could. No one could have done more. Let us go see to Lissy now."

She compelled herself to walk slowly, her arm resting on Helen's shoulder, when she wanted to run into the other bedroom, grab Lissy, and run with her to the doctor's house. I will not panic, she told herself. She sat down on the bed, willing her hand to stop shaking, and touched Lissy's forehead.

It was so hot that Roxanna shuddered. Lissy's skin was oddly clammy, and as she sat staring down at her sweat-soaked hair, the child shivered and opened her eyes. She reached for Roxanna. "Mama, make me better," she whispered.

Roxanna grasped Lissy's hands, fearful of their feverish heat. God give me strength, she thought as she stared down at her daughter.

"Mama?" Helen asked, her voice filled with terror.

Enough of this, Roxanna, she told herself. "Don't worry, Helen," she said calmly. "I am sure that Lissy will be fine. Hand me that pitcher of water and a facecloth. Very good, my dear."

She wrung out a cool cloth for Lissy's face and then took her by the hand, kissing her fingers one by one. "Now you must try to sleep, my love," she told Lissy. "I'll be here with you. Helen, go to my bed. You need to sleep so you can help me tomorrow."

She held Lissy all night, crooning to her as she sobbed with the fever. In the morning she left Lissy in the care of the scullery maid and Helen, and hauled herself into the saddle for a half-day in the field, after sending the groom for Dr. Clyde.

She watched the farm laborers, some of them newly recovered from the flu, and then she did not care anymore. She turned the Empress toward Moreland, hoping that Tibbie would be well enough to take her place in the field. And if he was not, well, then, it didn't matter, not the harvest, or the animals. Nothing mattered but Lissy.

Dr. Clyde could promise nothing, and do little but offer fever powders of dubious value, and advice that might or might not bring about a change in Lissy's condition. He could only visit every other day, peek into the sickroom, and say "h'mmm" in that way of all doctors, and shake his head. As much as she clung to his visits as a sign of hope, she began to dread the familiar sound of his footsteps on the stairs.

"You're doing everything I would do," he assured her one afternoon as June began to turn into July with no change in Lissy's condition. He picked up Lissy's hand, frowning at her limpness. "Where's our old Lissy?" he asked, more to himself than to Roxanna. "This damnable flu just doesn't let go." He tried to smile, but it was a failed attempt. "And it preys on anxious mothers, too. Lady Winn, can you remember when you last slept?"

Roxanna stared at him stupidly, then shook her head. No, I cannot, she thought, or even when I last ate something. She could only look at him, as though he had the power to change the situation, and then look away, aghast at the helplessness in his eyes.

"Roxanna, you need some help here," he said. "I wish I could think of anyone who could help you that isn't already tending the sick."

"I just wish it would let go of her," Roxanna said as she squeezed out another cloth to wipe Lissy's body, feeling as wrung and pummeled as the rag she held. "She is so thin now."

Dr. Clyde could only nod. "Does she ever speak to you?" he asked, his voice low.

Roxanna nodded. "Sometimes. It doesn't always make sense." She glanced sideways at the doctor, and noticed how his own eyes were closing. Poor man, she thought. For two months and more now you have watched your patients sicken and die. She touched his hand, drawing back quickly when he gasped and leaped to his feet, startled out of his somnolence.

"Go home, Dr. Clyde," she said softly. "We'll manage here."

Manage what? she asked herself as he rode away, chin tipped down against his chest, swaying as though he already slept. She watched him from the upstairs window, wanting to call him back. What for? she thought. My child is dying and I can only wring out cool cloths and pretend that I am doing something to help her.

"Winn."

She turned back to Lissy, whose eyes were still closed. "What?" she asked, coming closer.

Lissy opened her eyes suddenly, and looked around as though she expected to see someone. "Winn," she repeated, then closed her eyes again to begin her cycle of coughing and then struggling to breathe. Roxanna held up her daughter so she could get an easier breath, breathing along with her until she felt light-headed and even more useless than before.

While Lissy dozed fitfully, Roxanna tiptoed from the room. She peeked in on Helen, but she was sleeping, too, exhausted from watching. Roxanna went downstairs, standing in front of the bookroom door for a long moment, as if wondering why she was there. Finally, she squared her shoulders and went inside. I have put this off too long, she thought as she reached for a sheet of paper and the inkwell. *Lissy wants him, too. I hope we will not be too much trouble, but I cannot face this alone.*

Chapter 18

"In the thirty-eight—nearly thirty-nine—years that I have known you, brother, I disremember your ever asking my advice on any subject. Let me savor the moment."

Lord Winn looked up from the contemplation of his mother's favorite silverware pattern and into his sister's eyes.

"You're right, of course, Clarrie," he replied. "But damn it, why hasn't she written me?" He broke off a corner of the cinnamon bun on his plate and regarded it moodily before flicking it out the open window. "French cooks have no clue when it comes to cinnamon buns. Even Lissy would sniff at these. Why doesn't that stubborn woman write?"

Clarice patted her lips with her napkin and continued her perusal of him. "My dear brother, only think how fast this dear little creature has gone from widow to wife, and under what circumstances. She needs time."

"I know, I know," he said impatiently, leaning back in his chair. "But when I was there in March . . ." He paused. *This isn't something to confess to a sister,* he thought, then hurried on with the narration before he lost his nerve. "Well, she was awfully glad to see me." He smiled at the memory. "Awfully glad, Clarrie." He ran his fingers around the inside of his collar.

His sister reacted as he thought she would by increasing the candlepower of her stare. "Winn, you told me you were there not more than thirty minutes!" she declared.

"It's true," he confessed, feeling the blush travel upward from his navel to his hair follicles.

"And that part of the time you were visiting with Helen and Lissy?" she continued inexorably. "Winn! Really!"

Trust a big sister to make a grown man feel like a boy, and not a bright boy, either, he thought sourly. "Yes, really!" he retorted, out of sorts with Clarice and wondering why he had invited her to Winnfield. "We didn't waste a minute. Clarrie, must you smirk?"

Clarice laughed, and he directed his attention to the silver pattern again, disgusted with himself.

"I had no idea you were such a ladies' man," she murmured, a smile in her eyes.

"No, no!" he protested. "Not *any* lady's man, Clarrie. Just that lady's man. I don't know what it is about Roxie Rand." Well, yes I do know, he thought, but I'll be damned if I need to catalog a sexual primer for my older sister. I've never been so excited by a woman as I am by my own wife. "And you don't need to grin about it, Clarrie," he admonished.

She promptly wiped the smile off her face, but couldn't disguise it so easily in her eyes. "Brother, I am just remembering some comments from you earlier this year. Something about 'never wanting to be trapped in a matrimonial snare again.' Correct me if I am wrong," she concluded.

He could only sigh in exasperation. "Clarrie, cut line, won't you?" he declared. He took a turn about the breakfast room, pausing at the sideboard for a piece of bacon, and waving it at her. "I asked her to let me know how she felt about our relationship. I have heard nothing from that time to this!" He ate the bacon, wishing Clarice would not give him that feather-brained look. "Oh, what?" he snapped in irritation.

To his surprise, she went to him and kissed his cheek. "Winn, you're really dead in love, aren't you?"

He nodded, miserable. "I thought I loved Cynthia, but what I felt was only a pale cousin to this. And what's worse, I miss Lissy and Helen, too. This isn't fair!"

Suddenly the room seemed too small to hold him. He wanted to stride out of doors and walk for several miles until he felt more in control of himself. Roxie, I will have to go on my own forced marches if you do not come to the rescue, he thought grimly.

"I seem to remember also that you were pretty adamant about not wanting any children of your own, too," Clarice reminded him. "Did you ever mention that to Roxie?"

He thought a moment, chagrined. "Too many times, I fear," he confessed. "I really should go to Moreland, throw myself at her feet, and tell her I have been an idiot."

Clarice nodded, to his increased irritation. "You were pretty stupid, Winn," she agreed, her eyes merry. "Now don't poker up! Let me have the fun of scolding you, and then tell you that I will do whatever I can to further this relationship. Only ask, Winn."

He nodded then, grateful she was his sister. "Thanks, my dear," he said, flinging himself into his chair again. "I suppose I can go see her this fall, whether I hear from her or not."

"Why wait that long?"

He nodded. "Why, indeed? I'm too old to play games, Clarrie. I just wish this were her idea, too, and not mine alone."

Clarice was about to reply when the door opened. "My lord, the mail is here. Shall you read it now, or do you wish it in the bookroom?"

He waved his hand at the butler. "The bookroom, Spurgeon. No. Wait. Bring it here."

The butler set down the correspondence and left the room. Winn glanced at the pile, then looked away. "Bugger it," he muttered.

But Clarice was going through his letters. "Really, Winn, your language," she murmured as she sorted the mail. She let out a triumphant laugh and dangled a letter in front of his face. "Winn, does this handwriting look familiar?"

He pounced on the letter, ripping it open, filled with joy he had not felt since March. "She wrote, Clarrie, she wrote!" he declared in triumph as his eyes scanned the page.

As he read, his eyes eager, his heart pounding, the horror dawned on him slowly. He read the letter again, certain that he had missed a joke somewhere, a phrase that would turn the nightmare on the closely written page into a huge jest. After his third perusal, he stared at Clarice, who was regarding him with an expression that went from delight to fear as she watched his own face.

"Winn, what is it?" she demanded, when he could say nothing.

Wordless, he pushed the letter toward her, and leaped to his feet. He jerked the door open and leaned into the hall. "Spurgeon!" he shouted. "I need you immediately!"

He glanced back at Clarrie, who was on her feet now, her mouth open. "Clarrie, I had no idea," he said, feeling the tears start in his eyes. "Tibbie has been ill for months, Meggie Watson is dead, and Lissy . . . Oh, Clarrie!"

"Maybe it is not that serious," Clarice said, hurrying around the table to clutch his arm.

He took the letter from her. "Roxie would never tease about this. Those children are her life. And here I am at Winnfield. Damn you, Spurgeon! Where are you?"

It took him only a few minutes to pound upstairs and change into riding pants and his old campaigning boots, talking to Clarice as fast as he thought of things. "Can you follow me soon? I'll leave it to you to contact my bailiff and find someone to come along who can take over, at least temporarily. Can you bring along some servants, too? Damn it, where are my saddlebags?"

He stopped in the middle of the room, ready to scream. In a second Clarice was holding him close. His arms went around her and he sobbed into her hair. He could hear her murmuring something, but all he could see was Roxie's face, and then the letter, scarcely legible, written by someone exhausted and incoherent with worry. He cried at his own stupidity, havering around Winnfield like a mooncalf, full of self-pity and ill humor, when his wife needed him so badly.

I have left out so much, he thought as he snatched up the reins and threw himself into the saddle. He looked back at Clarice, a better sister than he ever realized before, who had run after him to the stables.

"Don't worry about anything," she was telling him as Ney danced about, impatient as he was to be off. "I'll write a little note to Fred, and organize things here. Chickering can pack your clothes, and I have a good idea what Roxie will be needing."

Roxie needs me, he thought as he blew a kiss to his sister and galloped from the stable yard, taking the fence cleanly. She needs me.

It became the refrain that kept him in the saddle mile after mile. He stopped at noon for a meal, then was too impatient to eat it, thinking of Lissy near death and Roxie watching at her bedside. He tossed a coin at the tavern keep as he snatched up some bread and beef and forked his leg over Ney again.

Snatches of her letter came back at him as he rode into the afternoon of a beautiful summer day. "If you can spare the time," and "Truly I do not wish to trouble you," harrowed him as Ney pounded along the Great North Road. All she can see is what a great lot of trouble she has been, he thought. She cannot fathom how much I love her and her daughters. I would do anything for you, my love, he thought. Pray God I do not have to bury your daughter for you. I do not know that even together we could bear that. I know I could never face it alone.

He reached the North Riding as the sun was low in the sky. His mind was on Roxie, but as Ney trotted along, Lord Winn wondered where the field laborers were. There should have been many of them on the roads at this hour, returning to their homes, but there were so few. This influenza has taken its toll, he reflected. He had seen the flu in Spain, and soldiers too exhausted to level a musket or drag themselves into the saddle. A man could be pronounced well by the impatient surgeons, but still die if he could not rest sufficiently.

He was weary of the saddle himself as Ney climbed steadily into the foothills of the Pennines. Just another mile, he thought. And then there was Moreland, the elms offering slanting shade to the estate's approach as the sun finally set. It was a different sight from the bare branches of March, more welcoming. He spurred Ney for a final effort. Where *was* everyone?

The groom was nowhere in sight as he ducked his head and rode Ney into the stable. Damn the man, he thought as he dismounted and hurried to remove his horse's saddle. Five Pence and the mare he had left for Roxie looked at him with interest. He glanced in their mangers, and cursed to see them empty of grain. The water troughs were dry, too. I will fire that man on the spot, he swore as he grained and watered all three horses. He will never work in this shire again.

The groom rode into the stable as he was preparing to leave for the house. Hot words were on Lord Winn's lips, but he watched from the gathering shadows as the man dragged himself from the saddle and leaned against his horse, scarcely able to stand. He stayed that way a long time, and then Lord Winn cleared his throat.

The groom glanced around as though his neck pained him, then sighed with relief. "Thank God you've come, my lord," he said, not letting go of his horse's mane.

Winn came out of the shadows, observing at close range the perspiration on the man's face, and the paleness of his skin. He took him by the arm. "Are you ill, too?" he asked, his angry words forgotten.

The groom nodded, shivered, and allowed Lord Winn to lead him to a perch on the grain bin. "We've all had it, my lord. Tibbie can just barely manage in the mornings, and I oversee in the afternoons." He protested when Lord Winn took the saddle from his horse, then could only stare dumbly, as though trying to gather strength for a trip up the stairs to his quarters.

"How long have you been doing this?" Winn asked as he stabled the groom's horse.

"Not long. Two weeks? Before that, Lady Winn was in the saddle all day, even after Felicity took sick. I don't know when she slept." He paused, too tired to say more.

Winn helped the groom to his quarters, promising to send

someone with food later. The man only shook his head and closed his eyes.

His mind deep with disquiet, Lord Winn ran into the house. It was dark, as though no one lived there. "Roxie?" he called, his voice tentative.

There was no answer. He hurried to the stairs, and could make out a little light on the first landing. He took the stairs two at a time, dreading what awaited him. A single candle flickered in a sconce at the top of the stairs, casting weird shadows on the slowly moving lace curtains. He hurried down the hall, calling Roxie's name.

And then Helen was standing in the hallway by the only room with a light in it.

"Helen," was all he said. With a sob she ran down the hall, her arms out, to fall into his welcoming embrace. He knelt and hugged her close, breathing in the dearness of her, grateful down to the depths of his soul that she was on her feet and appeared healthy.

Finally she pulled away from him a little and ran her hand over his face, as though she could not believe he was real. "You came," she said simply, and his heart turned over.

She took his hand then and led him to the room with the open door. "Mama," she said from the doorway. "Mama."

Roxanna was sitting in a chair by the bed, her head bowed forward as if in sleep. She jerked awake at Helen's quiet words and looked around wildly as he came forward and gripped her by the shoulders. She closed her eyes again, as though in prayer, then rested her cheek against his hand. "Thank you for coming," she whispered. "I am so tired."

He knelt beside her and took her hand. "Roxie, I left the moment I received your letter."

She opened her eyes, but her vision rested on the quiet form in the bed. "I didn't mean to trouble you . . ." she began, then shook her head and was silent.

"Who ever said you were trouble?" he whispered as he looked at Felicity, lying so unnaturally still.

She squeezed his hand and started to reply, but Lissy moved then, and she dropped his hand and reached for her daughter, touching her forehead. As he watched, she dipped a cloth in water, wrung it out, and carefully ran it over Lissy's bare little body, so still again under the sheet.

"She is so thin," he whispered. He touched her arm, wincing to see her ribs so prominent. "And so warm."

Roxanna finished her work, standing a moment over her daughter, breathing along with her, then sank into the chair again. "She does not eat much," she explained, her voice toneless. "Dr. Clyde says that the fever will go away eventually, but I do not know that Lissy can last long enough to find out."

She was silent again. He glanced at her to see silent tears coursing down her cheeks. Such hopeless tears, he thought. He touched her face, wondering if she had cried this way for Anthony. Of course you did, my darling, he thought as he took out his handkerchief. Is this never going to end for you?

The dimness of the room bothered him. "Can I light some candles?" he asked.

Roxanna shook her head. "The light bothers Lissy's eyes. Oh, Fletch, how kind of you to come," she said, as though just realizing that he was in the room.

"When did you last sleep, Roxie?" he asked as he pocketed his handkerchief.

"I can't remember exactly."

"When did you last eat?"

She shrugged and looked away, as though it was of little importance to her. "I think it was yesterday. Yes, I'm sure it was . . ." Her voice trailed off as she stared at her daughter. "I should eat, though. You see, Winn . . ." she began, and then stopped.

"What?" he asked.

"Nothing that can't keep." She directed her attention to her daughter again.

He rested his hand against Roxie's cheek a moment, then left the room, taking Helen with him. "Come, my dear, let's light some lamps downstairs. Can you cook?"

She smiled at him. "I've been learning. Sally is in the kitchen now, fixing some soup for us."

Below stairs, he shook hands with the scullery maid he only dimly remembered from Christmas, overriding her shyness by sticking his finger in the pot of soup, rolling his eyes, and pronouncing it excellent. It is tasty, he thought as he took up a spoon for a further dip from the pot. In a few years upon retirement, Mrs. Howell may have a worthy successor. He turned to Helen.

"Now, my dear, if you will set the table in the breakfast room, and Sally, if you will brew a pot of coffee as fine as that soup, I'll try to coax Lady Winn downstairs for a bite. Helen, can you watch Lissy while your mother eats?"

Helen nodded and glanced at Sally, who smiled back. "We've

both been doing that, sir. Sometimes Mama kicks up a fuss when we make her leave, but we insist at least once a day."

Lord Winn put his hands on the girls' shoulders. "I could have used you two at Waterloo," he said, his heart lifting as the light seemed to come back into their faces. "Come on, now, step to it. I'll get your mother downstairs."

While Helen set the table, humming softly to herself, he lit lamps in the breakfast room, entrance hall, and sitting room. He paused in the sitting room to blow dust off the piano lid and raise it. He played a tentative chord, pleased that the piano was still in tune. He looked at the music on the stand, seeing the little melody he had written earlier that spring for Helen. He played it, standing by the piano.

"I know that one by heart, Winn," Helen said from the doorway. "And I have been working on the Scarlatti, like you said."

He turned around to smile at her, pleased to note that she had brushed her hair and pulled it back into a bow. "Come, my dear. Let's go upstairs again and talk your mother into dinner. Do you think I will have any luck getting her to go to bed afterwards?"

"Not at all," Helen said. "She just sits in that chair and dozes."

"Not tonight she won't," he said firmly as he took her hand and walked down the hall. "I mean to do that in her place."

"She's stubborn," Helen said, her voice uncertain.

"So am I, dear. So am I."

He was prepared for real resistance, but Roxie offered little. He put it down to her general exhaustion. She nodded at his suggestion for dinner, and he had the good sense to agree with her rider that she return promptly to Lissy's room. "Of course, Roxie, anything you say. Isn't that what I promised the blacksmith?" he replied as he winked at Helen, who grinned back and seated herself in Roxie's chair.

Roxie, you've been losing weight, too, he thought as he took her by the hand and led her downstairs. The lights made her blink at first, but she gradually relaxed and allowed him to seat her at the table.

He looked at the table in pleasure. Helen had put out good china and crystal, and the place mats and napkins gleamed so white against the dark wood. It was a room of pleasant memories, too, of Felicity peeking around at him, waiting for cinnamon buns. And now . . . The pain of seeing Lissy lying so still upstairs washed over him again and he hung onto the back of the chair where he had seated Roxanna. The moment passed and he seated himself, nodding to Sally to serve the soup.

"You should have written me sooner," he said mildly as he sat and watched his wife eat, wondering at her ravaged beauty and its power over him. You are much too thin, but I am captured all over again, he thought. Beyond the misery of the moment, there was something different about her that he could not quite put his finger on. When she made no reply, he gave his attention to the soup, and then bullied Roxie into a second bowl, and a glass of sherry, too.

He poured himself another cup of coffee, preparing for an assault on Roxie's plans to return to Lissy's room. "Now then, my dear . . ." he began, and then stopped, looking at her. He grinned, raised the cup in a toast, and finished his coffee. So much for my strategy.

Roxie was asleep, her head nodding over the table, her hand still wrapped around the stem of the sherry glass. "You poor dear," he whispered as he got up quietly and eased the glass from her hand. He picked her up and carried her upstairs, marveling again how light she was. She smelled faintly of lavender, and his heart was full.

He thought she might wake when he laid her on her bed, but she only sighed and rested her hand on her stomach, relaxing completely as though she knew she could surrender to sleep, now that he was there. He lighted a branch of candles and the lamp beside the bed, looking around in appreciation at the new wallpaper and draperies. I could easily prefer this place to that slab of stone I live in, he told himself. I certainly prefer the company.

He removed her shoes, and considered leaving it at that, then changed his mind. Better to take the pins from her hair and divest her of her dress, he reasoned. He sat on the edge of the bed, taking the pins from her hair, spreading it out to flow over the pillow. Roxie slumbered on, captured by sleep. I could whistle "Lilliburlero" and accompany myself on the drums and you would not wake up, he thought, smiling to himself.

She parted company from her dress without a whimper. He pulled her arms from the sleeves, remembering how boneless she was that first morning in his bed, satiated with love. And now you are exhausted by Lissy's illness, he thought, fingering her wedding ring.

She looked more comfortable without her dress, but he continued, untying the cord that held up her petticoat. It was while he was sliding Roxie out of her petticoat that he noticed his wife had a little company.

"What's this, Roxie?" he asked out loud as he ran his hand

lightly over the slight bulge below her middle. "Oh, Roxie, no wonder you didn't want to write," he said as he rested his hand on her belly.

He sat back a moment, moved beyond words, then touched her again, delighting in the experience. So we made a baby in March, he thought, and I can cup my hands around three and a half months of our child. As he sat there, he felt the tiniest flutter under his fingers, like someone tapping lightly. "Oh, God," he breathed, and it was a prayer of gratitude.

The strength of the woman lying on the bed humbled him. How could you do it? he thought. How could you take on Tibbie's work, and watch Lissy, and suffer Meggie's death? And all this time you were probably in the throes of morning sickness, if I can remember anything my sisters complained about. I think our child is determined to be born.

Sitting there with his hand resting on his baby, he considered the matter. "In all this long agony, why didn't you say anything, my love?" he asked her sleeping body. He had his answer almost before the words were out of his mouth, and he could only wonder at his stupidity. How many times have I insisted to you that I did not want children? he berated himself. You must be terrified that I will find out and be furious.

"It can keep then," he said as he gently replaced her petticoat. "We can wait until Lissy is out of the woods. I can't wait to hear how you're going to bring up this subject, my dear wife!"

He laughed softly as he covered her with a sheet, kissed her cheek, and strolled out of the room on air. He was still smiling when he relieved Helen in the sickroom. "Go to bed, my dear," he whispered. "I'll watch tonight."

She stood up and allowed him to sit in her place, then sat down in his lap, leaning against him. "I missed you," she said softly. "We all did."

"Even your mother?" he asked, his eyes lively. He kissed the top of her head and settled Helen comfortably on his lap. He prepared for a long night of thinking and watching, his mind on the child lying so still in the bed, but his heart on the woman in the other room and her careful secret.

Chapter 19

Fortified with a pot of Sally's coffee and a Fielding novel, he kept awake all night. Around midnight, Helen staggered off to bed with a wave of her hand, and he returned his attention to the child before him.

Lissy slept in odd little spurts, muttering to herself, turning from side to side to find a cool place, and then sitting upright once to stare at him, speak nonsense, then lie back down. He made her drink the heavily sugared water on the nightstand, and sponged her down several times. Her skin was tight and dry, and warm enough to worry him. Just watching her was a draining process, he decided. No wonder Roxie looked like the walking dead.

His wholehearted admiration for his wife grew as the night dragged on. How on earth had Roxanna managed to tend Lissy and the estate, too? Whoever thinks women are weaker vessels never knew Roxie Rand, he thought. He counted the months on his fingers, and concluded that their son or daughter would be born around Christmas. Such a lovely gift.

As much as he loved Moreland now, he wanted his first child to be born in the family seat at Winnfield. We can spend our summers here, he told himself as he sat Lissy up to take her fever powders.

"Good girl," he said out loud, when she swallowed the bitter liquid without complaint. To his gratification, she opened her eyes at the sound of his voice and turned her head to stare at him. Her lovely eyes looked so wide now in her thin face that she seemed almost a caricature.

"Winn."

That was all she could manage, and it was such an effort that tears started in his eyes. As he laid her back down on the bed she tried to reach for his hand. He took her lightly by the fingers. "Hang on a little longer, my dear," he pleaded.

She slept then, and he dozed, too, waking before dawn to hear a carriage on the front drive. He stood up and stretched, his neck on fire from his awkward position in the chair. He pulled back the draperies to see, and could just make out the Manwaring carriage.

After a glance at Lissy, he tiptoed from the room and hurried down the stairs. He grabbed his sister and gave her a kiss as she came up the front steps.

"Honestly, Winn," she protested, a smile on her face. "We only parted company yesterday!"

"That's how glad I am to see you," he replied. He looked beyond her to the others leaving the carriage. "And you brought an army. Thank God for that. Clarrie, when was the last time I told you I loved you?"

Clarice grimaced. "It escapes my memory, brother." She introduced him to a tall young man who came next from the carriage. "Here is David Start, your new bailiff," she said as they shook hands. "Annie here will go to the kitchen or wherever she's needed, and Mrs. Mitchum is your housekeeper until the redoubtable Mrs. Howell returns." She handed a heavy basket to the bailiff. "Here we have lemons and jellies and potions galore. Lissy will not dare to remain sick."

He put his arm around her and led her into the house. "Such a lovely old place," Clarice murmured. "Is Roxie asleep?"

"Yes, and thank goodness for that," he said, helping her with her cloak. "Oh, Clarrie, she was burned right down to the socket."

"I can imagine."

He shook his head, amusement welling up in spite of the situation. "No, you really can't, my dear."

He only grinned at her quizzical expression, and then waited while she dispersed her help to various locations. She took the basket from the bailiff, and told him to wait there while she settled herself upstairs with Felicity. "And then the sun will be up, and Lord Winn will show you to Tibbie's house."

"Clarrie, you are a real general," Winn commented as they climbed the stairs. His sister only snorted and dug him in the ribs.

All joking ended as she stood silently over Lissy, shaking her head. "Flu is such a vile illness," she whispered, "never letting go until it is too late." She touched Lissy's arm and leaned over her. "Well, my dear, we shall see what can be done yet. Since you're a child of Roxie's, there's fight in you yet."

She removed her bonnet and allowed him to lead her to the next door. He opened it quietly. "Roxie's still asleep," he whispered, looking in on his wife, who lay in the same position he had left her in. "I wish she would stay in bed herself, but I am sure she will be up soon."

Clarice nodded. "Roxie would never stay in bed, but between the two of us, when she sees that we can manage, she might allow herself to rest."

He closed the door and leaned against it. "She really needs to rest, Clarrie. Roxie is expecting a baby." He grinned. "That March visit may have been brief, but it was potent, apparently."

She gasped and hugged him. "Winn! This is wonderful!"

He nodded, pleased to share the news with his sister. He put a finger to her lips. "I only discovered it last night when I removed her dress. Don't say a word. She has no idea that I know, and really, she doesn't show much."

Clarice took his arm as they walked back to Lissy's room. "I suspect she is afraid to tell you. I can't blame her."

"Nor can I, my dear," he agreed. "I shall have to dance very fast to repair my wounded credit. And Clarrie, I *am* delighted. In fact, I can't imagine why I had such a crack-brained notion about not wanting a child of my own."

Clarice touched his face and stood on tiptoe to kiss his cheek. "Brother, it was probably a combination of too much war at home *and* abroad." She went into Lissy's room. "Now go downstairs and show David Start what he is to do. Then go to bed yourself. I think yours will be the night shift."

"Oui, mon capitan," he said.

"Winn, you're a nuisance," she said affectionately as she bent over Lissy.

"Before I sleep, I think I will compose a little note to Lord Whitcomb," he said, his hand on the doorknob.

"Whatever for?"

"Call it pride. If we are to remain here, off and on, in the North Riding, it's time to mend that particular fence."

Clarice looked dubious. "Since when did you become a diplomat?"

He grinned and closed the door softly behind him.

When Roxanna opened her eyes, her room was bright with sunshine and there was a vase of roses on her nightstand. I must be dreaming, she thought. She sniffed the roses, grateful that her morning sickness had receded enough to permit pleasure again at sharp fragrances. She settled more comfortably on her side, her hand going almost automatically to her belly. The baby was moving now; she was sure of it.

She sat up then and threw back the covers. "Lissy!" she exclaimed.

"Lissy is being quite carefully watched, my dear," said an unfamiliar voice from the window seat.

Roxanna looked around quickly, and then smiled. "Oh, Lady Manwaring," she said, relieved to recognize her visitor.

"Clarice to you, Roxanna," said the woman as she set down her knitting. "Your husband is quite the bully. There I was, minding my own business on a visit to Winnfield, when your letter arrived. He drafted my services, plus those of a bailiff, housekeeper, and servant from his estate. Annie is watching Lissy."

"Thank God," Roxanna said as she lay down again. She wiggled out of her petticoat, which had twisted up around her waist. "Thank you for getting that dress off me last night."

"Oh, well, yes," Lady Manwaring replied, just a hint of laughter in her voice. "Now, my dear Roxanna, why don't you just go back to sleep? Annie is watching, and I will take over from her in an hour."

"You're sure? Where is Helen?"

"I'm sure. My brother—remember, he is a bully—convinced Helen to ride out with David Start, the new bailiff. She knows all the fields and can give him some real assistance." Clarice came closer. "Roxanna, you are raising a very capable daughter. Tell me your secret."

"She had no choice, the same as I," Roxanna said simply. She lay down again, and offered no objection when Clarice straightened her pillow. "Yes, Helen does know the estate. Heaven knows we've ridden around it enough lately. Fletch is right about Helen, of course."

Clarice laughed. "Well, don't ever tell him! That sort of confidence makes husbands intolerable." She touched Roxanna's cheek. "My dear, go back to sleep. There's nothing going on here right now that we cannot deal with."

Roxanna closed her eyes. I'll never sleep, she thought. When she woke, the afternoon sun was slanting in the window, and Clarice had been replaced by Lord Winn.

He sat in the chair by the bed, hand on his cheek, reading the book in his lap. She lay still, not wanting to attract his attention yet, and soaked in the familiar sight of his spectacles scooting out to the end of his rather long nose. He is a handsome man, she thought. I wonder if our baby will have green eyes, too?

"Fletch," she said, to get his attention.

He smiled at her, closed the book, and took off his spectacles. "Well, my love, you look less like a potter's field candidate now than you did yesterday. Feel better?"

"Oh, I do," she said. "My love," is it? she asked herself. He tugged the blanket a little higher on her shoulders and went to the fireplace to give the coals another stir. "How is Lissy?" she asked when he returned to her side, sitting on the bed this time. She wanted to touch him, to rest her hand on his leg to assure herself that he was there, but she did not. "I pray she is no worse."

"About the same. We're just continuing what you were doing so well, my dear. Dr. Clyde looked in on her, and pronounced us capable. I thought about asking him to look at you—"

"Oh, no!" she said hastily, eyes wide. "I am fine. Only tired."

He raised his eyebrows. "Don't like doctors, do we?" he asked.

"I am not the patient here," she said firmly.

"Of course you are not," he agreed, his voice serene. "You're not sick. You're just . . . tired."

"And now I must get up," she said.

"I'd rather you just rested," he said, putting his arm across her so she could not move.

She looked up at him. "Clarice is right. You are a bully," she whispered, and let him give her a hug. She clung to him, trying to press his strength into her own body, so thankful to have him here.

"I'm not going anywhere, my dear Roxie Rand," he assured her finally. "Plenty of time for this later."

Not after you find out, she thought as she released him. I have to tell you.

"Winn, I need to—"

But he was getting up now, and retrieving his book and spectacles from the chair.

"What you need is a hot bath. I promised Clarrie I would tell her when you woke up. The tub's already in front of the fireplace. I think she enlisted Inca runners to bring in hot water, so I will leave you now."

He was gone with a wave of his hand and a wink. When she made her appearance an hour later in Lissy's room, he was feeding Lissy. She stared at him and tiptoed closer, resting her hand on his shoulder in her surprise. How does he do that? she thought, watching the wonderful sight before her. Everything she had offered, Lissy had rejected, turning away. And here he was, spooning down oatmeal without a complaint.

"You're a wonder, Fletch," she marveled when Lissy finally closed her eyes and he lowered her back to the bed. "She wouldn't eat so much for me."

He set down the bowl. "My dear, as a former colonel commanding, I am not used to disobedience in the ranks. I think she knew I meant it when I ordered her to open up." He took her hand and leaned back, sniffing the air. "Ah. I love that lavender. If she will eat a little more each day and gather her strength, she might outlast the fever."

Roxanna nodded, her heart too full for words. Tell him, Roxanna, she thought, tell him now while he is mellow.

"Fletcher, you really should know something."

"What, my dear? That I am handsome and charming, and more than you ever dared dream of in a second husband?"

She laughed, then put her hand over her mouth when Lissy moved. "No! That you are aggravating and tyrannical and . . . and quite essential to my peace of mind right now," she finished in a rush, disappointed with herself that her courage failed, yet wanting to tell him how she felt at the moment.

He was about to reply when Mrs. Mitchum opened the door. "Lord Winn, there is someone below to see both of you," she whispered, her eyes on Felicity.

Winn raised his eyebrows. "Who, pray?"

"Lord Whitcomb," she replied. "I put him in the sitting room. Shall I tell him you will be down?"

Roxanna put her hands to her mouth and shook her head. Mrs. Mitchum looked at her, a question in her eyes, but Lord Winn only smiled at the housekeeper, as though this was the best news of the week. Roxanna stared at him in horror.

"Yes, Mrs. M. Tell him we'll be down directly," he said.

When Mrs. Mitchum closed the door, Roxanna leaped up and retreated to the far corner of the room. "I will not go down there," she said, her voice low with emotion.

"I think you should," Winn said, coming to her side and putting his arm around her. "You see, I wrote him this morning and told him what was going on here."

She wriggled from his grip, her eyes wide. "You did what?" she gasped. "Suppose he does something. Suppose . . ."

He took hold of her more firmly this time. "There is nothing by law that he can do, because you are my wife. Let me remind you that Felicity and Helen are his nieces. I think he has a right to know how they are. Don't you?"

She thought a moment, then nodded reluctantly. "Still, he frightens me," she said.

Winn put his arms around her. "I know, Roxie, I know. You're about to be reminded of one of the sterling benefits of marriage."

He tipped her chin up with his finger and looked right into her eyes. "You don't have to face things alone anymore."

There was nothing she could do except nod. He smiled and kissed her forehead. "Let's go face the lions, Roxie. I think you might also discover that they are not as frightening as you remember. At least, this is my suspicion."

She took his hand as they went down the stairs, clutching it tighter and tighter as they approached the sitting room, loosening her grip only when Fletch winced and declared, "If you cut off my circulation, I'll be minus fingers, too, my dear. How many parts can a man lose?"

She paused at the door for a deep breath. Helen was inside, playing Mozart, and it steadied her as much as Winn's hand on her shoulder.

"Excellent!" Winn said. "You always were one to ride toward the sound of guns, Roxie." He opened the doors. "Ah, Lord Whitcomb. Grand of you to come."

The door was open; there was nothing she could do but follow her husband inside, holding her breath until she felt light-headed, then letting it out slowly when Marshall Drew held out his hand to her. She hesitated, then felt the pressure of Lord Winn's fingers on her shoulder. You are a bully, she thought as she extended her hand finally and shook Lord Whitcomb's hand.

"Good evening, Marshall," she said, wishing that she could sound brave. I must say something. What's a conversational opener for a villain? "I'm glad you could hear how Helen has been progressing. That's lovely, my darling," she said to her daughter at the piano.

Helen beamed at her. "Shall I continue, Mama?"

Roxie felt herself relaxing. "Yes, of course." She indicated the sofa across the room. "Perhaps we could sit here?"

She sat as close to Winn as she could without climbing into his lap, recalling with painful clarity her last tête-à-tête with Lord Whitcomb in the vicarage. The memory left her unable to say anything. To her relief, her husband picked up the conversational baton and wielded it like a marshal. His voice was relaxed and genial, and she couldn't believe her ears.

"Lord Whitcomb, we wanted you to know how Lissy was. She seems to be gaining in strength, but it's still early days, I am afraid."

Whitcomb nodded. "We've had our share of influenza, too." He looked at her. "I heard that Tibbie was ill, but he must have recovered remarkably, Roxanna. Your fields are quite the envy."

Roxanna smiled in spite of herself and sat a little taller. "I was bailiff until a week or so ago," she said.

"You are to be commended then," Marshall Drew replied. He paused, then looked at Helen, who was concentrating on the sonatina. "She is well?"

"Yes, thank God," Roxanna said gratefully, warming to his concern. "The flu seems to pick and choose."

Marshall nodded. He rose. "I do not intend to stay long, of course, but I would like to see Lissy."

"Of course," Winn said, when she hesitated. "I do have a favor to ask of you first."

Lord Whitcomb smiled, and she further relaxed her grip on her husband. She remembered that smile, too, and was glad to see it again. "Whatever I can do, please know that I will."

"I haven't asked Roxanna yet, but I am certain she will agree. Will you take Helen back to Whitcomb for the rest of the week?"

Roxanna bit her lips to keep from screaming out loud and dug her fingernails into her husband's hand. He merely raised her hand to his lips and kissed her fingers.

But Winn was still speaking, as though he conversed with his best friend, and not the man who had tried to shame her and steal her daughters. "I'm sure you can see that Helen could use a change of scenery, and it would give Roxie some relief, too. Will you consider it?"

She held her breath, praying that Whitcomb would say no. To her amazement, tears came to his eyes. He looked away from them toward Helen, who was starting Scarlatti now, her head moving in time to the rhythm. He did not speak until he was firmly in control again.

"Yes, of course, Lord Winn," he replied. "I would be delighted, and I am sure I speak for Agnes, too." He turned to Roxie then. "If it is agreeable to you, Roxanna."

Suddenly she understood, and felt tears of her own. *And I thought I loved Fletcher Rand before,* she told herself as she looked at her brother-in-law. *I wonder if I would have the magnanimity to attempt what he is doing? Anthony would; surely I can do no less. One mustn't be outdone by one's husbands.*

"Yes, by all means, Marshall," she replied. "It would be a relief to me to know that Helen was in good hands while we are so occupied with Lissy right now."

Marshall sighed. "Very good. May I go invite Helen myself?"

She nodded. "Do tell her that we will let her know how Lissy goes on."

He went to the piano and sat next to her daughter, their heads together. She watched them and swallowed, reminded of other days.

"Does he resemble Anthony?" Winn asked quietly.

She nodded. "Sometimes it gives me a start." She looked at her husband. "When was the last time anyone told you that you are remarkable?"

It was his turn to blink and look away. "I never was remarkable before I met you, Roxanna," he said finally as Lord Whitcomb returned to the sofa.

He was smiling. "She agrees. I will send 'round my groom in the morning for her. Thank you."

"You're welcome," Roxanna said, when her husband seemed unable to respond. She took another deep breath and held out her hand to Lord Whitcomb. "Come, let me take you to Lissy. Fletch? I think Helen is stuck on that andantino. Can you untangle her, my dear?"

She climbed the stairs slowly with her brother-in-law, thinking her own thoughts, grateful for the gathering dusk, but more at peace than in months. They entered Lissy's room, where Mrs. Mitchum watched.

Roxanna remained in the doorway while he sat on the edge of Lissy's bed, touching her cheek, then kissing her forehead. He spoke softly to her, and she couldn't tell if Lissy was capable of response, but her heart went out to him. I can forgive, she thought. It costs nothing except a little pride, and the rewards are infinite.

Lord Whitcomb joined her in the doorway again and they went silently down the stairs. He paused at the bottom and took her hand. "Roxanna, please let me know how she goes on. If there is anything I can do . . ."

She smiled. "Remember her in your prayers, of course. Beyond that, we can only wait. Thank you for coming."

She opened the door for him. He looked back at her, some of the bleakness gone from his eyes. "Roxanna, I hope you can forgive me someday," he murmured.

"I will work on it," she promised. "Good night, Marshall."

She returned to the sitting room, standing in the doorway to watch her husband and Helen practice the andantino. I would like to hold moments like these in my hands forever, she thought as she stood there. I love him so much, and must face the blinding truth that if we can somehow go on this way, I will only love him more.

He turned around then at the piano bench and motioned her forward. She shook her head. "You two continue," she said. "Since everything seems to be in control, I will sit with Lissy for a while and then go to bed."

He nodded and blew her a kiss. "I can recommend the Fielding, if you like a ribald tale. Only don't lose my place. I'll be up to take over in an hour."

She smiled and turned away, but he called her back. "I meant to tell you, my love. David Start thinks you are a fine bailiff." He turned back to the piano and played a lavish chord while Helen giggled. "Yet another male shot from the saddle by Roxanna Rand. Good night, my dear."

By rights, the week that followed should have been a dreadful one, but it was not. She could only marvel what a little more sleep and the support of people who cared did for her outlook. The first night she woke up after midnight, her heart pounding, terrified that Lissy was alone. Snatching up a shawl, she ran to her daughter's room, only to discover Lissy sleeping and Lord Winn involved in Henry Fielding. He merely looked at her standing in the open doorway, put his finger in the place, and whispered, "Do I have to take you back to bed?"

That only gets me in trouble, she thought as she quietly closed the door behind her and returned to her room.

And while Lord Winn slept during the day, Clarice divided the time with her, making her eat, with a certain loving tyranny that made Roxanna suspect that all the Rands were cut from the same cloth. Annie cleaned, Mrs. Mitchum cooked and supervised, and Roxanna found herself with little to do except tend her daughter and rest.

Lord Winn joined her in Lissy's room in the afternoons, doing nothing more than sitting with his long legs propped up on the bed, reading aloud to Lissy from a book of nursery rhymes. "I am not sure she hears me," he explained, "but one never knows."

"I never took you for a reader of nursery rhymes," she said as she gathered herself comfortably in the chair and admired the way her husband's hair curled so neatly over his collar. He needed another haircut.

"There's probably a lot you don't suspect that I know, Mrs. Rand," he replied, a twinkle in his eyes. "Besides that, she's a little young for Fielding."

Clarice's husband, Lord Manwaring, arrived two days later in a post chaise, fortified with more lemons and oranges and another Fielding novel for his brother-in-law. He took his turn in the sickroom, too, moving with surprising agility for one so formidable.

"I wouldn't have it any other way, Roxanna," he insisted, when she assured him that they could manage without troubling him, too. "Clarice and I have been through enough of these sickroom dramas to easily outdistance you and Winn." He kissed her cheek. "Besides, m'dear, what are relatives for?"

What indeed? she asked herself as she tied on a bonnet for a stroll in the orchard at the end of the week. She thought then of her brothers in India, and those wretched card games they forced her to play, when they were all young together in Kent. I have been dealt such a hand this year, she thought as she admired the little apples. It was not a hand I would ever have chosen willingly, because of the force of circumstance, but I have done the best I could with it. I will have to face Lord Winn and tell him about the baby. If he chooses not to remain with us, I can manage that, too, because I have to. Fletch is always insisting that I never do things by halves, and he is right. There is no other way to live.

She looked across the Plain of York, hazy now in July's welcome warmth, a checkerboard of fields and pasture. I hope I am lucky enough to hang onto my husband and my daughters. When he says he does not want children, perhaps he does not mean it.

"Oh, I say, Roxanna," called Fred from the front steps. "Please hurry!"

She looked up, her nerves snapping suddenly at the unexpected tremor in his voice, shouting to her across the lawn. Please, God, she prayed silently, as he hurried toward her. She looked up at the open window in Lissy's room, and there was Fletcher, leaning out, his head bowed. "No," she said out loud. "It cannot be. We have all worked so hard."

She ran past her brother-in-law, and into the house, bursting into the room to stop in horror at the sight of Clarrie in tears, clutching her brother, who was sobbing, too. They stood in front of Lissy's bed, as though to hide death from view. "No," she insisted, as though there was no other word. "It cannot be."

Lord Manwaring pounded up the stairs behind her and stood, leaning against the door, trying to get his breath.

"Oh, I declare, you two," he said in disgust, shaking his head at his wife and brother-in-law. "Lissy, I hope you do not think all adults are cloth-witted. Maybe your mama has more sense."

Roxanna gasped and pushed aside her husband to gape at Lissy, who sat up in bed staring at all the commotion. She pursed her lips in that familiar way that made Roxanna sob out loud, and looked at her mother.

"All I did was ask for some food," she explained. Her voice

was rusty from little use, and her head wobbled from weakness, but she was completely coherent, and even a little impatient. As Roxanna put a shaking hand to her cool forehead, she smiled at her mother. "I really would like a cinnamon bun."

Clarice sobbed louder. Fletcher threw himself into a chair and stared at the ceiling, tears on his face. Roxanna found herself weeping, too, even as she clung to her daughter.

"Lissy, let me speak to Mrs. Mitchum about a cinnamon bun," said Lord Manwaring, picking up a bowl. "In the meantime, perhaps you would let me feed you this applesauce?"

Lissy nodded and opened her mouth obediently, like a little bird. Even Lord Manwaring had to pause a moment, and his voice was less assured. "It seems that we are the only sane people in the room. There is no accounting for relatives. How sorry I am that you had to learn this at such a tender age. Open wide for your Uncle Manwaring, Lissy."

"Well, my dear, let us take these glad tidings to Helen at Whitcomb," said Lord Winn as he helped her into the barouche. "I think I am sufficiently recovered not to make a cake of myself in front of Helen's uncle."

She smiled at him and scooted closer as he rested his arm across the back of the seat. "I know I cried enough for two," she said, then blushed. And heaven knows I have been eating enough for two lately. I simply *must* speak to this man.

She couldn't do it. They rode in silence, and soon Lord Winn was asleep. Dear tired man, she thought, and leaned back into his slack embrace, closing her eyes, too.

She woke as the carriage stopped at the steps of Whitcomb, then touched her husband's face to wake him. His eyes snapped open and he looked about wildly, then chuckled, embarrassed. "Roxie, let's go to bed when we're through here. I could sleep for a week."

She opened her mouth to speak and he kissed her suddenly. "There," he said, satisfied with himself. "I have been wanting to do that—and other things—for considerably more than a week. Oh, yes, and to tell you that I love you, Roxie. Body and soul, heart and mind, through and through. Indefatigably, even, which will probably be a good thing, considering your unflagging interest in my various parts."

And so she was blushing fiery red as Lord Whitcomb came down the front steps, a question in his eyes. "Tell me it is good news," he demanded as Lord Winn helped her from the barouche.

She nodded and touched his arm. "It is, Marshall. The fever is gone. We wanted you and Helen to know right away."

Then Helen was there, throwing herself into her mother's arms, and hugging Lord Winn, who almost made a cake of himself again when he told her the welcome news.

"We will drive over tomorrow, if we may," Lord Whitcomb said. "May I keep Helen here until then? We're working on a little project for Lissy which we need to finish."

"Of course you may, Marshall," Roxanna said without any hesitation. "And you'll bring Agnes and stay to dinner?"

"With pleasure," he replied. He turned to Helen. "My dear, go inside and bring out our painting." He watched as she skipped inside, then took Roxanna's hand. "I really do owe the two of you an apology," he began, his voice low and hard to hear. He looked at Lord Winn. "My actions of this winter were reprehensible beyond belief. Even now I cannot imagine what was in my mind."

Roxanna covered his hand with her own and took a deep breath. "Marshall, I wish you would not harrow yourself up over this," she began.

"But Roxanna, I forced you to such a desperate act," he insisted as he released her hand.

She shook her head, wondering at the peace that came over her. "If you had not forced my hand, I would never have married Lord Winn. Now, that would have been horrible." She took her husband's hand. "I cannot imagine life without him now. Thank you, Marshall, for what you did. I am in *your* debt, for I love Fletcher Rand."

Lord Whitcomb stared at her, then smiled at Lord Winn, who swallowed and looked away. "Sir, you are a lucky man. Roxanna, we'll see you tomorrow for dinner."

He hurried back into the house, unable to continue. Roxanna found a handkerchief in her reticule and handed it to her husband, who blew his nose vigorously, wiped his eyes, and helped her back into the barouche. They rode in silence past the end of the lane and the vicarage now occupied by another, then Lord Winn called for the coachman to stop.

"We'll walk the rest of the way," he told Roxanna as he helped her down.

They started across the cow pasture. "Walking's good for you," he said, then stopped to take her by the shoulders. "Roxanna, if you love me so much, why didn't you write me in March?"

She stared at him. "But I did! I waited and waited for a reply." She sighed and put her arms around his neck. "Oh, dear! I knew I had waited too long, so I sent the letter to Northumberland, and not to Carlisle. Did you not receive it there?"

Lord Winn pulled her close to him, his arms tight around her. "Oh, no! Two days before we were to go to High Point, they were cleaning the chimneys there and someone managed to burn down that wretched pile. I never went to Northumberland."

She laughed and cried and tried to ignore the Ayrshire cows that were heading toward them, curious about this invasion of watering pots in the pasture. "So you never knew in March that I loved you amazingly?"

"Never knew," he repeated, his lips on her hair. "Suspected, but hell, that's not the same." He pulled her closer. "And, Roxie, excuse me for asking, but in such proximity as this, I cannot help but observe that someone has come between us."

She was silent for a long moment. "I was afraid to tell you, Fletch. Remember all those things you said about not wanting any children?"

He winced. "I did haver on, love."

"You did. When I did not hear from you, I assumed you had changed your mind about wanting to alter our relationship. I couldn't tell you about the baby then." She rested her head against his chest. "And you know how I like to put off bad news."

He pulled back from her and placed his hand lightly on her belly. "I said a lot of stupid things, didn't I? How kind you will be to overlook them. And I will overlook your procrastination," he added generously.

"You knew, didn't you?" she asked after a moment, her voice lively with good humor. "You have been so careful of me lately. How did you know?"

"Well, it became a little obvious when I separated you from your dress! I may be a cloth-head, dear wife, but when it moved under my hand—Roxie, what a feeling."

Roxanna kissed him. "You really don't mind?" she murmured.

"Mind? I think I can stand the strain of parenthood." He patted her belly. "I'm already so good at fathering. Why waste such an education? Do let me tell our daughters." He peered at her. "Do you mind if I call them that? They seem like my own."

She didn't mind. Somewhere in her heart, she knew Anthony wouldn't mind, either. "By all means, you tell them, my love."

They walked along slowly, and soon Moreland came in sight. Roxanna stopped, remembering her anxious walk last fall and her first view of the dower house. "In for a penny, Lord Winn," she said.

"In for ten pounds, Lady Winn and company."

Epilogue

Winnfield
Dec. 15, 1817

Dear Clarrie and Fred,

Please know you two are the first with the news—Roxie was delivered of a son yesterday afternoon at 3:30 o'clock. He came out squalling and complaining and Roxie said he was just like me. You'll also be pleased to know, Clarrie, that I resisted the urge to tease her back just then. Poor dear, Roxie looked like she had been run over by a wagon. But I was brave. I either held her hand or rubbed her back through the whole ordeal, and only felt a little faint when I heard him cry for the first time.

We're going to name him Robert Newell Anthony Fletcher Winfrey, which seems quite a handle for something so small. He has Roxie's high-arched eyebrows and my green eyes, and he's long. Heaven knows where she stashed him all those nine months. Lissy and Helen are delighted. We've all taken a turn at changing nappies, but the menu will be Roxie's domain. Amabel wrote her last month about hiring a good wet nurse, but you know that Roxie does nothing by halves. Anyway, as Tibbie would say, "T'bonny lad is grazing on a good pasture."

And so are we all. By all means, please come for Christmas, as planned. Roxie will enlist us to do her work, and she can crack the whip from a chair by the fire while Rob dines.

How did I get so lucky, Clarrie? I'm giving Roxie an emerald necklace for Christmas. Don't tell her. As a joke, I've also framed a sketch I drew of Roxie giving Tibbie a ten-pound note in front of the dower house. Guess which she will prefer?

Love and Kisses from the Proud Papa,
Winn

P.S. Fred, should I wake up and act sympathetic during those 2 a.m. feedings, or just keep sleeping? Rush your reply, please.
W.